— ♡ —

*The Highest Praise for*
**Bleeding Hearts**

"Never quite a cozy and never quite tough, this tale combines the best of both styles to stunning effect."
—*Publishers Weekly*

"Haddam's usual deft writing, skillful plotting, and gentle humor . . . refreshing and entertaining."
—*Booklist*

"First-rate . . . a must read."
—*Rendezvous*

"A tightly woven, carefully structured mystery, with sufficient clues integrated into the telling to make the ending increasingly inevitable but not quite predictable."
—*Mystery Scene*

"Once you get to know Gregor and Bennis and Father Kasparian, I guarantee you'll want to come back for more."
—*Indianapolis News*

"A rattling good puzzle, a varied and appealing cast, and a detective whose work carries a rare stamp of authority . . . This one is a treat."
—*Kirkus Reviews* (starred review)

— ♧ —

### And the Other Holiday Mysteries by Jane Haddam

#### Not a Creature Was Stirring

"Vintage Christie [turned] inside out . . . *Not a Creature Was Stirring* will puzzle, perplex, and please the most discriminating readers."
—*Murder Ad Lib*

#### Precious Blood

"A fascinating read."
—*Romantic Times*

#### Act of Darkness

"Juicy gossip abounds, tension builds and all present are suitably suspect as Demarkian expertly wraps up loose ends in this entertaining, satisfying mystery."
—*Publishers Weekly*

## A Great Day for
## the Deadly

"Haddam . . . plays the mystery game like a master. . . . A novel full of lore, as of suspense, it is bound to satisfy any reader who likes multiple murders mixed with miraculous apparitions and a perfectly damnable puzzle."
—*Chicago Tribune*

## A Stillness in
## Bethlehem

"A high-quality puzzler."
—*Publishers Weekly*

"Classic mysteries are back in vogue, and Jane Haddam's . . . Gregor Demarkian series is one of the finest."
—*Romantic Times*

## A Feast of Murder

"Haddam offers up a devilishly intricate whodunit for fans of the classic puzzler. . . ."
—*Tower Books Mystery Newsletter*

# bleeding
# hearts

---

## jane haddam

BANTAM BOOKS
NEW YORK  TORONTO  LONDON
SYDNEY  AUCKLAND

BLEEDING HEARTS
A Bantam Book

PUBLISHING HISTORY
Bantam hardcover edition published February 1994
Bantam paperback edition / February 1995

ISBN 0-553-56936-8

*Published simultaneously in the United States and Canada*

Bantam Books are published by Bantam Books, a division of Bantam Doubleday Dell
Publishing Group, Inc. Its trademark, consisting of the words "Bantam Books" and the
portrayal of a rooster, is Registered in U.S. Patent and Trademark Office and in other
countries. Marca Registrada. Bantam Books, 1540 Broadway, New York, New York 10036.

this book is for

*meg ruley*

who got this started
and keeps it going
and thinks better of me
than I do

*bleeding hearts*

*prologue*

———

*on the night
father tibor got
arrested* . . .

# 1

"Bennis," Father Tibor Kasparian said, his Russian-accented voice coming over the speakerphone in thick bright blobs, like elasticized marmalade. "Bennis, you have to help me. I have finally been arrested and now I want to get out."

It was seven o'clock on the evening of Friday, February 1, and Bennis Hannaford was hunched over her brandnew Macintosh, putting the finishing touches on last year's operating budget for Holy Trinity Armenian Christian Church. She had a Benson & Hedges menthol in an ashtray near her left hand. It had been burning away, untouched, for a good three minutes. She had a mug of coffee near her right hand. It was half drunk but stone cold. On the display screen in front of her she read:

NOVEMBER 16TH—9:22 PM—$28—GIVEN TO
ANNIE LEMBECK, HOMELESS PERSON, KNOCKED ON RECTORY
BACK DOOR. OFFERED DINNER. WAS REFUSED.
OFFERED APPLE. WAS ACCEPTED. LISTENED ONE HALF HOUR
TO STORY OF ALIENS TAKING OVER MAYOR'S OFFICE.
STORY MAY HAVE MERIT.

There were hundreds of entries like this one. They filled up the little stack of computer disks Father Tibor had turned over to her on New Year's Eve. Bennis had spent weeks reading them and wondering if Father Tibor had anything else to do. She knew perfectly well Father Tibor had something else to do. He had to get arrested, for one thing. She wondered where he found the time.

The entry under the entry she had just read said:

NOVEMBER 16TH—9:25 PM—ONE APPLE—GIVEN TO
ANNIE LEMBECK, HOMELESS PERSON . . .

Bennis picked up her cigarette, tapped away the long
column of ash that had accumulated on the end of it, and
took a drag.

"It's seven o'clock," she said. "I thought you told me
you were going to get arrested at three."

Father Tibor sighed. "Father Ryan said we would get
arrested at three. I think Father Ryan is a little out of date."

"Which means what?"

"Which means protesting restrictions against street
vendors in downtown Philadelphia is not the same as protesting the Vietnam War in front of the Pentagon. Everybody was very nice until the very last minute, and then it
was our fault."

"What was your fault?"

Father Tibor sighed again. "It was Stephen Hartnell
from First Congregational. He had taken some cold medicine and he got sleepy. He got so sleepy he fell over, and
he's a big fat man, so the thing he was standing next to fell
over, and the thing was a big flimsy can full of glass bottles
to be recycled, and the next thing we knew there was glass
all over the road, and they made a big crash, and this policeman panicked and shot his gun into the air, and then there
was a dog—"

"Never mind," Bennis said. "What about the street vendors?"

"The street vendors will be fine, Bennis, but it will not
be because of us. Reverend Casey from African Methodist
got up and gave a speech about how it was racism; when
the immigrants needed to be street vendors they could do
it without any interference and now when it is African
Americans who need to do it there are registration require-
ments and licensing fees. All of which is probably true, but
the important part is that Reverend Casey got to say it on
Channel Five—"

"—ah—"

"—and now everybody is talking about compromise.
Will you come and get me, Bennis? I have to pay a twenty-

five-dollar fine and I left my wallet at home. If you're busy, I could call Donna Moradanyan—"

"Donna's Tommy's got the flu. I'll come get you. What precinct are you at?"

"I'm not at a precinct. I'm at the superior court. I will go back now and listen to the arraignment of the prostitutes. They are very young, Bennis."

"I know."

"This is a remarkable country, Bennis. People who were born and brought up here do not understand. How long do you think you will be?"

"Twenty minutes, maybe."

"All right. I will go back and listen to the prostitutes. There is one, Bennis, I do not think she is sixteen."

Bennis was sure there were several prostitutes at Tibor's court who were not yet sixteen, and maybe one or two who were not yet fourteen, but she didn't have a chance to tell Tibor so. The speakerphone's speaker stopped crackling and went to a hum. Bennis leaned over her coffee and shut the sound off. Her cigarette was burned to the filter. She got out another one and lit up again. Her head ached faintly. It always did that when she worked too long at the computer. She took a long, deep drag on her cigarette, promised herself to quit smoking again for Valentine's Day, and stood.

"Money," she told herself, and then, "note."

Her computer was at the curved center of a built-in workspace in one corner of her bedroom. The edges of this workspace were twin piles of mess. Bennis rummaged around in the closer of these messes and came up with a piece of paper and a Bic medium-point pen.

*Christopher*, she wrote, *I had to go out. Go up to the fourth floor and ask Donna Moradanyan for the key. Eat something. See you later. Bennis.*

She grabbed a roll of transparent tape and her coat, started for the hall, then stopped. She checked the pockets of her jeans for money and decided she needed more. She went into the kitchen and raided her cookie jar for the three hundred dollars she kept there. For all she knew, Tibor wasn't the only member of the demonstration who needed

twenty-five dollars for the fine. She might as well be prepared.

She let herself into the hall, fastened the note to her
door with tape, and went downstairs. There was light
showing through the crack under the door of old George
Tekemanian's first-floor apartment. She thought about
stopping, but didn't. If she got talking to old George, she
could lose an hour.

She let herself out on the stoop and looked up and
down Cavanaugh Street for cabs. There were none at the
moment—there was no traffic of any kind—but Bennis
knew it wouldn't be long before a taxi showed up. Cabs
liked Cavanaugh Street.

Bennis sat on the bottom step to wait. Across the street,
Lida Arkmanian's town house was lit up like a lighthouse
and festooned with hearts and ribbons—Donna Moradanyan's first foray into decorating the street for Valentine's
Day. Two blocks up, light spilled out of the plate-glass
windows of the Ararat Restaurant, darkened periodically
by the shadows of waitresses and diners moving back and
forth in front of the big main arc light. Bennis stretched her
legs and considered lighting another cigarette, and then she
saw the cab.

It was a cab with its occupied light glowing, but there
was always a chance it was going to drop its fare on Cavanaugh Street, so Bennis stood up and went to the edge of
the curb to wait for it. It did stop on Cavanaugh Street,
up beyond the Ararat, in front of the narrow brownstone
Howard Kashinian had renovated and turned into two duplex apartments. One of those two apartments he had kept
for his own great-aunt Melina. The other he had sold to
Hannah Krekorian after Hannah's husband's death. It was
Hannah Krekorian whom Bennis saw get out of the cab
now, her stout little middle-aged-to-getting-old figure moving briskly against the wind. The wind was very bad. February was always a cold time in Philadelphia. This February
was starting out to be brutal. Hannah scurried quickly to
the first step of her stoop, then turned around.

At the curb, the street-side passenger door to Hannah's cab remained open. Bennis watched, fascinated, as

first one trouser-clad leg and then another emerged from it. The legs were followed by a body and then a head, all unnaturally elongated, all sticklike and stretched. What a tall, thin man, Bennis thought. And it was true. He was immensely tall and emaciatedly thin. He looked like some sort of flexible rod with a coat attached to it. From this distance, Bennis couldn't make out any of the detail of his face—the best she could do was note that the coat was an expensive one, obvious from the way it moved and the way it hung and the things it didn't do in the cold—but there was something about him that seemed familiar, and the familiar thing was not pleasant. Bennis reached for her cigarettes, thought better of it, rubbed her hands together in the frigid breeze. The tall, thin man shut the curbside door and paid the driver. He walked over to Hannah Krekorian and took her arm. The two made their way up the steep cement staircase to the brownstone's front door. Bennis stepped halfway off the curb and began to signal for the cab.

He does look familiar, she told herself. Why does he look familiar? He wasn't anyone who lived on Cavanaugh Street. He wasn't anyone she'd known growing up on the Main Line either, although that would have made more sense. Most of the people on Cavanaugh Street were either Armenian immigrants or the children or grandchildren or great-grandchildren of Armenian immigrants. Some of them were tall, but after a certain age all of them ran to fat. None of them had that fine-boned fragility that made a person, male or female, look more ghostlike than real. Even Gregor Demarkian, who was six foot four, was a big massive solid man, not an elegant one.

I have seen that man before, Bennis told herself. I really have.

Then the cab pulled up to the curb and she had to get into it. That was always the way things seemed to work out. She got curious about something and something else came along to prevent her from satisfying her curiosity. It was the way the universe was organized. There was something cosmic out there that was trying to get her. There was—

—there was a distinct possibility that she was getting her period.

She leaned over the front seat and told the driver, "Superior court."

The driver gave her a strange look, but took gamely off.

Bennis sat back and sighed. She told herself she could go over to Hannah's tomorrow and just *ask* who it was. That was what would make the most sense.

Then she closed her eyes and let the cab take her across town, lulling her even in the Friday-night traffic, making her drift off to sleep in spite of the weekend lights. When they pulled up in front of the superior court building, she was nearly snoring.

"Hey, lady," the cabdriver said.

Bennis came to and reached for her wallet.

Back on Cavanaugh Street, a gust of wind coming up the stairs as Gregor Demarkian opened the front door to let himself in, tugged at the tape Bennis had used to fasten her note to her brother Christopher to her door, ripped the note away, and sent the note and the tape both spiraling down the dark center of the stairwell.

## 2

Hannah Krekorian had never been a pretty woman. In fact, she had never been pretty at all, even as a child. That might not have mattered if she had had flair, like Sheila, who was really plain but knew how to make herself up. It might not have mattered if she'd had brains or talent or humor or anything else that could provide an aura of fascination. Instead, Hannah had been a stocky, plain child with a good heart who had become a stocky, plain woman with a good heart. There were advantages in that. Her husband had married her for what he called her "generosity." Her friends stuck by her for what they called her "helpfulness." She had been elected to the parish council four times because of her universal reputation as a "good Christian woman." The problem was, Hannah Krekorian did not want to be a good Christian woman. She wanted to be what Lida Arkmanian had been, when they were all growing up together on Cavanaugh Street. She wanted to be the most beautiful girl in the class, the natural prom queen, the undisputed choice to represent the spirit of spring at the annual citywide Armenian Festival. Most of all, Hannah wanted to be the kind of woman men just couldn't help being attracted to.

It was so cold on this night, the tips of Hannah's fingers were turning blue. The joints of her fingers felt too stiff to handle the key to her own front door. The bones in her face seemed made of stone. She was being silly and she knew it. She wasn't a girl anymore. She was fifty-eight years old, and so was Lida. Sheila Kashinian wasn't much younger. All of them had grandchildren. None of them was going to be chosen to represent spring this year or any year in the future. What good was it going to do her, wishing her life had been different when she was seventeen?

The key turned in the front-door lock. Hannah pushed against the door and couldn't make it budge.

"Here," Paul Hazzard said, coming up behind her. "Let me do that. It's so cold out here, I can barely breathe."

Actually, it was Hannah who could barely breathe. She'd been having trouble with breathing ever since Paul Hazzard had come up to talk to her, back at the coffee break during her meeting for the Friends of the Matterson Settlement House. The Matterson Settlement House was one of Hannah's "charities." She kept on with it—as she kept on with the Friends of the Philadelphia Public Library and the Friends of the Calliman Museum of Art and the Friends of the Boswell Theater of Modern Dance and all the rest of it—because the meetings gave her someplace to go and the other members of the organization gave her somebody to talk to. Hannah had people she could talk to on Cavanaugh Street, of course. She did a lot of real and well-appreciated work for the church and the Holy Trinity Armenian Christian School. She was surrounded by people she had known forever. It just wasn't enough.

Wasn't enough for what? she wondered now, watching Paul get the door open and stand back to let her pass. She'd been so restless lately, so dissatisfied, and she didn't know why. She stepped into the foyer of her brownstone and turned on the foyer light. The doorway to Melina Kashinian's apartment was dark. Melina Kashinian was eighty-nine and probably already in bed. That's what's really wrong with this place, Hannah thought. Everybody goes to bed too early. And they all go to bed alone.

What?

Paul Hazzard had shut the door behind himself and was now waiting expectantly. Hannah could feel herself blushing hot and hard, as ashamed of herself as if she'd just dropped her drawers in public. It was no good at all to tell herself that Paul Hazzard couldn't read her mind. Where had a thought like that come from?

"There's an elevator over here," she told Paul Hazzard, "just for me. My apartment starts on the third floor."

"It's a floor-through?"

"It's a floor-through duplex. I don't think there are any buildings on Cavanaugh Street with more than one apartment on a floor. Not anymore. It was different in the old days."

The elevator door opened. Paul Hazzard put his hand against the rubber safety edge and let Hannah go in first.

"In the old days, this was a tenement neighborhood," he said, nodding. "I'm impressed with what's been done to it. Most of the tenement neighborhoods have become slums."

"Most of the tenement neighborhoods *were* slums," Hannah said. "I always tell my grandchildren that that's what I grew up in. A slum. My grandchildren live in suburbs, of course. My children wouldn't live anywhere else."

"What about you? Why do you live here?"

"Why not?" Hannah shrugged. "I've lived here all my life. And my children did well. All our children did well, and the grandchildren who are grown did well, too, and we've had a little private urban renewal. It's very comfortable here."

"I wish it were comfortable where I live," Paul Hazzard said. "I've still got the town house my I-don't-know-how-many-greats grandfather built before the Revolutionary War, but the neighborhood's not what it was. To put it mildly. The neighborhood's downright dangerous."

"Oh, yes," Hannah agreed. "So much of the city is dangerous these days."

She had been holding her finger on the "open door" button. Now she released it and the door slid closed. Her head felt stuffed with cotton and very floaty. It was as if she had had a good strong cocktail to drink. Hannah never had anything to drink except a glass of wine at Christmas. Her mother hadn't approved of drinking, and her father had done too much of it.

The elevator cab slid upward, silent. Paul Hazzard studied the pattern of the wallpaper on the cab's sides.

"Here we are," he said as the cab bounced to a stop. "Why are all the foyers in this building dark? It isn't safe."

"Cavanaugh Street is always safe," Hannah told him. "I don't think there's ever been a crime here, not really, except one Halloween we had an attempted robbery."

"Only attempted?"

"Somebody coshed the thief with a—I don't remember what it was. But it was all right, you know. Nobody got hurt and they caught the thief and we didn't even have to go to court because there was a plea-bargain."

"Wonderful," Paul Hazzard said.

Hannah found her apartment key, wondering why her fingers were still stiff. She did not wonder why she still couldn't breathe. Paul Hazzard was the handsomest man who had ever said two words to her in her life, never mind asked her to dinner, which he had done. He was the tallest and thinnest and most Wasp-looking man she had ever met.

Hannah got her apartment door open and stepped into her own front hall. Paul Hazzard came in after her and Hannah found herself wincing. It all looked so—so stodgy. So solid and middle-aged and graceless. The big square club chairs in the living room. The hand-tatted antimacassars. The doilies her grandmother had made, badly, from spools of undyed thread. What had she been thinking of?

She scurried quickly into the living room, to the little glass panel in the built-in bookshelves that hid what she had always thought of as her "bar." Now that seemed pretentious as hell. It wasn't a bar. It was a bookshelf with a couple of bottles of Scotch on it. They were probably the wrong kind of Scotch.

"Well," she said. "I don't keep much in the way of liquor, but I do have some Scotch. If you'd like to have something to drink while I'm getting dressed . . . ."

"Do you have Perrier water?" Paul asked. "Or Poland Spring? Something like that?"

"You don't want a real drink?"

Paul Hazzard shook his head. "I gave all that up years ago. You have to be so careful with alcohol. It doesn't take anything at all to get dependent. But you should have something if you want . . . ."

"No," Hannah said. "No, I don't drink. I never have. I stick to diet soda and coffee."

"I'll bring you some apricot herb tea. It's better for you. Caffeine does terrible things to your intestines. And as for diet sodas—" He shrugged. "Chemicals," he told her. "You know."

"Of course," Hannah said, although she didn't know. "I do have some mineral water."

"I've gotten really serious about taking care of myself these last few years," Paul Hazzard said. "It's so important when you pass fifty. If you don't take control of your life, you'll really go to pieces."

"Oh," Hannah said again. "Yes."

"I've even started working out with weights. I'm not bodybuilding, you understand. At my age, that wouldn't be appropriate, and it probably wouldn't be healthy. But I've started strength training. You ought to try it. It does wonders for me."

"Weights?" Hannah was worse than bewildered. "I thought women couldn't—I mean—"

"Nonsense," Paul Hazzard said. "There are lots of women in the class I take. Young ones and old ones and middle-aged ones. It's a myth that women aren't suited for exercise."

Hannah brightened. "That's right. You're a doctor. Mrs. Handley told me."

"I'm not that kind of doctor. I'm a clinical psychologist. A Ph.D."

"Oh."

"But I do know a lot about health and nutrition. I have to. It's a myth that medicine can treat parts instead of the whole. Even psychologists have to concern themselves with the whole person. Especially psychologists."

"Oh." How many times had she said "oh"? Hannah couldn't remember. She looked around a little wildly and remembered she had promised to get some mineral water. She fixed her attention on the kitchen and headed in that direction. She had to do something, she really did, because she just couldn't *think*.

"Mineral water," she said under her breath. "I do have mineral water. I just don't have Perrier."

Paul Hazzard was following her. "Of course, all that about the whole person is very nice—and it's absolutely essential that you get in touch with your inner child, I insist on that with all my clients—but the fact is, there isn't any whole person to concern ourselves about if there isn't a person at all. If you see what I mean."

"No," Hannah said breathlessly. "I'm sorry. I'm not very well-read in this kind of thing—"

"The lights in your foyer," Paul Hazzard said.

"The—?"

"They ought to be on."

"Well, I suppose they should, but—"

"It's not sensible to say that there's never any crime on this street. There's crime everywhere. It's a sign of the times. It's a wholly dysfunctional society."

Hannah had reached the kitchen. The door was shut. She pushed it open and looked in on the usual spotlessness. It amazed her how much time she spent cleaning. What did she do it for?

"The mineral water will be in the refrigerator," she said. "Would you like it in a glass with ice?"

"In a glass will be fine. No ice. I wish you'd pay attention to me about the lights."

"I am paying attention to you about the lights."

Paul Hazzard propped himself up against the kitchen table. His legs looked impossibly long. His body looked impossibly lean. His gray hair was as fine and smooth as spun silver. Hannah had a hard time believing that he was real.

"I *am* paying attention to you about the lights," she said again, "it's just that—I don't think you realize—well, Cavanaugh Street isn't like other places. It really isn't."

"We all think our own neighborhoods aren't like other places. We all feel safe for a while. And then something happens."

"Did something happen to you?"

"Oh, yes. At least, I was the secondary victim. Who it really happened to was my wife."

"Your wife?"

Hannah felt a spurt of panic go through her, but it subsided. Paul was a widower. He had said so back at the meeting. She remembered that now. There was a small bottle of Colorado Sunshine Naturally Carbonated Water on the top shelf of the refrigerator door. Hannah got it out and looked around for a bottle opener. She used to keep bottle openers all the time. They were a necessity. Then flip-tops had come in and she'd got out of the habit. She opened her miscellaneous utensil drawer and stared into it.

"Just a minute," she said. "I'll find something to open this with in no time at all."

"Let's get back to my wife," Paul Hazzard said. "Don't you know what happened to her?"

"No. No, of course I don't. Should I?"

"Oh, yes." Paul Hazzard was nodding. "You really should. It wasn't that long ago. And it was in all the papers."

"What was?"

"My wife's murder," Paul Hazzard said simply. "A man broke into our town house one night to rob the place, and stabbed her through the heart."

## 3

Every once in a while, Caroline Hazzard was required to remember that she had once had a stepmother. When that happened, she became extremely agitated and had to go immediately to Group. Caroline had several Groups, and a psychotherapist, too, but when the subject was Jacqueline Isherwood, Caroline stuck to her Healing the Inner Child Workshop. After all, Caroline had been a child when her father had married Jacqueline—Caroline had been five. She remembered with perfect clarity the day Jacqueline had moved into the town house on Society Hill. This tall woman with the heavy perfume and the immense fur coat. This cawing female with her Miss Porter's School accent and her field-hockey legs. This—stranger, really—whom she was now supposed to love. Hadn't they realized that love couldn't be commanded like that? Hadn't they considered the *effect* it might all have on her? If it had been only one incident in an otherwise adequate life, it would have been different. Caroline's life had not been otherwise adequate. Caroline's life had been an epic of emotional neglect and dysfunctional conditioning. That was why, now, at the age of forty-two—

Now, at the age of forty-two, Caroline was sitting at her desk in her office off the back hall of WPBP, trying to remember just what equipment she needed to bring home with her so she could take it to Westchester tomorrow to give her demonstration. She had written the list out last night and put it in her bag so she would have it when she needed it, but somehow it had gotten lost. She had reminded herself during coffee break this morning to come down to the office to check it all out as soon as she got a chance, but she never did get a chance. Coffee break had been difficult and lunch had been impossible. She had called her Overeaters Anonymous buddy, but she hadn't been able to get through. Then the day had gone on getting worse and worse, and here she was.

Seven-fifteen. Sitting in the office. Trying to remember

what to bring. What Caroline Hazzard did for a living was to produce a local public television show on home improvement for women. Once or twice a week, she gave lectures on home improvement for women to women's groups. The lectures were always project-specific. How to design an addition. How to build a staircase. How to replace a floor that had rotted from mildew and humidity with one that wouldn't rot anytime soon. Caroline liked solid, practical projects that women could go home and start work on immediately. She liked specific step-by-step information that could be followed to inevitable success. She liked to see women empowered. She wanted to help women build their self-esteem. It was just that there was something wrong in her, that was all. It was just her programming that was off. That was why she couldn't ever seem to feel empowered or full of self-esteem herself.

There was a spray of crumbs across the corner of her desk—her sister Alyssa's crumbs, from the Peak Freans Alyssa had been eating when she'd dropped in to visit half an hour before. It was Alyssa who had made Caroline think of Jacqueline Isherwood. Alyssa always did things like that. Alyssa was a saboteur.

They were *all* saboteurs.

Caroline leaned forward and pressed the intercom buzzer. A moment later the speaker crackled and Sandy's voice said, "Yes? Miss Hazzard? Can I do something for you?"

Caroline felt momentarily guilty. Sandy must have a life of her own outside the office. It couldn't be right for Caroline to make her stay late just because Caroline couldn't make up her mind what to do next. What was Sandy doing down there, at her desk in the typing pool, with no work to do and nobody to talk to?

If there was something Sandy wanted, it was Sandy's responsibility to ask for it. That was what they taught you in Group. It was a symptom of codependency to think you had an obligation to read other people's minds.

"Sandy," Caroline said. "Yes. I need some help. Could you come in here for a minute?"

"I'd be glad to."

"Bring your copy of the Westchester itinerary with you

if you have it. I seem to have misplaced mine for the moment."

"I have it, Miss Hazzard. I'll be right in."

Was that a tongue-click of annoyance Caroline heard, coming at the end of Sandy's sentence? Caroline didn't like Sandy much. She didn't think Sandy liked her either. If it had been up to Caroline, Sandy would have been replaced by another secretary practically immediately. It was not up to Caroline. Sandy was a member of the typing pool, assigned to assist Caroline when Caroline needed assistance. She was also WPBP's star hire under the Americans with Disabilities Act. She wasn't going anywhere soon.

The door to Caroline's office opened and Sandy came in, walking a little heavily on the brace that propped up her withered right leg. The leg was withered because something awful had happened to it when Sandy was a child, but Caroline could never remember what. The leg seemed less important to Caroline than Sandy's weight, which put Sandy definitely on the pudgy side. People like Sandy were beyond Caroline's comprehension. She didn't understand why they didn't do something about themselves.

Sandy put a thick sheaf of papers down on the edge of Caroline's desk and sat herself in the visitor's chair, stretching her braced leg out along the carpet. She was wearing a new pink sweater and a chipped front tooth. It was just like her, Caroline thought, to spend her money on clothes instead of dentistry.

"Well," Caroline said, forcibly stopping herself from saying "I'm sorry." She said "I'm sorry" far too much. They were always pointing that out in Group. It was part of Sandy's job to stay late, not a special favor Sandy was doing Caroline.

Sandy was looking at the sheaf of papers. "I've got the itinerary right here," she said, "and a copy of your lecture and your materials list. Have you packed your materials yet?"

"No," Caroline said.

"I can pack them for you if you like. You're going to need the compass. That can be tricky. And you're going to need the plane. I hope you don't have trouble carrying it."

Normally, of course, nobody would have trouble carrying a compass and a plane, but Caroline's weren't the ordinary kind. Specifically, they weren't the ordinary size. Back when the show had started, Caroline had tried using standard-size equipment. It had made demonstrations difficult, on the air and off, because the equipment had been much too small for the audience to see properly. Now Caroline had her equipment custom-made. Her plane was the size, and the weight, of a brick. Her compass was a good two feet along the pivot. Her protractor could have been used as a fan in the Plaza Hotel's Palm Court. Carting this stuff from one end of the mid-Atlantic states to the other was exhausting.

At the bottom of Sandy's sheaf of papers was a copy of the poster Caroline took with her everywhere she was to speak. Sitting as she was, Caroline could look right down at the part in her own black hair.

She got out of her chair and went to the window. It wasn't much of a window. It looked out on the low roof of the building next door, which was about to collapse from neglect.

"Sandy, did you see my sister come in, or leave? My sister Alyssa?"

"Yes, Miss Hazzard, of course I did. She stopped by on her way in and her way out."

"Stopped by where?"

"At my desk, of course."

"Alyssa stopped at your desk?"

"Yes, Miss Hazzard, she almost always does. If she has the time."

"How extraordinary," Caroline said, completely at sea. "Well, that's very nice of her, I suppose. Did you talk about anything?"

"Not anything in particular. She had some cookies."

"Alyssa always has cookies."

"It must be nice to be able to eat like that and stay so thin," Sandy said. "I gain weight if I so much as look at fudge."

"It's a kind of addiction," Caroline said. "Alyssa is addicted to food. She can just kid herself that she's not because she never gains weight."

"Oh," Sandy said.

"We're an addiction-prone family. We all are. Even my brother James. Did Alyssa tell you what she'd come here to talk to me about?"

"No, of course not."

"Did you know I used to have a stepmother? A woman named Jacqueline Isherwood."

"Isherwood?"

"Jacqueline Isherwood Hazzard."

Sandy looked surprised. "The one who was murdered? Really? I'm very sorry. That must have been awful for you."

Caroline shrugged. "I suppose so. A lot of things have been awful for me. I was very damaged as a child."

"I should have made the connection," Sandy said slowly. "I always knew your father was the psychologist. And it was in the papers at the time."

"What was?"

"That she was married to the psychologist. That her husband—"

"Yes," Caroline interrupted hastily. "Yes, I see. Well, it was four years ago, for goodness' sake. There's no reason it should have stuck in your mind. You weren't working here then."

"I was in high school then."

"Oh, I wouldn't expect someone in high school to pay much attention to the papers, or even to the six o'clock news. I was just wondering, you know, about Alyssa. About anything she might have said."

"I really don't know what you mean, Miss Hazzard. Your sister didn't say anything in particular. Hello. How are you. Would you like one of these cookies. That kind of thing."

"She didn't say anything about my stepmother?"

"No."

"Or about my father?"

"Oh, no."

"Or about *me*?"

"She asked me if you were in your office when she first arrived, Miss Hazzard. I'm afraid I don't quite understand—"

"No, no," Caroline said, talking too fast again. "Of course you don't. Why should you? I'm sorry, Sandy.

Would you pack up for me, the way you offered to? And as soon as that's done, we can both go home. You'll probably be glad to get away from this place."

"I won't mind."

"No, no, of course you won't. Of course you won't. Here, let me get the compass for you, I had it to work on the ell plans with, I lost my regular one this morning—oh, *damn.*"

"Miss Hazzard?"

"Never mind." Caroline had dropped the compass on the floor. She picked it up and put it back on her desk. She was trying to avoid looking at her shoe, which had a stripe of white leather across the toe. The stripe of white leather was now marred by a splotch of black, where the point of the oversize pencil the compass held had hit it.

"Are you sure you're all right?" Sandy asked. "Could I get you something? Maybe you want one of your tranquilizers?"

*One* of her tranquilizers? How did Sandy know she took more than one kind of tranquilizer? And who *else* knew? God, this was really awful. This was a disaster. She was losing it completely. What did they call it in Group? That feeling you get that you're more stoned on your own than any dope could make you.

"I have to go to the bathroom," Caroline said. She edged around the side of her desk and then around the chair Sandy was sitting in, looking at the ceiling, looking at the floor, looking at nothing. "I just have to go to the bathroom again. I'll be right back."

"Are you sure there isn't anything I can get you?"

"Of course I'm sure, Sandy. I'm fine. Don't worry about me. I'll be right back."

Caroline was at the door to the hall now. She whirled around and plunged out into it, into the dark, and as she did, it occurred to her that it was a metaphor.

She was always plunging out into the dark.

She was always falling into the abyss.

It would be easy enough to blame it on Alyssa and Alyssa's taste for the sensational, but Alyssa was just as much a victim as Caroline was.

They were both victims of Jacqueline Isherwood Hazzard.

And of their father.

There was a window open in the ladies' room, blowing cold polluted air in from the streets of Philadelphia.

Caroline had never been as glad of the smell of carbon monoxide in her life.

*4*

"All I told her," Alyssa Hazzard Roderick was saying to her husband Nicholas, her voice thick with the exasperation it manufactured like mucus anytime she had to deal with her sister Caroline, "all I told her was that it was inevitable, which it is, and that there was nothing we could do about it, which we can't, and which is just saying the same thing all over again, but you know what I mean. Believe it or not, I was trying to do some good for all of us. I thought if I could talk to her calmly off the home turf, I might be able to get her to see reason."

"Caroline?" Nick asked mildly.

Nick was a decidedly rotund man in his early fifties, a kind of Santa Claus with black curly hair, and Alyssa loved him as madly as she had on the day she'd first met him, when she was twenty-four. That was years and years ago, of course. Alyssa had been forty-five on her last birthday, although she didn't really look it. Four pregnancies and four miscarriages in four years hadn't managed to put any weight on her. She was as willowy and fragile-looking as she had been as a teenager. She was also decidedly fond of food. One of the things she liked about Nick was that he was decidedly fond of food too, and disinclined to get all neurotic about it the way so many of the other lawyers in his firm did. One of the other things she liked about him was that he looked so at home here, in this town house where she had grown up. Soon after their wedding, Alyssa's father had turned the top floor into an apartment for them, and they'd been living in it ever since. Every once in a while Nick suggested that they build a house out in Radnor, since they could afford it, but the suggestion never went anywhere. There were thirty-five hundred square feet on this floor of the house alone. They were very comfortable.

Nick was sitting in a yellow wingback chair next to the great marble fireplace in their living room, paying no attention at all to the legal pad he had in his lap. He had been working on something when Alyssa came in, but he had stopped as soon as he'd seen his wife had need of him. Alyssa liked that about Nick too. There was nothing in his life more important than his relationship with her. Since there was nothing more important in Alyssa's life than her relationship with Nick, it worked out splendidly.

Alyssa was sitting on the edge of the couch, eating her way methodically through a gigantic chocolate-chip cookie. She had bought two of them in the pastry shop on the corner before she'd come upstairs. Nick's was sitting on an arm of the wingback chair, untouched.

"The thing is," Alyssa said, "you really can't blame Candida. I mean, no matter how embarrassing it's going to be for us, under the circumstances, it only stands to reason."

"Does it?"

"Oh, yes." Alyssa nodded sagely. "I mean, what is Candida, really? She's just a kind of modern-day courtesan or something. She was Daddy's mistress and before that she was Thomas Brandemoor's mistress and before that she had some Greek or other from a shipping family. She lives on men."

Nick picked up his cookie and took a bite out of it. "We used to have a word for that kind of woman when I was growing up. And it wasn't 'courtesan.' "

"Call her anything you want, Nicholas, the fact is that she's got to be pushing fifty. And no matter how shrewd she's been with money—and my guess is that she's been very shrewd—well, she can't be what we'd really call rich, can she?"

"She might not be what you call rich," Nick said, "but she's rich enough for me. Kindly remember that I checked her out for the family back when she first took up with

Paul. She owns that house she lives in out in Bryn Mawr. It's got to be worth a million five."

"That's very nice, Nicholas, but a really big book would make her more than that. Just think of the advances they pay some of these people nowadays. Ten million five sometimes. I've heard of it."

"I just want you to take off your rose-colored glasses," Nick said. "You're always looking for the good side to everybody. So Candida DeWitt is going to write her memoirs. So you make excuses for her."

"She doesn't need an excuse to write her memoirs, Nick. People do it every day."

"I know they do it every day." Nick sighed. "That's not the point. The point is that the selling angle for these memoirs is the death of your stepmother—"

"Oh, I know."

"—and the fact that Candida and Paul were screwing like rabbits the whole last two years of your stepmother's life—"

"I don't think Jacqueline was capable of screwing like a pickle-jar top. She was a poisonous woman."

"I don't care if she was Mrs. Attila the Hun. The point, Alyssa, is that it is extremely unlikely that Candida is going to write these memoirs simply to make a little money. If she needed a little money, we could give it to her. Did you get the impression, when you talked to her, that she would be willing to accept a settlement?"

The chocolate-chip cookie was lying, half eaten, in Alyssa's lap. She had tucked her feet up under her and was now sitting more or less in the lotus position on the edge of the couch. Nick was so intelligent about these things; he really was. He was so good at starting at the beginning and thinking things through to the end. Maybe that was what he got from being a lawyer.

Alyssa picked up the cookie and took yet another bite of it.

"Candida," she said slowly, "didn't really seem to be after much of anything. At least, not much of anything from me. She just—announced it all. Like a town crier giving the news."

"But it was her idea for the two of you to meet?"

"Oh, yes," Alyssa said.

"Why you? Why not Caroline, or James? Why not Paul?"

"I don't think Candida and Paul are speaking, exactly," Alyssa said. "That's because of all that stuff with the police when Jacqueline died, which Candida has a perfect right to be upset about, because Paul behaved like an ass. I don't know if she's ever met James. And as for Caroline—"

Alyssa and Nick shot each other very, very meaningful looks. They both knew Caroline better than they wanted to.

Nick said, "Even assuming it makes sense that of all the people in the family, she'd call you, isn't it a little odd that she'd call anybody at all? Why didn't she just sell her book—is the book sold?"

"What? Oh, yes. I mean, it's not written yet, you know, but I think there's an agreement already signed for the book when it's finished. From Bantam, I think she said."

"There, then. She's sold the book. Why didn't she just go ahead and write it? Why warn the family of a thing of this kind?"

"Maybe she was just being straightforward and above-board."

Nick sighed. "This is Candida DeWitt we're talking about. She didn't play field hockey at Westover. She managed to get an amicable palimony settlement out of a Greek shipping tycoon. Don't talk crazy."

"Maybe it was a compulsion with her, then. Maybe she's one of those people who just can't keep their mouths shut."

"If she were one of those, she'd be dead by now," Nick said. "I'm sorry, Alyssa. I probably like all this as little as Caroline does. It doesn't feel right to me. Did Caroline have anything useful to say when you talked to her?"

To Alyssa's mind, Caroline never had anything useful to say. To be incoherent and hysterical was the essence of being Caroline. She got up and brushed the crumbs of the now-demolished cookie off her skirt. The maid would vacuum in the morning the way she vacuumed every morning.

"Caroline"—Alyssa made her way to the drinks cart to pour herself a glass of wine—"was being positively apocalyptic, complete with pop-psych jargon, of course. God, I'm sick of pop-psych jargon. It's been a bore ever since Daddy took up with it."

"It's made a very nice pile of money for everybody involved," Nick commented. "How do you mean, Caroline was apocalyptic? Was she making threats?"

"Oh, no. Caroline never makes threats. She doesn't even threaten suicide anymore now that she went into therapy. No, you know, she was just talking about the cosmic significance of it all."

"The cosmic significance of Candida DeWitt's memoirs?"

"Of course not. The cosmic significance of Jacqueline's dying. In Caroline's mind, Jacqueline did it deliberately. She knew Caroline had just started therapy, so she got herself killed to avoid the inevitable confrontation. I'm putting it badly. But it doesn't make much sense even when Caroline explains it herself."

"But what did she think of Candida DeWitt's memoirs?"

Alyssa shrugged. "She was against them, of course. I mean, we all are, aren't we? No matter how understanding I'm being, I'd just as soon not see all that raked up again. Do you suppose she'll get on talk shows, talking about the sex?"

"She might."

"It would make Daddy absolutely livid. Caroline's going to make Daddy absolutely livid too. She was nattering on and on about what she was going to say to him as I left. I don't envy him that conversation, I tell you. Why he puts up with it, I don't know. Daddy's always telling those people who come to those seminars he runs that they shouldn't put up with anything at all."

"Well," Nick said judiciously, "he hasn't been giving very many seminars the last few years."

"That's true," Alyssa said.

"Maybe he doesn't feel up to holding out against your sister Caroline. She can be something like a force of nature."

"That's true too," Alyssa said.

"Why don't you pour me a glass of wine while you're up," Nick told her. "Some kind of sherry if you have it.

You should try not to let this upset you too much, if you know what I mean."

"Oh, I know what you mean, all right." Alyssa found a bottle of Harvey's Bristol Cream and poured Nick an over-size glass of it, just the way he liked.

Really, she thought. Families were such a pain. So very impossible. So very—so very *there*. If it were up to her, she would redesign all their personalities. Daddy and Caroline would be interested in opera instead of psychology. James would be terribly respectable and very concerned about the poor. The only one she would leave the same would be herself. She might not be perfect, but she was very, very, very, very sane.

She handed Nick his glass of Harvey's Bristol Cream and drifted away in the direction of the front window, which looked down the hill into what must once have been a thriving urban enclave but was now not more than a collection of concrete overpasses, twisting into the blackness like prophecies of ugliness. Maybe they should move out to Radnor someday. Maybe they should move permanently away, to somewhere like Bermuda.

"Do you know what I think?" Alyssa asked Nick without turning around to face him. "I think it was the worst possible thing that Caroline never married. It's made her too caught up in herself."

5

James Hazzard sometimes wondered what he would have done with his life if he had been born fifty years earlier than he had. He had visions of what it had been like during those fifty years. He had received them from the ranks of black-and-white movies he kept in the media room off his office. MGM, Warner Bros., RKO, Fox—every one of them had made its contribution to the image of the Gypsy fortune-teller, that fat old woman in dirty clothes, hunched over a crystal ball in a filthy trailer parked on a darkened patch of ground at the edge of town. Every one of them had seen fit to make the prophecies real and the Gypsy women embodiments of evil. Maybe they had to do that because, being Hollywood, they were pathologically afraid of older women. Maybe they were just being silly. Surely any Gypsy fortune-teller whose prophecies were real could make a million dollars on the stock exchange and not have to live in a filthy trailer.

James Hazzard's office was in a four-story brownstone in one of the few nice residential neighborhoods left in central Philadelphia. A discreet brass plaque fastened to the center of the pearl-gray front door was all there was to mark the building as a place of business. The plaque said

### JAMES HAZZARD
#### ASTROLOGER

in upright Roman letters identical to the ones used to announce the existence of the society gynecologist next door. James Hazzard's suits came from Brooks Brothers. His shoes were custom-made at John Lobb in London and sent to him by Federal Express. He had been in a filthy trailer once, when he was a sophomore at Brown, but that was just to get laid. The girl involved had had as much prophetic insight as a Pet Rock. James didn't have much prophetic insight himself, but he did have a talent for reading people. He knew what they wanted and what they hoped for and— best of all—what made them afraid. When the time came to put up or shut up, he always knew what to *say*.

James's office was a large room that took up most of the space on the brownstone's second floor, carpeted in pearl gray like the door downstairs, painted in cream, hung with house plants that spilled green leaves out of planters into the vast empty overhead space made by the twenty-foot ceiling. Science, that was the ticket. All of the people who came to James Hazzard liked to believe they were disciples of science, although of an alternative and More Humane kind. They wanted to feel connected to the force of the universe and get in touch with their feminine side. They wouldn't have sat still for one minute in a dirty trailer, or by the side of an old woman who had not taken care of her teeth. They were all desperate and they were all miserable and they were all scared to death.

Now it was seven-thirty and James's last appointment for the evening had just walked out the door. Her name was Katha Parks, and she was a kind of meta-example of fear and trembling. She had the most successful catering business on the Main Line, a personal income of well over two million a year, a Ferrari Testarossa, a vault full of jewelry, and a vacation house in Montego Bay—and she was frantic. That was the only word James had for it. Frantic. She worked out three hours a day. She never let more than eight hundred calories pass her lips in any twenty-four-hour period. She refused to see her maid until she'd put on her makeup. It was crazy. And, James thought, the richer and more successful they were, the crazier it got. That was why people like Katha Parks were willing to pay $1500 an hour for a personal charting session with James Hazzard himself.

James made his way around the huge marble copy of a drafting table he used instead of a desk, went to the office door, and looked out into the hall. Light spilled down the stairwell from the third floor. James went to the rail and called up.

"Max? Are you still there?"

"I'm still here," Max called back.

James winced. Max was sounding definitely swish, angry-swish, the way he did when some fool woman came on to him and wouldn't take no for an answer. James didn't mind the swish in itself—he was a cosmopolitan man with a tendency to regard sex as a pleasant activity no matter whom he did it with, or of what sex—but he did mind what it represented, which was an impending explosion. It had been a long day. James wasn't ready to deal with Max in one of his revolutionary-warrior moods. He wasn't ready to deal with a telephone operator with a bad attitude. He wanted a strong cup of coffee with a shot of Scotch in it followed by a long, pleasant dinner at the Harmony Café.

James went around the stairwell and climbed to the third floor. The light on the landing was not on—Max was always saving electricity and being a Friend of the Earth—

but the light coming from Max's office was enough. James went in and found Max sprawled out in the swivel chair behind his desk, looking like a cross between a college student and a life-style ensemble in one of the better sportswear catalogues. Max was a devotee of $100 jeans and $600 plaid lumberjack's shirts. James sometimes thought Max kept Ralph Lauren Polo in business all on his own.

"Coffee just perked two seconds ago," Max said, not looking up. He was frowning at a stack of papers in front of him. James recognized columns of figures and got bored. "Pour some for yourself, will you? I've got to finish up here before we talk."

"When you finish up here, are you going to tell me what pissed you off?"

"Dina Van Rau pissed me off. You're going to have to raise the admission prices to the seminars. To at least three fifty a head. There's no way around it. Expenses are up and the profit margin is down."

"I've been thinking about John Calvin," James said. "About the theology that said some people were born saved and other people were born damned and you could tell the difference because the saved people had more material wealth. Does that sound familiar to you?"

"Pour me some coffee too," Max said. "I've got to go out tonight to one of those places where they serve nothing but herb tea and bean sprouts. God, I hate the healthy foods movement."

James hated the healthy foods movement too. He especially hated the part of it where people like his father thought you were an unenlightened mess in need of immediate therapy if you had a cocktail every night before dinner. He poured two cups of coffee, doctored them both liberally with Johnnie Walker Black, and passed one over to Max.

Max had finished with his columns of numbers. He took the coffee James was handing him, put his feet on his desk, and said, "Your sister Caroline called. Not five minutes ago. She was hysterical."

"Caroline is always hysterical. Was it something in particular this time?"

Max nodded. "Candida DeWitt, that's what it was. Apparently nobody got around to telling her what was going on until today, and then your sister Alyssa just blurted it all out, and now Caroline—"

"—is acting like a Victorian virgin with the vapors. I'm glad you took the call instead of me."

"I don't mind talking to Victorian virgins with the vapors. Especially your sister Caroline. She's like listening to the Donahue show. Do you suppose she is a virgin?"

"I haven't the faintest idea."

"It would be really wonderful if she were. Nobody's a virgin anymore. I think virginity's a very frustrating thing, don't you? As soon as you try to do anything with it, you lose it."

"Was all that supposed to make sense?"

"It makes perfect sense," Max said lightly. "Never mind. Are you all worried about Candida DeWitt?"

James took a long sip of his coffee, which was smooth and soothing and just the right kind of bitter for the end of a working day. Oddly enough, he wasn't in the least bit worried about Candida DeWitt. The death of Jacqueline Isherwood and the circumstances surrounding it had driven Caroline half crazy and embarrassed Alyssa and Nick, but they had been good for James. SOCIETY VICTIM WARNED, the headline on the *National Enquirer* said, and it was followed by a story about how "psychic James Hazzard, the victim's stepson" had told his stepmother she would die a violent death within the month if she didn't take steps to protect herself, which, of course, she hadn't, so she did. It was all a lot of nonsense. James had never claimed to be a psychic, just a "trained astrological counselor," whatever that meant. He had certainly never warned Jacqueline that she was about to die a violent death. He had never warned Jacqueline about anything. God, how he had hated that woman. Prissy, frumpy, uptight, and absolutely humorless—James just knew Paul had married her for her money. There couldn't be any other reason. James himself hadn't said four words a day to her for the last five years before she died. Jacqueline made his skin crawl.

SOCIETY VICTIM WARNED, the headline said, and then another one, in an even less respectable outlet: PERILS

OF DISBELIEF. In any rational world, that sort of publicity should have been enough to kill half his business. The people he dealt with had a positive allergy to anything that smacked of low rent. Instead, his business had actually increased, and increased most dramatically in the level of his private consultations. It was as if all these people read the supermarket tabloids, and more than half believed them, on the sly. It was as if the entire upper-middle-class population of the United States had taken a step backward and sideways, into a new Dark Age of superstition and insanity, into a dream-world full of cackling demons that stayed just out of sight. James himself did not believe in astrology. He knew perfectly well that the stars and the planets were not where his charts said they were. He'd taken more than one astronomy course in college. He didn't believe his fate was tied up with some cosmic force in the universe either. He didn't think there was any cosmic force in the universe. He didn't think there was any such thing as fate. He just—

His mug was more than two-thirds empty. He topped it up with coffee and Scotch—with a lot of Scotch—and then realized Max was staring at him. James raised his glass in a toast and said, "Here's to nothing. What's the matter with you?"

"It's you we ought to be worried about," Max said. "You look definitely odd right now."

"I was indulging in a very dangerous activity. I was letting myself get ethics."

"Oh, don't do that. We'd go broke."

"I know."

"Maybe you can get ethics after you retire. You can write a big exposé of the New Age movement and make a million dollars going on talk shows and telling the public how you ripped them off."

"If I did, thirty psychics would go on with me and tell the public how they never rip anybody off, and the audience would believe them. Do you ever wonder what's wrong with people these days?"

"Not if I can help it."

James took a deep swallow of coffee and Scotch and

sighed. "Are you sure that was all Caroline wanted, to talk about Candida DeWitt?"

"Absolutely. Except for the usual, of course. Your dysfunctional family. How long you were going to be content to stay mired in denial before you came to your senses and decided to take control of your life."

"Nothing about Fred Scherrer?"

"Fred Scherrer." Max was puzzled. "The name's familiar, but I can't place it. Is it someone we know?"

"It's someone I know. He's a lawyer."

"Oh," Max said, comprehending. "*The* lawyer."

"Exactly. *The* lawyer."

"Not a mention, darling. Why? Was she supposed to say something about him?"

"No," James said. "As far as I know, he doesn't have anything to do with this at all. But I think it's funny. You know. I think it's funny that he hasn't turned up."

"Well, he's hardly hiding, James. Scherrer's a famous lawyer. I don't think he's been hiding in a hole in the ground ever since your stepmother was—ah—how should we put it?"

"Murdered," James said. "And Fred Scherrer hasn't been hiding in a hole in the ground. He's defended two more famous people and done a lot of civil liberties work that doesn't make such a splash in the papers. That's not what I mean. I mean it's funny he hasn't turned up about this."

"About Ms. DeWitt's memoirs."

"Exactly. Even Candida hasn't mentioned him. And that's odd."

Max got up and got himself more coffee and more Scotch. "Everything's odd around here," he said, dropping the swish. "It makes me tired sometimes, how odd it all is. Does it really matter, if Candida DeWitt isn't putting this lawyer in her memoirs?"

"It would matter more if she was," James said. "I think I'm the only one who realizes it, but Fred Scherrer is far more potential trouble to the family than Candida DeWitt ever could be. Candida DeWitt gives good television, but she doesn't actually know anything."

"And Fred Scherrer does?"

"Yes," James said slowly. "I can't be absolutely sure. I've never tried to test it—but yes, I think he does."

Somewhere behind James, still standing next to the coffee and the Scotch, Max coughed.

It was an uncomfortable cough that sounded a little strangled, and James understood it perfectly.

## 6

Mary Elizabeth Poodiak had changed her name to Candida DeWitt four days after her twenty-first birthday, four days after the earliest date on which it would have been legal to change it. With the change, she had gone through the psychological equivalent of shedding a skin. The young woman who emerged from the Philadelphia courthouse as Candida DeWitt was not the same as the one who had gone in as Mary Poodiak. She walked differently. She spoke differently. She had a different glint in her eye. She felt like a bird coming out of an egg. Where before she had been hard and smooth, now she was a Personality. Where before she had been brittle and tough, now she was—what? Candida had never been able to put it into words, but it was the part of her that had attracted the richest and most accomplished of men, and gotten her exactly what she wanted out of them. It was the part of her that suited her purposes so well, she never had to be hard or mercenary. Candida DeWitt was a woman who genuinely liked men, in all their maleness. She enjoyed listening to baritone voices yelling imprecations at football coaches. She was made contented by the soft swearing frustration of a conglomerator attempting to broil a steak in an electric oven. She could go to sleep to the sound of a hammer hitting nails. A woman who genuinely liked men and made very few demands on them beyond the financial—in certain times and under certain circumstances, that combination could be worth the weight of Jumbo the Elephant in gold, and it had been. This big house in Bryn Mawr was not all that Candida

DeWitt owned. She had a nice tidy portfolio of stocks, a very interesting collection of municipal bonds, and a judicious selection of rental properties to see her through a comfortable old age. Memoirs or no memoirs, Candida DeWitt was set for life.

Of course, what Candida had been engaged in all these years was a kind of whoring. She knew that, although the frowsy little blonde who had come out to stay for the weekend didn't seem to. The frowsy little blonde was an assistant editor at Candida's publishing house, and she was supposed to be helping Candida put together a detailed outline of the book she had contracted to write. In the process, the frowsy little blonde—Casey Holder, Candida told herself, I have to remember that her name is Casey Holder—was doing everything in her power not to recognize the truth of just about anything at all.

Candida DeWitt had been intelligent about her body as well as her investments. She had kept herself reasonably trim and reasonably attractive, without indulging in the kind of obsessional dieting that turned middle-aged women into walking skeletons, like Nancy Reagan. Candida knew a lot of women like that. She didn't envy them. She didn't envy anyone. As far as she knew, she had a perfect life.

Well, almost.

If she'd had an absolutely perfect life, she wouldn't have been writing this book.

Casey Holder was sitting cross-legged on the rug in front of the living room fireplace, frowning down at photocopies of Candida's original sample chapters. She'd been pawing through them all night, as if she expected to find something new there.

"Of course, the really delicate thing," Casey Holder said, "will be deciding how to handle the murder and everything that came after it. Linda told me to bring that up especially. She said the strategy on that ought to be planned right from the beginning."

"Linda" was Linda Bell, the real editor on Candida's book. Linda was also the president of this division of her publishing company and a reputed expert in how to make best sellers. Candida had wondered from the first if that could really be true. When Candida talked to Linda, she always got the impression that Linda hadn't read the last few chapters Candida had written.

"I don't think we have to worry too much about the murder," Candida said now. "I did put it in the very first chapter. Or something about it, anyway."

"Of course you did!" Casey Holder was encouraging. Candida wondered what that meant. So far, she had noticed an odd thing about publishing people: They never told you anything you had written was rank awful even if they thought it was. It was as if they expected you to explode at the very suggestion of real criticism.

"If there's something wrong with the way I did it," Candida said, "I can always change it. I do try to be reasonably accommodating, you know."

"Oh, you're very accommodating," Casey Holder said. "There isn't anything Linda wants changed about the first chapter. It's *perfect* just the way it is. It's very arresting."

"So to speak."

Casey Holder was oblivious. "The tension that chapter creates is just perfect, and it goes right to the heart of what people are going to want to read. And you follow it with the two chapters on the senator, and that's good too, because the senator is always interesting to people who like gossip. And after the senator, well, things are very straightforward."

"They were fairly monotonous, from what I remember."

"Yes. I see. The point is, the real charge, the real excitement in this book the way you have set it up so far—it was you who set it up this way, of course, I mean, we're going by your original proposal. It wasn't our idea to put the murder first."

"Of course it wasn't."

"All right, then, you see, the way you've set it up, the real interest is going to be in the murder."

"Of course," Candida said again. "I want the real interest to be in the murder."

"So do we," Casey Holder said, "so do we. But then the question becomes how you're going to handle it, you see."

"No."

"No?"

"I don't see why I can't just tell the story and get it over with," Candida said reasonably. "Start at the beginning, write through the middle, and stop when I come to the end."

Casey Holder looked distressed. "But there are issues. You must realize that. There are legal issues, for one thing."

"What kind of legal issues?"

Casey Holder was being brave. "There are libel issues, for instance. If you're going to speculate on the identity of the murderer—"

"I'm not going to speculate on anything."

"If you're even going to hint, or slant the story in such a way that an inference couldn't help being made—"

"I'm not going to do any such thing," Candida said. "I've been entirely open about what I intend to do. I don't know who killed Jacqueline Isherwood Hazzard. Nobody knows. Nobody has ever been convicted of the crime."

"Oh, convicted." Casey Holder shook her head. "Convicted isn't everything."

"It is in the United States legal system," Candida said firmly. "Innocent until proven guilty. That's what the Constitution says."

"Yes. Of course. But in your outline—"

"I say that I will reveal information never before published." Candida nodded vigorously. "And I will. I will reveal a lot of information never before published, because I have a lot of information never before published. But that information won't be the identity of the murderer, because I don't have that."

Casey Holder was getting very uncomfortable. She was squiggling around on the rug like a baby too young to turn over yet, frustrated at being unable to move. Candida stretched out her right leg and used the toe of her high-heeled pump to press a button imbedded in the floor. That would buzz the kitchen and bring the maid, who could be sent off for coffee and liqueurs. Maybe coffee and liqueurs could cheer things up.

"Come now," Candida said. "You must have realized you weren't going to get the name of the murderer. You must have realized you couldn't."

"I think Linda was hoping you'd heard some rumors. . . ." Casey sighed. "Things like this are so fascinating. Real murders among real people. That's why true crime books sell so well. And of course, you know what Gregor Demarkian says."

"Gregor Demarkian." Candida processed the name through a couple of times and finally came up with a definite image. "Oh, yes. The detective. I've heard of him."

"I thought you'd know a lot more about him than I do," Casey said, "living on the Main Line and he's from Philadelphia and everything. There are stories about him in the *Inquirer* all the time."

"How do you know what stories are in the *Inquirer*? Do you mean publishing people in New York read the newspapers from Philadelphia?"

"Our clipping service clips articles about Demarkian for Linda Bell," Casey said. "Linda's wild to get him to do a book about his cases. She said it would be absolutely the hit of the season. He hasn't been interested so far though. I don't think he likes publicity."

"What is it he always says that you think I should have heard of?"

"He says somebody always knows the identity of the murderer." Casey sat up and stretched. "He says even in really famous cases like Lizzie Borden and Jack the Ripper, there were people who knew what happened. They just never told and the truth never came out."

"I suppose the murderer always knows what happened," Candida said. "There's that."

"It's not just the murderer. It's people around the murderer. People who know the murderer."

Candida shook her head decisively. "I don't see what good that would do. If the murderer was some passing tramp, or a hophead looking for money for drugs, well, the murderer himself might not know he'd committed the murder ten minutes after he'd committed it. He might not remember a thing."

"But Jacqueline Hazzard wasn't killed by a passing tramp," Casey said. "At least, that's not what the police thought at the time."

"The police thought a lot of things at the time," Candida

said, "including that I committed that murder myself to get Jacqueline out of the way so I could marry Paul. It was a damned good thing I'd been photographed shaking hands with the President of the United States at a fund-raiser for the homeless in Los Angeles twenty minutes after the crime was supposed to have been committed. The police think a lot of things."

"I suppose they do," Casey said. "Never mind. I guess Linda and I were really hoping that you were the one— well, you know—that you were the person who knew what really happened, and that you'd *hint*."

"My dear girl," Candida said. "If I did anything like that, I'd be sued. These are educated people we're dealing with here. They don't put up with nonsense of that kind. They make you pay for it."

There was a soft sound of footsteps, rubber soles against hardwood floors, and Candida's maid came into the room, still in uniform and looking expectant.

"There was something you wanted, Mrs. DeWitt?"

Candida DeWitt had never been married, but she understood that after a certain age that was not an asset. She called herself a widow and provided no further information.

"Louise," she said now, "I'd like a cup of coffee, if you wouldn't mind getting it for me. Perhaps Ms. Holder would like a cup of coffee too."

"Coffee," Casey Holder said. "I don't think so. Unless you have decaf?"

Candida kept her expression neutral. She didn't keep decaf in the house. It tasted like cow's piss.

"We have herb teas," she suggested instead. "Red Zinger, I believe, and—Sleepytime?"

"Yes, Mrs. DeWitt," Louise said. "We have Sleepytime. We also have Mandarin Orange and Lemon Zinger."

"Mandarin Orange," Casey said quickly. "That will be perfect."

"I will bring along the honey in case you like it sweet," Louise said. Then she turned around and disappeared.

Candida stared at the empty space where Louise had been and thought hard. It was so difficult to decide what to do sometimes. She had always been a very easygoing sort. She had always had to be. She had never operated out of revenge before. She found it very difficult to understand what it would be best to say or who it would be best to talk to or when it would be best to sit still and not move at all.

This did not seem a time for sitting still. Casey Holder was gazing up at her, half-fascinated and half-tense, an anxious young woman who would always resent other women, for reasons she would never be willing to explain to herself.

"You know," Candida told her, "if what you really want is some kind of hint, you ought to talk to Fred Scherrer. If your Gregor Demarkian is right and somebody always knows, then Fred Scherrer is definitely the man who knows about *this*."

## 7

Fred Scherrer had been interviewed for *60 Minutes* by Ed Bradley, and in the middle of that interview he had declared—in a sound byte that made the air—that he could defend Saddam Hussein in an Israeli court and get him off. Fred Scherrer was fifty-two years old, and for the last thirty of those years he had been the most famous defense attorney in America. He might have been the most famous lawyer in the history of America with the exception of Clarence Darrow. He was certainly a phenomenon. Illiterate teenagers in southern Georgia knew his name. Associate justices of the United States Supreme Court cursed him over cocktails in the bar of the Burning Tree Country Club. Millions of middle-aged women with a lust for blood and an insatiable curiosity about capital cases snapped up the books he wrote for $22 a pop, making him the only lawyer on record to have a book spend one hundred sixty-four weeks on *The New York Times* hardcover nonfiction best-seller list.

If one of the middle-aged women with a lust for blood had met Fred Scherrer, she might not have been impressed. He was not a physically prepossessing man. Five foot seven, a hundred fifty-four pounds, kick-sand-in-my-face thin running to wrinkles and paunch—from a distance, Fred Scherrer resembled the sort of man who spends his life working at the post office but never has quite enough juice to get promoted off the carrier routes. It was only face-to-face that he began to be impressive.

Right now Fred Scherrer wasn't even being impressive face-to-face. He had shut himself down, in a way, turned all the interior emotion off, blanked himself out. He always did that while he was waiting for a jury to come in, which was what he was doing. He was being especially impassive, because there was no doubt whatsoever what verdict this jury would bring back. Getting Saddam Hussein off in Jerusalem was one thing. Getting Chuckie Bickerson off in Westchester County was something else. This was the sort of case Fred took for practice. Chuckie Bickerson had kidnapped a fifteen-year-old Mount Vernon cheerleader from the parking lot of her school at four o'clock in the afternoon in full view of her boyfriend, the junior varsity cheerleading squad, and the sour-faced Puritan English teacher who served as adviser to the Glee Club. The phrase "asking to get caught" came to mind, but Fred found it ludicrously inadequate. And dumb? Good God. Talking to Chuckie Bickerson could give a normal person a migraine. Chuckie had raped and murdered the cheerleader, of course. He'd raped and murdered a few other girls too, and when the police finally caught up to him—which, after the stunt in Mount Vernon, wasn't too difficult—they'd found the bodies of those girls in Chuckie's basement, just lying there stacked up against the vinyl-covered furniture and stretched out on the industrial-grade rug. The smell had been awful.

Chuckie's smell was awful too. It was as if the sourness of his sweat were woven into him, unremovable by soap. Fred would never have taken his case if Chuckie hadn't insisted on pleading innocent.

Ass.

Chuckie stirred in his seat, stretched his arms, shook his head. "I got to go to the bathroom," he said. "Where's that guy that takes me to the bathroom?"

"Maybe he's gone to the bathroom himself. He'll be back in a minute, Chuckie. Just hold your water."

"I *been* holding my water," Chuckie said. "I been holding *myself*. Why didn't you let me get up there and talk?"

I didn't let you get up there and talk, Fred thought, because I didn't want to be witness to a lynching. He said, "The defendant doesn't have to testify, Chuckie. And it's generally a good idea if he doesn't. Prosecutors can be very tricky bastards."

"I could have explained myself," Chuckie objected. "I mean, I had things to say."

"I know you did, Chuckie."

"I could have told them all about those girls. The things they said to me. The things they did."

"I know."

"Once you've screwed 'em, their lives are ruined anyway," Chuckie said. "My mother told me that. A woman's virtue is all she has. If she loses it, she might as well be dead."

"Your mother must have been a very interesting woman, Chuckie."

"Oh, she was. Except she wasn't really my mother. My real mother went away somewhere. Why didn't you tell them about the eyes?"

"The eyes?"

"Yeah, you know. When somebody gets murdered, the picture of the murderer stays in their eyes, and all you have to do is look. But my picture didn't stay in any of their eyes. So I couldn't have murdered them."

"It was a case of multiple serial suicides."

"Suicides," Chuckie said firmly. "That's the ticket."

"There's Sergeant Devere," Fred said. "If you're going to the john, you'd better do it now."

"I still say you should have told them about the eyes," Chuckie said. "That would have cleared up everything."

Fred stood up and waved to Sergeant Devere, who nodded and began to come across the front of the courtroom to them. Sergeant Devere didn't like Chuckie any more than Fred did, but Sergeant Devere was a professional. In fact, as far as Fred was concerned, Sergeant Devere was awesome. If Devere ever started to play poker for serious, he'd get rich.

"Chuckie wants to go to the bathroom," Fred told Sergeant Devere. "I'd like to go for a walk, if you get what I mean."

"Of course," Sergeant Devere said. "I'll take Mr. Bickerson out back for a while."

"I don't see why I always have to be out back whenever you take a walk," Chuckie said. "I've seen trials on television. The accused guy doesn't always have to go out back."

"Judge's orders," Sergeant Devere said.

"Maybe it has something to do with the fact that the first day here, you grabbed a paperweight during recess and tried to take a policewoman hostage."

"Self-defense," Chuckie said sullenly. "You can't blame a guy for what he does in self-defense. I'm being railroaded here."

"Right."

"Mr. Bickerson?" Sergeant Devere said.

Fred moved away from the table, giving Devere room to work with Chuckie's shackles. Chuckie was wearing shackles because on their *second* day in court, he'd tried to kick the bailiff in the groin. Fortunately for the bailiff, Chuckie had seen karate kicks only in the movies. He'd never before actually tried to do one.

Fred left the courtroom, looked around the corridor outside—newspeople everywhere; more cameras than a store that was going out of business on Broadway—and then made his way to the stairs. He went down the single flight to the basement and along the corridor there to the cafeteria. He found Sydney Mellerstein, his junior partner, sitting alone at a table against the wall, drinking coffee. Fred got a cup of coffee for himself, paid for it, and went over to join Sid.

"Jury's still out." He sat down.

Sid sighed. "They must be staging an orgy. They couldn't be having trouble coming to a decision. How's Chuckie?"

"Chuckie's Chuckie."

"That's too bad. I picked up our messages before I came down here. You got a call from Caroline Hazzard."

The coffee the cafeteria served in this courthouse was terrible. In Fred's experience, the coffee the cafeterias served in all courthouses was always terrible. The coffee served in the cafeterias in state legislative buildings was worse. Fred doctored his cup with enough milk and sugar to produce something on the order of a mocha egg cream, and put Chuckie Bickerson firmly out of his mind.

"Caroline Hazzard," he said. "Now, there's a blast from the past—the recent past, but the past. I wonder why it was Caroline who called instead of Paul."

"Maybe because Paul has sense enough not to bother you with hysterical phone messages when you're right in the middle of a murder trial."

"Hysterical. That's right. Caroline is the hysterical one. Always talking about her inner child and how hard she's working to heal her addictions. What did she want?"

Sydney took a long swig of his coffee. He grimaced. "She wants to hire you. She wants you to work for free. You owe it to the family. You can't let that woman get away with this."

"Let what woman get away with what?"

"Let Candida DeWitt get away with publishing her memoirs," Sid said. "That's what this flap is all about. Candida DeWitt is publishing her memoirs. I refrained from telling Ms. Hazzard that I intend to camp out all night in front of the door to my local bookstore when the time comes, just so I can have the first copy I can get my hands on. Whew. This is going to be a pip."

"I wonder how graphic she'll get," Fred mused. " 'Mr. Fortune Five Hundred Empire Builder may look self-possessed in public, but in private he likes to be dressed up in diapers and fed a bottle of baby formula.' "

"Do people do things like that?"

"They do considerably worse. I hope she gets *very* graphic. I'll defend her in the libel actions for free. It'd be worth it for the publicity. It'd be worth it to see Candida again. I wonder how she is."

"I always thought you rather liked her," Sid said. "I liked Candida better than I liked any of them, at least at the time. Of course, they were all under a lot of strain."

"You could say that. They're probably still under a lot of strain. I knew Paul at Harvard, you know."

"Yeah," Sid said. "I know."

"He was very successful at that—stuff he does. Enormously so. I suppose that's where Caroline picked it up."

"He married a rich woman," Sid said. "It's funny how nobody ever mentions that. Nobody mentioned it at the time. Paul had made a fair piece of change, but she had serious money."

"That's true." Fred nodded. "And there was that house, right in the middle of Philadelphia—that belonged to her originally, didn't it?"

Sid snorted. "You shouldn't let Harvard cloud your judgment. It belonged to her all right, but Paul was always going around saying how it had been in 'his' family since whenever, that 'his' great-something grandfather built it. He would outright lie about it."

"I'm sure he still does," Fred said. "I think the family name was originally Hazuelski. His father changed it. Paul was Hazzard at Harvard. But it—got around."

"Did it matter?"

"In a way. In those days. Yes. Of course, I was an outsider too, a public school boy on scholarship—but I like being an outsider. It doesn't bother me. Paul was from Philadelphia and he was almost-but-not-quite, if you know what I mean. A second-string prep school. A dancing class but not the right dancing class. Invitations to the big deb balls but not to the really important little ones. I remember wondering at the time if Paul was marrying Jacqueline for love or for position or for simple obsession. I don't think I ever reached an answer in my own mind."

"Why did she marry *him*?" Sid asked curiously.

Fred laughed. "Because she was a thoroughly ridiculous woman, that's why. Jacqueline was the sort of rich woman who has love affairs with projects. The recovery movement was her project. Or maybe Paul's career in the recovery movement was her project. I don't know."

"Whatever," Sid said. "They're always saying in the

papers that you know who really did it. They're always saying you're the only one who knows."

"The only way I could be the only one who knows is if I'd done it myself," Fred said, "and I didn't. I'm glad to be able to say I was in Gstaad at the time. You shouldn't read the tabloids, Sid, they're bad for you."

"You read them," Sid said.

"The Bickerson jury will be returning to the courtroom in three minutes," a woman's low voice said pleasantly through the loudspeakers hanging above their heads. "Will all principals please return to the courtroom. The Bickerson jury will be returning to the courtroom in three minutes . . ."

Fred checked his watch. "Hour and a half. Maybe they sent out for Chinese."

"Maybe Chuckie will throw another fit when the verdict is read." Sid got to his feet. "Is he really that dumb, or is he putting on an act? I keep thinking nobody could be really that dumb."

"He's really that dumb." Fred got to his feet himself. "But she isn't. I wonder what it is she thinks she's up to."

"Who?" Sid demanded.

"Candida DeWitt," Fred said, leading the way back out into the corridor. "She really isn't a stupid woman, you know, and this memoir thing is damn near terminal idiocy. So she's got to be doing it on purpose."

"Right." Sid sounded dubious.

"I wonder what she's up to," Fred said again. "I wonder if I paid her a visit if she'd tell me."

8

Gregor Demarkian was out to dinner with a friend who had been with him in the FBI, but that was all right. Lida Arkmanian had a key to his apartment. She had a key to old George Tekemanian's apartment on the first floor of this same building and a key to Hannah Krekorian's place up the street, but for some reason Lida had keys to neither Bennis Hannaford's apartment nor Donna

Moradanyan's. There was no significance in this. Keys got passed around on Cavanaugh Street the way baseball trading cards had before they got valuable enough to collect. Keys came and went too, until somehow they mysteriously disappeared, and then somebody had to ask Gregor to jimmy a lock.

Since Gregor's key was the only one she needed for the moment, and since it hadn't disappeared, Lida was thinking about keys in only the most desultory way, because she was tired and drifty-headed and really in need of an early night. She had spent the past several hours making pastries of various kinds, for no good reason at all. God only knew she didn't need to eat more desserts than she already did, and Gregor needed it even less. God only knew she had better things to do with her time than cook—or did she? That was a very hard question to answer. Lida didn't know what a fifty-eight-year-old woman was supposed to do with her time. She just knew that she'd been feeling restless all evening, and wondered if she ought to take a vacation. She was much too jumpy to sit still, and so it had seemed the perfect solution to do some serious cooking and let her nerves do some good for somebody while she couldn't make them calm down. Now it was eight-thirty and she was coming empty-handed out of Gregor Demarkian's third-floor apartment, having left a pile of halvah in his refrigerator tall enough to qualify as a foothill. She felt like a complete idiot.

Not such good decorations this time, she thought, giving a last look at Gregor's apartment door. It sported a single large metallic red-and-silver heart in honor of the upcoming Valentine's Day, but nothing as exuberant as Donna ordinarily put up to celebrate a holiday. Donna Moradanyan decorated this entire town house, inside and out, and most of Cavanaugh Street on any excuse at all, and did it with energy too. One Christmas, she'd wrapped the entire front façade of Holy Trinity Armenian Christian Church in ribbon and tinsel until it looked like a package. One Halloween, she'd decorated a lamppost on Cavanaugh Street to look so convincingly like the Devil, someone had called a cop. This time Donna's heart didn't seem to be in it, so to speak. She didn't seem to have the fire.

February, Lida murmured to herself, starting down the stairs. February. That's all it is. I ought to get Hannah and go to the Bahamas until the good weather comes back. That would cheer me up.

She reached the half-landing, looking down the stair-well at what she expected to be nothingness, and stopped. There was definitely not nothing on the landing outside Bennis Hannaford's apartment door. There was a tall young man with longish hair and an immense down parka, look-ing agitated. He must have heard her coming. He turned, caught sight of her on the half-landing, and relaxed a little.

"Hello," he said. "I'm sorry if I startled you. The front door was unlocked, so I just came in—"

—the front door was always unlocked. Gregor was al-ways lecturing old George and Bennis and Donna about how they ought to remember to lock it—

"—but now that I've gotten up here, I've knocked and knocked, and nobody answers, and I just don't know what to do. I'm Christopher Hannaford."

"Oh," Lida said, feeling instantly better. "Oh, yes. Ben-nis's brother. She told us you were coming."

"She doesn't seem to have remembered I was coming," Christopher said. "She isn't home."

Lida came the rest of the way down the stairs to the second floor and looked thoughtfully at Bennis's door. "I think I know where she is," she said. "She must have gone to pick up Father Tibor at the demonstration—"

"Demonstration?"

"It was a protest of some kind he was involved in. I'm not really sure of the details. Anyway, she must have gone to get him, and not expected to be long, and then things happened to hold her up. Somehow, with Father Tibor, things always happen to hold you up."

"I've heard." Christopher grinned. "I get regular re-ports about Father Tibor and old George Tekemanian and Gregor Demarkian and Donna Moradanyan. Which one are you?"

"I'm none of those," Lida said. "My name is Lida Ark-manian."

"Oh, I've heard of *you*," Christopher said. He stepped back a little and tilted his head to one side. Lida flushed and turned away. He made her—he made her so conscious of the way she looked. A small woman, still relatively thin—although not as thin as she had been—and relatively shapely, in spite of the fact that she'd had five children and—oh, who was she kidding? How old was this man? Forty? Less than forty? Her stomach stuck out. That was why she wore dresses with full skirts with elastic waistbands. After five children, anybody's stomach would stick out, unless you had one of those operations, the way movie stars did and—what was the *matter* with her?

"You don't look at all the way Bennis described you," Christopher Hannaford was saying. "She makes everyone on Cavanaugh Street sound so foreign."

"Some of us are foreign," Lida said. "Father Tibor came from the Soviet Union. When there was a Soviet Union."

"Getting to be a crazy world, isn't it?"

"Yes," Lida said. "I read somewhere last week that the Swedish government is going to privatize their post office. Sweden. It's hard to believe it."

"We're probably going to nationalize our parking garages," Christopher said. "It's just an itch for change, that's all. It goes through the world every once in a while. It's been going through me for the last six months."

"Has it?" Lida said. "I think I've been experiencing something similar. Restlessness. Restlessness but no real need to do anything in particular. Are you the one who's the poet?"

"I'm a deejay out in California. I write poetry sometimes."

"You publish your poetry in *The New Yorker* and in *Poetry* magazine. Bennis shows them to me sometimes."

"I'm flattered. I never thought Bennis took my poetry seriously. It doesn't pay enough to keep me in coffee beans."

"I wish I could do something like write poetry," Lida said. "All I seem to be able to do is cook."

Christopher kicked a toe at Bennis's closed door. "I suppose I'll just have to camp out here on the landing and wait. She can't be all night, can she? And I've got a book to read. In fact, I think I've got six. I hit one of those huge Barnes and Noble stores right before I got on the plane."

"Ah," Lida said, looking toward Bennis's darkened doorway herself.

It was very odd. She didn't feel restless anymore. She didn't feel self-conscious. She was really very relaxed. That strange feeling of being on trial and sure to be found wanting had disappeared. Maybe it was just that Christopher Hannaford didn't seem to be looking at her anymore. Not looking at her to any purpose, at any rate. Maybe it was just that she finally knew what it was she was supposed to do.

"You can't stay here," she told him. "It could be hours before Bennis gets back. Father Tibor is definitely not reliable when it comes to time. And you must be hungry."

"I'm always hungry," Christopher said. "Why? Is there a restaurant—"

"There's a very good restaurant just a couple of blocks away," Lida said, "and you can go there if you like, of course, but that wasn't what I meant. I meant you should come across the street with me. That's where I live, across the street. That big window on the second floor of the building immediately opposite this one is my living room."

"You can't see it from here," Chris said.

"No," Lida agreed, "but you can see it from the living room windows of all four of the apartments in this building, and what's more important, you can see all their living room windows from mine."

"Meaning when Bennis gets in, I'll be able to see her window light up."

"Exactly. Of course, we will leave a note on the door before we go, just in case you would rather watch television or read one of your books instead of watch for lights in Bennis's window."

"I don't want to put you to any trouble. I know it's late, or getting that way—"

"You won't be any trouble at all. I will be glad to have the company. I have that big town house, and there isn't anybody to live in it but me. It gets very lonely sometimes."

"Bennis said something in one of her letters about your giving room to some refugees."

"Oh, yes," Lida said, "I gave rooms to refugees. I gave

rooms to quite a few refugees. But refugees are just like anybody else. They like to have places of their own. Mine found very nice apartments. We keep in touch. Do you like Armenian food?"

"I don't know," Chris said. "I've never had any."

"Well, we'll try it anyway," Lida said, and then, suddenly, she was embarrassed again, she didn't know why. She stuck her hands into the slash pockets of her chinchilla coat and searched around frantically for a pen and a piece of paper. Why she expected to find them, she didn't know. She never kept anything in the pockets of that coat except a little loose change. She was still in awe of the fact that she owned it.

Chris had come up with his own pen and paper, rooted out of the duffel bag he had brought instead of a suitcase. If Lida hadn't known he was rich, she'd have taken him for one of those rootless men who always seemed to be thumbing rides just above the exit ramps when she took the superhighway. Still, she was more sophisticated than that. She knew that people who came from old money often dressed like tramps, as a kind of statement. She knew that from Bennis.

Chris finished his note, looked at it thoughtfully, and then nodded to himself. He took his Swiss army knife out of his pocket and opened it to one of the smallest blades.

"This will hold it up," he said, "and she'll know it's really me. I've got the ultimate model, you know. It's even got a knife and fork and spoon."

"Big enough to eat with?" Lida asked doubtfully.

"Big enough to eat with if you're Thumbelina," Chris said.

"Let's go across the street," Lida said. "I'll give you a knife and fork and spoon big enough to eat with if you're the Green Giant. Or whoever it was that Jack met. I'm not very good at fairy tales."

"Neither am I."

Lida felt perfectly at peace. She was silly to chide herself about the amount of cooking she did. She had been cooking since she was a girl. It was an excellent mode of communication with people she only barely knew. It was a completely safe zone of human endeavor. Once she'd started talking about cooking, she hadn't been afraid of Christopher Hannaford in the least.

Feed them, Lida Arkmanian told herself. If you feed them, the feeding will blot out everything else.

It always had before.

## 9

Very much later, at ten twenty-two, when the windchill was down to minus forty degrees and the sidewalks felt like ice, Bennis Hannaford finally got home with Father Tibor Kasparian in tow. She had a couple of other people in tow too. Father Ryan. Father Carmichael. Father Papageorgiou. Reverend Kress. Cold or no cold, Bennis had the window she was sitting next to all the way open. She was puffing frantically on a Benson & Hedges menthol and seriously considering taking to dope.

"We can't possibly sit in at the mayor's residence," Father Carmichael was saying, "because he's got pit bulls."

The cab pulled up in front of Holy Trinity Church. Bennis shoved her hands in her pockets, came up with a wad of money, and peeled off a few bills for the cabdriver. The driver took them and asked,

"Are they always like this? Aren't they supposed to be holy people?"

"I don't know what they're supposed to be," Bennis said. "You can keep the change."

"*Very* nice."

"I'm getting out," Bennis said to the collective clergy. "This is where we're all going. You guys should get out too."

The collective clergy didn't seem to have heard her. Bennis landed on the sidewalk and walked back along the side of Holy Trinity into the little courtyard onto which Father Tibor's apartment fronted. She had her hands in her hair and her mind on something else. She was thinking she

really ought to get out of there and go back home to see if
Christopher had arrived.

"Idiots," she said to the air.

Nothing happened. No priests or ministers rounded
the corner from the church. No sounds of vigorous arguing
split the night air. They were probably still back there, taking up space in the cab.

Bennis went back out along the side of the church and
around to the front again. It was too cold to sit still and she
was too exasperated to want to. She found the Fathers and
Reverend Kress standing in the little plaza in front of the
church steps, stomping their feet in the cold but otherwise
oblivious of it. They were discussing tactics for mounting
an assault on Independence Hall.

"It would be a purely symbolic gesture," Father Ryan
was saying, "but it would be wonderful symbolism."

"Gentlemen," Bennis said.

And then she stopped.

Holy Trinity Church was much closer to the building
where Hannah Krekorian lived than Bennis's own apartment building. It was close enough so that Bennis could
now get a good look at the tall man in the coat who seemed
to be taking up Hannah Krekorian's night. They were coming back from somewhere again, which meant they must
have been out together in the meantime, but Bennis didn't
bother about that. She got up as close to the edge of the
church's property as she could, so that she had a clear look
at the man's face.

That was when she got a very rude shock.

"Good God," she said. "Where did Hannah pick *him*
up?"

Father Tibor tapped her on the shoulder. "Bennis? Will
you come to the apartment for some coffee? We need to
pay you back for all you have done."

Bennis was still staring at the man. He had taken Hannah's key now, the way well-brought-up men used to do
when she was younger, and he was opening the building's
front door. He hadn't changed at all since the last time
Bennis had seen him. He didn't have a touch of loss or grief
in his face.

"Bennis?" Father Tibor asked again.

"Yes," Bennis said. "I'm coming. Just a minute. I'll be right there."

Paul Hazzard, Bennis thought.

Paul Hazzard with Hannah Krekorian.

Just *wait* until Gregor Demarkian hears about this.

*part one*

———

*hearts
and flowers...*

*o n e*

*1*

Gregor Demarkian had been living on Cavanaugh Street for something over two years, and in that time he had developed a routine for what he thought of as his "normal" days. "Normal" days were days when he was not involved in any extracurricular murder case, or traveling, or being hauled off from one place to another to "consult" with people Father Tibor Kasparian thought needed his advice. "Normal" days were normal in spite of the fact that there were fewer of them than of the other kind. It was odd how that worked. Gregor had sworn at enough alarm clocks in his time to believe that he ought to have loosened up and done away with schedules completely, now that he was retired. Instead, he might as well have been back in Virginia, coming in every morning to the Department of Behavioral Sciences. That was what Gregor Demarkian had done his last ten years with the FBI. First he had organized and then he had run the Department of Behavioral Sciences, which had the job of conducting federal searches for interstate serial killers. During the decade he spent in the FBI before that, he had done all sorts of things, none of which he would now describe as "normal." It was enough to make him wonder about people—and even about himself. His schedule was as rigid now as it had been when he'd held a mandatory staff meeting every Monday through Friday at eight A.M.

These days, what Gregor held every Monday through Saturday at seven A.M. was breakfast at the Ararat Restaurant. He would have held it there on Sunday too, but the Ararat wasn't open then. The Melajians, who owned it, went to church on Sunday mornings. Some of the people Gregor usually met for breakfast went to church on Sunday mornings too. Father Tibor Kasparian had to, or there would be no liturgy for the rest of Cavanaugh Street to attend. Old George Tekemanian hadn't missed a Sunday since the day he was married. He had been twenty-three then and was well over eighty now. Even Bennis Hannaford went most weeks, in spite of the fact that she'd been brought up Protestant Episcopal and not in the Armenian church. Only Gregor stayed away consistently. He wasn't sure why. He had nothing against religion. He had nothing against hearing Tibor preach and listening to the choir sing the kyrie eleison. He even believed in God on and off, depending on how his life was running. When it went badly, he tended to think there was an almighty out there, determined to get him. No, no. It was none of the usual things. It was just that church somehow didn't seem—right—to him.

The seats are hard, Gregor told himself now. They hurt to sit in for even a little while, and the liturgy goes on for hours and hours, and before it's half over you want a club chair and a great big mug of old George Tekemanian's hot buttered rum.

It was ten minutes to seven on the morning of Saturday, February 2, and Gregor was in no danger of being asked to go to church. He had just come out the door and down the stoop steps of the brownstone where he had his apartment—and where old George Tekemanian, Bennis Hannaford, and Donna Moradanyan had theirs. He began walking up the street toward the Ararat. He stopped every once in a while to check out the decorations Donna Moradanyan had put up for Valentine's Day. If he hadn't known that Donna went to church regularly, he might have suggested she go. As it was, he thought he ought to suggest something. Donna was definitely off her feed. These decorations—the big silver-and-red heart on their front door; the red and white metallic streamers wrapped around every lamppost; the crepe paper cupid with his crepe paper bow and arrow on the façade of Lida Arkmanian's place between the first and second floors—these decorations were nice, but they lacked Donna's usual obsessiveness. It was as if she just hadn't been able to work up any enthusiasm for hearts and flowers this year. Always before, Donna had loved Valentine's Day.

Gregor got to the Ararat, tugged at its plate glass front door, and found it locked. Linda Melajian looked up from where she was folding napkins at a table in the center of the room and nodded. Linda Melajian was what the old people on Cavanaugh Street called a success story. She had gone away to an Ivy League college in New England and gotten a wonderful education—but then she'd come back again. Now she helped run the family business and taught English to new immigrants two nights a week in the basement of Holy Trinity Church.

"Sorry," she said as she turned her keys in the lock and got the door open. "I'm running late this morning. Don't ever tell my mother you caught me still folding napkins at seven o'clock. Or nearly seven o'clock. What time is it? Hannah Krekorian woke me up at quarter to six, if you can believe it, all hot to place an emergency catering order for a party she wants to give next Friday night. I'd keep an eye out for her today if you don't want to go. I think she's going to ask the whole street."

It was customary in this neighborhood that anybody who gave a party asked the whole street. Gregor shrugged off his overcoat and slid it down the wall-side bench of the window table where he had his breakfast almost every morning. The coat bounced against the glass with the softest of ricochets. Gregor went back to the front desk and took one of the copies of the *Philadelphia Inquirer* that were kept for sale next to the cash register. Linda would put it on his bill.

"A party next Friday night," he said, going back to his booth. "With such short notice, will anybody come?"

Linda laughed. "This is Cavanaugh Street in February. They'll come in costume if they're asked to. Hannah wants fifteen pounds of *loukoumia*, can you believe it? Mickey's going to have to cart the stuff over there in a wagon. In several wagons."

*Loukoumia* was the Greek and Armenian name for what the rest of the world called Turkish delight—but in Armenian neighborhoods, and Greek ones, nothing was ever called Turkish anything, unless somebody was trying to start a fight. Gregor opened the paper, saw the headline (DEFICIT GROWING WORSE), and decided to read the comics instead. He hated parties. He especially hated the kind of parties where the hostess felt it necessary to have fifteen pounds of *loukoumia*.

"Let me see," Linda said. "A ham and cheese omelet, three eggs. A side of hash browns, a side of breakfast sausage, two orders of rye toast with butter, and a pot of coffee. Did I leave anything out?"

"Could I have it ham and cheese and mushroom?"

"Sure. I didn't think you ate mushrooms. No cholesterol."

"Now, Linda."

"Never mind," Linda said. "Where's old George this morning? Where's Father Tibor? Usually you people descend on me in a gang."

Gregor shrugged. "Tibor had a late night with that protest of his. Old George has a cold and isn't supposed to go out. I'm supposed to bring him back some muffins."

"He isn't really sick, is he?" Linda asked quickly. "If he's really sick, I'll go over there myself with some *hav abour*. I know he likes *erishtah abour* better, but chicken soup is better than lamb soup when you're sick, and old George is getting up there—"

"Old George isn't getting up there," Gregor said. "Old George is already there."

"Right. Don't worry about the muffins. I'll put a box together and go myself."

*Doonesbury* had a sequence about the deficit. Gregor sighed and closed the paper. "While you're there," he said, "bring some of that *hav abour* to Donna Moradanyan. I don't know what's wrong with her lately. She just isn't behaving like herself."

Linda Melajian looked startled. "You don't know

what's wrong with Donna Moradanyan? Really? I'd have thought it was obvious to everybody."

"You would?"

"Well, of course," Linda Melajian said. "I mean, after all—"

Gregor never got to hear what Linda meant, or what was after all. The plate glass door blew open so forcefully, it rattled all the other plate glass windows facing the street. A gust of wind hit the stack of folded napkins on the table where Linda had been working and scattered them across the floor. Salt and pepper shakers jumped, and copies of the *Philadelphia Inquirer* rippled in the breeze. Bennis Hannaford stood in the door, wearing jeans, a turtleneck, a flannel shirt, a pair of L. L. Bean Maine hunting boots, and a bright red scarf. Gregor thought she had to be freezing, out in the cold like that without a coat. Bennis didn't seem to be noticing the temperature.

She had a stack of computer printouts under her arm. She grabbed them in her right hand, held them in the air, and announced: "Gregor, I've got the most outrageously awful thing to tell you."

## 2

Gregor Demarkian had reason to know that Bennis Hannaford was not a flake. In spite of the way she liked to act in public—which was as a cross between a Barbara Stanwyck madcap debutante from a thirties movie and Agatha Christie's Mrs. Ariadne Oliver—she was in her way a brilliant businesswoman and certainly a successful writer. What she wrote was sword-and-sorcery fantasy novels, but Gregor was not the kind of person to whom genre fiction simply didn't count. Especially genre fiction that sold that many copies and made that much money. Of course, Gregor had never actually read anything Bennis had written. He'd tried on several occasions, but he was always brought up short by the unicorns. Bennis always had unicorns in her novels. She always had witches and dragons and sorcerers too. It made Gregor dizzy. Tibor and old George Tekemanian had read the whole series, though, and they said the work Bennis did was wonderful.

The problem with Bennis, as far as Gregor was concerned, was not the flakiness she liked to pretend to, but the driving determination she liked to indulge. That, Gregor knew, was the key to Bennis. Out in the world somewhere, Gregor was sure, there were hundreds of other women who wrote as well as Bennis did. There were probably dozens who published as frequently and were as well reviewed. None of them had a tenth of the energy, or the bullheadedness.

Unfortunately, Bennis did not restrict her application of drive, determination, energy, or bullheadedness to her professional life. She brought those things to everything she did, including eating breakfast in the morning. She caused herself a lot of trouble.

Now she threw her sheaf of computer printout paper on top of Gregor's *Philadelphia Inquirer*, said, "Hi, Linda" and "Could I have a pot of really muddy black coffee and a full sugar bowl?" and threw her red scarf on top of Gregor's coat. Then she sat down and put her chin in her hands.

"Just guess," she said, "what I found out last night."

Gregor Demarkian did not like to guess things with Bennis Hannaford. He suspected Bennis of setting traps. He said, "I don't know. Wasn't your brother supposed to come in last night? Has he got a new job?"

"He's got the same job he always had," Bennis said, "and he's fine and all the rest of that and he's sleeping in. It's not about Christopher, for God's sake. What do you take me for?"

I take you for a prime pain in the nether regions, Gregor told himself, but he didn't say it out loud. "I take it whatever awful thing you've found out is about a person. You've got that news-about-a-person expression on your face. Who is it?"

"Hannah Krekorian."

Gregor blinked. "That's odd. This seems to be Hannah's day. Linda was just telling me that Hannah got her out of bed this morning, trying to place a catering order for a big party she's decided to hold this Friday night."

"Did she really?" Bennis said. "I take it this was a spur-of-the-moment thing?"

"Linda seems to think so."

"I bet it's a get-acquainted party," Bennis said. "That would just fit. Oh, I really can't believe this is happening."

"A get-acquainted party for Hannah Krekorian?" Gregor said.

Linda Melajian came up carrying a tray holding two large pots of coffee, two saucers, two cups, two spoons, two napkins, and an immense sugar bowl. Bennis said, "Thanks a lot," poured one of the coffee cups two-thirds full of evil black liquid, seemed to fill the rest of the cup up with sugar, and bent over her computer printouts. Linda picked up Bennis's coffee cup and put a saucer under it.

"Back in a minute with breakfast," she said.

Bennis looked after Linda's retreating figure. "I suppose you ordered one of those breakfasts that are a kind of suicide pact with your arteries. I ought to lecture you about it but I just don't have the time. Listen. Yesterday afternoon Tibor had that demonstration at City Hall or wherever with Father Ryan and Father Carmichael and all those people—"

"The demonstration about the street vendors. I remember. In protest against the city raising the licensing fee or something like that."

"Right," Bennis said. "Well, about, I don't know, maybe seven o'clock last night, I get a call from Tibor that he's been arrested and he owes a fine and can I come down and pay it. Which is all right, because I knew that was probably coming when the day started. So I packed up all the money I could find in the apartment—"

"Which was probably too much," Gregor interrupted automatically. "You keep too much cash around. You're going to get robbed."

Bennis ignored him. "Anyway, I got all this money together because I knew I was going to get down to the courthouse and find out there were five other people too broke to pay their fines and then what was I going to do, so I took the whole wad and I went out onto the street to find a cab. And I did. Right away. That's because just as I got out there to look for one, Hannah Krekorian came home in one. With a companion."

"So who was this companion?" Gregor asked. "You make it sound like Jack the Ripper."

"I think Jack the Ripper is very apt. Although I didn't recognize him then. He was too far away. A really tall, cadaverously thin man in a good coat. It wasn't until I got back that I realized who it was."

"Because you'd been thinking about it," Gregor said slowly.

"Not at all." Bennis was indignant. "I wouldn't get this worked up just from speculation."

Oh, yes, you would, Gregor thought, but he didn't say that either. Instead, he took a long sip of hot black coffee and tried to be encouraging. "You saw him again, I take it? Hannah and this person were still on the sidewalk when you got back?"

"If they had been, they would have frozen to death. It was hours, Gregor. No, they must have gone out to dinner or something. They were getting out of a cab at Hannah's place again when I got home with Tibor and the rest of the clergy—and I won't do that again anytime soon; good Lord—and since I was standing right there at the church, and that's a lot closer, I got a good look at his face."

"Which you recognized," Gregor said.

"I most certainly did."

"Well?" Gregor asked her. "Who was it? It couldn't really have been Jack the Ripper. Nobody alive today knows who that was."

"Maybe I just mean he was the next best thing. It was Paul Hazzard. Does the name ring a bell?"

"I don't know," Gregor said slowly.

Bennis nodded. "That might have been the year your wife was so sick. The year of the trial, I mean. Otherwise, I think you'd remember it. It was a kind of national soap opera, complete with press leaks and stolen tape recordings and I don't know what else. Everybody thought the state of Pennsylvania had him nailed—Paul Hazzard, I mean—and even now just about everybody's sure he killed his wife. It's just that he had Fred Scherrer for a lawyer, so he didn't get convicted of it."

Linda Melajian came up to the table with another tray. "Here you go," she said, starting to set down dishes. "The coronary bypass surgery special."

## 3

Gregor Demarkian knew enough about the way the courts operated in the United States—and especially about the way the courts operated in cases of murder—not to have any illusions that the guilty were always convicted or the innocent set free. He had sat in a courtroom in Tupelo, Mississippi, and watched a man he knew had slaughtered five young women set free for insufficient evidence. He had sat in the FBI office in Salt Lake City and waited for word that the state of Utah had put a man he was sure was innocent to death by firing squad. The vagaries of the political system were the primary reason he was opposed to the death penalty in spite of the fact that he had worked for so much of his career with perpetrators who in every moral sense deserved to be dead. In favor of the death penalty or not, consciousness of the arbitrariness of organized justice notwithstanding, Gregor still believed implicitly in the principle of innocent until proven guilty. There were times when he had privileged knowledge, when he knew a verdict was wrong because he possessed information the jury did not have. In cases in which he had no more information than the jury had had, or even less, Gregor went with the decision their deliberations had settled on. He would have eaten dinner at the house of an acquitted poisoner with no qualms at all. "Everybody's sure he killed his wife" was not the kind of information Gregor Demarkian allowed to influence his life.

The sausages at Ararat were round spiced patties from Jimmy Dean, his favorite. He cut one in quarters and speared a piece.

"I remember the case now," he said. "There was a whole lot of nonsense about an antique dagger."

"It wasn't nonsense, Gregor. It seemed like the only explanation at the time. It was a dagger that her grandfather had brought back from some Pacific island he'd gone to in the early twenties. I remember seeing it once when I was about eight years old. I went there for a birthday party for Jacqueline's sister Juliana."

Gregor was surprised. "You went there? You mean you knew the woman who was murdered?"

"Not exactly." Bennis shook her head. "Jacqueline Isherwood was a lot older than I was—my sister Myra's age, in fact. I think Jacqueline and Myra went all through boarding school and college together. I only really knew Juliana, and by the time Jacqueline was murdered, Juliana was dead."

"How?"

"Overdose of Seconal when she was twenty-six. Juliana was not a very stable person. We weren't very good friends or anything. The Isherwood girls were all very serious about psychology. And you know how I feel about psychology."

"Mmm." Gregor speared another piece of sausage and thought about it. "Wasn't there something impossible about that dagger? Wasn't it that there wasn't any blood on it or—"

Bennis sighed. "There wasn't any blood on it, that was the thing. And there should have been, because the dagger was sort of ridged—it had millions of little cut-out patterns in it and it would have been impossible to clean all the blood out of it in such a short time, and Jacqueline was found less than an hour from the time she was killed—"

"By the husband?"

"Yes, Gregor, I think so. You can look in here." Bennis tapped her stack of computer printouts. "That's just about everything ever printed on the case. I subscribe to one of those networks, you know. Your computer plugs into it and then when you want some information you just ask and out comes all this. It's very helpful. Like with the dagger. The police thought the dagger had to be the murder weapon because the wound was so odd. One of the true crime magazines had the police drawings of the cross-sections the autopsy people made. Apparently, if you looked at Jacqueline from above, what you saw was the round hole where the sharp point went through her chest and then a little curved depression to the right. Your right, as you looked at it. But if you looked at the cross-section, it got stranger."

"I think it's strange enough the way it is," Gregor said. "A little curved depression? Where? In her skin? In her clothes?"

"In her skin," Bennis said. "She wasn't wearing many clothes, just a bra and a pair of panties, and it wasn't much of a bra. That was in the papers at the time too. It was one of the reasons so many people thought Paul Hazzard must have killed her. Who does a woman walk around in front of in nothing but her bra and panties, especially in her living room, if not her husband?"

Gregor Demarkian's wife, Elizabeth, had never in her life walked around in front of him in her bra and panties. He ate some hash browns and wondered why any woman would do that.

"Cross-sections," he said finally.

Bennis grabbed the computer printout and pulled it toward her. "Here's the cross-section. The doctor who did the autopsy testified at the trial that he didn't usually do cross-sections of this kind, but the odd shape of the depression bothered him, and so he did. Take a look at it. You can't tell from this angle, but the hole the sharp part made— the part that actually pierced Jacqueline Isherwood's heart—was perfectly round."

Gregor looked. For a tissue cross-section, the outline was strikingly clear. He wondered if the magazine that had published it had tidied up the edges to make a better illustration. What Bennis had looked like this:

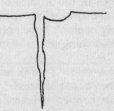

Gregor pushed the printout back to her. "Do you have a picture of the weapon that probably wasn't the weapon? Or doesn't your computer service do photographs?"

"They come over the fax. Really, Gregor. You're going to have to catch up with technology one of these days. It's wonderful, the things we can do with microchips."

"The only microchips I want to hear about are deep fried and made of potato," Gregor said. "Do you have that picture?"

"Of course I do."

Bennis rifled through the computer printout again, found a loose sheet of paper, and passed it over. On it, Gregor found a smudged black-and-white photograph of a very curious weapon, a round, needlelike shaft point attached to a sharp-edged curved handle, ornately carved. It looked like this:

Gregor studied it for a moment, then handed it back to Bennis. "The objections were well founded. There have to be a million ridges in the surface of that thing. It would have taken days to make a good job of cleaning it, and even then you probably couldn't have gotten everything. Not if you'd plunged that thing into a woman's chest. What's it made of?"

"Iron," Bennis said. "I think some of the decorative scrollwork may be copper or brass."

"Well, iron or copper or brass, cleaned or not, right shape or otherwise, I wouldn't have believed this was the weapon in a murder in twentieth-century America under any circumstances—except maybe if it had been found sticking out of the woman's chest when the police arrived at the scene, and even then I'd have questions. People just don't do things like that."

"Like what?"

"Like use antique daggers to do their nearest and dearest in. What for?"

Bennis frowned. "Well, it was right at hand, wasn't it? It was hanging there on the wall. Maybe there was an argument—"

"Try to picture it to yourself," Gregor said patiently. "You're having a royal bust-up with your father. The two of you are yelling and screaming at each other. You're so furious, you want to kill him. So you walk to the wall, take this extremely odd-looking thing out of the brackets holding it up there, walk back to your father, who has been standing still for all this in the meantime—"

"Oh," Bennis said. "Maybe it didn't happen that way. Maybe it was premeditated. Paul Hazzard decided to kill his wife. So he waited until she was alone and not expecting anything, then when her back was turned he took the dagger down from the wall—"

"Why?" Gregor demanded.

"Why what?"

"Why take the dagger down from the wall," Gregor insisted. "It's a highly individualized weapon. Using it would be like announcing there was something out-of-the-way about this death. Why not bring a Saturday night special, or a flic knife? Go down into central Philadelphia and pick something up on the street. Go to New York and pick something up so nobody could connect it to you. You could get it in any of a dozen ways, but you'd have the kind of thing a hopped-up street tough would bring with him if he broke into the house, and that would make the police much more likely to think it was a burglary instead of you."

"I see what you mean," Bennis said. "But Gregor, Jacqueline Isherwood Hazzard wasn't killed with a Saturday night special or a flic knife. She was killed with something that made this funny wound."

"I know," Gregor acknowledged. "That's how we can be sure this was not a premeditated crime. It was probably entirely spur-of-the-moment. It just wasn't committed with that silly dagger."

"Then what was it committed with?"

Gregor shrugged. "Some perfectly common item the killer had on him, or her, at the time. Some ordinary instrument nobody would connect with homicide on a day-to-day basis, but that just happens to be lethal if used in the wrong way. That kind of thing."

"Like what?"

"I don't know, Bennis. This is your murder mystery. You're the one who came barging in here to tell me that Hannah Krekorian was seen coming home in a cab with a man you've decided has murdered his wife."

"Gregor—"

Gregor cut his omelet into strips with the edge of his fork, then picked up a piece of toast and bit into it.

"Hannah Krekorian is a grown woman," he said. "If she wants to keep company with a man, it's her own damned business and none of yours. Paul Hazzard was tried and acquitted of the murder of his wife over four years ago. It is the business of the judicial system of the state of Pennsylvania to determine his guilt or innocence, not yours. Persisting in accusing this man of a crime after he has been duly acquitted—and when you have absolutely no specialized knowledge of your own—is un-American and probably immoral in a larger sense. Stay out of this, Bennis. You are not Hannah Krekorian's mother and she's not yours."

"I'm just trying to look out for somebody I care about," Bennis said sullenly.

"You're just trying to meddle," Gregor told her, "and I won't have it. Now, order yourself some breakfast. Here comes Father Tibor with a gleam in his eye."

Bennis poured herself more coffee and sank farther down onto the bench. "I think you're being completely unreasonable," she said. "You can't let people go running off to cut their own throats. It's not good for them."

It was Gregor Demarkian's opinion that most of the trouble in this world had been caused by people who thought they knew what was good for other people better than the other people themselves, but that was an argument he and Bennis had had several times, and he wasn't going to get into it again.

Instead, he moved closer to the window along his bench and let Father Tibor Kasparian slide in beside him.

"It's a wonderful morning," Father Tibor said. "Father Ryan and Father Carmichael have come up with a plan for decisive political action, and it is not completely stupid."

## *t w o*

### *1*

There was a funeral being set up at Holy Trinity Church when Gregor passed it, going home alone after a breakfast that had been too long and composed of too much food. He had Bennis Hannaford's stack of computer papers under his arm. Bennis had errands to do in downtown Philadelphia and no particular interest in keeping the information, or the paper it was printed on. "After all," she said through a haze of cigarette smoke, "I got it for you. I thought you'd be interested. Things have been . . . quiet around here lately." It was certainly true that things had been quiet around here lately. The world of extracurricular murders seemed to be going through a recession. Gregor still wasn't sure he wanted Bennis thrusting four-year-old unsolved cases under his nose and insisting he do something about them—and why? Just because Hannah Krekorian had had dinner with a man who had once been accused of the crime? Gregor knew what Bennis was hinting at, but he thought it was absurd. Hannah Krekorian was a stocky, stodgy middle-aged woman. She was almost old. She was no more interested in romance, or capable of inspiring it, than Gregor was interested in the Super Bowl chances of the Philadelphia Eagles. Or was it the Flyers? Bennis and Donna had season tickets to both the football and the hockey games, but Gregor could never remember which team played which.

# two

Setting up for an Armenian funeral was a complicated thing. The Armenian funeral liturgy was a complicated thing. Gregor wondered if Tibor would read it in Armenian, to limit the amount the family could understand. The priest who had read the funeral liturgy for Gregor's wife, Elizabeth, had insisted on reading it in English. Gregor had been ready to kill him and worse well before they actually got to the grave. That was what the problem was with all this "celebrating your ethnic heritage" stuff. Everybody ran around singing the praises of ethnicity, talking about how rich and wonderful it made their lives to be part of an ancient culture. They forgot that that culture had content. In the case of the Armenian funeral liturgy, that content was sin. There he was, standing at the edge of a heaped mound of white roses that covered what was left of his wife, listening to a priest who had known neither of them pray for her release from her iniquities. Iniquities, for God's sake. Elizabeth. It hadn't made Gregor feel the least bit better when friends came up to him afterward and said that the Greek service was really much worse. He may have been raised in an ethnic neighborhood by a mother who never shed her immigrant's accent, but he was thoroughly an American in all the most important ways. He thought there was something faintly unpatriotic, and possibly even treasonous, about sin.

Gregor went on past the church—Tibor would be in there soon, making sure he had everything he needed; there was no point to Gregor's calling in at the rectory for the rest of the day—and to the steep stoop of his own brownstone. He looked at the single large heart fastened there and shook his head. He wished he understood women. He wished he understood *rabbits*. He had been praised a million times for the insight he had into the minds of murderers. He thought he did pretty well at figuring out who would do a murder and why and how and what kind. He did better than pretty well when the murderer was a John Wayne Gacy or a Son of Sam. What he didn't understand were ordinary people living ordinary lives. They couldn't all be like Bennis. They couldn't all be erratic and pigheaded. Some of them had to make sense.

He went up the steps to the front door, let himself into

the foyer—the front door was unlocked; the front door was always unlocked; it didn't matter what he did or what he said—and stopped outside old George Tekemanian's apartment. George's lights were on. A low murmur of voices was drifting into the foyer, punctuated spasmodically by sudden bursts of laughter. Gregor knocked and said, "George? It's Gregor Demarkian."

There was a sound of footsteps moving rapidly over hardwood—definitely not old George's footsteps; George was sure on his feet even at eighty-odd, but he hadn't been that fast in twenty years—and Donna Moradanyan stuck her head into the hall.

"Oh, Gregor," she said. "Come on in. We're just playing with George's new toy."

"My grandson Martin gave it to me," George said from deep inside his apartment. "It is to compensate me for the diet his wife has put me on because I am sick. Come in, Krekor. This is a wonderful thing."

"It is a wonderful thing." Donna stepped back to let Gregor past. She was a young woman in her twenties, tall and blond and strapping-healthy. Donna reminded Gregor of the young women he had known in the Midwest when he was first working for the FBI, young women who played tennis and touch football and swam laps and still didn't have a place to put all their energy. Gregor knew both of Donna's parents. They were younger than he was by fifteen years, but they had grown up on Cavanaugh Street. Donna's mother was a small, round woman in the classic Armenian mold. As a young woman she had been dark and beautiful. As a middle-aged mother she had run to the kind of weight called "pleasingly plump." Donna's father was very tall, like Gregor himself, but he was dark and Middle-Eastern enough to play the ethnic friend in a new wave James Bond movie. Where Donna had gotten the blond hair and blue eyes was anybody's guess.

Gregor went into George's foyer, dumped the stack of computer paper on the foyer table, and shrugged off his coat. The table was a John Esterman reproduction. It must have set George's grandson Martin back a good three thousand dollars. Gregor tried not to think about how much money Martin spent on George's apartment. What Martin had wanted to do was move George out to the Main Line, where Martin lived with his wife and George's two great-grandchildren in a six-thousand-square-foot house with "grounds." Martin had done extremely well in the bond market. But George wasn't interested in moving. In fact, George was adamant about not moving. Martin had done the next best thing, to his own mind, and brought the Main Line to George. He'd bought this building, turned it into floor-through condominiums, gutted this ground floor apartment for George, and reconstructed the place to be what he called "pleasant." He'd bought George a lot of expensive furniture. He'd arranged for a cleaning woman to come in twice a week. George had balked at the idea of someone coming in every day to cook, so Martin had given that up. Instead, he'd started to give his grandfather presents, gadgets, grown-up toys. Gregor thought Martin sat down in front of the Sharper Image catalogue once a month and picked the most ridiculous and most ridiculously expensive thing.

Of course, what Martin had done for George was not all that unusual on Cavanaugh Street. In a way, it was the entire explanation for Cavanaugh Street. All these older women with their town houses and their Bermuda vacations and their fur coats—it wasn't their money that was paying for it, or the money their husbands had left either. In Gregor's generation, only one or two people, including Gregor himself, had managed to do better than low average in a financial sense. Lida and Hannah and all the rest of them had brought their children up on Cavanaugh Street when Cavanaugh Street was not much better than a slum. They had watched their husbands die of early heart attacks from working three jobs to put the children through college. They had lived on rice and beans to make sure they could send money enough for meat to their precious Karens and Stephens and Lisas and Alexanders, away at law and medical school and in need of protein to keep up their strength. It was the Karens and Stephens and Lisas and Alexanders who had made good. And paid off. Cavanaugh Street was a tribute to American upward mobility and Armenian family sense.

Old George was sitting in the overstuffed chair next to

his fireplace, surrounded by what seemed to be a pile of shiny socks. On the table next to his right arm was a pile of food that looked like nothing Angela Tekemanian had ever prescribed for a diet for anyone. Angela had been a nutritionist before she went to law school. She tended to favor the low fat and the aggressively green. Gregor supposed the food on the table had come from Linda Melajian and Ararat. Old George had a plate of *boerag* on his lap. The socks had been made into balls and then—what? What had happened to those socks? And how many pairs of socks did old George Tekemanian own?

"Come in," George said again. "Come in, come in. You must see this thing. And you must eat some food."

"Martin and Angela are due in at six o'clock," Donna told him. "George doesn't want to be caught with the loot. He says Angela is beginning to get very, very sticky."

"Angela is always sticky," George said. "But she means well. This last time, though, Krekor, she talked for thirty-five minutes about arteriosclerosis. I tried to tell her if I don't have it now, I'm not going to get it, but she wouldn't listen to me."

"Angela never really listens to anybody," Donna said.

"Watch what I do to these socks, Krekor. It is a wonderful thing."

George reached to the table and took a pair of socks from behind a tall box of *patlijanov dolma*. The socks were rolled into a ball and not shiny at all. He put his plate of *boerag* back on the table and replaced it with what looked like a small white plastic box. Then he held the socks in the air and grinned.

"Here," he said. "Observe."

Gregor tried to observe. The socks went into the box. The socks came out of the box. The socks were turned over and went half into the box. Gregor couldn't follow it. Suddenly old George was sitting there with his hands still and the box closed, and the socks were shiny.

Gregor walked over, took the socks out of old George's hands, and held them in the air. They seemed to be coated in clear plastic.

"What is this?" he asked. "What did you do to them?"

"They're vacuum sealed," Donna Moradanyan said.

"It was Angela's idea this time," old George said. "With this device, you can do many wonderful things. You can freeze vegetables absolutely fresh. You can keep chicken without its skin in the freezer for months, without having to worry about freezer burn. You can have healthy food all the time, and never have to worry about going off your diet."

"We've been vacuum-sealing George's sock collection all morning," Donna said. "Next we're going to start on his ties."

Old George put the newly-shiny socks on the pile and the vacuum-sealer device back on the table. He grabbed a couple of *dolma* out of the large box and started to eat.

"We will keep the ties for when Tommy gets home," old George said. "Also the *loukoumia*. Tommy has gone to play group at the church school, Krekor. He likes it very much."

Tommy was Donna Moradanyan's very small son— three years old now, Gregor thought, though he had to work at it to remember. Tommy had been born the first year Gregor had been back on Cavanaugh Street. That much he was sure of.

"Play group," Gregor said. "That ought to be interesting. I can see Tommy now, marching up to old Mrs. Hogrogian and saying 'I'm not particularly happy with these weather conditions we're having today, are you?' "

"Tcha. That's Father Tibor's fault," old George said. "Reading the child Aristotle before he was even out of diapers."

"He read the Aristotle in Greek," Donna said, looking out the window to Cavanaugh Street. "I don't think Tommy understood a word of it. He just liked sitting on Father Tibor's lap."

"Aristotle he may have read in Greek, but the big art book he read in English and also the story about King Arthur and the knights." Old George shook his head. "He is a very bright child, Tommy. You can't blame him. Tibor used the words and Tommy learned the words and that was that."

"I don't think that's something Tommy ought to be blamed for," Gregor said seriously. "All you hear about these days is children who can't read and teenagers who don't know how to say anything but 'like' and 'man' and 'huh' and 'duh.' I think it's a good thing Tommy is getting a good vocabulary."

"I didn't say it wasn't a good thing in the long run," old George said.

"I think it's a good thing even in the short run," Gregor said.

Donna was still looking out old George's front window. She didn't seem to be listening to them.

"Donna?" Gregor asked.

Donna started. "Oh," she said. "Yes. Excuse me. I must have been daydreaming."

"You do a lot of daydreaming lately," old George said, sounding sharp.

"I did a lot of daydreaming as a child too," Donna told him. "Well. I'd better get upstairs. I've got work to do before I go to pick up Tommy. We'll come in right after lunch if it's all right with you, George."

"You come in for lunch," George said. "I have still got very much food."

"Yes. Well. Maybe we will. I'll see you two later, okay?"

Donna gave them both a little tight smile and retreated into George's foyer. Gregor watched her extract her parka from under his coat and head for the door. She must have stopped in to see George after dropping Tommy at play group. Was she really desperately unhappy, or was Gregor imagining things? It was at times like this that he missed his wife, Elizabeth. Elizabeth would have known how to read Donna Moradanyan. She had even known how to read J. Edgar Hoover. Gregor had relied on her for everything, and then she had died.

There was a crock of *tutumov rechel* next to George's white plastic box. Gregor stuck a finger in it, came up with a little blob of jelly, and stuck it in his mouth. Linda Melajian's *tutumov rechel* was always so sweet.

"All right," Gregor said. "So something is wrong with Donna Moradanyan, and nobody wants to tell me what. That's par for the course. Nobody tells me anything."

"It is not a question of nobody wants to tell you, Krekor. It is a question of you have not asked."

"I'm asking now," Gregor pointed out.

Old George nodded. "I know that, Krekor. I am thinking of how to go about it so that you understand. You see, Tommy is going to play group now, every day for two hours in the morning."

"So? Don't tell me Donna is feeling old and wishing he'd always be a baby? She's got more sense than that."

"Donna is not wishing he would always be a baby, Krekor. It is Tommy we are concerned with here, not Donna. When Tommy goes to play group, he meets all kinds of children, more than he knew before."

"So?" Gregor asked again.

"So," old George said, "he is an intelligent child. He takes after, I think, his mother. He goes to play group and he notices that almost all the other children there, they have fathers. Most of them, they have fathers to come home to. Some of them, they have fathers who are divorced, they have to go somewhere to visit. But almost all of them, Krekor, have fathers."

"Ah," Gregor said. "I take it this is upsetting him?"

"You could put it that way," old George said.

"Well, what about Peter? I know he's not very responsible, but he is the boy's father and he doesn't live that far away. Hadn't he got a job in New York last time we heard?"

Peter Desarian was the young man who had gotten Donna Moradanyan pregnant and disappeared—except not quite, because Gregor had gone off to find him. To say that Peter Desarian was "irresponsible" was a little like saying that Adolf Hitler had had something against the Jews. Old George Tekemanian had gone very stiff at the mere mention of the young man's name.

"If we have heard that Peter is having a job in New York," he said, "it is on jungle drums, Krekor. Peter does not write."

"Does Donna want him to?"

"No, Donna does not want him to. But this does not solve our problem now. There was an incident, you see. With Tommy."

"What kind of incident?"

"It was back in November, when you were away at that conference. It happened one afternoon at Lida Arkmanian's house."

"What incident?" Gregor insisted.

"It happened because of nothing," old George went on serenely. "It was a Saturday afternoon and we were all sitting around in Lida's television room, watching the Walt Disney *Pinocchio* on a tape. We were eating too, Krekor, you know what Lida's house is like, the television room is just off the kitchen to make it easier to get snacks—"

"*George.*"

"Yes. Krekor. You see, Tommy got hysterical."

"What do you mean, hysterical?"

"Hysterical," George repeated. "He burst into tears and leapt into Donna's arms and started screaming and crying and ranting and raving—like a crazy person, Krekor, or like a tantrum, and then, when Donna and Lida tried to calm him down, when they rocked him and soothed him, he started asking over and over again, 'Why doesn't my daddy love me? What was the wrong thing I did to make it so my daddy doesn't love me?'"

Gregor winced. Old George was an eerily good mimic. It was as if Tommy Moradanyan were there in the room.

"Oh, dear Lord," he said. "That's a mess."

"Yes," old George agreed. "That's a mess. It's what I was trying to get across. Tommy is a very bright child, but he's a child. He understands about half of things, which in this situation is the worst possible thing. And there is something more, Krekor. I think, in the months since then, the problem has been getting worse."

"Worse how?"

"I don't know. I am not a psychiatrist, Krekor. I am not even Ann Landers. I know only that Donna is very upset. And she is getting more and more upset every day."

"She hasn't talked to you about it?"

"She wouldn't talk to me about it, Krekor. I am not her confidant."

"What about Lida Arkmanian? Or Bennis? Isn't Bennis her best friend?"

"Bennis is her best friend, but if they have talked about

this, I don't know. Women talk about everything together when they are friends, Krekor, do they not?"

"I don't know. I've never been able to figure out the first thing about women."

"I, Krekor, have been able to figure out that whatever it is I think I am doing right, I am doing wrong, but this may not be universal. Robert Redford may have a different experience."

"Robert Redford has a different experience from all of us," Gregor said, getting up. "Do you think I should talk to her? Do you think there's anything either one of us can do?"

"I think we should leave her alone to work it out for herself. You know how upset they all get when they think we're meddling. Of course, they all meddle themselves the first chance they get, but this is human nature. Isn't that right?"

"Of course it is," Gregor said, and supposed he even believed it. After all, he had spent his life meddling in one thing or another. He hadn't even been able to retire without finding a way to go on meddling.

He went out into old George's foyer and picked up his coat and Bennis's computer printouts.

"I'll be back later today," he said. "I'm glad you're looking so much better than you did yesterday."

"Angela came in and threatened to nurse me back to health," old George said. "That always fixes me right up."

## 2

Up on the third floor a few moments later, Gregor got his door open, threw his coat onto his coatrack, and looked at the sheaf of computer papers he still had under his arm. He thought about going up to Donna Moradanyan's apartment, but decided against it. Old George was right. Donna wouldn't welcome his meddling. If she wanted his help, she'd come along and ask for it. He threw the bolt on his door with a satisfying *click* and went into his kitchen. It didn't matter to him that nobody else on Cavanaugh Street ever seemed to lock anything. He was a man of the world. He knew better. He threw Bennis's computer paper onto his kitchen table and went hunting around for coffee.

"Hazzard," he said to himself absently. "Paul Hazzard."

It was impossible, really. He couldn't stop himself. All the time he'd been down at old George's, even when he and George had been talking about Donna Moradanyan, some part of his brain had been thinking about Paul and Jacqueline Isherwood Hazzard. And why? Bennis hadn't said a single really intriguing thing about the case. He had no new evidence and no hope of getting any. The investigation was four years old and probably of no interest to anybody but melodrama enthusiasts like Bennis Hannaford and writers for second-rate local newspapers and supermarket tabloids. And yet . . .

"It's that damned dagger, that's what it is," Gregor said to the air.

He had a jar of instant coffee in one hand and a white coffee mug in the other. He put them both down on the counter next to the sink and drifted over to the kitchen table. He made terrible coffee. Tibor made worse coffee, but that didn't make his own any better. It was like the difference between arsenic and cyanide. One might be a little less strong than the other, but they were both lethal. He paged through the computer printouts and shook his head.

"Newspaper stories," he muttered to himself in disgust. That's all these pages held—old newspaper stories, old magazine stories, clips and items from several dozen sources. The computer service Bennis subscribed to must be some kind of media research vehicle. It wouldn't help him any. If there was anything Gregor had learned after twenty years in the FBI, it was that newspapers almost never got anything right.

He got his kettle, filled it with water, and put it on the stove. Then he went to the phone hanging on the wall near the refrigerator. It took a little thought to decide who would be best to call. It was a question of who had access to what information and who owed whom a favor. Finally, he made up his mind and punched a number out on the touchtone pad.

"Philadelphia Police Department," the woman on the other end of the line said, answering. "Commissioner's office."

"This is Gregor Demarkian. I'd like to speak to Robert Cheswicki, please."

"If you will wait a moment, I'll see if he's in."

Gregor waited for her to ask him to spell his name. When she didn't, he got a little nervous. Secretaries and telephone operators who didn't ask him to spell his name usually got it wrong. He had been transformed into "Greg Marks" by more people in more places than he wanted to count. This time he was lucky. Either this woman was better at names than most of the people Gregor had dealt with, or Bob Cheswicki was very good at deciphering mangled messages.

"Gregor," Bob said, sounding as sunshiny and beamy as he looked in person. Gregor had always thought there was something *wrong* with an assistant commissioner of police who was cheerful all the time. "Where did you come from? I haven't heard from you in ages!"

"I've been leading a reasonably quiet life the past few months, believe it or not. Nobody's thrown the corpse of a taxi dancer into John Cardinal O'Bannion's lap. Nobody's camped out on my doorstep and insisted I do something about the weird things her mother-in-law has started to do with food. It's been very boring."

"You don't sound bored," Bob said judiciously. "I take it you've found something to perk you up?"

"I've found something to annoy me," Gregor admitted. "I was wondering if you'd do me a favor. If you'd get me some information I need."

Bob Cheswicki was cautious. "If it's about a current case, I might not be able to—"

"No, no, no," Gregor said. "The case is old. Very old. Four years old, in fact. I thought we'd work out a trade. Wednesday, I'll buy you lunch at La Vie Bohème, you'll bring along everything you can get your hands on about the murder of Jacqueline Isherwood Hazzard."

There was silence on the other end of the line. Then

Bob came on again, and he sounded strangled. "Gregor, if you know something we don't know about that case, all I can tell you is we want to hear it. You don't know how we want to hear it. There are still men in this department who blow up every time they think about Paul Hazzard getting off, and I'm one of them."

"I don't have any new information," Gregor told him. "I'm just—curious."

"That's enough for me." Bob was definite. "If you get curious enough, you might actually come up with something. Twelve o'clock?"

"Perfect."

"See you there."

The phone went to dial tone, and Gregor hung up.

I must be crazy, he thought.

I don't have anything to go on. I haven't got a hope of getting anything to go on. And now Bob Cheswicki is going to be keeping his fingers crossed I find a way to jail Paul Hazzard, if not actually execute him.

Why do I do these things to myself?

## *three*

### *1*

There were people who thought Paul Hazzard was a fraud—a con man with all the right credentials and a telegenic face, but no conviction. There were other people who were afraid he wasn't a fraud, that he believed all the nonsense he spouted, that he thought he was making sense. The reality was a little more complicated. Paul Hazzard did not lack conviction. He believed absolutely that most of the people in the world were exactly what he said they were: masses of addictions and post-traumatic stress disorders, shamed out of any hope of acquiring self-esteem on their own, in denial. There was a virus loose in the world, the virus of shame and guilt, the virus of hidden abuse. This was not like ordinary abuse. Paul thought that ordinary abuse, like battering and incest, was probably easier on everyone, because there was no confusion that it was what it was. Hidden abuse was insidious. It was made up of sideways glances and offhand refusals. It thrived on hierarchy and competition. It was the essence of "standards." It didn't surprise Paul Hazzard at all that middle-class Americans were so miserable. The highest standard of living in the history of the world, an almost unprecedented freedom of action, access to art and information so wide and cheap it would have made John Stuart Mill giddy—none of that mattered because none of the people Paul Hazzard dealt with could climb out of their pain long enough to experience the world around them. These were the people Paul Hazzard helped—or used to help, when his seminars were crowded, and his books sold millions of copies. He was sure he helped them. They came up to him wherever he went to speak and told him how he had changed their lives.

What complicated this situation was twofold. In the first place, Paul Hazzard wasn't stupid. In the second, he had his suspicions. His lack of stupidity surfaced in what had become cynicism about the socioeconomic composition of his audience. He hadn't failed to notice that really poor people had no interest in healing their shame or finding the child within. Maybe they were too damned distracted by worrying about where the rent money was going to come from and figuring out how to get their children two blocks down the street to school without being shot. Maybe they were poor because they were distracted. That's what a lot of people in the field would have said. Paul had always found meetings of recovery leaders shocking. Paul had been brought up in a fairly liberal family. It was liberalism of a haphazard and unthoughtful kind, but it was liberalism nonetheless. Recovery leaders talking together always sounded like caricatures of Republicans in *The Nation*. The poor were responsible for their poverty. Bad things never happened to good people. Bad things happened because you hadn't done your grief work or because you hadn't owned your anger or because you resisted turning responsibility for your life over to your higher power. Recovery was all about taking responsibility for your life by giving up control of it—and if you didn't do both those things, it was no surprise if you ended up drinking muscatel out of a paper bag on the Bowery. Anything could be an addiction. All addictions were progressive, incurable, and ultimately fatal. If you didn't do something about yours, whatever happened to you was your own damned fault. Maybe you were trying to punish yourself.

Paul Hazzard's suspicions had to do with sex—and he never expressed them to anybody. If he had, in this place and in this climate, he would have been lynched. This did not mean he did not believe his conclusions were true. It did mean that he understood how to operate in his environment, which was what he would have called (in one of his seminars) an "important life skill." Feminism was everywhere. It would get you if you didn't watch out. He couldn't let anyone know what he really thought, which was this: Grief work and healing your shame and discovering your inner child and owning your anger and recognizing your abuse and all the rest of it were very necessary, but they were necessary only *for women*. The party line in the recovery movement was that women outnumbered men at seminars and in support groups because women were more in touch with their feelings than men. Women were more enlightened. Men had bigger problems and a stronger will to denial. Paul Hazzard thought this was hogwash. Women outnumbered men in recovery because women experienced the world differently than men did. Women found addictive what men could take in their stride. Women were damaged by blows men would hardly notice. Women were weak. Paul Hazzard knew all this because he knew himself. He'd smoked two packs of cigarettes a day for twenty years. Then, on his fortieth birthday, he'd taken all the cigarettes in the house and thrown them in the garbage. He'd had a bad couple of months. He'd been impossible to live with. His temper had been hair-trigger and irrational. Then the couple of months was over and he was fine. He'd never smoked another cigarette. He'd never had the desire to smoke another cigarette. Contrast that to the women in his groups, who talked about their "addiction to cigarettes" decades after they'd had their last smoke and came awake every morning wishing they could light up.

The other way women were different from men was in relationships. Yes, women were often abused. They were abused a lot if you counted the metaphysical level as well as the physical one. Paul believed they brought it on themselves. Women could never decide what they wanted from a relationship and stick to it. They were always changing their assumptions and expecting men to let them change the rules. They said they wanted to be independent, but when they were out of a relationship they were always declaring themselves to be "miserable." They said they wanted to be strong, but when their men slept with other women or batted them around the kitchen or drank up all the rent money, they accepted the first apology they got and went on trying to "keep the relationship together." It was enough to make you believe in a hereditary, sex-linked, sex-specific form of masochism.

Actually, Paul Hazzard liked masochism in women. It was useful. He had spotted it right away in Hannah Krekorian, even before he spoke to her. The way she stood. The way she walked. The way she nibbled guiltily on a cookie, as if indulging in chocolate chips were the moral equivalent of working as a camp guard in Dachau. Paul Hazzard knew the signs. And, since he had gone to that particular meeting in hope of meeting someone who would suit his purpose, he had been interested. It was too bad that Hannah was neither young nor pretty. Paul liked his women very young and very pretty. Unfortunately, he also liked them very rich, and the three things rarely went together, at least in women who were available to him. Even at the height of his career, when he had his own series on PBS and his books sold twenty-five thousand copies a week, there were certain women who had remained beyond his grasp. Very young, very pretty, very rich women wanted to marry rock stars. To find someone willing to take on a stodgy old psychologist, he had to make compromises.

He had to do something soon, or his life was going to fall apart. That was the problem here. Nobody had the faintest idea what Jacqueline's dying had done to him financially. Not even the children. The children just thought he was stingy. If he'd been stingy, he wouldn't be in this mess. Maybe he needed a few sessions at Shopaholics Anonymous. He didn't, of course. He wasn't some silly woman with even less sense than character who didn't know when to cut up her credit cards. He'd stopped shopping when he'd gotten worried enough.

He was sitting at the desk in the first floor study, looking at the phone he had just hung up. That had been Hannah, inviting him to a party she was giving this Friday night. She would have mentioned it when they went out to dinner, but his conversation had been so interesting, it had just put the party straight out of her head. Paul was sure there had been no party planned on the night he'd taken Hannah Krekorian to dinner. This was her way of making sure she saw him again. Paul thought it was a very good sign.

He left the study, made his way to the front hall, and climbed the stairs to the second floor. This house had thirty-five hundred square feet on each floor, but not many rooms, except at the top, where Alyssa and Nick had their apartment. The kitchen was in the basement. The living room, the study, and the library were on the first floor. The dining room and another reception room were on the second floor. Paul went into the dining room and looked around. Caroline was sitting at one end of the long table, eating shredded wheat and looking sour. She had her special small pitcher of skim milk and a glass of bloodred just-from-the-juicer juice beside her. James was sitting at the other end of the table, eating English muffins piled with butter and cream cheese and drinking coffee black. He looked happy as a clam. There was another difference between men and women, Paul thought. Men would never force themselves to eat things that made them feel sour. They'd eat what they wanted and take the consequences. Women were always saying they wanted to make their own standards instead of living up to the standards set by men, but you could no more get them off one of their ridiculous diets than you could turn Waikiki Beach into the diamond as big as the Ritz.

Paul got himself a cup of coffee from the sideboard and put it at a place midway down that side of the table. He got cream cheese and butter and bagels from the sideboard too, and sat down. Caroline glared at him.

"Of course you realize this is sabotage behavior," she said frostily. "You both know how important it is to me to stick to this diet. You're both afraid that if I change, things won't be so pleasant for you. So you eat that stuff where I can see you, hoping to make me lose control."

"I'd never try to make you lose control," James said airily. "I don't indulge myself in missions impossible. Did I hear you on the phone, Dad? Caroline says you've got a new paramour but she's so young you don't want anybody to know."

"I think you ought to consider the entire etiology of eating disorders," Paul said to Caroline. "You don't need to lose weight. You're thin as a rail. What are you doing on a diet?"

"I'm on a maintenance diet."

"You're in denial," Paul said. "This is some kind of incipient anorexia nervosa. Your dieting is out of control."

"Don't tell *me* when I'm out of control," Caroline snapped. "You don't own my emotions. I own my emotions. You've got no right to tell me how I feel."

"I'm not telling you how you feel. I'm just trying to point out—"

"You're just trying to manipulate me, that's all you're doing. That's all you've ever tried to do. You were a manipulative and withholding parent from the beginning, and you know it. You just hate knowing I know it. You just hate it that you can't use it on me anymore."

"Could we try not subjecting me to it anymore?" James said. "It's Sunday morning. Maybe we ought to go to church."

They both stared at him blankly.

"Well," James said, "it would have to beat having another one of these arguments. These arguments are the pits. And they never get anywhere."

"I have a right to express my anger."

"I have a right not to listen to it."

"That's not true," Caroline said quickly. "I have a right to express my anger and I have a right to be listened to."

"I don't know where you got that from—scratch it; yes, I do—but in case you haven't heard, slavery has been illegal in this country since the Emancipation Proclamation. And slavery is the name for the condition where some people have an absolute right to some other people's time. I *do* have a right not to listen to it. And now I would like to discuss something else."

"I don't have to stay here and be subjected to this abuse." Caroline stood up. Her shredded wheat was half eaten. Her juice had barely been touched. Paul wondered what it was the juice of. Radishes? With the juicer, you never knew. Caroline stalked to the dining room door and stopped. "You can try as hard as you want to keep me under your thumbs, but it won't work," she declared. "I'm a *survivor*."

Then she turned her back to them and stalked away.

Down at his end of the table, James was eating his way through the last half of his last English muffin, sinking his teeth into two inches of cream cheese, catching the overflow of butter with his tongue. Paul watched him curiously. James was unlike either of his other children. Nothing bothered James.

"Caroline," James said carefully, "is furious with me. She left her tote bag in the front hall last night, and when I came home I tripped over it. She was very put out."

"Did you do it on purpose?"

"No," James said. "It wouldn't have occurred to me. Putting a frog in her bed, that would have occurred to me. Maybe I'll do it sometime. I was a little potted, if you want to know the truth. I went drinking with Max and we had a better time than usual. When I tripped over the tote bag, I jabbed myself with that oversize compass of hers. I'm still bleeding."

"I don't suppose it was anything serious," Paul said dryly.

"It's not. I was wearing boots. Are you all right? You were talking on the phone, weren't you? Do you have another lady?"

Paul buttered his bagel carefully. "I don't have another lady, exactly. I've met a woman I rather like."

"Really? What's her name?"

"Hannah Krekorian."

"Armenian," James said judiciously. "Or at least her husband was. I suppose that's her married name."

"It is. And believe it or not, she's not twelve years old. She's damned near as old as I am."

"Well-preserved?"

Paul thought of Hannah's dumpy figure, her plain, uninteresting face. "Not exactly," he said. "She's just someone I'm comfortable with. I'm going to go to a party at her house this coming Friday night. A crush with cocktails, I think."

"On the Main Line?"

"No," Paul said. "On Cavanaugh Street. In the city. You know about that. There was a piece in the *Inquirer*."

"Home of the Armenian-American Hercule Poirot." James laughed. "Well, I hope you're prepared. Maybe this woman is a friend of Gregor Demarkian's and she took up with you only because Gregor Demarkian wants to meet you because Gregor Demarkian has decided to look into all that about what happened to Jackie and so—"

"For Christ's *sake*," Paul said. "I don't even think that's a pleasant suggestion. What's gotten into you?"

"Nothing's gotten into me. I just think the coincidence is funny. Your Hannah what's-her-name probably doesn't even know Gregor Demarkian. But with Candida writing her memoirs and all—" James shrugged.

"Candida's memoirs are going to be mostly about sex," Paul said, "no matter what the rest of you think. I know that woman. Don't bring up all that about Jackie in front of Caroline. She'll get hysterical."

"She'll get hysterical anyway. She can manufacture excuses for hysteria more efficiently than I could ever give her causes for it. You want another bagel? I'm getting up."

"No," Paul said. "No, thank you. I'm fine for now."

Actually, he was hungry as hell, but he didn't want James to notice that. Paul was always telling James that James ate too much. Which James did. But James didn't care. Paul took a sip of his coffee and sighed.

Paul wasn't worried that Gregor Demarkian might want to look into the death of Jacqueline Isherwood Hazzard. He didn't think there was anything about that that Gregor Demarkian could find—or anything he could do about anything he did find. There were other reasons why a man might prefer not to court a woman with a detective in attendance.

Of course, Paul told himself, he had no reason to expect that a detective would be in attendance. James was right. Hannah Krekorian probably didn't even know Gregor Demarkian. Living on the same street and sharing an ethnic heritage did not add up to acquaintance in modern Philadelphia. And what could he do even if Hannah did know Demarkian? It was really too late to turn back now.

Hell, Paul Hazzard thought, it was worse than too late.

Any retreat from where he was standing at that moment would be a form of suicide—and he didn't mean the psychic kind.

## 2

Fred Scherrer was in his second hour of listening to the woman with the black eye when the phone call came. He would have put the caller off with an excuse if it had been anyone on earth except who it was. The woman with the black eye had no name she could remember. She had been sitting in Fred's Park Avenue living room since four o'clock that morning, when she had been released into Fred's custody by St. Dominic Hospital. She was five foot three, one hundred pounds, and reasonably young. Fred guessed she was in her early thirties. Her hair was dyed ash blond. She wore a pair of clean blue jeans that were a little too long for her and a flannel shirt that was much too big for her in the shoulders. The clothes belonged to a paralegal in Fred's firm named Mary Ann. This woman had no clothes of her own because they had all been torn off. When she was found, she was lying curled up on a bench in Bryant Park, wearing nothing but a bra. According to the hospital, she had been subjected to multiple rapes. According to the hospital, she was suffering from shock. According to the hospital, there was nothing anybody could do for her except give her food and wait. They had been perfectly happy to release her into Fred Scherrer's custody. If they had still been a Catholic hospital, they wouldn't have been allowed to. The rules set down by the archdiocesan office of Catholic Charities would have forbidden it. But St. Dominic had not been a Catholic hospital for some five years now. It had been taken over by the city, and by the city's bureaucrats. This woman was unidentified, uninsured, and black. She was not their problem.

She was, Fred thought, one of the most gracious women he had ever seen. She moved with such precise politeness, she might have been an instructor in a school of etiquette. The nurses had taken one look at the color of her skin and said: welfare. Fred didn't think so. She'd been found in the wrong part of town. Bryant Park did not normally cater to a welfare population. Manners like these had to be learned.

Sitting with your hands folded and unmoving in your lap and your legs pressed together at the ankles was not a skill routinely taught at P.S. 37. Maybe Mary Ann had noticed the discrepancies too. Mary Ann was how the woman with the black eye had come to be sitting in Fred Scherrer's living room. Mary Ann had been waiting for a friend of hers in the emergency room of St. Dominic Hospital when the woman with the black eye had been brought in. Mary Ann's friend had cracked her wrist trying to do a handstand in the Crystal Channel Saloon.

Sid came into the living room from the kitchen and mouthed "Candida DeWitt" as obviously as he could into the air behind the woman with the black eye's head. Fred looked at Mary Ann, nodded slightly, and got up. Mary Ann was sitting on the floor at the other woman's feet. She was listening intently as the woman with the black eye went on and on in a pleasant uninflected voice about how *affecting* the Monet exhibit had been at the Guggenheim, or maybe it wasn't the Guggenheim, she got these museums all mixed up sometimes, she could never remember what they were called.

Fred reminded himself that it was time for him to give Mary Ann another lecture about how she ought to go to law school. She would make a very decent lawyer and a very committed one. Then he followed Sid out to the kitchen and closed the door behind him.

"She hasn't budged. She doesn't seem sleepy either. Candida DeWitt is on the phone?"

"That's right. I know you said not to bother you, but I thought—"

"No, that's all right. Did you get in touch with anybody else? Who'd be the D.A. on this if they ever caught the perpetrators?"

"Raymond Barsi. I talked to him half an hour ago. He's lighting a fire under the police department."

"I'll light a fire under the police department if he doesn't," Fred said. "You talk to our people at the *Daily News*?"

"Yeah. At the *Post* too. I didn't have any luck at the *Times*."

"We'll get the *Times*," Fred said. "Don't worry. I'll turn

this into the black version of the Central Park jogger case. This *is* the black version of the Central Park jogger case. They just don't know it yet. Could you believe that hospital?"

"Yes," Sid said.

Actually, Fred could too. He could believe a lot of things. Even Chuckie Bickerson hadn't made him feel like he'd gotten lost in one of Franz Kafka's nightmares, and Chuckie Bickerson made practically everybody feel like that. Fred stretched and scratched his head. "All right. Let me talk to Candida. Have you found a rental nurse yet?"

"Not rental nurse, for God's sake, Fred. Private duty nurse. Yes. She'll be here at ten."

"Fine."

"Phone's off the hook," Sid said.

The phone receiver was lying on its side on the kitchen table. There was no hold button on this set. Candida had probably heard every word Fred had said to Sid. Fred wondered what she'd thought of it. Fred had never been able to decide, with Candida, what really impressed her. Candida did not give much away.

Fred picked up the receiver and said, "Candida? This is Fred."

"Fred," Candida said. Her voice sounded like music. "Hello. I was beginning to wonder if I had been cut off."

"If you had been, you should have called right back," Fred told her. "I'm always happy to hear from you. I'm sorry about the delay. Things are a little crazy here at the moment."

"Things are always crazy where you are, Fred. I'm used to it. To tell you the truth, I called to ask you a favor."

"So ask. Anything I can do."

"I was wondering if you could come down to Pennsylvania for the weekend. This coming weekend."

Fred cast an involuntary glance in the direction of his living room. By the time the weekend rolled around, they would know who this woman was, and what they were going to do with her, and whether there was a hope of catching the men or boys who had hurt her. They would be involved in warehousing her, that was all. Nobody needed Fred for that.

Fred sat down in the nearest kitchen chair. "Of course I'll come to Philadelphia," he said. "I'll be glad to. You're not in some kind of trouble, are you?"

"Oh, no," Candida said. "No, of course not. Not legal trouble, or anything like that. You'll stay with me, of course. I've got a perfectly nice guest room with its own Jacuzzi."

"I'll be delighted. You sound worried."

"Oh, I'm not, not really. I just need some advice, and I couldn't think of a better person to give it to me."

"You don't want to give me a hint?"

"No, no. It's something I'll have to show you. You'll see. And don't make too much of this. You know how you get."

"Overwrought," Fred suggested.

"Overzealous," Candida amended. "I'll see you— when? Friday? Saturday?"

"I'll be down Friday afternoon, if you don't mind having me that early."

"I don't mind at all."

"Good," Fred said. "And Candida? I'm glad to hear from you."

"I'm glad I called," Candida said. "I'll see you Friday."

Then she hung up.

Fred sat still for a while in his chair, tapping his feet against the oversize kitchen floor tiles. It wasn't that unusual that he should hear from Candida DeWitt—although he'd never been invited to her house before. They had been in touch on and off since Fred had wound up Paul Hazzard's murder trial with an acquittal. They contacted each other randomly and tentatively, as if neither one of them were entirely sure what they wanted to do besides that.

It was unusual to hear such a note of strain in Candida's voice. Candida was never strained. She was never angry or upset or indiscreet either. It went with the territory.

"I wonder what Paul's doing to her now," Fred said to himself, out loud, as if Sid were in the room and he could ask for some input. Then he got up and replaced the receiver gently in its cradle.

Once he started talking to himself, he knew it was time to stop thinking and start taking action.

Action always made him feel a million times better.

## 3

Out in Bryn Mawr, Candida DeWitt sat in her living room in front of her fireplace, contemplating the white spray paint that now defaced the fireplace's fieldstone façade. She didn't mind the spray paint much. That could be removed. She didn't even mind the message.

### DEATH TO YOU

it said in oversize letters, but that was silly and melodramatic. If that had been the beginning and end of it, she would never have taken it seriously. No, it wasn't the fact of the spray paint or its message that bothered her. It was how it had been done.

None of her locks had been forced.

None of her windows had been opened.

At no point had her alarm system gone off or even started to go off.

What that meant was that the person who had painted this message on this fireplace had entered Candida's house with a key and known the house well enough to disarm the security system. Candida could think of only a handful of people who could do that, and they were all connected to Paul Hazzard.

One of the reasons they had suspected Paul of murdering Jacqueline to begin with was the fact that none of the locks had been forced in that house either, and none of the windows broken, and the alarm system hadn't gone off in spite of the fact it was armed.

The similarities made Candida DeWitt very, very uncomfortable.

## *four*

### 1

La Vie Bohème was not Gregor Demarkian's idea of a restaurant. It wasn't even his idea of a comfortable bordello. La Vie Bohème was one of those places with too many spider plants and Boston ferns in the windows that faced the street, too much space between the tables in the main room, and too much fondness for silverware that was supposed to be a work of art on its own. Gregor Demarkian had a lot in common with the bluff old colonels who went to lunch in Agatha Christie's novels, although he didn't think he had anything at all in common with Hercule Poirot. Gregor liked his chairs comfortable and his food in substantial quantities. He wanted peace and quiet while he was eating and a large cup of coffee when he was finished. He wanted sensible food like steaks and prime rib and menu listings in plain English—unless, of course, he was eating Armenian or Chinese. The problem with La Vie Bohème was that it played Ravel without ceasing, served its coffee in delicate little bone china contraptions no bigger than the pieces of a dollhouse tea set, and listed steak on its menu as *boeuf à l'anglaise.* Fortunately, the steak was an excellent two-and-a-half-pound porterhouse and the chairs, though gratingly elegant, were large. That was why Gregor agreed to go there, and why La Vie Bohème was Bob Cheswicki's favorite restaurant. Of course, the prices were outrageous. That went with the territory. Gregor knew that from twenty years as a federal agent, dealing regularly with local law enforcement personnel. There was always one restaurant in every town that high-level police officials truly loved, but that they couldn't afford on their own. That was where you took them when you wanted their cooperation.

Gregor went from Cavanaugh Street to La Vie Bohème by cab. It was too far to walk, and what he would have had to walk through would not have been safe. It bothered him, what had happened to Philadelphia. The Philadelphia he'd grown up in had not been like this—and it was not just poverty that made the difference. This new president said he would pump a lot of money into the cities. Maybe that would work. Gregor liked the sound of it. His instincts, however, ran in the opposite direction. Money would be nice. It might even be essential. *Attitude* was what really mattered. The police he met these days didn't seem to think they could do much about crime. The schoolteachers he met at the library lectures he sometimes gave and the mini-conventions he was asked to speak at mostly thought their students were stupid and not worth much more than the effort it took to warehouse them. "It doesn't matter if it's the African baseline essay or Shakespeare," one of them had told him over cookies and punch at the Art Institute. "These kids are never going to be able to understand either." Then there were the people themselves, bumped into in convenience stores and newsstands, corner diners and taxi stands and bus stops. Everybody seemed so tired. Everybody seemed so *lost*. It was as if Philadelphia were a wind-up toy beginning to wind down. Gregor kept half expecting a big hand to come down from the sky to tighten the spring.

Since no big hand came out of anywhere to do anything, Gregor got out of his cab in front of La Vie Bohème, tipped the driver less handsomely than Bennis would have—really, Bennis was outrageous—and made his way across the sidewalk to La Vie Bohème's front door. It was a big blond wood door with a brass handle big enough to be God knew what. The sign that said LA VIE BOHÈME was a tiny brass one screwed into the door at eye level for a tall woman, engraved with letters so small they were unreadable. The energy might be going out of things in general, but some people had more than you wanted them to have, Gregor thought. And they always expended it on things like this.

Gregor let himself into the air lock, shook the slush and rock salt off his shoes, and went on through to the reception area. Bob Cheswicki was standing at the reservations desk, talking to a tall brunette woman with a rhinestone snood holding her hair at the back of her neck. Bob Cheswicki, Gregor remembered, had recently been divorced. His wife of fifteen years had finally gotten sick and tired of being married to a cop. Gregor wondered how much time Bob spent chatting up the ladies. There were men who needed to be married. There were men who never would and never could be any good on their own. Gregor didn't know if Bob Cheswicki was one of these or not. He could see that the young woman at the reception desk was not impressed. She probably saw streams of well-paid businessmen every day. Why should she be impressed with a cop?

Bob saw Gregor come in and straightened up a little. "Here's Mr. Demarkian," he said. "Only three minutes late."

"There was a lot of traffic," Gregor said.

The young woman at the reception desk put herself out at least as far as giving Gregor a smile. Gregor Demarkian, after all, was Somebody in Philadelphia. He got his name in the papers and his face on the six o'clock news. There had even been an article or two about him in *People* magazine. The young woman grabbed a pair of enormously large, beribboned and tasseled menus out from under the surface of her desk, stepped into the foyer, looked straight into Demarkian's eyes, and said, "Follow me, sir. It's right this way."

Then she turned her back and Bob Cheswicki winked. "Think I'd do any better if I told her I was Batman in my spare time?" he whispered into Gregor's ear.

"No," Gregor said.

"She just gave me all kinds of grief about bringing my briefcase to the table," Bob said. "Apparently, it isn't done at La Vie Bohème. I wish you'd brought a briefcase."

"It looks like I should have brought one to take away what you brought to give me. What's in that thing?"

"Everything," Bob said solemnly.

The young woman had stopped halfway across La Vie Bohème's main room. She was looking back and waiting patiently, a little frown on her face. There was a hanging fern just above her head whose tendrils fell so close to her hair, they made her seem as if she were wearing a hat. Gregor got a weird image of her starring in something called *Sheena, Queen of the Jungle*. Had there really been a movie of that name, when he was younger?

"I suppose we'd better move," Bob said.

"I was just riding in a cab," Gregor said, "thinking about how awful everything's gotten and how everybody's attitude is all wrong."

"We *had* better get moving. You've got Februaryitis. Never mind. A nice complicated murder will clear that right up."

The young woman with the menus was beginning to look very angry. She was working hard not to, but Gregor knew the signs. He began to move toward her between the unidentified greens and spider plants.

Bob was probably right, Gregor thought. He probably did have Februaryitis, or whatever you wanted to call it. There was probably nothing wrong with the country that couldn't be cured by a couple of weeks vacation in the Caribbean.

If that wasn't it, then he must be getting old.

## 2

Whether or not bringing briefcases into La Vie Bohème was de rigueur, it was certainly implicitly discouraged. La Vie Bohème's chairs were large and wide, but its tables were anything but. Gregor was reminded of the old-fashioned soda shoppes that had littered the neighborhoods of Philadelphia just before the Second World War. They'd had tables like this. Round. Small. Made of cast iron tortured into curlicues and flourishes and painted white. The tables at La Vie Bohème had glass tops. That was the only difference. The soda shoppe tables had only more contorted cast iron. Gregor remembered never having room to put his ice cream sundae down without worrying it would fall off. Now he wondered—as he wondered every time he came here—how he was going to cut his meat without upsetting it and everything else onto the floor. This was the kind of thing that bothered Bob Cheswicki not at all. He ordered a bottle of wine to split between the two of them—"I'm taking the day off. I wanted to enjoy myself while you were paying for it"—and began to pull papers out of his briefcase and spread them around the table. The glass top of the table was covered by a pearl-gray linen tablecloth. It slipped.

"Have the *boeuf américaine,*" he told Gregor while he got his presentation in order. "It's a slab of prime rib two and a half inches thick. They've got the hottest horseradish this side of the Atlantic Ocean. What exactly do you know about Jacqueline Isherwood Hazzard?"

The waiter arrived with their bottle of wine. It was a vintage Margaux that probably listed for over a hundred dollars a bottle. Bob really did intend to make him pay. He also did not intend to let the waiter pull any nonsense. The waiter went through the ritual of the wine tasting. Bob went through it muttering under his breath about evidence protocol. Gregor ordered the *boeuf américaine.* So did Bob. The waiter did not so much leave as escape.

"You've got to call their crap around here," Bob said to the waiter's retreating back. "They can be unbelievably pretentious."

Gregor felt like pointing out that pretentiousness was at least part of what the people who came here were paying for. If all you wanted was really good beef, there were half a dozen steakhouses in the city who could give you that at one-fifth these prices. Gregor poured himself a glass of wine and tasted it. It was good, but not nearly as good as it would have needed to be for Gregor to consider it worth what it cost. He put his glass down on the table and said, "Back to Jacqueline Isherwood Hazzard. She was a friend or acquaintance or something of Bennis Hannaford's sister Myra, by the way, but I suppose that's natural. That's the real Main Line."

"Oh, she was real Main Line, all right," Bob Cheswicki said. "Original Main Line, if you know what I mean. Railroad money. Lots and lots of it."

"The town house she and her husband lived in was hers?"

Bob nodded. "Through her mother's side of the family. It goes back to before the Declaration of Independence. That's her mother's side of the family all over, if you want to know. They've got lineage that sounds like it was made up by David O. Selznick. *Four* signers of the Declaration of Independence. *Nine* members of the Continental Congress and *sixteen* who attended the Constitutional Convention in one capacity or another. So much background, you're surprised they didn't strangle on it, except maybe they did. By the time Jackie's mother married Jackie's father, the mother's side was stony-broke and not a hope in hell of recouping their losses. Not in that climate. Jackie's mother was an only child."

"And in those days young women of good family didn't go into business," Gregor said. "Yes, I see. But there was money on the Isherwood side?"

"Oh, yes, you bet. Lots and lots of it. It came to Jacqueline, of course. She was an only child too. Not very attractive though. At least I think she wasn't."

"You think?"

Bob Cheswicki shrugged. "By the time I saw her, she was in the morgue, and nobody is attractive in the morgue. I've seen pictures of her, of course, but you can never tell with pictures. People who take very bad ones can be very good-looking in real life."

"Fair enough."

"But I also figure she wasn't very attractive because she married Paul Hazzard. I mean, this is *serious* Main Line money we're talking about here. Sure, we get a case or two a decade of some debutante running off with her ski instructor, but it happens a lot less than the public wants to think. These women have their heads screwed on straight ninety-nine percent of the time. They don't marry nobodies unless they have to. They know they can do better than that."

Gregor had finished about half his glass of wine. He topped up and thought about what Bob had just told him.

"From what I understood," Gregor said cautiously, "Paul Hazzard wasn't a nobody. Of course, if what you mean is a nobody in Main Line social terms, I understand, but—"

"No, no," Bob insisted. "I mean a *nobody*. This is—thirty years ago at least we're talking about here. When they were married, I mean. Paul Hazzard was a psychologist with a degree from Harvard and another one from Johns Hopkins. He had a very respectable practice and a decent income. He'd just written his first book. But he was still nobody. There was nothing at all to indicate that he'd turn out to be the psychological guru best-loved by just about everybody. I think, if you'd told one of the people who knew Paul Hazzard when he was first married to Jacqueline, if you'd told that person then that Paul Hazzard would eventually write a book that would sell two and a half million copies in hardcover—he'd have laughed in your face."

Gregor thought he ought to get hold of this book. In his experience, books did not sell in the millions of copies like that without having something interesting about them.

"Maybe there was a way to tell," Gregor told Bob. "Maybe Jacqueline Isherwood saw something in Paul Hazzard that everybody else missed. I don't know what it's like these days, but when I was young, women used to pride themselves on being able to do that."

"Maybe," Bob Cheswicki said. "But you have to go back to the background. It's not the kind of chance one of these women would normally take, unless, as I said, she had to."

"Meaning you think Jacqueline Isherwood Hazzard was just plain enough not to be able to command the sort of husband she wanted in the marriage market she would ordinarily have been expected to compete in—I have to keep reminding myself we're talking about thirty years ago here."

"I know what you mean," Bob said. "But it's not much different in those circles even now, you know. It comes from having so much money, you never really have to work. What do you have left to compete for except each other?"

"Do the men compete for the women?"

"The men are spoiled brats."

"Let's get back to Jacqueline and Paul," Gregor said. "They got married and then what?"

"And then nothing," Bob told him. "They got married and they were happy, as far as anyone can tell. There were three children, all Paul Hazzard's from a previous marriage. Caroline, James, and Alyssa. The children all went to the best private schools and then to the Ivy League. Paul wrote his book and started giving seminars on, I don't know, that stuff."

"Healing the shame within," Gregor offered helpfully.

"That's the kind of thing," Bob said. "It's all over the place now. I can never seem to make it stick in my head. It stuck in everybody else's head though. Whoosh. And it wasn't just Hazzard. It was dozens of people. Have you ever heard of the inner child?"

"Of course."

"Do you know what it is?"

"Not exactly."

Bob Cheswicki sighed. "I don't know what it is either. I went into Waldenbooks the other day to buy myself the new Ed McBain, I went into the wrong section and there they were. Books about the inner child. Dozens of them. And those seminars. Did I tell you Paul Hazzard used to give seminars?"

"I don't know," Gregor said. "I've heard he used to give workshops, but I never was sure what they were workshops in."

"Owning your anger," Bob Cheswicki intoned solemnly. "Learning to nurture yourself. I've read the titles. And don't ask me what they mean, because I don't know. What I do know is what he used to charge. Three hundred dollars for a single all-day session—that's three hundred dollars *a head*. Seven hundred fifty dollars for what was called a limited weekend, meaning Friday evening, all day Saturday, and Sunday breakfast. One thousand two hundred dollars for a full weekend, all three days, morning to night. One thousand five hundred dollars for the four-day, Thursday through Sunday, marathon special. Except he didn't call it a special."

Gregor was shocked. "Did anyone come? Who would pay prices like that?"

"Lots of people," Bob replied. "A typical limited weekend at, say, the Sheraton, would draw about six hundred people—and at the height of his popularity he'd have limited weekends scheduled three times a month and booked up six months in advance. The marathons were much better attended. He'd hold those about once a month and he'd get about a thousand people at each of them, and they were booked up well in advance too."

"It must have been a brutal schedule. He must have been exhausted."

Bob Cheswicki shot him a cynical little smile. "He wasn't exhausted at all. He didn't do much more at any of these things but give a speech at Sunday breakfast or maybe open the conference on Thursday or Friday night. He hired what he called workshop leaders to do the actual sessions. He paid them minimum wage."

"And they put up with that?"

"The assumption was that they were learning so much doing what they were doing, they should have paid him. And yes, they put up with it. Hell, they even believed it. I talked to some of them."

The waiter returned, carrying salads and a pepper grinder the size of the baton the grand marshal carried in the Tournament of Roses parade. Gregor and Bob both waved pepper away and grabbed their salad forks.

"So," Gregor said. "You keep talking about Paul Hazzard's career in the past tense. Is it over?"

"Pretty much," Bob admitted. "It would have to be, wouldn't it?"

"Because he went on trial for killing his wife? Because people think he did kill his wife in spite of the fact that he was acquitted."

"It doesn't matter if people think he killed her or not," Bob said. "In fact, it's probably worse if they think he didn't—from the point of view of the workshops, I mean. Look. What Paul Hazzard was selling—what all these guys are selling, really—is the theory that we make our own reality. That much I understand. We can be victimized, you know, and warped by our parents, but once we get into recovery and take control of our lives, well, then it's a different story. If bad things happen to us, it's because we secretly want them to happen to us—"

"Don't be ridiculous," Gregor said sharply.

"I'm not being ridiculous," Bob insisted. "I know this is all contradictory as hell, but nobody seems to care. They just go on and on like this. And think of it from the point of view of a young woman who is thinking of spending seven hundred fifty dollars for one of Hazzard's workshops. If you were that young woman, would you really want to learn the secrets of life from a man whose wife was randomly murdered by a tramp? What kind of reality would you think Hazzard was making for himself?"

"But Bob, for God's *sake*."

"I know, I know. But trust me, Gregor, that's the way people in this movement think about things. After the murder it was as if Paul Hazzard were jinxed. The people who thought he was guilty didn't want to know him because nobody does want to know a murderer if they can help it, except maybe those strange women who want to marry one once he's on death row; don't let me get into that. The people who thought he hadn't done it didn't want to know him either though, because—well, I just explained that. Nobody signed up for his workshops. Nobody sent in for his inspirational audiotapes. The sales of his books went way down and one of them even went out of print. I'd guess his income went from about a million five a year to less than fifty thousand."

Gregor gnawed a piece of radicchio, winced at its bitter flavor, and took a sip of wine. "That shouldn't matter, should it? You said Jacqueline Isherwood was a rich woman. Her money wasn't entailed or tied up in any way?"

"No, it wasn't entailed," Bob Cheswicki said, "but it turned out not to have been willed to Paul Hazzard either. There was money left in trust for the upkeep of the Philadelphia house. They can all live there forever for nothing, basically. The trust pays for the repairs, the light bill, the electricity, everything. There was money left in trust for the three children too, but to be paid out only on Paul Hazzard's death. There was nothing at all left to him."

"Not even an income?"

"Not even an income."

"But why? I thought you said they got on well together."

"I didn't actually say they got on well together," Bob said. "I said the marriage was mostly uneventful. As to Jacqueline Isherwood Hazzard's will, I think the intention was twofold. With the children—they're not such children now, by the way; they're in their forties—anyway, Paul Hazzard had put quite a bit of money into annuity trusts for the children while business was good. None of them was rich in the classic manner, and all of them had to do at least some work to live the way they liked to live, but they were mostly all right even without a share of Jacqueline's money. And as for Paul Hazzard, well. There was a little problem with Paul Hazzard in the last year before Jacqueline died. Seems he was keeping a woman."

The waiter came back to check on their progress with their salads. It was clear from his face that they hadn't progressed enough. Gregor and Bob both ignored him.

"I didn't think," Gregor said, "that women were kept these days. I thought it was out of fashion."

"Her name is Candida DeWitt—or that's what she calls herself—and she most definitely likes to be kept. Oh, she owns her own house out in Bryn Mawr and a stack of securities in her own name and all the rest of it, but idiosyncratic as the arrangements might be, what she definitely is is kept. Expensively kept. And she comes right out and admits to it."

"Ah," Gregor said. "So Jacqueline's will was a form of revenge."

"I don't know," Bob admitted. "That's what the prosecution alleged at the trial, of course, to present motive. Paul Hazzard thought Jacqueline was going to leave him because of Candida DeWitt. Paul Hazzard needed Jacqueline's money. Paul Hazzard killed Jacqueline to get Jacqueline's money. But the truth of the matter is, we didn't really have a shred of evidence that Jacqueline knew about Candida

DeWitt. The only thing we were absolutely sure of was that that will was a surprise to Paul Hazzard."

"What made you sure?"

"Paul Hazzard made us sure. When he heard about it, he made a very public and very nasty scene. In front of sixteen witnesses, by the way, including four police officers and a district court judge."

"Where was he told about the will?"

"The contents came out at the inquest. He should have heard about it before that, of course, but he was tied up doing seminars and the lawyers hadn't been able to get hold of him long enough to tell him. He blew a fit, Gregor. I saw him."

"Funny, isn't it? I've never met the man, but from everything I've heard about him, he doesn't sound like the kind who'd be likely to blow fits."

"I think all these psychologist guys are a little nuts underneath."

"I still don't understand about the motive," Gregor said. "If Paul Hazzard was bringing in a million five a year—by the way, was that net or gross?"

"Net before taxes."

"Net before taxes. Well then. Even after taxes, even after this mistress of his, he must have had something left."

"Don't bet on it."

"From a million five. Did he buy sports cars? Did he gamble?"

"Nope. He just didn't pay attention. It adds up, Gregor. It really does. Fifteen magazines every time you pass a newsstand. A sweater you see in a catalogue and like so you order it in all six colors. Fifteen pairs of shoes. Day after day. Week after week. Year after year. It adds up. I can show you the balance sheets if you like. We subpoenaed them."

"Aren't they confidential information?"

Bob Cheswicki shrugged. "I made you an official consultant to the police department for this case ten minutes after you called. I got the chief's permission. We're paying you a dollar."

"Wonderful," Gregor said.

"You can look over the records all you want," Bob Cheswicki said, "but it still comes down to the same thing. On the night Jacqueline Isherwood Hazzard died, Paul Hazzard wasn't broke, but he was the next best thing to. And by the time he got finished paying Fred Scherrer's bill, he really needed money."

*f i v e*

*1*

Christopher Hannaford got up late on Thursday morning because he got up late every morning. Out in California, the radio show he did started at midnight and went to six A.M. In California, this was a schedule he liked. Waking near noon, wandering across the vast empty expanse of his loft space to his Pullman kitchen, making coffee: All in all, it was a very good routine for composing poetry in his head. In spite of the fact that the radio show made him quite a bit of money—and the poetry made him no money at all—Christopher persisted in thinking of poetry as what he "did." He even had reason to think that way. Monetary awards notwithstanding, modern poetry in the United States was a structured field with its own set of rewards, and Christopher had won all of them. He'd had an issue of *Poetry* magazine devoted entirely to his work. His pieces had appeared in *The New Yorker* and *The Atlantic* and *The New Kenyon Review*. He'd been asked to read at the 92nd Street Y in New York City. Christopher had once told his sister Bennis that poetry was the only thing he had ever been able to take seriously. That wasn't quite true—there were one or two women he had taken *very* seriously— but it expressed the one thing he had ever had trouble expressing, so he went with it. Christopher Hannaford took poetry so seriously, he had never actually told anybody he committed it.

Since Bennis had a one-bedroom apartment, Christopher was sleeping on the fold-out living room couch. The couch faced the oversize living room window that looked out on Cavanaugh Street. Halfway up this window there was a plant ledge covered not with plants, but with papier-mâché models of castles with moats, populated by miniature knights on horseback and damsels in pointed hats and dragons breathing painted fire. Bennis always made models of Zed and Zedalia when she was revising her books. Zed and Zedalia were the principal kingdoms in the fantasy world she wrote about. Zed was a country ruled by a king. Zedalia was a country ruled by a queen. They displayed, Bennis had told the *New York Times Magazine*, the differences between the masculine and the feminine principles in government. Christopher had read that quote and then called to ask her if she'd meant it. She'd told him not to be a damned fool. She had enough trouble keeping track of her characters' names without worrying about turning them into analogies of God only knew what.

At the moment, both the masculine and the feminine principles of government seemed to have succumbed to the dragonic one. Christopher sat up a little and contemplated the pointed tail, the red spurts of flame, the scaly back. These models had to be a form of automedication. That's all there was to it. Bennis couldn't need this kind of detail to write. Christopher contemplated making himself a cup of coffee. He contemplated getting up and taking a shower. He contemplated reading one of Bennis's books. It had been years, since the publication of *Zedalia in Winter*, since he'd tried.

Bennis's living room window looked directly across the street into another living room window, a much bigger living room and a much bigger window than Bennis had. Christopher lay propped up on the back of the couch and watched the furniture in that living room do nothing in particular. He imagined Lida Arkmanian coming in from downstairs or upstairs or the back hall, rearranging things, doing away with dust. Did she do her own dusting? Christopher didn't think so—women who owned town houses of that size rarely did any domestic work at all—but he could imagine her dusting. He could imagine her straightening shelves and washing down counters too. He had never found those things particularly alluring activities. He didn't do any of them himself and he never asked the women he knew to do them, or even asked them if they could. He just found something he liked—half-attractive and half-comforting, oddly enough—in thinking of Lida doing them.

There was a small brass Tiffany carriage clock on the end table to the right of the couch. Christopher picked it up. It had that kind of ornate lettering he found so hard to read. Positioned so that he could imagine the rococo numerals as a species of decorative dots, he saw that it was two minutes to twelve. It was too late for lunch, that was certain, unless he wanted to ask today and wait until tomorrow. He didn't want to wait until tomorrow. And dinner would be better anyway. Less light.

Christopher got out of bed and went down the hall to Bennis's bedroom. Bennis was out. Christopher thought she was doing that on purpose these days, so that he had a chance to sleep. He went to the suitcase he had left on the small bench at the foot of Bennis's bed and looked through it. Christopher Hannaford had never been much for formal clothes. The closest he had ever come to wearing a suit was the blazer-and-tie combination required as a kind of quasi-uniform by his New England prep school. He'd worn a tuxedo or two to a wedding or two. He'd had to, because he was always being asked to serve as an usher or a best man. He always managed to get the jacket off and the tie untied and his sleeves rolled up in the receiving line. He didn't have anything formal with him. He just didn't want to look poor. He didn't tell himself that Lida was too fine, too good, too pure to care about his financial status. He thought any woman in her fifties with a lot of money who was asked by a younger man to go out to dinner would be a damn fool not to worry about his financial status.

Fortunately, Christopher Hannaford was very well off. He was well off enough to play around with late-night radio shows and writing poetry, because his father had been considerably better than well off. Christopher found jeans and a workshirt and a sweater in what he thought of as the "insufferable snot with Hatteras connections" style and put them on.

Actually, the thing about the radio show was that it might cease to be playing around very soon. That was part of the reason he had come east to stay with Bennis. He wanted to ask her advice about this offer he'd gotten. It was amazing, really. Seven children in the family, and Bennis was the only one of them who had inherited the Hannaford genius with money. Christopher put on a pair of clean socks, shoved his feet into his cowboy boots, and headed out of the apartment.

Coming out into the cold air of Cavanaugh Street, standing at the top of the stoop and watching children run down the sidewalk and older people walk by, only pretending not to look at him, Christopher almost lost his nerve. People were so connected here. Everything was so public. A couple of dozen people were going to see him ring Lida Arkmanian's doorbell. What would happen then?

If Bennis's experience was anything to go by, what would happen would be a full-blown gossip circus, stopping just short of Peyton Place details. "The really incredible thing about what goes on around here," Bennis had told him, "is that everybody is absolutely convinced that everybody else is falling in lust left, right, and center but it never seems to occur to anybody that when that happens, people mostly do something physical about it."

Right. Bennis often sounded like that, off paper. Christopher knew what she meant. He went down the steps to the sidewalk, looked both ways in a perfunctory manner, and jaywalked across the street to Lida's front door.

Lida's front door had two gigantic crepe paper cupids on it. They seemed to be engaged in a duel with their arrows. Christopher was betting on the one with the silver dust in his eyebrows. He had the face of a cherub who could commit a murder and get away with it.

Christopher pressed the doorbell and stepped back to wait. He expected a maid. What he got was the grating scratch of an intercom coming on and Lida's voice—it hardly sounded like Lida's voice; it hardly sounded like anything human—saying,

"Yes? Who is it, please?"

The intercom button was hidden behind the left side of the silver-dust cupid. "Lida? This is Chris Hannaford. Did I get you at an awkward time?"

Click. Dead air. Static. Cough. "Christopher. When I buzz, the door will open. You can come right in."

"Where will I find you?"

"I'll come to the living room. Just a moment."

Click. Dead air. Buzz.

Christopher hated this sort of thing. Of course, nobody wanted to be a servant anymore. He didn't blame them. It was an awful life and there weren't many chances for advancement. He simply wished there were better alternatives than all this grate and buzz.

He got the front door open just in time and quickly pushed his way into the foyer. It was high-ceilinged and elegant and very, very clean, exactly as he remembered it. The living room was on the second floor. He went up the stairs.

Lida was wearing a pair of charcoal-gray wool slacks and a white silk shirt. She reminded him of the older women Saks sometimes used to model clothes for their suburban catalogues. He stopped at the edge of the stairs he had just come up and smiled.

"Hi," he said. "I did get you at an awkward time."

"No, no." Lida shook her head. "I was upstairs trying to make a Valentine train, out of cardboard, to fill with candy. For Donna Moradanyan's son, Tommy. Have you met Tommy?"

"The short one with the Rhodes scholar vocabulary," Christopher said.

"I do not believe he is short for a boy of three. I'm afraid I wasn't having very good luck. I'm not very artistic. That's Donna's department."

"I'm not very artistic either. Maybe I could help you out anyway. I could hold the tape or keep the sides of the train standing upright while you try to figure out how to fasten them together."

"Don't be silly. You don't want to waste your time like that. You have so much to do."

"I don't have a single thing to do except sleep on Bennis's couch and eat her out of house and home. Which is hard, by the way, because food gets delivered to her door more regularly than the mail. Really. I'd like to help. It would keep me out of Bennis's hair for a while and let her get some work done."

Lida turned away from him. Christopher could see the lines of tension in her back, under the thin layer of silk. She had her hair knotted at the nape of her neck, the way ballerinas liked to do. The loose hairs there seemed to be standing on end. Christopher felt his own skin getting very, very hot.

"All right," she said, turning back to him. "It's quite a climb. I have a little workroom in the attic."

"Let's go, then."

"Yes," Lida said slowly, "let's go."

Christopher let her get a little way up the stairs before he started after her. This was where he had to be careful. This was the hardest time. He was as sure as he could be that they both wanted the same thing. It wouldn't be a good idea to presume on that and rush things.

Rush things?

Sometimes Christopher Hannaford found himself astounded that any man and woman anywhere ever managed to end up in bed with each other. Getting there the first time was such a mess of conflict and confusion.

Lida stopped two-thirds of the way up the stairs and looked back at him. She looked tense and hurt and confused.

"Aren't you coming?" she asked him.

"Oh, yes," Christopher said. "I'm definitely coming."

He thought it would be the better part of valor not to point out to her that, under the circumstances, she might just have made a very dirty pun.

*2*

Alyssa Hazzard was one of those women who kept her life busy with Projects, the kind of Projects that required committees to stage benefit balls and get their pictures in the paper. Unlike some of the women who worked with her on these committees, she did not deceive herself about what she was doing. Some people maintained that society charity was a fraud. Alyssa Hazzard agreed with them. Obviously, if any one of them had been seriously interested in raising money for AIDS research or providing operating funds for the Philadelphia Cancer Hospice, they could have done more for either cause by just donating the cost of the dresses they would wear to the parties they gave to raise money. That was what critics didn't understand. They always bought new dresses to wear to charity parties, and the dresses always cost a minimum of eight thousand dollars apiece, and if you added that all up . . .

Actually, Alyssa never bought new dresses for charity parties. She made do by recycling clothes through the better thrift shops and by being good at alterations on her own. She had a Balenciaga she had worn three times, getting away with it by claiming that it was a vintage dress and an artwork and a homage to her mother. In another life Alyssa wouldn't have bothered with benefit balls at all. She had taken them up only after Jacqueline had been murdered and Paul had gone on trial. It was very interesting the way all that worked. All her friends had stuck valiantly by her side the whole time Paul was in the dock. They had called her daily and urged her to be brave and made a big point of inviting her to be on their committees. Then, after the trial was over, it was as if she had ceased to exist. The phone calls stopped—and when she made phone calls of her own, they weren't taken and they weren't returned. The invitations to be on committees stopped too, and the invitations to parties, and the quick little morning flurries asking her to lunch or to a visit to a gallery. A court had proclaimed Paul Hazzard innocent of the murder of Jacqueline Isherwood Hazzard. Alyssa's friends seemed to think they knew better.

Alyssa didn't have the same trouble with the women who ran the benefit balls because the women who ran the benefit balls did not know that she was Alyssa Hazzard. They knew her only as Mrs. Nicholas Roderick, informally called Ali, which she had allowed to be assumed to be a diminutive of Alice. Her picture had appeared in the newspapers quite often during the trial. Her picture had appeared on the television news too. She had stuck by her father throughout it all. She wasn't unhappy that she had done it. In this crowd it did her no harm. None of these women ever read anything in the papers that didn't mention their own names. None of their husbands looked at anything but the front pages and the financial sections.

Alyssa did more than hide her home life from the women she worked the charity circuit with. She hid the charity circuit from her family as well. Nick, of course, she did not hide. She needed him as an escort when she went to parties and she needed him to figure out the money when there was money to figure out, because she wasn't very good at it. Caroline and Paul and James were another matter. Alyssa supposed they knew she did these things. Their newspaper reading was as selective as everybody else's, but Paul at least glanced through every page of any paper he bought, just in case he saw something that inspired him. Caroline probably restricted her reading to Dear Abby and Ann Landers and Dr. Joyce Brothers. As for James—there was no telling what James did, but once he had made a joke about the company she kept, so Alyssa assumed he had heard or read something. The point was that no member of her family except Nick knew anything *in particular* about what she did, and Alyssa wanted to keep it that way.

Alyssa had every reason to believe that her family was no more interested in learning about her life than she was in having them learn about it. That was why she was so shocked when she came out of The Silver Unicorn after her luncheon meeting for the steering committee for the Turkish ball to benefit the American Heart Association and saw That

Woman waiting at the curb. That That Woman was waiting was undeniable. As soon as Alyssa came through The Silver Unicorn's doors, That Woman straightened like a soldier and walked half a step forward.

That Woman was how Alyssa Hazzard Roderick tended to think of Candida DeWitt. It was not for the usual reasons. Candida didn't look like the Other Woman. She looked like a Main Line matron. Alyssa had not cared for her step-mother, Jacqueline. In her opinion, Jacqueline was so awful, Paul was a saint for not having had affairs with every female he'd come across during the entire course of his second marriage. Except, of course, that he may have. The problem with Candida DeWitt, to Alyssa's mind, was when she had surfaced. Just around the time Jacqueline died. Just around the time the police were looking for a good motive to hook on to Paul. Alyssa was sure Paul would never have been arrested if Candida hadn't been on the scene, making such good newspaper copy.

It was too bad, really. On a metalevel, so to speak, Alyssa rather liked Candida DeWitt.

Candida moved forward again, getting closer. Women from the committee were coming out of The Silver Unicorn in little clubby clumps. They all seemed to be laughing in that oddly harsh way women do when they reach middle age and go to too many parties. Candida came up to Alyssa's side and said, "Alyssa? I don't know if you remember me."

"Call me Ali," Alyssa said in a pleasant voice, very much lower than the one Candida had used. "Or call me Mrs. Roderick."

Candida's eyes lit with understanding. "I see. They don't know who you are. You seem to have done better with that than I have."

"Done better with that?"

"You don't think it's been any different for me, do you?" Candida asked. "I try to put my lack of social engage-ments these days down to the fact that I'm getting older, but I know it's not that. None of the kind of men I'm attracted to is the least bit interested in having a mistress who might very well have killed her last lover's wife."

"But you couldn't have killed her," Alyssa said. "That was proved absolutely at the time."

"So what? People just cough politely and say, well, you never really know. And they're suspicious enough to believe it. Will you walk with me a little while? There's something I want to talk to you about."

"Why me? Why not Caroline or James? Why not Paul?"

"I don't know why you," Candida said, "but you're the one I seem to talk to. And I will admit I think you have the most sense. If we go west, we'll be heading in the right direction for you to find a cab when the time comes. All right?"

It was true. When Candida DeWitt wanted to talk to one of the family, Alyssa was the one she talked to. When the family wanted to talk to Candida, they sent Nick. Cars had begun to pull up at the curb. Nobody offered to give Alyssa a ride. They knew she always refused.

Alyssa and Candida began to walk west, not hurrying, not strolling exactly. It was far too cold to stroll.

"Did you tell the family about my book?" Candida asked after a while. "I suppose they might have known under any circumstances. It was announced in a few places."

"I told them," Alyssa said. "They weren't very happy."

"I wouldn't have expected them to be." Candida shrugged. "Really, there's no way to make everybody happy in situations like these. You just have to go ahead and do what's right for you. That's all I'm doing, you know."

"I know. It still isn't very pleasant for the rest of us."

"Yes," Candida said. "The question in my mind is, is it something more than just not very pleasant for one of you?"

"What is it exactly that you mean? They're upset, Candida. They're very upset. So am I."

"It's odd, you know. With all the nonsense Paul spouts about thinking with your heart and not your head, he's a very controlled man. All of you are very controlled people, really. Even Caroline."

"If you expect to get an argument out of me over that, Candida, you're very wrong. It's always been my contention that Caroline puts it on more than she really feels it."

"Well, I don't know about that. I just meant she isn't an abandoned, spontaneous, spur-of-the-moment sort of person. She thinks things through."

"I suppose she does." Alyssa didn't suppose anything of the kind. To her, Caroline was not the sort of person who "thought things through." Caroline was not the sort of person who thought. Caroline was the sort of person who planned. There was a difference.

Candida was biting her lip. "What I'm trying to say," she said carefully, "is that I don't think, if I knew one of you had done something, oh, unkind, say, or threatening, I don't think I'd put it down to a moment of impulsive spite. I think I'd have to assume it was very deliberate."

It was worse than cold. It was freezing. Alyssa shoved her hands into her coat pockets. She had her best cashmere-lined gloves on, but they didn't help.

"Is there a point to all this?" she asked Candida. "Has somebody done something? Has Caroline taken to calling you up in the middle of the night and threatening to do you in?"

"Nobody's called me up in the middle of the night." Candida seemed to be contemplating some kind of revelation and then deciding not to reveal. Alyssa was intrigued. Candida went on. "I want you to look at something. It arrived in my mailbox just this morning."

Candida snapped open the button clasp on her bag and brought out a clean white envelope. Alyssa knew from its size and shape and the quality of the paper that it was an engraved, or at least thermoplated, invitation. She took it out of Candida's hand and opened it up.

" 'The pleasure of your company is requested at a reception,' " she read. "It's one of those all-purpose invite cards the jewelry stores make up. For a party for this Friday night. So what? Who's Hannah Krekorian?"

"Hannah Krekorian," Candida said judiciously, "is the woman your father took to dinner *last* Friday night."

"Is she really?" Now Alyssa was more than intrigued. "She has to be reasonably loaded. I wonder why I've never heard of her."

"I don't know if she's loaded or not," Candida said. "What I want to know is how this invitation ended up in my mailbox."

"She invited you to a party."

"I don't see why. I've never met her. And even if she wanted to meet me, which she might, given one thing and another, she wouldn't invite me to this party. She's already invited Paul. In fact, unless I've gotten very bad at reading this kind of thing at my age, which I don't think I have, she's in the way of giving this party in honor of Paul. Not that she would tell Paul that, of course."

Alyssa handed the invitation back. "I can never get over how good your sources of information are. They're much better than James's, and he says he's channeling one of the oldest souls in the universe."

"They're good because they have to be good." Candida dropped the invitation back into her bag and snapped the bag shut again. "There are only two places this invitation could have come from, you know. One of them is Paul's study, or wherever he put this invitation when he got it. It was handed to him, I expect. That's why the envelope was blank when whoever sent it to me wanted to write my address on it."

"I see," Alyssa said. "You think one of us sent this to you. Me or James, maybe, but not really. You're much more likely to suspect Caroline or Paul. I think Paul has more sense than this, you know."

"Maybe he does."

"I don't see why any one of us would want to bother, just to embarrass you. We'd embarrass Paul as well. We've all had more than enough embarrassment."

"I'm sure you have."

"Where was the other place it could have come from?"

Candida looked at her oddly. "Hannah Krekorian, of course."

"I thought you said you didn't know Hannah Krekorian."

"I don't. It's who else this Hannah Krekorian knows that makes me think there's a chance, an outside chance, that this invitation might have come from her. Do you know who Gregor Demarkian is?"

"Of course."

"Hannah Krekorian is a friend, or at least an acquaintance, of Gregor Demarkian's."

"So?" Alyssa was blank. What could the woman be getting at? "I don't see why this woman's friends are an issue. And you just said, just a second ago, that she'd never invite you to this party."

"Well, that's true enough, as long as you assume that the purpose of this party is to put something on for Paul. But what if the purpose of this party is altogether different? What if it's to put something on for Gregor Demarkian?"

"But why?" Alyssa insisted. "Why would Demarkian want to cause embarrassment to you and Paul? Do you know Demarkian?"

"Of course I don't know Demarkian," Candida said in exasperation. "But Gregor Demarkian is a detective, Alyssa. And the Philadelphia Police Department is not happy leaving the murder of your stepmother as an officially unsolved crime. If you would just put two and two together—"

"But why?" Alyssa demanded again. "Why now?"

"I don't know."

"It doesn't make sense."

"No," Candida agreed. "It doesn't make sense. So that brings us back to square one. Somebody at the house sent me this invitation, hoping I'd use it and wind up with egg on my face. It wasn't a very good idea."

"It obviously didn't work."

"No, it didn't work. It did get me angry. That's not a very good idea either, Alyssa. I'm not a very pleasant person when I'm angry."

"Well, go be unpleasant to somebody else," Alyssa said, tugging her collar up against the wind. "I didn't send you that thing. I wouldn't. I wouldn't want the trouble it would get me into. Go pick on Caroline or Paul."

"I'm not going to pick on anybody," Candida said.

They had reached an intersection, how many blocks west of The Silver Unicorn, Alyssa didn't know. Candida stepped to the edge of the curb and shot her hand into the air. A taxi appeared out of nowhere and pulled up beside her.

"I'll let you take this one," she told Alyssa. "I want to

walk awhile longer. You should think of the things we were talking about."

"What things?"

"What we were talking about," Candida insisted. She had the cab's door open. She was waiting politely.

Alyssa got in the cab and recited her address mechanically. Now, what was this all about?

But the driver pulled out into traffic, and Alyssa didn't have a chance to ask. She looked back at the sidewalk. Candida had disappeared. She thought of the invitation. She decided it made no sense at all.

Even Caroline, who hated Candida with even more venom than she hated most women, wouldn't do anything like this.

If Caroline wanted to make Paul look like a world-class horse's ass, she'd find a way to do it in worldwide syndication.

*s i x*

*1*

The engraved invitations that Hannah Krekorian had
sent out to everyone she knew on Cavanaugh Street had
not been made up especially for this party. They were stock
invitations with blanks on them for date and time. They
could be ordered from Tiffany's by the hundred. All the
older women in the neighborhood had them. There had
been a craze for them about a year before Gregor Demarkian
moved back to Philadelphia. They went out of local fashion
almost as quickly as they had come in. Almost nobody used
them anymore. That Hannah did struck most of her friends
as very odd. It also struck Gregor Demarkian as useful. The
nice thing about stock invitations that hadn't been especially
made up was that there were always more of them hanging
around somewhere. All Gregor had to do to get one for Bob
Cheswicki was to call Hannah and ask her if she minded if
he brought a friend. Of course, Hannah thought he was
talking about a woman. Gregor could hear the alarm in her
voice. Everybody on Cavanaugh Street expected him to
come to his senses and marry Bennis Hannaford one of
these days—in spite of the fact that both Gregor and Bennis
thought any such move would mean they were equally
certifiable. Hannah couldn't help herself. No matter how
much she might want to discourage Gregor from veering
from the path that local gossip had already laid down for

him, she couldn't bear the idea of *not* seeing who he would bring. Gregor asked for the extra invitation when he ran into Hannah in Ohanian's Middle Eastern Food Store on Wednesday morning. Hannah brought it over to Gregor's apartment herself on Wednesday afternoon. Gregor didn't tell her what he was up to. He knew perfectly well she wouldn't want a police officer who was still vitally interested in the case against Paul Hazzard at the party she was giving for Paul Hazzard. Even if she said the party wasn't for Paul Hazzard.

"It'll be all right," Gregor told Bob when Bob arrived at his apartment at six-thirty on Friday, "because she doesn't have the faintest idea who you are. Does Paul Hazzard?"

"He might know I'm an assistant commissioner of police," Bob said, "but he wouldn't know I've got any interest in the case. Why should he?"

"He probably won't even know you're an assistant commissioner of police." Bennis came into the living room from Gregor's kitchen, nibbling on a *dolma* she had found in his refrigerator. Bennis was wearing what Gregor thought of as "one of her Bennis outfits." It was a long, straight dark dress with a plain neckline and close-fitting sleeves, sewn all over with tiny black and silver beads. Bennis looked wonderful, very twenties-glamorous and exotic, but Gregor had the uneasy feeling that she was wearing more on her back than it had taken Donna Moradanyan to buy her last car. Bennis finished the *dolma* and licked her fingers.

"There really isn't any reason he should recognize an assistant commissioner of police," she said reasonably. "It's not like Mr. Cheswicki is the commissioner himself. The commissioner is always on television and being interviewed in the newspaper and whatever. Assistant commissioners are . . . anonymous."

"It's still a good thing we're not lying about his identity," Gregor said. "Just in case."

Bob looked bemused. "I wish you were clearer about what it is you wanted me to do at this thing. I'm sure it will be a nice party and the food will be wonderful, but—"

"Aren't you happy to finally get a chance to meet Paul

Hazzard in person? After all these years of hearing about him?"

"Well, I am," Bob said. "It will be interesting."

"Maybe it will also be helpful," Gregor told him. "I don't know. I suppose I'm not sure what I'm looking for either. I just want someone else there whose impressions I can trust. Just in case."

"That's twice you've said that." Bennis took her pack of cigarettes out of her evening bag. "Just in case of what?"

"Just in case Paul Hazzard really is the murderer," Bob said cheerfully. "Gregor's been going crazy with the material I gave him last week. I think he's almost as interested in it as he would have been in a fresh case. We've started a pool down at the department about how long it's going to take him to come up with a theory."

"I've got six theories already. Don't you think it's time to go?"

Bennis shot a look at Gregor's little table clock and sighed. "We're going to be early as hell, but we always are, and if we don't go, you'll make me crazy pacing around worrying we'll be late. Do you know what it is you're trying to do here tonight?"

"I think so," Gregor said.

"He usually does," Bob Cheswicki pointed out.

Bennis had a big cashmere shawl to wear outside instead of a coat. She picked it up off the back of Gregor's couch and wrapped it around herself.

"If we're going to go, we ought to go," she said. "Maybe Paul Hazzard will be there too, getting ready to help Hannah greet the guests. Then you two can have him all to yourselves for fifteen minutes."

## 2

Gregor Demarkian was almost always the first person to arrive at any party. He was so distressed at the idea of being even a minute or two late, he sometimes arrived at his dental appointments a good fifteen or twenty minutes early. Tonight, however, he wasn't going to be close to being the first on the scene—and it bothered him to realize he should have anticipated that. Old George Tekemanian was waiting impatiently for them in the hall when they came downstairs. They had agreed to walk old George over, and old George had been ready to go by quarter after six. So, apparently, had the rest of Cavanaugh Street. Gregor held the door open for old George while Bennis and Bob Cheswicki went down the steps to the street. When Gregor emerged into the night air, he suddenly saw what looked like a slow start to a Mardi Gras. Everybody seemed to be out. Everybody seemed to be dressed up. The neighborhood looked as wild as it did when Donna Moradanyan was really in the mood to decorate. Gregor saw Sheila Kashinian—in four-inch heels, too much makeup, and her best blond mink—hanging off Howard Kashinian's arm. He saw Mary Ohanian, and Linda Melajian's mother, Sarah, gotten up in "party dresses" of the kind that used to be popular for "semiformals" in the early sixties. He saw Linda Melajian herself, in silver studs and leather, looking as if she were about to be married to a punk rock guru. The only people on the street who looked the least bit normal, or even sane, were Lida Arkmanian and Bennis Hannaford's brother, Christopher. Lida was wearing a dress. Christopher was wearing a suit that didn't look like it belonged to him. They were standing at the bottom of the steps to Lida's town house, talking.

"Everybody wants to see what Hannah's gentleman caller is like," Bennis said. "I should have known."

"We won't be the first ones there," Bob Cheswicki agreed.

"If Paul Hazzard did murder his wife," Bennis said, "this will be practically as good as an execution. Can you just imagine it, he shows up a fashionable twenty minutes after the hour, and forty people leap out at him and yell 'surprise!'"

"Nobody's going to yell 'surprise,' " Gregor said.

"They ought to."

Gregor knew what Bennis meant. He turned toward Hannah's apartment and began to march briskly down the street. Old George kept pace in that springy, self-satisfied way that meant he was thoroughly enjoying himself. It wasn't a very long walk. Gregor passed the Ararat Restaurant, which seemed to be closed. That made sense to an extent. Certainly none of their usual customers from the neighborhood was going to show up tonight. It didn't make sense in another way, because a lot of the business the Ararat did these days was with tourists. The *Inquirer* and the *Star* had both given the place wonderful reviews, and now a steady stream of people trekked out here from the other neighborhoods of Philadelphia and the towns of the Main Line to eat *yoprak sarma* and *lahmajoon*. With any luck, these people called before they came. Gregor passed Ohanian's Middle Eastern Food Store and saw that that was closed too. One of Donna Moradanyan's red-and-silver hearts dangled in the larger of the two front windows. Under it was a huge plate of *mamoul* cookies made in heart shapes and covered with *naatiffe* frosting and the sign GIVE YOUR SWEETHEART A TRADITIONAL ARMENIAN VALENTINE'S DAY!

Oh, well, Gregor thought. Around here, people took what holidays they wanted and adopted them. Gregor was waiting for Donna Moradanyan to get really interested in Hanukkah or Rosh Hashanah.

Hannah Krekorian's building was very close to Ohanian's, almost directly across the street. Gregor went purposely to the corner and pressed the button for the walk light, in spite of the fact that both Bennis and old George Tekemanian were jaywalking. Nobody on Cavanaugh Street had the least realistic sense of how dangerous the world was, or what it took to protect yourself from the terrible things it could do to you. Gregor got his walk light and walked, catching up to Bennis, old George, and (traitor) Bob Cheswicki on the other side. They had waited for him.

"We all want you to go first," Bennis said. "This is going to be a nuthouse."

"Don't look at me," Bob Cheswicki said. "I don't know what's going on around here."

Sheila and Howard Kashinian waved to Gregor and

Bennis and old George Tekemanian. Sheila gave Bob Cheswicki a sharp, appraising look. They went upstairs and through the doors. They were followed by all six of the Devorkian girls, three sets of twins between the ages of fourteen and sixteen. The Devorkian girls weren't paying attention to anybody.

"Let's go," Gregor said with a sigh. "If we don't do it now, it's only going to get harder."

## 3

Whether or not it would have gotten harder was moot. Whether or not it was a nuthouse was not. Bennis's instincts had been deadly accurate. The stairway that led up to the landing that Hannah's apartment opened onto was jammed—in spite of the fact that it was still a good six minutes before the official starting time of this party. Gregor, Bennis, old George, and Bob found themselves sandwiched among the Devorkian girls—who were impossible—and six old ladies known to the street only as Mrs. Manoukian, Mrs. Karidian, Mrs. Vartenian, Mrs. Baressian, Mrs. Astokian, and Mrs. Erijian. They were all over ninety. They were all dressed in black. They were each and every one of them as formidable as Cerberus. They were a group of people that anyone on Cavanaugh Street who was giving a major party had to invite, because not to would be grossly impolite, but who could safely be anticipated to not show up. This time they had shown up. Gossip, Gregor thought, was a wonderful thing.

Hannah was standing just inside her own front door, greeting people in a flurried way that made Gregor think she hadn't intended to greet them formally. In spite of the stiff invitation, she had been thinking of this as just an extended version of "having people in." Standing next to her was a very tall, very thin man in his mid-sixties. He had a full head of silky gray hair and a very square jaw. Gregor looked at Bob Cheswicki and Bob Cheswicki nodded. Gregor looked back and decided that, to him, Paul

Hazzard was an unpleasant-looking man. Women, it seemed, positively adored him.

Bennis leaned over. "I'll tell you what happened," she whispered in Gregor's ear. "Paul Hazzard called Hannah this morning around ten and asked her if he could come over early and help out. Hannah said yes. Paul Hazzard showed up around five. About fifteen minutes ago Paul Hazzard finally figured out what he'd gotten himself into. I'll bet he was appalled."

It was Hannah Krekorian who was appalled. The Devorkian girls had said their hellos and gone charging across the living room to the table of food set up against the streetside window. They were well padded as it was, and determined to get more so. Hannah was staring over old George Tekemanian's shoulder and looking shocked. Gregor thought she must just have seen the old ladies.

"Do you figure that bunch behind us are the Furies or the Fates?" Bennis was still whispering in his ear.

"Shhh," Gregor said.

"They stare at me in church," Bennis said. "In a group. In concert. They think I'm a scarlet woman. One of them stopped me on the street about six months ago and told me to be careful about you. Promising a man something you never get to the altar to deliver could unhinge his mind."

"Good God," Gregor murmured.

"Krekor!" Hannah Krekorian said, sounding worse than desperate. "How good of you to come. I would like to introduce you to a friend of mine. This is Paul Hazzard. Oh, and this is Bennis Hannaford. And George Tekemanian. And—and—" Hannah looked at Bob Cheswicki doubtfully.

Gregor said, "Robert Cheswicki. Bob. The friend I told you about."

Hannah was so distracted by the old ladies, the information didn't take. "Bob Cheswicki," she repeated. Then she turned a little and said in the shrillest voice Gregor had ever heard her use, "Mrs. Manoukian! It's such an honor! How delightful it is to see you!"

"I'll bet," Bennis said, whispering again.

Gregor poked her sharply in the ribs. Paul Hazzard had

stepped back slightly and was looking them over. To be precise, he was looking at Gregor. It seemed Bennis had been right. Paul Hazzard hadn't recognized Bob Cheswicki's name. He hadn't noticed much about Bennis Hannaford either, and that was unusual in Gregor's experience. Old George Tekemanian might as well not have existed. Gregor didn't think old George's existence had even registered on Paul Hazzard's brain. Nothing seemed to be registering on Paul Hazzard's brain except what he was concentrating on, which was Gregor Demarkian. His concentration was making Gregor very uncomfortable.

"Maybe I should do something to break the spell," Bennis said. Whispering again. "Maybe I should go up and ask him if he killed his wife."

"Behave yourself," Gregor told her.

"I'm going to do nothing of the kind."

"Come with me," old George Tekemanian urged her. "There is rum punch. I heard Linda Melajian tell Mary Ohanian this morning."

Gregor thought Paul Hazzard looked as if he could use some rum punch. Paul had pulled very far back from his original place next to Hannah Krekorian. Somehow he had pulled them with him, so that they were now standing well away from the door and Hannah's problems with the old ladies. It was a neat trick. Gregor wondered if Hazzard had done it on purpose. If he had, he was a force to be reckoned with.

"Gregor Demarkian." Paul Hazzard had that odd sort of deliberately inflected voice Gregor thought of as "TV anchorperson." He cocked his head. "Gregor Demarkian," he said again. "I've heard a lot about you."

"If you read it in the paper," Gregor told him, "it was probably inaccurate."

"Very likely," Paul agreed genially. "But you are something in the way of being a famous man. Especially in the Philadelphia area."

"That's interesting," Gregor said. He meant that the tactic was interesting. He'd used it himself on one or two occasions, but always with psychopaths and street killers—the kind of people who were usually not well-educated enough to know what he was doing. He wondered how

Paul Hazzard would go on with it. There should be an attempt to outline the purported difference, to make Gregor look local (and therefore bush league) while Paul himself was made to seem more cosmopolitan in scope. In Gregor's case that was, of course, difficult to do if you stuck with the facts. The point of a manipulation like this is that facts had nothing to do with it. It was how you made your opponent feel that was the thing.

"I'm always very interested in anything that's going on in Philadelphia," Paul Hazzard said. "I'm afraid I don't always manage it. I'm in New York so much, I find it very difficult to keep up with the news."

"I never liked New York as a city," Gregor replied. "Of course, I never liked Washington either, and I spent a great deal of my time there."

"That's right." Paul Hazzard nodded his silky gray head. "You retired from the Federal Bureau of Investigation. I could never retire. I could never stand the way it would limit my scope."

"Oh, I don't know," Gregor said, "my scope seems to be far less limited now that I'm on my own than it ever was when I was with the Bureau."

"Does it? I think I'd find myself at loose ends."

"There's always something to keep my interest up. I like history, for instance. I never had enough time for historical research when I was directing a government department."

"History," Paul Hazzard repeated. "Do you like any particular period of history? Are you one of those people who knows the blood type of every soldier who fought at Antietam or do you plot the course of Napoleon's retreat from Moscow?"

"I'm interested in the history of crime, of course."

"Of course. Unsolved mysteries, I suppose."

"All the really unsolved mysteries," Gregor said, "aren't perceived as mysteries. They're the case of old Mrs. Smith who died so suddenly, wasn't it odd, but heart attacks happen that way. Except that it wasn't a heart attack and it was worse than odd, but nobody knows it, although one or two people may suspect. Either that, or the crime is unsolved because it's a simple case of random brutality. Street thug sees old lady with purse on street, goes up to old lady, sticks her with his flic knife, grabs her purse, disappears. As long as he takes only cash and gets rid of the purse at the first opportunity, it's the perfect crime."

"But his fingerprints will be on the purse," Paul Hazzard said.

"Yes, they will, but it won't matter. The chances are one in a million that the match will ever be made if he's picked up for something else. Our computer matching systems just aren't that good."

"I see." Paul Hazzard looked away. The room was too full of people. And there was too much noise. "That's rather disheartening to hear. I've spent much of the last four years thinking that a little mystery of my own would be solved any day now, cracked wide open finally by some cop somewhere picking up some junkie thief and running his prints. You did know I was once—involved—in the investigation of a murder?"

"Yes, Mr. Hazzard. I knew that."

"It was my wife who was killed," Paul Hazzard said. "My second wife. Jacqueline. They thought I'd done it, of course. They put me on trial for it, but I was acquitted. I suppose you knew all that too."

"Oh, yes."

"Do you suppose all these people know it?" Paul Hazzard gestured around the room.

Gregor thought of Bennis with her computer printout. "I wouldn't worry about it if I were you, Mr. Hazzard. It all happened a long time ago, and the state had a fair shot at you in a fair trial. Even if you did kill your wife, I doubt if anything could be done about it now."

"There could be new evidence."

"It would have to be very, very, very good new evidence. There are constitutional prohibitions against double jeopardy. The courts take them quite seriously. So do the police."

"I didn't kill my wife." Paul Hazzard had stopped looking around the room. He was doing his best to stare straight into Gregor's eyes. "I know it's asinine to make such a point of it after all this time, but it's true and the truth of it matters to me. I did not kill my wife."

Gregor said nothing.

"When I found her lying in the living room that night, I thought I was going crazy," Paul Hazzard said. "Except, of course, I wouldn't have put it that way then. Do you believe the universe is split in two?"

"What?"

"Never mind." Paul Hazzard seemed to straighten, although he hadn't been slouching that Gregor could tell. "I'd better get back to Hannah. I'm supposed to be helping out. I'm glad to have met you, Mr. Demarkian."

"I'm glad to have met you too."

"I'll bet you are."

Jab. Thrust. Sharp edge. Stab. Gregor was startled. The comment was such a change from Paul Hazzard's customary oversincerity. It almost made him human.

Paul Hazzard stepped into the crowd around Hannah near the door. Gregor looked around for Bennis and found her nearly at his elbow. She must have been eavesdropping on the whole thing.

"I don't like him," she said promptly. "Do you? He comes off to me like somebody who's after something."

"He probably is," Gregor said mildly.

"I don't see how you can let him take advantage of Hannah," Bennis said. "Really, Gregor. Sometimes I don't know what you're thinking."

As far as Gregor was concerned, most of the time Bennis didn't know what he was thinking. Gregor took this as a blessing.

"I'm hungry," he said as forcefully as he could. Then he took off as quickly as he could in the direction of the buffet table.

Since Bennis never ate anything at these parties until she had had at least one glass of wine, she didn't follow him.

## 4

Twenty minutes later, sated with *dolmas* and *dabgadz kufta* and Sarah Melajian's best *khorovadz biberr* and he didn't know what else, Gregor Demarkian sat in a chair along the wall next to Father Tibor Kasparian, drinking a large glass of *raki* and watching the movement in the room. Bob Cheswicki, Gregor noted, was where he had been all evening—just close enough to Paul Hazzard to know what was going on. Bennis had Tommy Moradanyan asleep in her lap while she sat on the couch next to Mary Ohanian. Their heads were bent so close together, Gregor decided they had to be talking about sex. Hannah Krekorian and Paul Hazzard were more difficult to figure. Paul seemed to be drifting aimlessly through crowds of people he did not know. Hannah seemed to be hovering around him anxiously, as if, if she took her attention away from him for even a moment, he would disappear.

"I did not say that I had met Mr. Hazzard before tonight," Father Tibor was chiding Gregor gently. He had a glass of *raki* too. His arrest seemed to have perked him up. "I said I knew more than you would think about the work he does. It is because of Sonia Veladian, Krekor, whose mother married that man with the mustache and later it turned out that the man was, well, you know, with Sonia when she was eleven. The mother threw the man out of the house when she found out. But still, the damage was done."

"And the mother took Sonia to see Paul Hazzard?" The problem with Father Tibor's stories was that they not only started in medias res, they started in media confusion.

"No, no," Father Tibor said. "Sonia was grown-up when she went to see Paul Hazzard, only not actually to see Paul Hazzard but to a—what do you call it—a support group. Yes. For grown-ups to whom things of this kind have happened as children. Sonia Veladian is older than Bennis, Krekor. She was older than Donna Moradanyan is now when she joined this support group."

"And did it help her?"

"Well, that is a curious thing, Krekor. It did and it didn't."

"Do you want to tell me about it?"

Tibor shook his head. "No," he said. "I don't. Not here and not now, at this party. I want to drink *raki* and relax a little. But come to my apartment tomorrow, Krekor, and I will tell you everything I know, and maybe we can find a way to get in touch with Sonia. Although I doubt it. The last I heard, she was in Somalia."

"Somalia?"

"She is with the U.N. It is a very complicated story, Krekor, but it has a good ending, I think. But I also think I do not like this man Hazzard. In principle."

"Oh, well," Gregor said. "A lot of people around here don't seem to like him on principle."

"There is not much to like." Tibor stood up. His glass was empty of *raki* and nearly empty of ice. He went three steps over to the table and poured himself some more. Across the room, Bennis stood up, put Tommy down on the place on the couch she had vacated, and walked over to Gregor.

"Hello," she said. "All in all, a very dull party. You'd think a major neighborhood scandal would manage to work up more tension than this. And Paul Hazzard. Didn't they say Eichmann was banal?"

"Hannah Arendt did," Gregor told her. "I don't think Paul Hazzard is banal. I think he's just minding his manners in a perilous situation."

Bennis laughed. "The old ladies got hold of him and positively grilled him. He kept doing all that appropriate closure behavior stuff to try to get out of it—you know, saying things like 'It's been very interesting talking to you, but I have to break off this conversation now'—and it was doing him no good at all. They were rolling right over him."

"They would," Gregor said.

Tibor came over with his full glass of *raki*. "You have been losing beads all evening," he said to Bennis. "Look at the door now. Someone has arrived whom I do not know."

They all turned to look at the door, where a pretty woman in her forties was standing, holding an invitation card and looking oddly sexy in a plain silk shirtwaist dress.

"Maybe it's one of Paul Hazzard's daughters," Bennis said. "He's got two. Maybe Hannah invited the whole family."

It was not one of Paul Hazzard's daughters. As Gregor and Bennis and Father Tibor watched, the woman walked a few steps into the apartment, held out her invitation card to Hannah Krekorian, and said: "You must be my hostess. I'm very glad to meet you. My name is Candida DeWitt."

## *seven*

### *1*

Later, Gregor would think how odd it was that Candida DeWitt had known exactly whom to introduce herself to, exactly where to go after she had come in the door. It bespoke careful planning of the kind that can sometimes make poor people rich, if they stick to it. It bespoke cleverness too. Gregor thought Candida DeWitt was very clever in the way the English used that word. She was smart and insightful about men and women and how they would behave in tense situations. She was good at putting herself first.

When the doorbell rang, Paul Hazzard had been holding forth to a little circle of women that included one of the old ladies (Mrs. Vartenian, looking fierce) and all six of the Devorkian girls. The Devorkian girls looked as awestruck as if they'd wandered into Madonna's dressing room. Hannah was hovering around at the edges. She seemed to have a compulsion to touch him, just a little, so gently it might never be detected. A light whispering rub of sleeve on sleeve. The side of a hand along the hem of a jacket. Paul Hazzard didn't notice. His face was lit up, as if a powerful light had gone on inside him. He was in his element. He had an audience.

"What you have to understand," he was telling the women clustered around him, "is that there are no hierarchies of pain. That's the worst of the sickness of the society around us. That's how that society keeps us in line. Here we are, so damaged we can barely function, and what do we hear? We hear that we shouldn't be, because somewhere in the next street or next town or next county or wherever, somebody has it worse than we do. And if we insist on naming our pain and owning our anger, we get hit with the big guns. Hiroshima. Dachau. How can we possibly say we've been damaged when people have been through things like that and lived perfectly good lives?"

"But that's true, isn't it?" Linda Melajian said. "My great-grandmother came from Armenia, and you should have heard the stories she used to tell about what happened to her. She had a baby and a husband, and they were both killed when the Turks came through during the massacres. She had pictures of them she used to keep in her room. But then she came here and married my great-grandfather and had other children, and she was fine."

"She was in denial," Paul Hazzard said promptly.

"I came from Armenia," Mrs. Vartenian said ominously. "In 1916."

"What you have to understand," Paul Hazzard said, "is that the human being is a delicate instrument. A very delicate instrument. Especially in childhood. Something like Hiroshima, or the concentration camps, or these massacres you're talking about—major traumas like these can affect the lives of the people who suffer from them forever. I'm not denying the power of experiences of that kind. What I'm trying to explain is that experiences that are much less dramatic may in reality be much more damaging. After all, the Nazis were the enemy. Nobody expected them to be anything else. Not even the children. A child is much more deeply and permanently hurt when someone close to him abuses him—when he's the victim of parental neglect, for instance."

"I've heard of things like that," Traci Devorkian said. "Junkies, usually. They get high as kites and don't clean the house or feed their kids for weeks at a time and the cops come in and the kids' beds are wet with pee and I don't know what and then it gets in the papers and the pictures are really gross."

"Pee?" Kelli Devorkian said. "Why would the kids pee in bed?"

"They don't have any control of their bladders," Debbi Devorkian said. "They haven't been brought up right."

"If our parents didn't pay attention to us for a couple of weeks, I wouldn't pee in bed," Kelli Devorkian declared. "I'd go out with Bobby Astinian and neck till my brains fell out."

"Shut *up*," Staci Devorkian said. "Mother is right over *there*. You'll get us all *grounded*."

"I was thinking of something a little more subtle than gross neglect," Paul Hazzard went on. "I was thinking of the kind of mother who always makes her children wait a minute before she gets them the milk they ask for, or always has one more thing to do—one more thing that takes only a minute—before she can look at the pictures they've painted or hear the story they want to tell."

"But that doesn't make sense," Linda Melajian said. "That sort of thing happens all the time. That's just life."

"Not really," Paul Hazzard contradicted her. "It's a kind of control. It's one of the ways parents ensure that their children stay within the preferred family pattern— within the preferred family sickness, if you will. Middle-class children today are really at much higher risk for permanent psychological damage than children were in earlier eras, or even than poor children are today. There's no excuse, you see."

"No." Linda Melajian shook her head. "I don't see."

"A child in a farm family in the eighteenth century with a critical and withholding mother could tell herself that her mother's behavior didn't mean her mother didn't love her. It was only that there was so much work to do and so little food and worries always about money. A poor child of today can tell herself the same kinds of things. But a middle-class child . . ." Paul Hazzard shrugged. "There's no way to escape reality for the middle-class child. The middle-class child *knows* her mother doesn't love her."

"I don't know," Marci Devorkian said firmly. "There seems something off about all this to me."

Candi Devorkian said, "Shhh!"

"I am ninety-seven years old," Mrs. Vartenian said,

"and I have lived long enough to say you are speaking nonsense."

"Oh," Candi Devorkian murmured. "Oh, dear."

It was impossible to tell if Paul Hazzard would have taken on Mrs. Vartenian. The general consensus later was that Paul Hazzard was probably smarter than that. A man didn't get very far as a psychologist—no matter how appealing his theories—without knowing something about people. Anyone on Cavanaugh Street could have told him that it was inadvisable to take on the old ladies unless you were willing to fight an emotional thermonuclear war. What interested Gregor was that Paul took this opportunity, and only this one, to stop the conversation. He had sailed right through Candida DeWitt's arrival, not even pausing in his pronouncements to register Candida's presence. His voice had sailed across the now-otherwise-quiet living room in the wake of Candida's self-announcement. His arguments had been as reasonably stated and complete as if he'd been giving them on the podium of the main convention ballroom in the Hilton Hotel. Candida DeWitt might as well not have existed until he decided she did.

Candi Devorkian's distressed "Oh, dear" still seemed to be floating through the air. Paul Hazzard turned away from her and her sisters and faced Candida with a noncommittal smile on his face. He looked as if he were addressing a saleslady. Candida, Gregor thought, had been subjected to this act before. She looked amused.

"Well," Paul said. "Candida. I didn't know you and Hannah were friends."

"We've never met before tonight," Candida said.

Paul Hazzard hesitated, frowning. This was not what he had expected. He didn't understand what he was supposed to do next.

"Well," he said again. "I'm at a loss. You have an invitation."

"Of course."

"Where did you get it?"

"It came to my mailbox in Bryn Mawr," Candida told him. "The way you would expect I'd get it."

Paul turned uncertainly to Hannah, who was standing just a little behind him. Gregor had never seen her face look so mutinous, so angry and upset. The contrast between Hannah and Candida DeWitt made Gregor uneasy. Candida was such a physically lovely woman. Hannah was so . . . solid.

Paul turned toward Hannah and raised an eyebrow. "Did you—?"

Hannah shook her head. "If Miss DeWitt is a friend of yours—"

"*Mrs.*," Candida said.

"If she is a friend of yours," Hannah went on doggedly, "then I am happy to have her here, Paul, but I did not send the invitation. I couldn't have. I didn't know who she was."

"I'm not a friend of Paul's," Candida said. "At least, I'm not anymore. He barely speaks to me."

"That's not true," Paul said quickly.

"I find it all very odd, really," Candida went on pleasantly. "Under the circumstances, it should be me who isn't speaking to him. After all, I'm not the one who tried to convince the police that he was the perpetrator in a murder they thought I'd committed."

"I don't get it," Traci Devorkian said loudly.

It was about time somebody intervened. Gregor kept expecting Bennis to leap up and do something. She wasn't moving. He got up instead. He was so bad at these things. It might really be much better if he went to the bathroom and forgot the whole thing.

At his side, Bob Cheswicki said, "Well, now I know why she's worth all the dough she gets. Holy cow."

Gregor wondered where Bob Cheswicki had come from. A moment before, he had been near the group around Paul Hazzard. It was as if he'd melted away from the scene of the action as soon as there was a sign of trouble. Some policeman he was turning out to be. That's what became of spending all your time behind a desk.

Gregor eased himself into the little empty space that had arranged itself around Paul Hazzard and Candida DeWitt like a magnetic field.

"Excuse me," he said. "My name is Gregor Demarkian."

Candida turned to him with interest. "Mr. Demarkian. I'm very glad you're here. I was hoping you would be here."

"Because you wanted to meet me?"

"Of course not. Because I knew your being here would make Paul very upset. Ask Paul. As far as he's concerned, everything I've done for the past four years or so has been just to make him upset."

"I don't know why you've done what you've done." Paul spoke angrily. "I don't know why you're doing what you're doing. It's pathological."

"A psychiatric term for everything," Candida said brightly. "He did try to get me arrested for the murder of his wife, you know. He told the police all sorts of things that weren't quite true. Fortunately, I had an ironclad alibi."

"All I did was answer questions," Paul told her. "All I did was exactly what my lawyer advised me to do, and even you said Fred Scherrer was a man worth listening to."

"Oh, he is. He's definitely a man worth listening to. I've been listening to him all this afternoon. On the subject of libel law."

"Candida, for God's *sake*."

Little ripples were going through the crowd now. Even Gregor, who was not sensitive to that sort of thing, could feel them. People had begun to speculate.

"What did she mean, the murder of his wife?"

"His wife was murdered?"

"Who is this person?"

Somebody in the crowd would know who "this person" was. That was inevitable. Of course, Bennis did know. Gregor wasn't worried about that. He could count on Bennis to be sensible in a situation like this. The trouble would come when some fool in the crowd would make the connection between Paul Hazzard and a newspaper story he had read once or a clip he had seen on the eleven o'clock news. Then he would blurt it all out, and then where would they be? Gregor stepped a little closer to the space between Candida and Paul. It made him think of the fifty-seventh parallel.

"Maybe I should get Mrs. DeWitt a drink," he said. "We have some excellent rum punch."

"Mrs. DeWitt is not going to stay," Paul Hazzard said.

"Of course I'm going to stay," Candida contradicted

him. "And I'd love some rum punch. It's exactly the sort of thing I have a craving for."

"You have a craving for sensationalism," Paul Hazzard said. "It's a form of personality disorder."

The tension in the room was so palpable now, it was like an ether made of fine wires. Hook it up to a battery and they would all be electrocuted.

"Rum punch," Gregor repeated. "Come with me. It's right over here."

There were more ripples in the crowd, more murmurs, a cough or two. Then Hannah Krekorian suddenly seemed to come to life. She had been standing frozen through almost all of Candida DeWitt's conversation with Paul. She had been so quiet, Gregor had forgotten she was there. Now she said "Oh!" in a loud, anguished voice that was so raw, it sounded like the wail of a wounded cat. Her thick, pasty face got red and her neck and chest, visible around the scooped-out neckline of her party dress, turned maroon. Never in his life had Gregor been made so aware of the fact that Hannah was a plain woman. Pain made her ugly.

"Oh," Hannah said again. She was half in tears and half in tantrum. She looked from Candida to Paul to Candida to Paul to Candida to Paul. Then she veered around in a great clumsy arc and ran for the duplex's spiral stairs. Going up to the second floor, Hannah was exposed to the shocked stares of everyone who was important to her on Cavanaugh Street. Even little Tommy Moradanyan was awake and staring. Hannah was clumsy and large and made a lot of noise. The stairs were delicate and shook under her weight.

"No, no," Lida Arkmanian said from the other side of the room. "This is not right."

"This is outrageous," Paul Hazzard announced. He wheeled on Candida DeWitt. "You were always a manipulator, Candida, but this is the first time I've ever noticed that you were a *bitch*."

Paul Hazzard gave Gregor a furious look that could have meant everything or nothing, and went shooting up the stairs after Hannah.

He looked ready to kill somebody.

## 2

*Now* the emergency support mechanisms went into operation. *Now* the women of Cavanaugh Street got moving. Gregor didn't know what motivated them. If he had been in their places, he would have done something before Hannah had gone running up those stairs and Paul had gone running up after her. Either that, or he would have followed them both. Actually, somebody did that. Mary Ohanian went sprinting up the spiral stairs and came back less than a minute later.

"She's locked herself in the bathroom up there and he's talking to her through the door," Mary Ohanian said, out of breath. "I don't think she's paying much attention to what he's trying to tell her."

"I wouldn't listen to a thing he tried to tell me," Sheila Kashinian announced. "Can you imagine?"

Gregor got hold of the sleeve of Candida DeWitt's dress and began to pull her out of the limelight. "If I were you," he told her, "I'd either retreat into obscurity or leave entirely. Leaving would be the better course."

"I suppose it would." Candida allowed herself to be led, but she was looking back at the spiral stairs. "I suppose I should stay long enough to talk to her. To tell her it wasn't Paul's fault. This wasn't something he set up to hurt her."

"Did he set it up at all?"

"Of course not. I just thought—"

Gregor had pulled them back toward the buffet table and the window. The space around the table was empty now except for Tommy Moradanyan, who had found the shrimp unattended and taken advantage of the situation.

Gregor poured a glass of punch and handed it to Candida DeWitt. He poured a glass of *raki* for himself.

"She'd be better off without him," Candida DeWitt said suddenly. "You do realize that, don't you? Paul Hazzard is very bad news. In spite of the fact that he didn't kill his wife."

"Do you know that for a fact? That he didn't kill his wife?"

"Oh, yes. I know it almost as well as if I'd been standing in the room when Jacqueline was stabbed. He ruined Jacqueline, you know. He—twisted her."

"Did you know Jacqueline before you met Paul?"

"The proper question would be whether I knew Jacqueline before she met Paul. I didn't. I did know her before he began to . . . work on her. That's what Paul does when he gets tired of women. He works on them."

"Did he work on you?"

"He tried. That was what was wrong with the way the police were doing their thinking. They believed—they insisted on believing—that Paul wanted Jacqueline dead so that he could be with me. But Paul didn't want to be with me. He had broken our—relationship—off nearly six weeks before Jacqueline died. It was the first time in my life I hadn't been the one to end it."

"Maybe he broke it off only because his wife told him he had to," Gregor suggested. "Maybe that was his motive. He broke it off under duress. He didn't want to. He rid himself of the duress. Then he could resume the relationship."

"If Paul was interested in resuming the relationship, he wouldn't have tried to hand me over to the police on a silver platter," Candida told him.

"True."

"Paul would never have wanted to be rid of Jacqueline. Whatever for? He was tired of her, yes, but she was useful to him and he had her completely cowed. She was really very stupid about men. Paul had affairs all the time and she never noticed. As long as Paul showed up for the family things her people gave and took her to the Assemblies every year and never got photographed with anyone else who belonged on the society pages, Jacqueline thought everything was all right."

"I've heard her described in much less flattering terms," Gregor said. "She seems to have—upset other people a good deal more than she seems to have upset you."

Candida shrugged. Her glass was empty. She handed it to Gregor and waited patiently while he refilled it. She was an old-fashioned woman in her way. She let men do things for her. It probably worked.

"Jacqueline," she told Gregor, "was an extremely easy woman to say things against. She was essentially stupid. She was arrogant in the way only really upper-class people can be arrogant. She was mostly oblivious of other people. Except that she wasn't oblivious of Paul. Which was her mistake. It's always a mistake not to be oblivious of Paul."

Activity had been going on in the room around them, feverish activity that Candida DeWitt had ignored and Gregor had failed to notice. Now he saw Helen Tevorakian coming down the spiral stairs, looking worried. He stopped talking to Candida DeWitt to listen.

Lida Arkmanian and Sheila Kashinian were waiting for Helen at the bottom of the stairs. Helen was more or less of Lida and Hannah's generation, and Sheila had been adopted into it by popular acclamation. Helen reached the foyer and shook her head. She was wearing a fussy dress pasted over with pink sequins. It made her look fatter than she really was.

"I don't know what's going on up there now. They're absolutely quiet, except that Hannah is crying."

"Is Hannah still in the bathroom?" Lida asked.

"I think so," Helen said. "You know how the bathroom is en suite?"

"Of course it's en suite," Sheila Kashinian said. "What else would it be?"

"The problem is," Helen Tevorakian said, ignoring this, "the bathroom door is on the other side of the bedroom from the bedroom door to the hall, and I can't get to the bathroom door because the hall bedroom door is locked now too, and I don't know what is going on."

"The bedroom door is locked?"

"Do you mean Paul Hazzard locked it?" Sheila demanded.

"I suppose he must have," Helen Tevorakian said.

"Why would he do a thing like that?"

Lida Arkmanian had had enough. "This is really impossible," she said. "Neither one of them is behaving like a sane person. We have to do something about this."

"Maybe Howard could go up and break down the bedroom door," Sheila suggested.

"I think it would do just as well if I went up there and knocked on the bedroom door," Lida said, "and told them both to stop it. Oh, when I get my hands on that man, I'm going to slap his face. Just let me up there."

Beside Gregor, Candida DeWitt stirred. "No," she called out in a loud, clear voice. "Let me go up there. I'll probably have better luck talking sense into Paul than you will."

Lida, Sheila, and Helen all turned in unison, keeping absolutely still as Candida crossed the room to the spiral stairs.

"I think you've done enough damage for one night," Lida said coldly when Candida arrived. "I think you ought to have the good manners to get out of here and let the rest of us clean this up."

"I didn't send that invitation to myself," Candida said mildly. "I find it interesting to speculate on just who did. What I said is true, by the way. I will have more luck talking sense into Paul than any of you would. I know what to say to him."

"She might have a point," Helen Tevorakian said reluctantly.

"Well, the good God only knows," Lida said, "I don't want to talk to the man. I just want to injure him."

"So do I," Candida said grimly. "And trust me, if I ever get my hands on him, I'll do damage to a far more sensitive stretch of his skin than his face. Have we agreed? Shall I go up there?"

"Yes," Helen Tevorakian said quickly.

Candida nodded to each of the three women in turn and hurried up the stairs. Helen, Lida, and Sheila looked at each other doubtfully.

"I hope we did the right thing," Helen Tevorakian said. "She seems like a very nice woman, but—"

"I know what you mean," Lida said. "The problem with strangers is that you don't know how they're going to behave—"

"I don't care so much about how she's going to behave," Sheila said. "What I want to know is what it is she thinks she's up to."

"It's so quiet up there," Helen Tevorakian said. "It was when I was upstairs too. I stood out in the hall and listened and listened, but all I could hear was Paul Hazzard pacing back and forth, not talking to Hannah or anything. And Hannah was crying, of course."

"Maybe they'll all come down soon," Lida said.

Sheila Kashinian snorted. "What do you think it is we're going to do then?"

"If we don't hear anything for five minutes, I'll go up myself and try to help," Lida said definitely. "That way we just won't be sitting here, waiting for the phone to ring, if you know what I mean."

"I used to sit around waiting for the phone to ring when I was engaged to Jack," Helen Tevorakian said. "Then, when he would finally call, I'd pretend I didn't recognize his voice."

"Don't let's get into all that now," Sheila Kashinian said. "We'll forget where we are and we'll never get anything done."

There was the sound of rapid footsteps upstairs, and then a hollow bang, as if a door had been opened too quickly and hit the wall behind it. Everyone looked expectantly at the top of the spiral stairs. Gregor expected to see a high-heeled foot emerge from the landing above. Surely the first person down would be Candida DeWitt.

There was the sound of more footsteps. There was what seemed to be a gasp. And then it started.

It was the loudest and highest scream Gregor Demarkian had ever heard in his life. It went on and on and on and on without stopping. It had a staccato backbeat to it that rent and pierced and punctuated its rhythm like the percussion section in an orchestra of manic depressives. Everyone in the living room froze. Gregor made himself move forward only with the most determined exercise of will he had ever made in his life.

"What *is* that?" Christopher Hannaford asked sharply.

That broke the spell. Gregor started running. Christopher Hannaford ran after him. Christopher was younger and therefore faster and got to the stairs first. They both went pounding up to the second floor.

The second floor landing was empty and dark. The only light to be seen was at the end of the hall, spilling out of an open door. Christopher went down there and stopped dead in his tracks. Gregor ran up to him and pushed him out of the way. Candida DeWitt was standing just inside the doorway. Her arms were wrapped around her waist and she seemed catatonic with shock.

The shocking thing was lying on the floor in front of her, right at the foot of Hannah Krekorian's king-size bed.

There was the body of Paul Hazzard, the face turned away from the door, half a dozen savage black punctures piercing the shirt at the center of the chest.

There was Hannah Krekorian herself, the front of her dress sodden with fresh blood, her hands holding a fancy curved-handled dagger that was covered with blood too.

Gregor didn't know what was making him colder.

The scene he was looking at.

Or the breeze that was coming in through the open bedroom window.

*part two*

———

*bows and arrows...*

*o n e*

*1*

A single pearl stud pierced earring was caught in the high pile of the carpet in Hannah Krekorian's guest room, just in front of the tall bureau next to the guest room bathroom door. Gregor Demarkian nearly stepped on it. He was pacing, as he had been pacing for nearly two hours, up and down the second floor hall and in and out of the guest room and the bathroom and around and around wherever he could find free space. Hannah's room was off-limits and the upstairs hall was full of people. One of the advantages of having an assistant commissioner of police in the house was the quickness of the service you got from the uniformed branch, and from Homicide too. Hannah's apartment had been full to the rafters of police less than ten minutes after Bob Cheswicki had put in the call. A mobile crime unit had pulled up to the curb outside in less than fifteen. Now the place was humming and buzzing and rumbling and exploding in flashbulbs. It would have been infested with reporters too, except that there was a police guard at the door downstairs. The medical examiner's people had brought an ambulance with them. Gregor had never understood why an ambulance was required to take a body to the morgue.

There was more than a pearl stud earring on the floor of Hannah's guest room. Obviously, this was a room she did not enter often, and that her cleaning lady felt free to ignore. There were all sorts of things twisted into the carpet down there. Bobby pins. Safety pins. Bits of paper and half-inch lengths of string. Gregor picked the earring up and left the rest alone. It wasn't evidence.

Gregor went back out into the hall. Bob Cheswicki was standing at the top of the stairs, looking flushed and tired. Beside him was a young officer in plain clothes, looking flushed and tired too.

"Gregor," Bob said. "Come here. This is Detective First Grade Russell Donahue. He's going to be our beard."

"Beard?"

"Mr. Cheswicki is going to conduct this investigation," Russell Donahue said, "and I'm going to pretend I'm conducting it, so that we satisfy protocol."

"Well," Bob said, "not exactly."

Gregor held out his hand with the pearl in it. "I found this in the guest room. Caught in the carpet all the way on the other side of the room from the hall door. Near the bathroom."

Bob Cheswicki and Russell Donahue looked at the pearl. "All right," Bob said. "Was Mrs. Krekorian wearing pearl earrings tonight?"

"No," Gregor told him.

"Was anybody else?"

"Not that I remember."

"I don't see that it would matter if anybody was," Russell Donahue said. "Even if somebody came upstairs on pretext of using the bathroom and went snooping around instead and lost an earring, so what? People do that all the time. And even if it was the murderer who did it, it wouldn't help us catch him. It wouldn't matter that he'd been in the guest room. The murder took place in the bedroom."

"Mmm," Gregor said.

"My guess is that Mrs. Krekorian lost it once, she doesn't even remember how long ago, and now you've found it," Bob Cheswicki said. "Give it back to her."

Gregor put the earring in his pants pocket. "Have you checked out what I asked you to?" he asked Bob. "I know it's very farfetched—"

Bob Cheswicki turned away, embarrassed. Gregor didn't blame him for being embarrassed. This was a mess of the first water. There was no way getting around it. It wasn't a case that could be hushed up. For one thing, Paul Hazzard had just been murdered at least apparently with exactly the weapon his wife was supposed to have been killed with all those years ago, and that had been a very sensational case. For another thing, Gregor himself had been on the scene—and the woman holding the bloody weapon had been Gregor's friend. Gregor could just imagine how the *Inquirer* was going to react to this one—and he had no illusions that the sensation was going to stay local for very long. Even if they managed to clear the case up in twenty-four hours, they were all going to end up on the cover of *People* before the month was out.

"Look," Bob Cheswicki said. "I'm not going to arrest her. You realize that. That's as a courtesy to you. At least I'm not going to arrest her yet."

"I know. Thank you. And if it's any consolation, I'll almost guarantee you that Hannah Krekorian has never in her life killed so much as one of those fish her husband used to catch and insist on everybody eating."

"Maybe." Bob sounded doubtful. "But she was standing there with the weapon in her hand, all covered with blood."

"I know."

"And she did have a motive."

"It was a pretty weak motive."

"No, it wasn't." Bob Cheswicki shook his head. "It was exactly the right kind of motive. She was furious. She was upset. The man had apparently put her in a very embarrassing position—"

"He had? Or Candida DeWitt had? If Hannah was going to stab someone, wouldn't it have made more sense to stab Candida DeWitt?"

"Why do you assume that anyone in this place was making sense?" Bob asked. "As far as I could tell by just looking at the body, the man was stabbed at least six times. That sounds like somebody out of control to me."

"Candida DeWitt—" Gregor ventured.

Bob was now nodding vigorously. "Yes," he said, "possibly. Even if she didn't have any blood on her. There's nothing to say she would have had, if she'd stabbed him and jumped straight away. That's one of the sane reasons I'm going to have for not immediately arresting your friend. Candida DeWitt certainly seems to have had a better motive."

"Then, there's the weapon," Russell Donahue put in. "It would be interesting to know how it got here."

"There's nothing to say it's the same one," Gregor said thoughtfully. "I mean, there's nothing to say it's the one that was found at the scene when Jacqueline Isherwood Hazzard died. Did the Hazzards keep it after all that?"

"That's a good question."

"And of course it might simply be a different whatever-it-is," Gregor said. "I've never been entirely sure what to call it."

"It's a dagger, Mr. Demarkian," Russell Donahue said. "And I don't think there could be two of them in Philadelphia. It's an extremely rare—um—artifact. It's supposed to be hundreds of years old and it came from some island in the Pacific. Papua New Guinea?"

"There's such a place as Papua New Guinea," Gregor said.

"I think what I'm trying to get at," Bob said, "is that whatever happened here, it wasn't what you were thinking about with the open window. It almost definitely wasn't. I can prove it to you."

"There's a fire escape right outside that window," Gregor said.

"I know." Bob Cheswicki looked around. "Come with me," he said finally. "Let me show you what I saw when I tried to work it out. It's easy as anything to see what I mean."

## 2

Paul Hazzard's body had already been removed from Hannah Krekorian's bedroom. Now there was a tape outline on the carpet and a smear of blood on the leg of the closest chair. The room was still full of people. Two men were bagging what they had picked up with the vacuum cleaner. A policewoman in uniform was on her knees in the bathroom, doing Gregor couldn't begin to imagine what. A man in whites was folding up what looked like oxygen equipment, but Gregor was sure it couldn't have been. In spite of all the help he'd given in all the extracurricular murders over the last few years, he still wasn't any good with crime-scene hardware. He hadn't been trained for it. The FBI investigated crimes, and in a few limited cases (such as in national parks or on Indian reservations) it even investigated ordinary murders, but by the time a Bureau agent reached the scene, the messy details had usually been reduced to a few dozen pages of ungrammatical official report. Every time Gregor thought he had finally figured out everything there was to know about mobile crime units, tech reports, autopsies, and physical evidence collection, some mysterious new gadget appeared out of nowhere and tripped him up.

Bob Cheswicki wound his way around the man in white and stood at the window.

"Look here," he said. "This window faces the hall door, right?"

"Right," Gregor said.

"It's a good fire escape they've got out there, by the way. One of the new stationary kind with handrails. Not one of those old rusty clunkers that fold up and half the time don't fold down when you need them. Anyway, the window is here, facing the hall door, and close to this wall"—Bob pointed—"which is the wall with the bathroom door in it."

"The bathroom door is all the way down there," Gregor said quickly.

"I know. It doesn't matter. What matters is if Paul Hazzard was standing here in the bedroom, talking to Hannah Krekorian through the bathroom door, which is what one of the witnesses said, I don't remember who—"

"Mary Ohanian," Gregor said. "She was the first one to go up and check. She came running down the stairs—"

"I remember," Bob Cheswicki said.

"You know," Gregor said thoughtfully, "that means the door to the bedroom must have been open, then. Later, when Helen Tevorakian went up, it was locked."

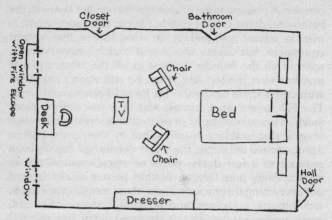

*Hannah Krekorian's Bedroom*

"Yeah. We'll get to that later. Thing is, you've got Paul Hazzard standing here, staring at the bathroom door, and that would put him sideways to the window. It would have been in his peripheral vision. Do you see what I mean?"

"You mean if someone came through it, he would have noticed."

"Exactly," Bob Cheswicki said, "and that's where we've got a problem with the window theory, because if Paul Hazzard had noticed someone coming through that window, one of two things would have happened. Either Hazzard would have called out, warned the rest of us that there was an intruder coming into the house—and we'd have heard it—or he would have fought his attacker, and we would have heard that."

"If it was someone he knew," Gregor proposed.

"He'd have cried out in surprise. He would have said something. There would have been some kind of noise, if not when the person first entered the room, then later when, what's her name, Helen Tevorakian, went up. I remember what she said as well as you do. She said it was completely quiet up here. All she could hear was Hannah Krekorian crying and Paul Hazzard pacing."

"And the door was locked," Gregor said.

"We're going to have to talk to all of these people again." Bob Cheswicki sighed. "In a formal capacity. You should talk to them too. In a formal capacity or otherwise. My point is simply that no matter what may or may not have happened in any other respect, what definitely did not happen was that a thief or other stranger came through that window and killed Paul Hazzard, or that someone Paul Hazzard knew came through that window and killed him. Not while he was standing here, talking to Hannah Krekorian, at any rate, and as far as we can make out, he did nothing else from the time he came upstairs to the time he was killed."

"Except pace," Gregor pointed out.

"That makes the window scenario even more unlikely."

"I suppose it does," Gregor said.

"I'll tell you something else." Bob was bouncing up and down on the balls of his feet. "Paul Hazzard wasn't killed by a stranger. At least, he wasn't killed by a street thief or any other kind of stranger he might have been worried about on the face of it."

"Why not?"

"Because we would have heard that too," Bob Cheswicki said. "He would have put up a fight. The only way anybody got six stab wounds into Paul Hazzard's chest like that is if they started from right up close, practically leaning into his arms. I know nothing is ever a hundred percent until you get the tech reports, but Gregor, I'll stake my life on it. It's the only way it could have been done. If it had happened any other way, we would have heard something." Bob Cheswicki burst out in a sharp little laugh. "Good God, do you know what I was just thinking of? All that touchy-feely stuff people like Paul Hazzard are into. All that trading around of hugs. Well, somebody gave him a hug this time, all right."

"I don't think that's fair," Russell Donahue put in faintly. "I mean, there's nothing wrong with a hug. I guess. I mean, just because this guy wasn't a, um—"

Russell trailed off. Gregor contemplated him seriously. Donahue was very young and a little more hip than police officers tended to be. He seemed unhappy with what he was doing and as if he wanted to be somewhere else. As Gregor watched, he took an aimless tour around the room and then returned to them, looking glum.

"I guess there isn't anything we can do here," he said. "We should get downstairs and talk to the people."

Gregor had never been in Hannah's bedroom before tonight. He had never had any reason to be. It was a pleasant, faintly expensive place decorated in gray and pink with a touch of white here and there. Looking through the bathroom door, he could see that the mirror in there was tinted pink too. There was a reason for that. Bennis had explained it to him once. Mirrors tinted pink made your skin look younger.

Gregor felt distinctly disoriented. He had known Hannah Krekorian all his life—or at least he'd thought he'd known her. They had been all through grade school and high school together. Gregor had served as an usher at her cousin Richard's wedding. If he closed his eyes, he could still see Hannah sitting on the stoop in front of the old unrenovated apartment house where her family had lived when they were all growing up, eight years old and taunting the hell out of him for striking out four times in a row at stickball. How had they all grown to be so old? How had they all grown to be so different?

Gregor looked through the bathroom door again, at the paints and powders and makeup pencils lying in rows in a compartmented glass tray that had probably been bought for the purpose. Gregor knew even less about women's cosmetics than he knew about crime-scene paraphernalia. He would never have guessed that Hannah had all those things. He would never have guessed that she would have wanted to. She had three times the makeup Bennis did, and Bennis was beautiful.

Did that matter?

He shook himself a little to bring himself to. "Well. Listen. You two are right. We ought to go downstairs. Only do me a favor."

"What's that?" Bob Cheswicki asked.

"Let me be the first one to talk to Hannah Krekorian."

## 3

The apartment was not so full of people anymore. Names and addresses had been taken. Extraneous people had been sent on their way. The very old ladies had gone home and the Devorkian girls had in all likelihood been ordered to bed. Hannah's living room looked randomly littered, as if a high wind had blown through it. Scraps of party napkins and half-filled glasses were strewn here and there. It made Gregor think of Pompeii. The volcano had erupted, and everything had been petrified in place.

Christopher Hannaford and Lida Arkmanian stood together near the fireplace, talking. Lida was standing very straight. Christopher was leaning against the mantel. When Gregor walked in with Bob Cheswicki and Russell Donahue, Christopher straightened.

"Krekor?" Lida said.

"Where's Bennis?" Gregor asked them. "I expected to find her glued to a policeman's side. Possibly the medical examiner's."

"Bennis took old George Tekemanian home," Christopher said. "He was looking a little peaked. She took Tommy Moradanyan too."

"Donna is still in the kitchen with Hannah," Lida said. "Making tea, I think."

Gregor nodded. "Are you going to take Hannah home with you? She's going to have to go home with somebody. I don't think she'd be able to sleep in that room even if the police didn't have it sealed as a crime scene, which they probably will."

Lida looked at Christopher and then down at her hands. "No, Krekor. Hannah is not coming home with me. She is going with Helen Tevorakian."

"Really?" Gregor said. "What's the matter? Did you two have a fight?"

"Of course not," Lida said.

"Everything's really very well organized," Christopher Hannaford put in. "Donna Moradanyan and Helen are with Hannah now, and then, as soon as the statements are taken, at least—" He frowned. "It is all right, isn't it? They're not going to—arrest anyone?"

"Do you mean that awful DeWitt woman?" Lida asked. "I hope they do arrest her. That *cat*."

"If they arrested somebody," Christopher said, "it wouldn't be Candida DeWitt."

"Who else could it be?" Lida demanded. Lida looked from one to the other of them. They looked back again. Lida caught her breath, shocked. "But that's crazy," she said. "Hannah? They can't possibly think Hannah killed that man. She's known him only a week!"

"She was the one with blood all over her and the murder weapon in her hands," Christopher said.

"Are you sure it's been only a week?" Gregor asked her. "Couldn't Hannah have known Paul Hazzard before that and never told you about it?"

"No," Lida said positively. "Met him casually or just been introduced, that possibly, yes, but not really known him, no. I would have heard about it."

"You two told each other everything," Gregor said.

Lida blushed bright red. "No. No, Krekor, that isn't what I mean. I mean that Hannah was not a woman who hid her feelings. When she was happy she was happy. When she was sad she was sad. And she was not—discreet."

"Unlike some other people we know," Christopher said, "who are sometimes too discreet."

Lida ignored him. "Hannah is a woman who talks, Krekor. She met Paul Hazzard at a meeting of the Friends of the Matterson Settlement House. It's one of her charities. They talked at this meeting and he brought her home and then took her out to dinner. That was one week ago today, assuming it is still Friday. Last Saturday morning, she called me about it."

"Umm. Has Hannah been acting oddly lately? Has she been different in any way?"

"Different? I haven't noticed anything different, Krekor."

"What about little things," Gregor asked. "Like, say, makeup. Has she been wearing more makeup than usual?"

"Krekor, what are you talking about? You know Hannah. You see her every day. If she had been wearing more makeup than usual, you would have noticed it yourself."

"Maybe. It's just that, upstairs in her room just now, I noticed she had a lot of it. A *lot* of it. Much more than Bennis has."

"Krekor, for goodness' sake. Of course Hannah has more makeup than Bennis has. Bennis doesn't need any and she's under forty."

"I think the theory is, the more you look like a model on the cover of a J. Crew catalogue, the more clothes you wear but the less makeup," Christopher said, "where, on the other hand, if you're a rather stodgy-looking middle-aged lady, you wear—"

"Stop it," Lida said.

"I'd better go talk to Hannah," Gregor said. "What about the two of you? Have you been asked to hang around here?"

"I just gave my statement to a police officer," Lida said. "I was finished just a minute or two before you came down. I was talking about going home."

"I was going to walk her there," Christopher said. "To keep the muggers at bay."

"We do not have muggers on Cavanaugh Street."

"We might someday," Gregor said. "I think Christopher is being eminently sensible."

"Thank you," Christopher said solemnly.

Gregor retreated. He liked Bennis's brother Christopher. He always had, even at the beginning, all those years ago, when he'd had reason to be very suspicious. The problem was that Christopher always seemed to be talking on two or three levels at once, like those books by James Joyce that Gregor had been forced to read in English class at the University of Pennsylvania.

He went into the kitchen. Helen Tevorakian was nowhere to be seen. Maybe Bob Cheswicki already had her someplace quiet, where they could talk without being interrupted. Donna Moradanyan was standing at the far end of the room, near the stove. She was talking quietly to Russell Donahue, who looked more uncomfortable than ever.

Hannah Krekorian sat at her kitchen table, her face set and emotionless, her hands folded on the tabletop in front of her. She had a cup of coffee that looked as if it hadn't been touched. It looked cold too. Gregor pulled out one of the other chairs and sat down as close to her as he could without actually touching her.

"Hannah?" he asked gently.

Hannah stirred slightly. "Krekor," she said. "I have been waiting for you to come. I was sure that you would come."

"Well, I came. I'm here. Why don't I ask Donna to get you a fresh cup of coffee? That one looks cold."

"They put rum in it," Hannah said. "That's why I didn't drink it. I didn't want to be drunk."

"A little rum right now won't make you drunk," Gregor told her. "You're in shock, you know. A little rum might actually be good for you."

"They took that woman into the study. That DeWitt woman. They took her there and now she's telling them that I killed Paul."

"Did you kill Paul, Hannah?"

"No."

"Did Candida DeWitt?"

"I don't think so." Hannah blinked, confused. "It was too *quiet*, you see. I thought he must have gone away. So I came out of the bathroom and there he was and that thing was on the floor next to him, lying there in the blood, and I just walked to it and I—I just picked it up. And it was cold, Krekor, it was so cold, with the window open and the door too, and the breeze coming through like that and I thought he must have opened the window, he must have been hot, and then I started screaming and I couldn't stop. She wasn't in the doorway then. She didn't come in until afterward."

"Afterward what?"

"After I started screaming," Hannah said simply.

Gregor got up. "Let me get you that coffee," he said.

"Let me get you that rum too. You're going to go home with Helen Tevorakian tonight. Did you know that?"

"I thought the police were going to arrest me and I would spend the night in jail."

"Nobody's going to arrest you."

"I should have realized from the beginning," Hannah said. "I should have known. What is it they say on the public service announcements for senior citizens? If it sounds too good to be true, it probably is."

"What probably is?" The coffee in the pot on the stove was still very warm, if not hot. Gregor got a clean cup out of Hannah's cabinets, poured it half full of coffee, took the rum bottle from the back of the counter, poured the cup most of the rest of the way full of rum, and topped the whole thing off with a gigantic helping of sugar. It was going to taste awful, but it would bring her out of this funk. He put the concoction down next to her elbow and said, "Drink that."

Hannah took a sip and made a face. "Too sweet," she said.

"Too good to be true," Gregor prompted her.

Hannah took a good, long swallow. She shuddered. "Yes," she said. "That was it. Too good to be true. Underneath, I don't think I ever fooled myself. Only on the surface. You know, Krekor, I am fifty-eight years old."

"That's right," Gregor said. "You would have to be, you and Lida. Because you're all a year older than I am and I'm fifty-seven."

"Yes," Hannah said. "And I've known it all along, you know, even when I was a little child. Except, of course, when you are a child, you think it will change when you grow older."

"What will change?"

"What you look like," Hannah said. "I remember being six years old and sitting in front of the mirror in my mother's bedroom and telling myself, 'When I grow up, I will be beautiful.' Well, Krekor, I am all grown-up and I am what I have always been. I am an ugly woman, and nothing on earth is ever going to be able to change that."

Then Hannah Krekorian put her face in her hands and burst into tears.

## *t w o*

## *1*

It was James who was home when the police called, and James who went to the morgue to formally identify the body—a ritual he was shocked to discover was impossible to escape. The police sent a car for him. James didn't know if they were worried about the dangers he would face trying to get a car of his own out of a parking garage or off the street (muggers), or the dangers the populace of Philadelphia would face if he tried to drive home after seeing his father lying on a slab like that, dead-white and looking faintly annoyed. Maybe they just thought it would be difficult to find a cab at—what?—eleven o'clock at night. James hadn't been thinking of it as "late" when he got the call. Coming out of the morgue, though, it felt infinitely late, some kind of metatime eternally stuck between the eleventh and twelfth tolls of midnight. James kept hearing the theme from *The Twilight Zone* playing in his head.

All the way home from the morgue, sitting up front next to the uniformed driver who seemed to view traffic as a form of war game, James thought about how odd Paul looked, dead. He looked odd because he looked the same. James had had to lean far over the body to be sure Paul wasn't breathing. He'd leaned so far he'd started to fall. The police matron had to catch him. After a while, James decided that there was a difference. Paul looked too thin. Paul had always been too thin, but alive he had covered it with personal magnetism and force of personality. James couldn't call it force of character. Christ only knew, Paul had never had any character.

The police driver pulled up to the door of the town house and waited at the curb while James got the front door unlocked. He was like a worried date or the kind of taxi driver women fell in love with. James got the door unlocked and let himself inside. There were lights on that hadn't been when he'd left. He felt instantly relieved.

"Who's home?" he called out. "This is James."

"James, it's Alyssa."

Musical voice pouring down from the second floor. Light on the second floor landing. James climbed the stairs.

"Alyssa? What are you doing here? Where's Caroline?"

"Caroline's working." Alyssa came out of the second floor sitting room to meet James in the hall. She looked frazzled and upset. Her wispy clothes seemed to be emotionally shredded, like frizzed hair. "She's in her studio. She's got the intercoms off. I can see her in the security monitor but I can't get her attention."

"She's been working like that for hours," Nick Roderick said, coming out to the hall too. "We left her just like that when we went out to dinner, and you know what she's like when she gets like that. She could be in there until morning."

"We heard it over the radio," Alyssa said. "We were at Palace of Glass, and then we went on to Dominique, you know, for dessert. And we were sitting in the bar, waiting for a table, when the news started, and it was the very first thing."

"The dagger's missing," her husband said. "That was the first thing I checked." He looked solemn. James thought he was hiding glee.

James went into the sitting room. The little glass drinks cart stood up against one of the love seats near the fireplace. James went over to it, filled a six-ounce glass with straight Scotch, and drank the Scotch down in a single long guzzle. Then he filled the glass again. He understood the attraction the idea of the "dysfunctional family" had for so many people. His own family was full of poisonous women.

"Don't tell any of my clients I'm doing this," he said.

"They drink herb tea and chant mantras when they're upset."

"Oh, James, be serious," Alyssa said.

"I am being serious. I am also going to get seriously drunk. And neither you nor anybody else in this house is going to stop me."

"I wouldn't try to stop you." Nick slumped into a chair. "I might even help."

"If Caroline tries to lecture me, I'll break her neck." The second glass of Scotch was finished. James modified his approach to the third—not straight Scotch in a six-ounce glass, but Scotch and Drambuie on the rocks in something larger; he was beginning to feel almost calm enough to be civilized—and took it over to the wingback chair. He sat and stretched out his legs. "I do not suggest," he said, "that you make a point of seeing people dead. It is very unpleasant. It is weird enough to make me start believing in channeling."

"I thought you did believe in it," Nick said.

"No," James corrected him. "I only sell it."

"You saw the body?" Alyssa said.

"Yes. That's where I just was. At the morgue, looking at the body."

"Why?" Alyssa was bewildered.

"Because somebody has to," Nick put in. "Somebody has to make a formal identification. It's standard procedure."

"But it isn't like Paul was some anonymous person on the street," Alyssa protested. "He was very well known. And wasn't he with people who knew him? Wasn't tonight the night he was going to that party we talked about?"

"I don't know," James said. "They didn't really tell me anything. I think they want a member of the family to make the identification. Don't ask me what they were up to. They just called."

"On the radio they just said he died at the home of an acquaintance," Alyssa said. "I should have thought to put on the eleven o'clock news. There probably would have been more."

"The radio mostly went on and on about his being

stabbed," Nick said. "That's why I went looking for the dagger. Is this beginning to look really strange to either of you two?"

"Jacqueline stabbed and Paul stabbed," James chanted. "That's not strange. That's a *plan*."

"James," Alyssa said.

"Maybe Caroline did it in a fit of psychic pique." James finished his drink and started pacing. "God, you don't want to look at a dead man's face. It's just too weird. It's just too normal. Paul looked more alive dead than he looked— Never mind."

"I don't believe Jacqueline was killed with that dagger," Alyssa said fiercely. "I don't care what the police said. I don't believe Paul was killed with it either. You just wait. There'll turn out to be some other explanation for why it's missing. It won't have anything to do with the crime at all."

Nick sighed. "She's been like this since we got home. I can't get it across to her that it would be too much of a coincidence. If the dagger is missing, it almost has to have something to do with the crime."

"Yes," James said slowly. He put ice in his glass and poured out more Scotch and more Drambuie. He felt sluggish and depressed, but his mind was still crystal-clear. It was going to be a long road to unconsciousness. It might actually take him the rest of the night.

"I'll tell you something I did hear," James said. "In passing, you understand. While I was hanging around the police."

"You weren't hanging around the police," Alyssa said.

"The dagger isn't the only thing the two deaths have in common," James said. "It's really very interesting. Candida DeWitt was there."

"What?" Alyssa said.

James finished his drink and reached for the bottle of Scotch. Again.

"I think that woman is persecuting us," he said. "I think she's following us all round, making things happen. I think she's going to end up murdering us all off, one by one."

## 2

Fred Scherrer came to Cavanaugh Street when Candida DeWitt called him. He sat next to her as she gave her statement to the police and wondered what good he was going to be. He could never do much for clients who weren't willing to listen to his advice. Candida DeWitt didn't listen to anyone. When he got to her at the scene, he told her she didn't have to tell anyone anything. She didn't have to make a statement of any kind. It was never a good idea to make a statement right on the spot like that. Even perfectly innocent people got confused. Fred was almost positive that Candida was innocent of the murder of Paul Hazzard. Over the years, he had developed an instinct for that sort of thing. It was an instinct no detective would ever be able to match, because it had been developed from years of listening to guilty people tell him the truth. It wasn't that no client had ever lied to him. Hundreds had tried. None had persisted. Fred was very good at making clients see that lying to their lawyer was a piece of idiocy. Their lives depended on Fred's knowing the truth and all the truth. But Candida wasn't giving off the right vibes, here. She wasn't the kind of quiet she would have been if she had stabbed Paul. She even seemed a little frustrated. Fred thought he understood. Candida was the sort of person who wanted her enemies alive and kicking. She wanted to watch the expressions on their faces when she got her revenge.

In spite of his advice, Candida insisted on giving a statement. She sat down with a very polite and very young detective in a badly-fitting suit, and answered everything he asked her but volunteered nothing. Fred did not have high hopes for this young detective's career. There were so many obvious questions to ask that didn't occur to him to ask. What was Candida doing at that party? When was the last time before the murder that she had been in contact with Paul? The young detective had to know who Candida was. If he hadn't started out knowing, by now he should have been told. Oblivious, he went on and on with his list of routine questions.

After it was over, Candida put on her coat, picked up her purse, and waited for Fred to lead her to the door. She waited with the air of someone who had done nothing more important than trade recipes with a friend.

Fred had driven his own car down to Philadelphia from New York, but he hadn't used it to come in to town from Bryn Mawr. He didn't know his way around the city well enough to trust that he wouldn't be the victim of a carnapping, crawling through the dark streets in a highly polished Mercedes-Benz. He'd engaged a taxicab instead, and paid for it too, both because of the long trip in from the Main Line and because he wanted it to wait. Fred Scherrer could bribe taxi drivers with the best of them. He was not cheap about baksheesh. The cab was waiting just a couple of blocks down when he and Candida came out of Hannah Krekorian's apartment building. The cab would have been closer, but Hannah's block was still clogged with police cars.

Fred walked Candida to the cab in silence, opened the door for her, helped her in. It was largely symbolic help—a gesture invented for hobble skirts and bustles—but Candida liked that kind of symbolism. Fred closed her door and went around the cab to get in himself on the other side. He leaned into the front seat and asked the driver to take them back to Bryn Mawr. Then he pulled the bullet-proof privacy shield shut and turned to Candida.

"All right," he said. "Now you're going to tell me what's going on."

"Of course," Candida said. She had her purse on the seat at her side and her hands folded in her lap and her legs crossed at the knee. She could have been Donna Reed playing the perfect ladylike housewife.

"Did you know Paul was going to be at that party? Did you go there to cause a scene deliberately?"

"Of course," Candida said. "I wouldn't have gone otherwise. I did ask you to come with me."

"And I told you I didn't like parties and I refused to come. I won't do that again. Have you known this woman, this Hannah Krekorian, a long time?"

"I'd never met her before tonight." Candida explained about the invitation. "I went to talk to Alyssa about it. For some reason, I thought she was the most likely one to have sent it. Not that I told her that. I implied I thought it was Caroline. It's not really Caroline's kind of thing though. That mess written on my fireplace, that's Caroline's kind of thing."

Fred rubbed his face with the palms of his hands. "You do realize how this looks? Paul has a new woman friend. You show up to put a damper on things. Paul ends up dead. Right now the two prime suspects in this case are Hannah Krekorian and you."

"I realize that."

"Do you also realize that the way the timing stacks up, at least from what I heard, you seem to have either stumbled on the corpse a second after Mrs. Krekorian turned Paul into one or else you turned Paul into a corpse a second before Mrs. Krekorian discovered him? That Demarkian man was doing timetables the whole time I was waiting for you, and I don't blame him."

Candida was serene. "There's a flaw in the timetables. I was there when that Helen person came downstairs. I remember what she said."

"What did she say?"

"She said the door to the bedroom was locked," Candida said. "She didn't see anybody or anything. She heard Hannah Krekorian crying and Paul pacing. But it could have been Hannah Krekorian pacing. It could have been anyone. She didn't *see* anything."

"Was somebody else missing from downstairs?"

"I don't know. There were a lot of people there. Over a hundred, I think."

"Did any of these hundred or so people besides you and Hannah Krekorian actually know Paul?"

"I don't know the answer to that either, but I think it would be an interesting line of investigation. All those workshops and seminars and support group meetings. It's always hard to say for certain that Paul didn't know somebody. If you see what I mean."

"Oh, I see. Are you all right?"

"I'm fine. I'm a little shook up, of course. I've never

seen a dead body face-to-face before. When Jacqueline died, I was out of state. And there was all that blood. And Mrs. Krekorian was hysterical. I suppose you heard about the dagger."

"I heard about it."

"There wasn't any blood on it the last time. It was absolutely clean. I wonder what this means."

"I don't know what it means."

"I'm glad I went there," Candida said. "I don't care if it will get me in trouble. Paul didn't care about that woman. He was using her in some way. Paul liked women young and pretty and thin as rails. I should know."

"He could have matured in his old age," Fred Scherrer said.

"He didn't. He just ran out of money. That's what this is going to turn out to be. Mrs. Krekorian is going to have some money."

"My, you're cynical. I don't think I ever noticed that about you before."

"I'm not cynical about everything," Candida said. "I'm just cynical about Paul. And now that he's dead, of course, it clears everything up. I know just what happened the last time."

"What?"

Candida took her purse off the seat and put it on her lap. She opened it up and looked through it until she found a gold cigarette case and a gold Dunhill lighter.

"I smoke five cigarettes a year," she told him, "always in moments of extreme stress. This stress seems to be extreme enough. What do you think?"

Fred Scherrer thought Candida DeWitt was a remarkable woman.

A *remarkable* woman.

### 3

Less than a minute after it happened, Lida Arkmanian's mind was somewhere else, on another planet, in another dimension, lost in space. It was anywhere but there in the bed in the master bedroom of her own town house, lying stretched out against Christopher Hannaford's side. It was doing anything but thinking about the way her body felt. Her body seemed to have parts she'd never expected the existence of. These parts were popping and shuddering and snapping like champagne inside a corked bottle. Lida thought about the tears on Hannah Krekorian's face and about Candida DeWitt. She thought about the man she had been married to for thirty-two years, who had loved her without limit but who had not been able to make her feel like this. She thought there had to be something terribly wrong with her. She went to start all over again.

"I shouldn't have given up cigarettes," Christopher said out of the dark. "This is the perfect moment." He began to stroke her hair, so gently she could barely feel it. "Lida?"

"What is it?"

"That's never happened to you before."

How could it be so cold under all these blankets? How could it be so *cold*? Lida pulled the quilt up to her chin. "Don't be ridiculous, Christopher. I am—over fifty years old."

"I don't care if you're over a hundred years old. That's never happened to you before."

Lida sat up. She had blankets all around her. It was dark. Nobody could see her. Why did she feel so exposed?

"All right," she said. "Yes. That never happened to me before."

Christopher put his hands behind his head and looked serious. "Did you like it?"

"Of course I liked it," Lida said. "What wasn't to like?"

"I don't know. Maybe it never happened to you before because you never wanted it to happen to you. I knew a woman once who said it was too threatening. Orgasms, I mean. They made her feel too vulnerable. So she didn't let herself have them."

"How did she prevent it?"

"I don't know."

"I think it's all the unorthodox things you do," Lida said carefully. It was impossible to talk about these things. It was only barely possible to think about them. "I think it's because you don't do—and you do—well, you know what I mean."

"Nope. I haven't done a single unorthodox thing yet. I haven't even gotten out the whipped cream. Never mind the cherries."

*"Christopher."*

"Seriously," Christopher said. "It's because of menopause. I've been assuming you've been through menopause."

No man of Lida Arkmanian's generation would ever have mentioned menopause to her. Even her doctor called it "the change." Lida was glad the room was too dark for Christopher to see her blushing.

"Yes," she said. "Yes, Christopher, I've been through menopause."

"I thought so. Gregor's always saying how you're a year older than he is, though God knows you look ten years younger. He should watch what he eats. Anyway, the thing about menopause is, once a woman goes through it, the orthodox way, as you put it, isn't usually the right way. It can hurt."

"Oh," Lida said.

"Not that I have anything against the orthodox way," Christopher said. "I mean, I'll do it hanging from the exposed beams in the family room if you want me to—"

"Christopher, for God's *sake*."

"—I was just trying to be a good sort. I have been a good sort, haven't I? It's been all right?"

"Yes," Lida said. "It has been better than all right. I just wish I didn't feel so . . . guilty."

"About the sex?"

"No," Lida told him. "No, not really. I feel embarrassed about the sex, sometimes, I mean it's been days, Christopher, and we haven't done anything else. Today I didn't even open my mail. Are you like this all the time?"

"Nope. But I am when I get a chance. Why not?"

"Why not." Lida sighed. "There doesn't ever seem to be an answer to why not. So here we are again. Do you know you're only two years older than my oldest son?"

"Does that bother you?"

"No." Lida sighed again. "That doesn't bother me either. It doesn't bother me that half the street probably knows what we're doing—and what does Bennis think? You come to visit her and then you just disappear."

"Bennis is smart enough never to ask questions she doesn't want the answers to." Christopher sat up. "I'm going to get a bottle of that New York State champagne we were drinking this afternoon. You want some chocolate? I'm starving."

"I'll take a glass of champagne."

Christopher got out of the other side of the bed, keeping his back to her. He whipped a robe around himself in no time at all and tied the belt. Lida was impressed. He had not been so careful when all this had started, and she had not told him that it embarrassed her when he walked around naked. He must have guessed.

Christopher came back to the bedroom with his arms full. He dropped the chocolate on the quilt—a little pile of heart-shaped dark-chocolate cremes from Godiva that Lida's daughter had sent—and handed Lida a glass.

"Here you are," he said, pouring champagne. "Do you know it's already two o'clock in the morning?"

Lida took a sip of champagne. "It's Hannah I feel guilty about," she said. "Not having her here. Not wanting her here. In spite of everything she has been through."

Christopher poured a glass for himself. "It's not as if she didn't have anywhere to go," he pointed out. "Helen Tevorakian offered to take her. You didn't abandon Hannah on Cavanaugh Street."

"Helen Tevorakian doesn't have half the room I do. And it's more than that. It's more even than that I didn't want to send you back to Bennis's to sleep tonight."

"Then what is it?"

"It's what it's always been," Lida said impatiently. "Always, even when we were children. I was the pretty one and she was the plain one. I got roses from secret admirers for Valentine's Day, and Hannah got cards from Helen and me. I had six boys ask me to our senior dance, and one of the five I turned down I fixed up with Hannah. I worry it was all too much."

"But what's that supposed to mean, too much?" Christopher asked. "It's not as if Hannah's life has been one unrelieved stream of failures with men. It couldn't have been. She was married. She has children and grandchildren."

Lida cocked her head. "On the day Hannah was married, right after the ceremony while she was standing in the receiving line to the dinner, Daphne Tessevarian walked up to her and said it was too bad she looked so fat in her wedding dress, but once she had children it wouldn't matter so much because she would be expected to gain weight."

"Ouch."

"Christopher, listen." Lida clutched the quilt to her chest—it kept slipping—and took another sip of champagne. It felt good. It tickled. "Listen," she said again. "Krekor is convinced that he knows Hannah and that Hannah could never have stabbed anyone, but I am not so sure. I am not so sure at all. What with Paul Hazzard, she was so happy, Christopher, she was thrilled, and then that woman showing up and everything falling all to pieces and in public like that, in front of everyone. And the man was stabbed six times at least, as if he were stabbed in anger. I don't think Hannah could think through a murder and commit it, but I think she might be able to kill someone like Paul Hazzard in anger."

"I think you're jumping to a lot of conclusions. You'd have to account for the dagger. You'd have to account for a lot of things. I think it's much more logical to suspect Candida DeWitt."

"Yes," Lida said softly. "We all want to suspect Candida DeWitt. It absolves us all of the responsibility."

"I feel responsible for only one thing," Christopher said. He finished off the last of the chocolate hearts and put his champagne glass behind him on the night table. Then he took Lida's champagne glass out of her hand and put it on the night table too.

"Let's go back to what we were doing," he said. "I'll bet you anything you want that I can get you to feel like that again."

"I thought that was impossible," Lida said. "I thought with men, once they—you know—I thought then they had to wait for a different night."

"I didn't say I could get *me* to feel that way again. I said I could get *you* to."

"Does this have something to do with whipped cream?"

"No," Christopher said. He stretched them both out on the sheets and then he kissed her. "Whipped cream is for when you're bored, and I am not bored. How about you?"

"No." Lida felt a little breathless. "I am not bored."

"Good."

Good?

Christopher got back under the quilt and Lida put her hand on his bare back.

He had a very nice back.

He had a very nice everything.

How long was she going to be able to get away with this?

## *three*

## *1*

Gregor Demarkian did not believe he would shield anyone from the consequences of murder, not even a woman he had known all his life. He was not so sure he would remain clearheaded in the face of evidence against her. It wasn't just a question of his having known Hannah Krekorian. It wasn't even a question of his having liked her. The real problem was his expectations. Here was a woman he had seen day after day for the past couple of years. He wasn't relying on what he remembered about them all from forty or fifty years ago. He had Hannah these days to consider, and Hannah these days was a heavy, talkative woman in middle age who paid more attention to the sound of her own voice than she did to what other people said to her. Hannah these days cooked too much food when her family came to visit, spent too much money on birthday and Christmas presents, and vaguely resented the very idea of Gloria Steinem. It wasn't that women like Hannah Krekorian didn't commit murder. Gregor had good reason to know that they committed it in batches. The problem was that they didn't commit *this kind* of murder. If Hannah had poisoned her family one by one and collected the insurance money, or put cyanide in the candy she handed out to the children who came to her door on Halloween, or overdone the insulin injections she gave to a failing old aunt or mother—those were the kinds of murders women like Hannah committed, and only after there were half a dozen bodies on the floor did anyone realize they were crazy. This sort of thing was something else. Six stab wounds into the chest of a grown man. It didn't fit.

The picture of him on the front page of the *Philadelphia Inquirer* didn't fit his image of himself, but he had expected worse, so he wasn't too upset. He'd never expected for a moment that he'd be able to escape publicity altogether. That was like believing the tooth fairy really did bring Tommy Moradanyan his quarters. Even Tommy didn't believe that. At least the headline on the *Inquirer* was more sensible than some of them had been in the past. It said

## PAUL HAZZARD FOUND DEAD

which was at least to the point. Unfortunately, the picture under the headline was not of Paul Hazzard but of Gregor coming out of the building where Hannah Krekorian had her apartment. Gregor supposed there was a picture of Paul Hazzard somewhere inside the paper. The subhead didn't bode well either. It said

### CHIEF SUSPECT IS CLOSE FRIEND
### OF GREGOR DEMARKIAN

as if the paper knew something neither he nor the police did. Surely Hannah was only half the chief suspect list? Surely Candida DeWitt was on it too.

Gregor got some change out of his pocket, fed it into the metal newspaper-dispensing machine, and pulled out a paper. He was standing at the corner of Calumet and Trell, half a block south of the bus stop. It was quarter after eight in the morning and he was bitterly cold. He should have taken a cab out from Cavanaugh Street, or waited until later in the day. The world wouldn't have fallen moribund and dead if he'd had his usual breakfast at the Ararat. The case wouldn't have solved itself either. He hadn't been able to face it. Linda Melajian and all the Melajians connected to her, Father Tibor, old George Tekemanian, maybe even Bennis—what would he have said? What could he

have said? It was much too early to assure them that everything was going to be all right.

Bob Cheswicki had asked Gregor to meet him at the
police station—"first thing in the morning," which to Bob
could mean anywhere between six and nine—on Calumet.
It was close enough to Cavanaugh Street so that Gregor
might have walked if it had been less cold and less dark.
Or maybe he wouldn't have. He shook his head. Cavanaugh Street was such a model of urban renewal, Gregor
sometimes forgot that so much of the rest of Philadelphia
looked like this.

The garbage piled up in plastic bags in front of the
stoops looked frozen into place. The young man standing
in the doorway of the building half a block up looked furtive
and faintly dangerous. Gregor wished the sun would come
out. Instead, just at that moment he felt a tinge of wetness
against his face, the hint of another bout of rain or snow
or hail. The streets were full of slush and his feet were wet.

Gregor took one last look at the paper—"Demarkian
emerges from murder scene" the caption to the front-page
photograph said—and went up the street to the station. As
he passed the building where the furtive young man was
hiding, the young man seemed to melt into the concrete
and stone. Gregor let himself into the station and got a
small shock. It was an ordinary police station in many ways.
It had a large waiting room with benches in the front. It
had a large area of cluttered desks in the back. The two
sections were divided by a long wooden counter where a
fat police sergeant sat. There were a couple of pay phones
on the wall directly opposite the counter. There were a set
of doors in one wall of the desk section, marked LOCK-UP,
UPSTAIRS, RECORDS, and REST ROOMS. Gregor didn't want to
ask why the rest rooms were in a place unavailable to the
general public. What really worried him was the bulletproof
glass. It was everywhere. It made a wall between the desk
section and the one with the benches in it, rising from the
countertop in a thick sheet no one could hear through. In
order to talk to the desk sergeant, you had to use a micro-
phone system like the ones they used in prisons. Bullet-
proof plastic, not glass, Gregor realized, looking at it more
closely. What it reminded him of was numbers joints in

downtown Washington, D.C. Things had gotten so bad, even the mob didn't feel safe. Gregor looked over the benches, which were empty. Maybe it was just too cold for any serious criminality on the streets of Philadelphia today. Gregor had been in rooms like this before. They were usually packed with people, no matter what hour of the day or night.

Gregor went up to the bulletproof wall. A sign above what looked like a telephone handset said PRESS BUZZER FOR ASSISTANCE. Gregor put the receiver to his ear and pressed the buzzer.

On the other side of the counter, the sergeant, an older African American man with white hair and large shoulders, looked up from the paper he was reading. When he saw Gregor, he came to the counter and picked up his half of the speaking mechanism. It really was just like a prison, Gregor thought. It would make him insane to have to work there.

"Yes?" the sergeant said.

"Gregor Demarkian for Bob Cheswicki."

"Entrance to your right. When you hear the buzzer, push hard, come in. Be quick."

With all the rest of the security around this place, Gregor would have expected the sergeant to ask for his identification. Gregor wondered if the sergeant hadn't asked because Gregor was expected or because the sergeant didn't expect trouble from a middle-aged white man in a good wool coat. If the latter was the case, Gregor could have told the sergeant a thing or two. John Wayne Gacy was a middle-aged white man in a good wool coat. John Wayne Gacy had killed God only knew how many people.

The door was cut out of the counter and the plastic protective shield like a line-drawing door in an old Warner Bros. cartoon. Gregor pushed through, then shut the thing behind him with a strong push. It resisted and sucked closed in its own time. The air in the desk section was staler and hotter than that in the section from which Gregor had just come. The baseboard heat registers seemed to be turned on full.

The name tag on the sergeant's uniform said E. WASH-

INGTON. Gregor took off his gloves and stuffed them in the pockets of his coat.

"Is all this really necessary?" he asked. "This looks like Beirut."

"Gangs," the sergeant said. He didn't look too worked up about it. "This *is* Beirut."

"You seem to be having a pretty quiet time this morning."

"Yep. Had a war zone here last night though. Sixteen people dead. Didn't even make the front page of the newspaper."

"No," Gregor said. "No, I don't suppose it would have."

"Bob Cheswicki's up on the third floor," E. Washington said. "He told us to expect you. Go right on up."

"Stairs only?"

"Used to have an elevator. Then the Hot Bloods rigged one of their Molotov cocktails to it, and for once the damned thing worked."

Gregor went over to the door marked UPSTAIRS.

"I'm going up, then," he said. "Have a quiet day."

"I can only hope."

Gregor thought about trying to make more conversation. Instead, he started climbing the stairs to the third floor.

## 2

The stairs were steep and there were a lot of them. This was an old building with ten- and twelve-foot-high ceilings, making for longer climbs. Fortunately, Bob Cheswicki was in plain sight when Gregor finally reached his destination. So were a lot of other people. Here was the population Gregor had expected to see downstairs where the sergeant was. Here were young men in black leather jackets and eye patches and face tattoos. Here were sharp-looking girls in high heels and not much else, chewing gum and swearing nonstop at everything that passed in a uniform. The young

men were manacled and handcuffed. The girls were free
but deprived of their handbags. None of the young men
was more than twenty. None of the girls was more than
fourteen. All of them had the rough-edged blue-red finger-
tips that were produced from too much skin-popping.

Bob Cheswicki was leaning over the shoulder of a uniformed officer who was sitting at a desk in the middle of
the room. The uniformed officer was checking something
on a computer printout. On the left side of the desk there
was a pile of Saturday night specials.

"Seventeen," the uniformed officer said. "That's what
it says here. Seventeen. We've only got fifteen."

"Okay," Bob Cheswicki said. "Take them all out and
strip-search them again. Get a matron for the girls."

The uniformed officer looked doubtful. "The Legal Aid
guy is downstairs."

"Send Stepanowski to deal with the Legal Aid guy."

"But—"

"For God's sake, Haraldsen. We're not trying to convict
them, we're just trying to disarm them."

"Right," Haraldsen said.

Bob Cheswicki looked up and saw Gregor. "Oh, good.
I get a reprieve. Hello, Gregor. Come along this way. We'll
let the officers get on with this mess on their own."

Bob backed away from Haraldsen's desk and made his
way toward the other end of the room. Gregor followed
him, weaving in and out among the young men and their
girls, excusing himself to uniformed officers not much older
than their charges. The officers looked tense as hell and
scared to death. The door at the back led to a corridor of
other doors, but not a very long one. Bob Cheswicki went
through the third door on his left and sat down at the desk.
The room was five by seven and barely large enough to fit
the two of them. The desk was piled six inches deep in
paper. Bob had a water maker and the makings of instant
coffee on top of his two-drawer green metal file cabinet.
The file cabinet was just the right height and size to serve
as a kind of side table. Bob found two clean styrofoam cups,
dumped heaping teaspoons of Folger's crystals into each,
and poured water. He handed one to Gregor.

"Sorry for all the confusion. Believe it or not, this is

what I do with myself these days. They have an official name for it down at headquarters, but it keeps slipping my mind. Bureauspeak. I'm supposed to 'mediate street conflicts.' If you can believe that."

"Gang wars."

"Exactly."

"Do you have a lot of them?"

"One or two a year in different areas of the city. Somehow, working on them lacks the satisfaction of working on something like the Hazzard case. Either Hazzard case. With the Hazzard case, you're likely to catch somebody."

"You didn't last time," Gregor noted.

"Oh, we caught him all right. We just didn't convict him. And yes, I still believe that in spite of what happened at your friend's apartment last night. Paul Hazzard killed his wife. There's never been a doubt in my mind. In the end, you know, he barely tried to deny it."

"Mmm," Gregor said. In his experience, murderers denied everything vigorously and often, no matter what the circumstances. "Let's not worry about the other Hazzard case for the moment, except where it might connect—"

"Like with the weapon."

"Exactly," Gregor said, "like with the weapon. I've been thinking about that weapon all night. In the end, I suppose it's the most important thing to be explained. What was it doing there? How did Hannah get hold of it? Who brought it into the house?"

"Maybe."

"Definitely. This is not some standard kitchen knife we're talking about. This is not a penknife somebody might carry around in his pocket. This is a valuable antique. I take it that by now somebody has verified that it was the same dagger?"

"They've verified that we've got every reason to believe it was the same dagger," Bob said. "The dagger that was on the wall in Paul Hazzard's living room is missing. The officer who picked up James Hazzard checked. And asked, of course."

"Of course. Did James Hazzard say when he'd seen it last?"

"No."

"Did he notice it missing last night on his own?"

"He says not."

"What about the position of the dagger?" Gregor asked. "One of the things I've never been able to get clear in my mind is where that dagger was on that wall. Toward the floor? At shoulder height? Higher?"

Bob Cheswicki considered. "It's one of those really old Federal houses," he said, "and the ceilings are fairly high, but this thing was placed in the middle of a bunch of others—there are dozens of weapons on that wall—at what would be about eye level for you. This is from what I remember, and it was a long time ago. But I think I'm accurate. You're a very tall man."

"Six four," Gregor said.

"So it was pretty far up," Bob concluded, "but not outrageously so."

"The point is that it couldn't have been taken by accident. Someone couldn't have stuck it into a pocket by mistake, without thinking. It would have had to have been reached for."

"Definitely."

Gregor tapped his fingers impatiently against a pile of papers on Bob Cheswicki's desk. "I don't like it. What do you think, by now, if you count my time with the Behavioral Sciences Department at the Bureau, I must have investigated hundreds of murders, wouldn't you think?"

"Well, yes, Gregor. But some of them came in sets."

"I know that, but that's not the point. The point is that in all that time, in the Bureau, out of the Bureau, it doesn't matter, never once have I found a case where a murderer used an odd or unusual weapon or an odd or unusual method unless he had to. *Had* to. Murderers do not go rigging up locked rooms or stabbing people with antique South Pacific ornamental daggers unless they have no alternative. This just doesn't make sense."

"I know it doesn't make sense," Bob said. "That's why I want you with us. To help make sense out of it."

Gregor got out of his chair and tried to pace. There wasn't much room. He kept bumping into furniture.

"Look at the murder of Jacqueline Isherwood Hazzard," he said. "Here is a woman in her own living room, in a house that was in all probability like all houses, meaning stocked with everyday weapons. I assume there were sets of steak knives in the kitchen?"

"I didn't check," Bob said, "but there must have been."

"Of course there must have been. Steak knives in the kitchen. Ice picks. Razor blades. Then there was that wall that the dagger was on. You said there were dozens of other weapons. Were there more obvious weapons?"

"What do you mean, more obvious?"

"Straightforward large knives," Gregor suggested. "This dagger is actually fairly small. How about something like a bowie knife or a small sword? Something closer at hand that would have been harder to miss."

"I suppose there must have been. Gregor, I just don't know these details off the top of my head."

Gregor waved this away. "We can check later, but what I'm saying only makes sense. There was no reason at all to use that dagger in the murder of Jacqueline Isherwood Hazzard."

"It wasn't used in the murder of Jacqueline Isherwood Hazzard," Bob put in quickly. "It wasn't what killed her. We determined that."

"It wasn't what killed her, but it was lying out next to the body or near it—"

"It was about three feet away on a small coffee table."

"Fine. It wasn't in its place on the wall. It was lying out where you would find it and jump to conclusions. And you did and you did."

"I didn't do either. I never believed in that thing as a weapon."

"Well, the police did." Gregor ran into the chair he had been sitting in and pushed it as far out of the way as possible, which wasn't very far. He was beginning to feel distinctly claustrophobic. "Bob, I'm not trying to make you look stupid. I'm not trying to make the Philadelphia police look stupid. I'm just trying to point out to you how nonsensical all this is."

"I know how nonsensical all this is," Bob said. "And the police were stupid. I mean, those officers were. Two of the least competent officers in Homicide."

"Last night," Gregor said, "Paul Hazzard is killed in

Hannah Krekorian's apartment with the same dagger that was suspected to have been the weapon in the death of his wife four years ago. So far so good. There are three ways that dagger could have made its way into Hannah's apartment."

"Shoot."

Gregor nodded. "Okay. In the first place, Paul Hazzard could have brought it himself. We talked about that a little last night. That officer of yours suggested that Paul Hazzard might have brought it as a kind of show-and-tell piece, a prop for him to use when he told people about the murder."

Bob frowned. "You didn't believe that, and I didn't either. The feeling I got last night was that the last thing Paul Hazzard wanted to discuss was that murder."

"I got the same feeling myself. He brought it up with me, but it seemed as if he were heading me off at the pass, if you know what I mean. Bring the subject up and get it out of the way so it doesn't come back to ambush you later in the evening."

"Right."

"The second possibility is that Hannah brought the weapon from Paul's apartment. The only reason she would have had to do that is if she were planning to kill Paul. She might not have realized that the weapon had been proven not to have been the one that really killed Paul's wife. She might have wanted to kill Paul Hazzard and throw suspicion back on the family. Or on Candida DeWitt."

"Candida DeWitt had an alibi for the murder of Jacqueline Isherwood Hazzard."

"Hannah didn't necessarily know that," Gregor said. He stopped pacing and sat down. He felt suddenly very tired. "I hate to admit it, Bob, but on one level this explanation has a lot going for it. Hannah is the kind of person who knows not quite enough about too many things. It's not impossible for me to imagine that she might have known the superficial facts about the murder of Paul Hazzard's second wife without having any of the details nailed down tight. And then there's the invitation Candida DeWitt received."

"I was wondering when you were going to get around to that."

"I've gotten around to it. Candida DeWitt has to have gotten it someplace. The most obvious place for it to have come from is Hannah herself. Of course, I don't see how Hannah could have known that Mrs. DeWitt would actually show up."

"She might have guessed," Bob said. "You ought to read more in the papers than the editorials and the sports pages, Gregor."

"Meaning what?"

"Meaning that the local papers and even a few of the national celebrity magazines have been full of it for the past few weeks. Candida DeWitt has a contract from some book publisher in New York to write her memoirs. The *Star* has been especially explicit about just how nasty relations still were between Paul Hazzard and Candida DeWitt."

Gregor rubbed his face with the palms of his hands. "It really is the most sensible explanation. Even the denouement is perfectly explicable. Hannah steals the dagger and invites Candida DeWitt to the party she's giving for Paul. Hannah kills Paul with the dagger with the intention of throwing the blame on Candida DeWitt. Hannah loses control and has hysterics and ends up getting caught red-handed. Literally. It makes more sense than anything else I can think of."

Bob leaned over and made himself another cup of instant coffee. "But you don't believe it," he said.

"No," Gregor admitted, shaking his head. "I don't believe it."

"Could that be because you know Hannah Krekorian? Could that be because you don't want to believe that someone you're close to could have committed a murder?"

"I've been asking myself the same question all morning. And do you know what? I don't think so. Oh, it's true enough that I'd rather it didn't turn out that Hannah had committed this murder. My life would be a lot more pleasant in a hundred ways if somebody else turns out to have done it. But it's more than that. This thing doesn't—fit somehow. It doesn't work. I can't make it come straight in my mind."

"It comes straight in my mind," Bob said. "Let me be honest with you, Gregor. Last night we didn't arrest Mrs.

Krekorian because we had some details we wanted to get straight before we made an accusation. This morning the only reason we haven't arrested her is because she's a friend of yours. And I don't know how much longer we're going to be able to extend the courtesy."

"I don't blame you," Gregor said. He thought about it. "Can we go do some looking? The both of us together, I mean, or me and Russell Donahue."

"It would have to be Donahue. I've got a full plate here and I'm not supposed to be involved in this investigation anyway. Do you have something in particular you want to do?"

"Yes," Gregor said. "I want to go out to Paul Hazzard's house."

"Just go out to his house?"

"Well, I'm willing to talk to anybody who might be there, but that's not really the point. I want to see that wall of weapons. I want to stand in the living room and really look at it."

"Why?"

"I don't know."

Bob Cheswicki shrugged. "Russ is going to have to go out there anyway. He might as well go out there this morning with you. Let me get hold of him."

"Thank you."

Bob Cheswicki unearthed his phone from a pile of papers and began to dial. "Gregor, do you know what you're doing? Have you got the least idea of what you're trying on?"

"No," Gregor said. "But I know I'm doing the right thing."

That was true too.

Gregor felt thoroughly optimistic for the first time since he'd heard Hannah Krekorian start screaming.

*f o u r*

*1*

Number 232 in *The Handbook of Daily Meditations for Code-pendents* said it very clearly: You are in control of your own availability. Caroline knew it hadn't been written to mean what she was making it mean at the moment. It meant you didn't have to be emotionally *there* for anybody you didn't want to be *there* for. It also meant that your time was your own. Nobody had the right to determine what you were going to do with it but you. That last part could be used to cover this, but not quite. Caroline didn't really know what the writer of *Daily Meditations* would have made of this situation, or what Melody Beattie, John Bradshaw, or her father would have made of it either. Her father had been through something very similar to this when Jacqueline died. It had had no effect on his philosophy as far as Caroline could tell. The recovery movement wasn't really prepared to take on institutional obligations like murder investigations and military draft laws and the requirement of all citizens to pay their income taxes. The recovery movement was much more comfortable with private and familial abuse. That way they could say over and over again that you were responsible to nobody but yourself. It didn't matter that it didn't make any sense.

Actually, to Caroline it did make sense. It was just a question of widening the vision a little. You *were* responsible to nobody and for nobody but yourself. You *were* in control of your own availability. It was the mark of a ravaged and codependent society that laws had been put in place to force you to behave otherwise.

*This situation*, as Caroline called it to herself, was the sight of Gregor Demarkian and a nondescript, vaguely black-Irish young man in an off-the-rack suit coming up the front walk. Caroline had seen them getting out of their cab when she looked up from her work just a few seconds before. Caroline was working at home, in the first floor living room of the town house she shared with her brother and sister (and until last night had shared with her father) because she knew from experience that her office was going to be impossible today. It didn't matter that it was Saturday. Half the people who would normally be at home in bed would come out just to see her. There she was, daughter of the dead man, orphaned by a couple of murders. The people who didn't come would call, and to their number would be added all the reporters who had managed to get a hold on this story and who wouldn't want to let it go. One or two journalists might easily get a book contract out of it. Caroline had a lot of work to do. She had a series of demonstrations in Boston next week. She had the next six months of shows to present in outline before the station's programming board next month. She had a show to tape this coming Tuesday night. If she had loved her father, she would have dropped it all, to do her grief work. She expected to be overwhelmed with rage at any moment, furious at him for abandoning her by dying. In the meantime, she had to draw illustrations for a set of cardboard panels giving step-by-step instructions for how to build a gazebo.

Gregor Demarkian and the young man in the off-the-rack suit reached the front door and rang the bell. Caroline toyed with the idea of not answering, and saying later that she hadn't been home. She decided against it. It was the kind of thing the police always caught you out at. Then they pretended to believe it made you look guilty. Caroline remembered that, too, from all the fuss about Jacqueline.

Caroline put her pencil down and got up and went to the door.

"Yes?" she said when she opened up. It was cold and windy outside. A blast of icy air hit her legs and penetrated the thin cotton of her black boxer pants with no trouble at all. Caroline shivered.

The young man in the off-the-rack suit took a leather folder out of his inside jacket pocket and flipped it open. "I'm Detective First Grade Russell Donahue," he said politely. "I'm investigating the death last night of a resident of this house, Paul Hazzard. This is a consultant for the Philadelphia police department, Gregor Demarkian."

"I know Mr. Demarkian from the newspapers," Caroline said. "Could you tell me what you want?"

"Well," Russell Donahue said, "we'd like to come in and look around, for one thing."

"Do you have a search warrant?"

"That's not the kind of looking around I meant, ma'am. At least, not at this point. Of course, we can go back and get a search warrant if you want us to. You are—?"

"My name is Caroline Hazzard. I was Paul Hazzard's daughter. I understand that you must be eager to look through my father's things. I understand you even have a right and an obligation to do so. But without a search warrant or some consultation with my brother and my sister?"

"Are your brother and your sister home?" Russell Donahue asked.

"No," Caroline said.

"I think Ms. Hazzard is operating under a misconception," Gregor Demarkian said. To Caroline, he looked fat and unappetizing and out of shape. Definitely in denial. "We don't want to look through your father's things, Ms. Hazzard. Far less do we want to search the house, at least at this time. What we are interested in this morning is the wall on which the antique weapons are kept. Assuming that they're still kept there."

"We want to see the place the dagger came from," Russell Donahue put in.

Caroline looked back over her shoulder. She could go on like this for a long time. She might even chase them away from the door this morning. But what good would it do her? They would only come back later, armed with warrants and a combative attitude. They would get what they wanted and be angry with her at the same time.

Caroline stepped back. "It's the first door on your left

as you go down the hall. The archway thing. I was working in there when you rang the bell.''

"Working at what?" Gregor Demarkian asked.

He had walked past her down the hall. Russell Donahue was right behind him. Caroline closed the front door and followed them both.

"I do a local cable television show on carpentry for women," she said. "I was drawing demonstration boards."

Gregor Demarkian was standing next to the coffee table where she had been working, leaning over her drawing of the gazebo's entrance-side elevation. "What's a demonstration board?"

"An instructional drawing."

"They're very colorful."

Caroline hated to have her things touched. It made her feel furious. It made her feel violated. It was a form of violation. It was a form of symbolic rape. She nudged him away from her drawings.

"They're colorful like that so that I can do demonstrations in front of large groups of people and no one will have to strain to see."

"I take it these are the weapons on the wall," Russell Donahue said.

Gregor Demarkian coughed.

Caroline turned her attention to the plainclothes policeman and the wall of weapons behind him, which did not need to be pointed out in that awkward and obvious fashion. The wall in question was covered over in weapons from side to side and top to bottom. The weapons were crammed in next to each other so thickly, it was in some places impossible to see the wall behind them. Japanese ceremonial swords. Milanese short knives with silver hafts and gold-inlaid holster sheaths. Arabic fighting daggers carved in intricate whorls and patterns. Caroline made a face. Paul had always been such a worshiper of death.

Gregor Demarkian walked up close to the wall and examined it.

"I've heard that the dagger in question, the one that was suspected in the death of your stepmother, is missing," he said.

"That's right." Caroline nodded. "My brother James looked for it last night, when he got word that Daddy was—that Daddy was dead. It was gone then."

"Was it gone earlier in the evening?"

"I don't know," Caroline said. "I don't know if James would know either. It's not as if we looked at it every chance we got. It wasn't even very noticeable. Not next to all the rest of this stuff."

"Could you show me where it belonged?"

Caroline crossed her arms over her chest. "Show yourself. It belonged in the rack that's empty at the moment. Next to that blowgun with the feathers on it."

"I see." Demarkian nodded. "How tall are you?"

"Five five," Caroline said.

"Could you reach it—the dagger, of course—could you reach it without straining?"

"I never tried."

"Will you try now?"

Caroline shrugged, came closer, and reached. She had to stand on tiptoe to touch the rack. She backed away.

"Five five," Gregor said again. "You said you have a brother and a sister. Do they live nearby?"

"They live here," Caroline said. "James has a room on the bedroom floor across from mine. Alyssa and her husband have the apartment at the top of the house."

"Fine. Is your sister as tall as you are? Taller?"

"We're about the same height."

"And your brother?"

"James is very tall. Almost as tall as you are. The way Daddy was very tall."

"Mmm," Gregor Demarkian said.

Caroline backed up a little and sat down on the arm of one of the chairs. "You know," she said, "if I were you, I wouldn't bother too much about us. About James and Alyssa and me, I mean. We're hardly the likely suspects in this case."

"Oh?" Russell Donahue was polite. "Who is?"

"I should think your two best bets would be Candida DeWitt and that woman Daddy was seeing, that Hannah somebody. She came to the house this week, you know.

On Tuesday or Wednesday. When I first saw her, I couldn't understand what it was Daddy was doing with her. I understood later, of course."

"Did you?" Gregor Demarkian asked. Really, Caroline thought. He ought to do something about himself. He ought to join an Overeaters Anonymous group. Food could be an addiction.

Caroline nodded. "Oh, yes. Usually, of course, Daddy was like all infantilized men. He liked girls better than he liked women, twenty-one-year-olds with IQs like golf scores and big china-blue eyes. Not to marry, of course. He was more sensible than that. But for fun. You know."

"So you decided that your father was interested in marrying Hannah Krekorian," Russell Donahue said.

"Not necessarily," Caroline told him. "I suppose she had a great deal of money."

"She was reasonably well off," Gregor said dryly. "*Is* reasonably well off."

"I assumed she had to be. Daddy is dead broke these days. After Jacqueline died, the book sales and the workshops dried up and there was his shopping addiction. He was absolutely out of control. Of course, he didn't think he was. Addicts never do."

"Right," Russell Donahue said.

Caroline squelched a sudden desire to explain it all to him—how shopping addictions were just the same as addictions to alcohol or nicotine or heroin; how addicts are helpless to control their own behavior; how addictions start out bad and can only get worse unless the addict gets into recovery. It all made perfect sense if you understood the theory, but so many people didn't want to understand the theory. About this one thing Caroline thought her father had been unquestionably right. The most serious disease in America today was not codependency. It was denial.

"The point I'm trying to make about this Hannah person," Caroline said carefully, "is that she was a world-class codependent. A real enabler. Right down to the martyr complex."

Gregor Demarkian looked blank. "Hannah Krekorian? With a martyr complex?"

"Of course. You could see it right away. It was in all that stuff she said about Mother Teresa."

Russell Donahue looked confused. "I don't understand. What does Mother Teresa have to do with any of this?"

"Mother Teresa is like a litmus test," Caroline explained patiently. "If you want to know just how sick our society is, measure the extent to which we insist that that woman is a saint."

"Oh," Gregor Demarkian said. "Now, wait a minute."

"But it's true," Caroline persisted. "Just look at what that woman is. If you can, I mean, because she really isn't anything. Or anybody. She's just a machine for meeting other people's needs. She's so full of shame and self-loathing, she doesn't believe she has a right to take care of herself."

Russell Donahue was standing next to the twin chair to the one Caroline was sitting in. He sat down himself, abruptly. Caroline felt wonderful. She almost felt high. It had been ages since she had confronted anyone with these things except other people who knew all the theories she did—and what was the good of that? People who had heard it all before thought they knew it all. They didn't really listen.

"Look," Caroline said. "We're each and every one of us born with a unique capacity to feel and think and love and create. There isn't anybody on earth who isn't born with that. Then, while we're growing up, in an effort to control us, our parents and the other adults around us try to make us feel unworthy. That's the key. We're all brought up to believe that we aren't worth the best that life has to offer, that we're means instead of ends, that we have to justify our existences. This is especially true for women, of course, because we've been assigned the role of nurturer and caretaker in society. But it's true of men too; they just have to fight through it a different way. To become whole, we all have to learn that we *are* ends in ourselves, that we deserve the best in life just by the fact that we exist, that we don't have to propitiate anybody or anything, that we don't have to apologize for ourselves. But that's the sort of insight Mother Teresa has never come close to. She's the ultimate diseased personality. She's not living as an end in herself. She's living for other people."

"Mother Teresa," Russell Donahue said slowly, "has spent sixty years of her life with her hands in pus and excrement to make sure that a lot of people too poor to eat have access to halfway decent medical care."

Caroline nodded sympathetically. "It's terrible, isn't it, to see someone throw away her life like that. She has such enormous energy. She could have had such a deeply fulfilling and emotionally significant life."

"Right," Gregor Demarkian said. "You were talking about Hannah Krekorian?"

"Oh, yes." Caroline sighed. "The thing to remember is that codependents in denial are very dangerous people. They're under such pressure and they've got such deep reserves of shame and self-blame and untapped anger and rage, they're likely to do anything. I met this Hannah person Daddy was going around with. I think she was a time bomb ready to go off. I think she did go off. Daddy wanted to go out and buy her a valentine, but I warned him against it. Women like that always take that kind of gesture as the next best thing to a proposal of marriage."

"Do they?" Gregor Demarkian asked.

"Trust me," Caroline told them emphatically, "when you get through all the nonsense you have to get through, that Hannah woman will be at the bottom of it. A world-class codependent, desperately unhappy and fanatically in denial. It's inevitable."

## 2

The young woman behind the desk at the florist's shop wanted $578.50 for the delivery of one hundred and one roses to Lida Arkmanian—and she wanted a few explanations too, although she wasn't going to ask for them and Christopher Hannaford wasn't going to volunteer them. The florist's shop was at the far end of Cavanaugh Street just where it dead-ended into Elman. There was an Armenian name on the sign outside and a pile of those powdered-sugar-covered Armenian cookies on a plate next to the cash register. Christopher had considered going to a florist somewhere else in the city. He hadn't seen what good he would do by it. The only person left on Cavanaugh Street who didn't know what was going on, or at least suspect, was Gregor Demarkian. It amazed Christopher that the man could be so dumb. Then he wondered what Gregor would think if someone told him about it. Then he gave that up. Christopher Hannaford had done some fairly obsessional things in his life, but obsessional thinking wasn't one of them. He had always been able to chuck useless lines of inquiry and occupy his mind with something else.

The other reason Christopher hadn't gone off Cavanaugh Street to buy the roses was that it would have been silly in the long run. Eventually the roses were going to have to be delivered. That would mean a florist's van and a lot of flowers going to Lida Arkmanian's door. How in the world was anybody going to hide that? It wasn't as if what was going to be delivered were one long white box.

Christopher paid for the roses in cash. Having spent much of his earlier life in serious debt, he didn't like credit cards. There was a box of heart-shaped chocolate-covered strawberry-creme-filled candies on sale on the counter, and he threw down three of those to eat on his way to breakfast. The young lady behind the counter glanced at the candies, nodded, and rang them up. Christopher had the uncomfortable feeling that she knew he liked to eat a lot of chocolate and that everybody else on Cavanaugh Street knew it too. Christopher just hoped the local radar didn't extend to his private practices in private places. The last thing he wanted in his life was a morning sitting across the table from Bennis, knowing that she knew that he liked to—oh, never mind.

The young woman behind the counter handed him his change. "Now, let me get this straight," she said. "You wanted the roses delivered today at two o'clock. Today."

"Yep."

"Not Valentine's Day."

"I've got something else cooking for Valentine's Day."

"Something bigger than this?"

"Yep."

"Well, that's going to be a gas and a half. If you order it through us, you better give us a couple of days' notice."

"They can't be there before two o'clock because she won't be home until one-thirty. She's got a meeting of the Armenian-American Heritage Library Association."

"I know," the young woman said. "My mother has that too. In fact, Lida will probably bring my mother home. I'll send the flowers over as soon as I see the whites of their eyes."

"Great." Christopher took one of the candies out of its wrapper and bit into it. "Thanks a lot."

"Have a nice day," the young woman said.

Out on Cavanaugh Street, it was ten o'clock and sunny, but still bitterly cold. Christopher was used to California, and this weather was beginning to annoy him. Didn't this city ever thaw out? He tried to remember how he had felt about it when he was growing up here. As far as he could recall, he hadn't noticed the weather. He finished the first of the candies and opened the second. Christ, he hadn't felt this good in he didn't know how long. He really hadn't. This was better than champagne and chocolate. This was even better than marijuana, and marijuana had been Christopher's favorite thing on earth until a combination of his own age and the stubbornness of the United States government in maintaining the illegality of it had made it too much trouble. Nothing would ever make *this* too much trouble. He wondered if she was sitting there in her meeting right now, thinking about him. Maybe she was thinking about the things they did instead, and blushing. She was always blushing. Christopher had never met a woman who was so easy to make blush. He finished the second candy and opened the third. He was working again. That was always the best sign. His pockets were full of scraps of paper with lines of poetry written on them.

He had reached the Ararat Restaurant. He stuffed the last corner of candy into his mouth and went inside. It was really terrible candy, nothing at all like the Godiva things he had been eating at Lida's the night before. He was going to have to buy Lida some more Godiva chocolates. He was eating her out of the ones she had at home.

Bennis sat alone in the window booth, drinking black coffee and reading the *Inquirer*. She looked up when he walked in and he waved to her.

"Linda," he said to Linda Melajian, who was going by with a pile of menus under one arm. "Can you get me a cup of coffee and a mushroom omelet? I'm going to be sitting over there with Bennis."

"Be right there," Linda Melajian said. "Isn't it awful? Don't you feel terrible? Helen Tevorakian was in here this morning, saying she didn't think Hannah would ever be able to sleep in that bedroom again."

"Well, it's terrible enough," Christopher agreed.

"Nobody can talk about anything else," Linda Melajian said. "You should have heard this place during the breakfast rush. We must have had fifty people in here. And then, of course, Gregor didn't show up, for the first time in I don't know how long. He always eats breakfast here when he's at home. I thought we were going to have a riot."

"Maybe you can stake out his apartment and catch him when he comes home."

"Don't joke," Linda Melajian said. "The way people are around here this morning, they're likely to do anything."

Christopher sat down opposite Bennis. Bennis looked up from her paper again.

"Well, well," she said. "The bear emerges from hibernation."

"I haven't been hibernating," Christopher said. "I was at the party last night."

"So you were. Of course, it's practically the only time I've seen you since you got here."

"I've been trying not to make a pest of myself."

"Is that what it is?"

"I've been having a very refreshing vacation, Bennis. Isn't that what vacations are for?"

"I just hope you know what you're doing."

"I *always* know what I'm doing."

Linda Melajian came over with a cup of coffee. Christopher thanked her and started drinking it. Bennis took her classic Hannaford sugar cravings out on coffee so sweet it was almost a syrup, but Christopher couldn't stand to drink coffee that way. He preferred his candy straight.

"Listen," he said, "believe it or not, I came looking for you because there was something I wanted to ask you. Something I think maybe I should have told Gregor Demarkian last night. Not that it's really anything important."

Bennis looked interested. "Do you mean you know something about the murder? I mean, of course you should tell Gregor if you know something about what happened last night. That's the whole point of an investigation. To find out what happened."

"It's not about what happened last night. It's about me. And Paul Hazzard."

"You? You knew Paul Hazzard?"

"Not exactly," Christopher said. "Not the way you're using the term. You remember that place you paid for me to go to right after Daddy died, the therapy place for compulsive gambling?"

"I remember you went. I also remember you didn't stay very long."

"You also know I haven't done anything but buy a lottery ticket once a month for years. You haven't had to bail me out, have you?"

"No," Bennis admitted. "I haven't."

"Okay, then. The thing is, the place I went to was run by Paul Hazzard's organization. He used to have some kind of corporate entity set up to keep all the pieces in place. Maybe he still does. Anyway, most of the time the man himself never went near the place. It was run by people he'd trained. But while I was there, he did show up just once for a couple of days."

"And?"

"And it was strange," Christopher said. "It was very strange. That was what I wanted to talk to Gregor about. I also wanted to tell him I'd had contact with Paul Hazzard before so it didn't come out later and look like Christ only knows what. But it's more than that. It's what happened while he was up there. In Vermont."

Bennis got out a cigarette and lit up. "You're being very mysterious," she said. "In fact, you're getting me very nervous. Does this whatever-it-is have something to do with you personally? Did you have a motive for killing that man?"

"It's not that," Christopher told her. "It's just that this thing—this thing that happened with Paul Hazzard—well, the implications could be not so good for your friend Hannah. It was something that happened with Paul Hazzard and an, um, older woman."

"Oh, Jesus," Bennis said.

Linda Melajian came back with a mushroom omelet on a plate with toast and hash browns. You got your cholesterol at the Ararat whether you wanted it or not.

Christopher reached for the salt.

"Let me explain the whole thing to you," he said to Bennis. "Let me start from the beginning."

*f i v e*

*1*

Years ago, when Gregor Demarkian had only recently met Bennis Hannaford, Bennis used to give him books. The books were always murder mysteries of the most traditional kind—Agatha Christie, Dorothy L. Sayers, Ellery Queen, Rex Stout—and always seemed to follow the same pattern. First a murder was committed. Then suspect A was designated most likely to have committed it. Then it was proved to be impossible for suspect A to have committed it. Then it turned out that suspect A had committed it after all. Of course, Gregor realized that not all these books had that identical plot. The problem was that many of them had. The pattern was fixed firmly in his brain. It insisted on coloring his expectations of what was going to happen next in his own life. It made him very uncomfortable. There was Hannah, the most likely suspect—so likely now that it was beginning to seem impossible that the murderer could be anyone else. Gregor kept trying to twist the picture and make the most likely suspect come out to be Candida De-Witt. It just wouldn't work. She hadn't had any blood on her at all. That wasn't conclusive, but it went a long way to make her a less likely prospect than Hannah. Then there was the weapon. Gregor had the feeling that under the circumstances, Candida DeWitt was the person with the least access to the ornamented dagger. She might have a key to Paul Hazzard's house left over from the days when she was on good terms with the family, but it was a long shot. Candida's relationship with Paul Hazzard had fallen apart just about the time when Jacqueline Isherwood Hazzard was murdered. If Gregor had been Paul Hazzard, after that murder he would have had all his locks changed. That wouldn't have been to keep out Candida DeWitt. She would have been a very minor problem. He would have wanted the locks changed to make sure no overly ambitious reporter could gain access by scaring up one of the stray keys that were sure to be lying around, given to friends who had promised to water the plants while the family was away on vacation or to building contractors doing serious repairs. Down in Washington, Gregor had known people who changed their locks every year, exactly because things like this happened. A house with locks in it that had been around for a while might be safe enough from random burglars, but it was likely to be as open as a bordello's front door to an entire collection of friends, foes, acquaintances, and strangers. Gregor knew what happened to house keys. He knew what had happened to his own.

Unfortunately, even if Candida did have a usable key to Paul Hazzard's house, that didn't let Hannah off the hook. There was still the blood to consider. There was still the motive to consider. Candida DeWitt might very well have hated Paul Hazzard. The newspapers and magazines all liked to pretend she did. Still, the sequence of events that had brought her to hate him was over four years old. There had been six stab wounds in Paul Hazzard's chest. This was a crime committed in hot blood. Would Candida's blood have been that hot after all this time? She hadn't been raving or upset by the time the crowd reached Hannah's bedroom *after* the murder. In fact, except for Gregor himself and Bob Cheswicki, she had been the most levelheaded one there.

Gregor sat in the chair next to the desk that belonged to Russell Donahue in the big bull pen of a squad room in the police station that served Cavanaugh Street—a much cleaner and nicer and less ominous place than the one where Gregor had met Bob Cheswicki earlier that morning—and tapped his fingers against Russell's copy of *Halberstam on Contracts*.

"Mary Ohanian," he said. "And Helen Tevorakian."

"You said that before," Russell told him. "We called. They're meeting you at two."

"Yes, I know. Russell, listen. If you could do anything at all at this moment, what would you do? Arrest Hannah Krekorian?"

"I don't know," Russell said. "I suppose so. Maybe I'd wait a few days. Maybe I'd talk to the district attorney first. I'd have to talk to the district attorney first in a case like this. There are a couple of things I might want to straighten out. There are one or two things about this case—"

"Yes," Gregor said. "I understand that. What I was thinking, though, was that it might be in the best interests of everybody involved if you did arrest Hannah Krekorian. Right away."

"What?"

Gregor stood up. "Not right away," he said. "Not right this minute. There are a couple of things *I* want to check out first. Mary Ohanian and Helen Tevorakian. Candida DeWitt."

"What about Candida DeWitt?"

"We have to talk to her. Today. But after that I think the best thing to do, assuming that everything still stands more or less as it stands now, is to arrest Hannah and get it over with."

"But why?"

"Because you would have arrested her if I weren't here mucking up the process. Because once you arrest her, everybody else in this case will relax."

"Except Mrs. Krekorian. She won't relax. It's no fun to be arrested."

"We'll work the timing right," Gregor said. "We won't let her spend any actual time in jail. We'll get the judge set up and the bail and all the rest of it. I don't want to persecute her, Mr. Donahue."

"Russ," Russell Donahue said. "It still won't be pleasant. Getting fingerprinted. Getting photographed. That woman will go all to pieces."

"She might," Gregor admitted, "but she'll go to pieces even worse at a trial. We want to avoid the trial."

"One way or the other, she's going to have to be at the trial."

"I'm trying to ensure that she won't have to be there as the defendant," Gregor said. "Let's try to get in touch with Candida DeWitt. Let's see if we can't go out there this evening and ask her a few questions."

"I'm not on duty this evening."

"You are now."

"I've heard about you." Russell Donahue sighed. "Sit down again, Mr. Demarkian. I'm going to go out and have Mary Lee Espicci call Candida DeWitt. She's better at getting appointments than I am. I'll be right back."

"Right," Gregor said.

He sat down again. Russell Donahue disappeared. Gregor picked up *Halberstam on Contracts* and noted that Russell's place was marked by a course registration receipt from the University of Pennsylvania Law School. Russell Donahue must be good. Penn didn't make allowances for students who worked full-time jobs in urban police departments. Penn didn't make allowances for anybody. If you wanted to be treated like a special case, you went to Penn State. Still, Russell must have convinced the law school to allow him to attend part-time. That was remarkable enough in itself.

Russell came back from wherever it was he'd gone and sat down again behind his desk.

"All taken care of," he said. "We're set up for seven-thirty tonight. I may even get to grab a hamburger for dinner. She's got Fred Scherrer with her, by the way."

"He came to pick her up last night," Gregor said. "I'm not interrupting a class?" He tapped *Halberstam*.

Russell Donahue shook his head. "I do contracts Monday, Wednesday, and Friday at nine. The department works around me. They're very good about things like this here, except sometimes for women. Lady working Burglary had to threaten a sex discrimination suit to get her schedule arranged."

"I'm surprised the law school admitted you as a part-time student."

"They didn't. I got shot. About three years ago. I was

in the hospital for months, and then when I came out I couldn't work and nobody knew if I was ever going to. So I took my disability and I got myself into the law school and I did two years straight. Then I got better and I could work again and I was running out of money and I was second in my class—"

"Right," Gregor said. "I'm impressed."

"Are you?" Russell Donahue suddenly looked distinctly odd. "That's good."

"Well," Gregor said. "I guess I'd better be getting out of here. Mary and Helen will undoubtedly be early."

"We'll get a police car to take you over. I'll bring a car and pick you up too. Six-thirty be all right?"

"That's a little early, isn't it?"

"We'll be going out to Bryn Mawr and there'll be the weekend traffic."

"Okay."

"Go right on downstairs and out the front door. I'll have a patrol car waiting for you."

"Okay," Gregor said again. Russell Donahue still looked distinctly odd. Now, what was this about?

Gregor got his coat off the back of his chair and shrugged it on.

## 2

By the time he got to Cavanaugh Street, Gregor Demarkian was feeling more than a little guilty about his plans for Hannah Krekorian. They made sense in the long run, but Russell Donahue had been absolutely right about the short run. Hannah was going to hate everything that happened to her. She wasn't going to remain calm. The whole scene was going to be an enormous mess, but he didn't see any way to get around it. If he didn't do something drastic soon, Hannah Krekorian was going to be arrested, tried, and convicted of the murder of Paul Hazzard.

Mary Ohanian and Helen Tevorakian had agreed to meet him at the back of Ohanian's Middle Eastern Food

Store. Mary couldn't take the time away from work to go over to Helen's. Besides, Hannah was at Helen's. Nobody wanted to bring Hannah into this more than they had to.

Gregor had the police car pull up to Ohanian's directly. He thanked the patrolman and got out. Cavanaugh Street was empty except for a florist's van in front of Lida Arkmanian's town house up the street. A man was climbing the steps to Lida's front door with what looked like a million roses in his arms. Gregor wondered why. Valentine's Day was almost a week away. He wondered who the flowers were from, too. Lida's children were usually more cutesy about Valentine's Day than that. They sent pink teddy bears with balloons that said, "I'm a fuzzy wuzzy bear and I wuv you!"

The display in front of Ohanian's window had changed a little. Now it consisted of a gigantic outline of a heart cut out of red cardboard and hung with white crepe paper streamers, inside of which was a collection of letters Gregor found it impossible to pronounce. He even found it impossible to concentrate on them. "Bdembrbdra Borgander!" Maybe. Maybe it was "Debgrvwzk Dekobgdr!" Gregor assumed whatever it was was something Valentine's Day–like in Armenian. Of course, the Ohanians had been in America for a couple of generations by now. They might not have gotten the words right.

Gregor let himself into the store, checked out a display of *pideh* tortured into heart shapes, and decided that the real danger in having Donna Moradanyan depressed came in the form of the efforts of other people to take her place. Gregor was positively nostalgic for the days of waking up to find his front door wrapped in pink metallic ribbon and dotted with sugar-candy cupids firing arrows at chocolate-chip-cookie hearts.

Krissa Ohanian was standing behind the counter when Gregor came in. She looked up and said, "They're in the back there. Mary's supposed to be doing a pastry inventory. I think they're talking instead."

Krissa Ohanian was Mary Ohanian's aunt, and one of those big, solid Armenian women who in another place and time would have been relied on to keep the family together through war and famine. Gregor didn't know if Krissa was married. He did know she clucked over Mary as if Mary were her own. Mary was barely eighteen years old. To Krissa, that qualified as being hardly out of diapers.

"Her father's absolutely livid," Krissa pointed out. "He was going on and on this morning about how he should have let Mary go to Wellesley instead of keeping her here at home, at least she wouldn't be mixed up in a murder. And he's livid at Hannah too. For inviting that man."

"Do people on the street think Hannah killed him?" Gregor asked, curious.

Krissa said no. "They all think it was that other woman, that Mrs. DeWitt. I'd never seen a fancy piece up close before. It was very interesting."

"Candida DeWitt looks like a suburban matron on the verge of being elected president of the garden club."

"It's not what she looks like, Gregor. It's what she *is* like."

If Krissa Ohanian had met Candida DeWitt on the street without knowing who she was, Krissa would have thought Candida was a very pleasant woman with good WASP social connections. Gregor was sure of it.

"I'm supposed to go in back here?" he asked, pointing behind the counter at a curtain.

"I'll let you through." Krissa pulled up the hinged countertop and stepped close to the cash register to let Gregor pass. "They're all the way in the back there. Just follow the light."

Gregor followed the light. The back of Ohanian's Middle Eastern Food Store was like a cave with stalagmites of cardboard boxes rising from the ground. Some of the boxes had words printed on them in English, but most of them didn't. A great many of the boxes had import stamps plastered all over their sides. Greek, Hebrew, Arabic—when the Ohanians said "Middle Eastern," they weren't fooling around.

The light led to an open space at the very back, where three boxes had been laid side to side and covered with a pair of worn terry-cloth dishtowels to make a table. Krissa had been absolutely right. Mary wasn't doing a thing about taking an inventory. Mary had a bottle of Coke. Helen Tevorakian had a bottle of 7-Up. They were both bent over a sheet of paper placed carefully on Mary's clipboard. It was not a sheet of paper that would tell anybody how many bags of pignolia nuts were on the shelves.

Neither Mary nor Helen looked up when Gregor came through. Helen was murmuring something about how Lida couldn't have been getting it right, it had to have been much earlier than seven twenty-two. Then Mary said no, seven twenty-two was just right, Helen forgot how early everybody was getting to the party.

Gregor Demarkian coughed. Mary Ohanian jumped guiltily and nearly fell off the packing box she was using as a stool.

"Don't sneak up on people like that," Helen Tevorakian chided him. "You could kill somebody."

"I wasn't sneaking at all," Gregor told her. "I walked right up to you two and you didn't even notice. What are you doing?"

"Making a timetable," Mary Ohanian said. "We thought, you know, that since you wanted to talk to us about what happened last night, we'd get it all written down. All the times and that kind of thing. We called people."

Gregor held out his hand for the sheet of paper. "I don't suppose it occurred to either one of you that you could leave the detecting to me? Or to the police?"

"Well, we don't want to leave the detecting to the police in this case, do we?" Helen demanded. "The police think Hannah killed that stuck-up little jerk."

"He wasn't little," Mary Ohanian said. "He was very tall. He was the thinnest person I ever saw in my life who didn't have an eating disorder."

"Maybe he did have an eating disorder," Helen said indignantly.

"Let me see that thing," Gregor insisted. "Right now."

Helen Tevorakian took the paper off the clipboard and handed it up. "It's just a rough outline. We know we're not professionals, Krekor. We're just trying to help."

"And you know what people in this neighborhood are

like," Mary put in. "Always hearing omens and sensing prophecies. You should hear Mrs. Kashinian on the subject of ghostly presences from the other side."

"Sheila says she heard a 'desperate moan' at just about seven o'clock." Helen Tevorakian was being as diplomatic as she could. "Sheila says it was coming from upstairs."

Gregor looked at the sheet of paper they had handed him. Amateur or not, it was a pretty fair job. That expensive private school the Ohanians had sent Mary to must have done some good. Gregor thought Mary's father ought to be ashamed of himself. He ought to have let Mary go on to Wellesley. Maybe they could get a few people together on the street and convince him to let Mary go next year.

The outline went into considerable detail. It was very neatly printed. And it was very well organized. "6:45 to 7:05—MAJORITY OF PEOPLE ARRIVE AT PARTY," it said, and then:

> 7:00 to 7:05—SHEILA KASHINIAN HEARS MOAN FROM
> SECOND FLOOR(?)
> 7:00 to 7:20—EVERYBODY EATS AND TALKS
> 7:22—CANDIDA DEWITT ARRIVES
> 7:27—HANNAH BURSTS INTO TEARS AND RUNS UPSTAIRS
> 7:33—PAUL HAZZARD RUNS UPSTAIRS AFTER HANNAH
> 7:36—MARY OHANIAN GOES UPSTAIRS TO CHECK ON THE
> SITUATION
> 7:39—MARY OHANIAN COMES DOWN
> 7:33 to 7:48—CANDIDA DEWITT TALKS TO GREGOR
> DEMARKIAN
> 7:42—HELEN TEVORAKIAN GOES UPSTAIRS TO CHECK
> 7:48—HELEN TEVORAKIAN COMES DOWNSTAIRS
> 7:48 to 7:50—DISCUSSION IN THE PARTY ABOUT WHAT TO
> DO NEXT
> 7:50—CANDIDA DEWITT GOES UPSTAIRS TO CHECK
> 7:52—HANNAH KREKORIAN STARTS SCREAMING
> 7:52:02—EVERYBODY RUNS UPSTAIRS TO SEE WHAT'S
> GOING ON

Gregor folded the page in his hands. "I'd like to keep this, if the two of you wouldn't mind."

"We made it for you to keep," Helen Tevorakian said.

"It isn't as complete as it might be. I have Hannah over at my apartment, of course, but the doctor's given her a sedative. And I wouldn't have felt right about questioning her."

"I'll talk to Hannah myself later," Gregor said. "Let me just clear up a couple of points here. Mary went upstairs right after Paul Hazzard did."

"That's right. Practically on his heels. Except not quite. If you see what I mean."

"What I'm interested in is what you found when you got there," Gregor said. "Was the door to Hannah's bedroom open?"

"Oh, yes." Mary nodded.

"Where was Hannah?"

"In the bathroom."

"No," Mary said. "The bathroom door was closed. And locked."

"How do you know that?"

"I saw Paul Hazzard try it. He rattled the knob and then he called out to Hannah. To Mrs. Krekorian."

"Did Hannah answer?"

"Not really," Mary Ohanian said. "She was crying, you know. She was totally hysterical. I could hear her."

"All right," Gregor said. "Did Paul Hazzard see you? Or hear you? Did he know you were there?"

"I don't think so, Mr. Demarkian. He never turned around. And Hannah was making a lot of noise."

"All right," Gregor said again. "That's clear enough, I suppose. Helen, let's go to you. You went up later. Why?"

Helen Tevorakian shot him a dry, self-deprecating smile. "*Why* isn't the question here, Krekor. The question is how we all managed the admirable self-restraint it took not to install ourselves outside Hannah's bedroom door the minute after Paul Hazzard ran upstairs. We were all itching to get up there."

Gregor laughed. "Noted. I'll take that as an explanation. You did go up there though. What did you find?"

"Nothing, really," Helen said. "The bedroom door was locked by the time I got there. I couldn't see anything."

"You're sure it was locked."

"Absolutely sure. I tried it myself."

"Then what did you do?"

"I listened. I stood very still outside in the hallway and listened hard."

"What did you hear?"

"Paul Hazzard pacing in the bedroom. Hannah crying. Still behind the bathroom door."

"Can you really be sure about either of those things?"

Helen Tevorakian considered it. "I can be sure about Hannah's crying. It was really very, very muffled. It would have been much clearer if there had been nothing between us but that one bedroom door."

"But you can't be sure about the pacing," Gregor prodded.

"I can be sure I heard somebody walking around in there. That was unmistakable. And Hazzard was in there, Gregor. I remember wondering if he was pacing around like that to keep warm," Helen said. "It was terribly cold in the hall. Frigid."

Gregor played with the piece of paper in his hands and frowned. "Mary, when you came upstairs and saw Paul Hazzard in Hannah's bedroom, was there a window open in that bedroom?"

Mary was alert. "You mean the window that was open later when we found the body? Oh, no, Gregor, it wasn't open when I went up. I could have seen the curtains blowing from where I was standing."

"And you weren't cold?"

"Not in the least. *I* remember thinking it was just like Mrs. Krekorian. She always keeps her rooms too stuffy."

"Is the open window some kind of clue?" Helen asked. "I read a murder mystery once where the murderer tried to change around the time the coroner was going to say the death occurred by putting the body in a refrigerator. Is that something like this?"

"I don't see how it can be," Mary Ohanian said. "When that kind of thing happens in books, it's always meant to change the time of death by hours. Nobody could have done that here. Mrs. Krekorian was in the bathroom. There were dozens of people downstairs. The murderer had to know the body was going to be discovered practically right away."

Helen looked stricken. "I have just been thinking about

the times again. It won't work out, will it, Krekor? That DeWitt woman wouldn't have had time to commit the murder. She would have had only two minutes."

"If your times are right," Gregor agreed, "she wouldn't have had time."

"I don't see how anybody would have had time," Mary Ohanian said. "Even Hannah. They were never alone up there for more than three or four minutes. How long does it take to stab a man six times?"

Actually, Gregor thought, it didn't take very long at all. It could be done in ninety seconds flat if you were fast enough and if you had the right things going for you. The most important thing you had to have going for you was surprise. You had to be someone Paul Hazzard did not expect could, or would, hurt him. You had to be someone with a reason for practically throwing yourself into Paul Hazzard's arms. Unfortunately, Hannah Krekorian fit both those conditions far better than Candida DeWitt did.

Gregor stuck the folded timetable into the inside pocket of his coat.

"I'm going to go over to see Father Tibor," he said. "Are you two going to be around all day if I need you? After the police see this timetable, they may have a few questions I didn't think of."

"I'm going to be around all day," Mary Ohanian said gloomily. "The way my father's behaving, he'll probably chain me in my room."

Helen stood up. "I'm going to go back and take care of Hannah. She needs taking care of. Any minute now, the full force of this is going to hit her, and she's going to have a nervous breakdown."

"I wish I knew why that window was open," Gregor said. "I wish I knew who opened it. Maybe it's time I talked to Hannah Krekorian myself."

"You talked to her last night," Helen Tevorakian said. "That's enough for the time being."

But it wasn't enough for the time being, and Gregor knew it. Every new fact he found was just making matters worse.

*s i x*

*1*

When the flowers came to Lida Arkmanian's house, Hannah Krekorian was sitting on the couch in Helen Tevorakian's living room, looking down on Cavanaugh Street from the living room window. The couch had its back to the window. She had to twist around to see that way. After the second armful of roses went in, she twisted back and stared at Helen's coffee table instead. The coffee table had a stack of books on it (*The Art of Picasso, Gauguin in Tahiti, Florentine Art*) and a big green ceramic frog. The frog reminded Hannah uncomfortably of the game they used to play as children, called Frogs and Princesses. The girls had always been the princesses, of course. The frogs had been the boys who chased them. Hannah couldn't remember if she had been chased much. She couldn't even remember if she had been happy to play. It was all so long ago. Nothing seemed real to her at the moment except Paul Hazzard's body dead on her bedroom carpet and her own dull ache. That was what she had been feeling today, a dull ache. All other emotion had been melted out of her. Paul. The party last night. That *woman*. Hannah was sure she ought to be angry at somebody. It took too much energy. It required a certainty she didn't have.

She twisted around to look at the street again. The street was empty. She turned around again and saw that Helen's heavy teakwood wall clock had advanced another thirty-five minutes. When? While she'd been staring at the street for the second time or while she'd been staring at the coffee table? How? It had been like this all day. It had been impossible.

Hannah got up and made her way to the back of the apartment. Helen's kitchen was covered with Valentine's Day cards from her children and grandchildren. Hannah had a load of cards just like these in her own apartment, which she couldn't get to. They used to pass out cards like that in school on Valentine's Day. There would be a cardboard box covered in crepe paper with a slit at the top, to act as a post office. The cards would be passed out at lunch. Hannah had a distinct memory of sitting in class all Valentine's Day morning, scared to death that when the cards were passed out, not a single one of them would come to her. Later she found out that all the other mothers were just like her own. They made their children send cards to every other child in the class, with no one left out. Hannah didn't know if that made her feel better or worse. She would have been grateful not to have been afraid.

Hannah got a cup out of Helen's china cabinet and put the teakettle on for water. Helen kept a little box of teabags next to the chocolate Ovaltine in her pantry and Hannah got that out too. Hannah didn't know if she wanted a cup of tea, but getting one was something to do. She wished she'd had the courage to go down to the Ararat this morning. She wished she knew what people were thinking. Most of all, she wished she knew if people were laughing at her. She wouldn't blame them if they were. Paul Hazzard, for heaven's sake. What had she been thinking of?

There was the scratchy sound of a key in a lock and then the whoosh of an opening door. Helen Tevorakian's voice sailed through the apartment. "She's around here someplace, Krekor," Helen said. "The only thing I worry about is that she might be sleeping."

The teakettle was spitting water and air. Hannah took it off the flame and poured boiling water into her teacup. She heard the front door close and said, "I'm not sleeping, Helen. I'm in here."

"She's in the kitchen," Helen said irrelevantly. "Come this way, Krekor. I don't know if you've ever been in this apartment."

Hannah didn't know if Gregor had ever been in this apartment either, but it hardly seemed to matter. She turned off the stove and sat down in front of her tea. She put a single spare teaspoon of sugar in it and waited for them to come in. Only Gregor entered. He was wearing his heaviest long coat and his longest scarf. He looked cold.

"Where's Helen?" she asked him.

"Helen's gone off someplace to do her laundry. She's trying to give us a little privacy."

"Did you ask her to?"

"Yes."

"Helen's very good at taking directions. Do you remember? She used to get ribbons for it when we were all in school."

"Mmm. I was just over at Father Tibor's apartment. He wasn't home."

"He went to lunch with somebody. Some young woman. I heard Helen talking to Sheila Kashinian about it on the phone. He'll be back around five-thirty or so. He promised."

"Good." Gregor unwound his scarf and draped it over the back of a chair. He took off his coat and threw that over the back of another chair. Hannah appraised him dispassionately. It was different for boys, she knew that. With girls, it was what you looked like and that was it. Unless you had a fairy godmother or the money for a good plastic surgeon, girls were born blessed or cursed. Boys could change everything with what they did. Gregor had not been considered especially attractive in grammar school or high school. As soon as he'd gone off to the University of Pennsylvania, all that had changed. As soon as he'd graduated, he'd become a catch. All the girls on Cavanaugh Street had wanted to go out with him.

Gregor sat down in the chair with the scarf on the back of it. "What's the matter?" he asked. "You're staring at me. Do I have my shirt on inside out?"

"No, Krekor. I was just thinking about us. You and me and Lida and the rest of us. When we were in high school."

"Were you? I try not to."

"It's all I seem to think about these days. Not just—not just since Paul died, you know, but from before. From when I first met him. It doesn't seem possible that that was only a week ago."

"I think I'll get myself something to drink."

Gregor got up, found hot water, found a cup, found a spoon, looked for coffee, and settled for one of the teabags instead. He put a cup of tea together and sat down again.

"Well," he said. "Here we are. Are you feeling all right?"

"Yes, Krekor. I am all right. Are the police going to arrest me?"

Gregor stirred uneasily. "I don't know."

"I keep expecting them to," Hannah said. "It only makes sense. There I was, standing over the body with a smoking gun. So to speak."

"Yes, I know, Hannah. But these things are more complicated than that."

"And you know I didn't kill him."

"I believe you when you say you didn't kill him."

"Yes." Hannah nodded. "There is a distinction there, and you ought to make it. But I didn't kill him."

Gregor took his teabag out of his cup, tasted the tea, made a face, and reached for the sugar. "Let's start further back now, to about the time you ran upstairs. You ran upstairs because the things Candida DeWitt was saying made you upset—"

"I ran upstairs because the existence of Candida De-Witt made me look like a damn fool," Hannah corrected him. "Excuse my language, Krekor, but I can't help it. I am very good at self-delusion, but even I have to quit sometimes."

"What do you mean by self-delusion?"

"I mean that I still don't know what Paul Hazzard wanted out of me, but whatever it was, it wasn't my *self*. He was not the kind of man who would be attracted to a woman like me. He didn't have to compromise. He could have Candida DeWitt."

"He doesn't seem to have wanted Candida DeWitt," Gregor pointed out.

Hannah waved this away. "He could have had a woman like Candida DeWitt. He could have had someone young. Do you know what my theory is?"

"What?"

"After the murder of his wife, Paul's business went downhill. That is common knowledge, Krekor, we don't have to speculate about that. He needed money but he had trouble finding women with money to marry him, because they did not want to put themselves in the same position as the wife who died. And I have money, Krekor. Not millions and millions and millions of dollars, but enough. All five of my sons pitched in together to make me a portfolio ten years ago, and they have managed it very well."

"Well," Gregor said, "that's a thought. But I think you're being a little too hard on yourself. You have a lot more to offer than your portfolio."

"Possibly, Krekor, yes. But not to a man. Not for romantic purposes."

Gregor started to protest, then looked away. Hannah smiled grimly. Oh, she had been right to be upset last night. She had been right. She had been making such a spectacularly *public* fool of herself.

Gregor cleared his throat. "All right, now. Let's go back to the point when you ran upstairs. Did you go straight to the bedroom?"

"I went straight to the master bathroom."

"You didn't stop anywhere along the way? You didn't take any detours? You didn't throw yourself on your bed or look in your closet or anything else like that?"

"No."

"Okay. Now, try to remember. When you went into your bedroom, were either of the windows open?"

"The windows?" Hannah drew a blank. "Of course they weren't open, Krekor. It's February. It's below zero outside at night."

"But you didn't check to see if either of the windows was open?"

"No, I didn't check, Krekor, but if one of them was, I didn't open it. You are being ridiculous."

Gregor shifted in his chair. "Let's try it from another angle," he said. "Did you at any time feel cold? When you first got up to the second floor? As you were crossing to the bathroom? Were you cold at all? Did you feel a breeze?"

"No, Krekor."

"Would it have been possible for you to take that route with the window closest to the bathroom wide open without your noticing either that it was open or that it was cold?"

"I don't know, Krekor. I was very upset."

"And you were crying," Gregor said.

"That's right."

"You were crying very loudly."

"Very loudly."

"Were you aware of it when Paul Hazzard came into the bedroom?"

"I don't know when he came into the bedroom, Krekor, but he did knock on my bathroom door. I assume it was when he first came in. I had not been in the bathroom long."

"You had the door locked?"

"Oh, yes."

"What did he say to you when he knocked on the door?"

Hannah thought it over carefully. "He called out my name," she said, "and then he asked me to talk to him and then he asked me to please come out."

"But you didn't do either of those things."

"Oh, no." Hannah shook her head. "I was crying too hard and I didn't have anything to say. And I looked awful. I always look awful when I cry."

"Did he go on trying to persuade you?"

"No, Krekor, he did not. He said only that he was going to stay right there in the bedroom until I came out, and then he started walking back and forth."

"You could hear that?"

"It was right outside the door, Krekor. It was very close. And I was listening for it, if you know what I mean."

Gregor had finished his tea. He stood up and put his cup in the sink.

"Did you hear anything else? Did you hear Mary Ohanian come upstairs?"

"No."

"Or Helen Tevorakian?"

"No."

"Did you hear anybody at all come into the room? Or the sound of the bedroom door closing?"

"No, Krekor, but you have to understand. I was crying. I was wailing. I was having what Bennis would call a 'world-class emotional binge.' "

"But you did come out eventually," Gregor said, leaning with his back against the counter. "Was the emotional binge over? Had you decided you wanted to talk to him?"

"No, Krekor, none of those things. I thought he had gone away." She paused and thought about it. "Because the sounds of the moving stopped. First he walked faster. And then he just stopped. I couldn't hear him moving out there at all anymore."

"And that was it," Gregor said. "You couldn't hear him moving. You didn't actually hear anything else."

Hannah shuddered. "He must have been dead, Krekor. I understand that now. But I didn't hear any of the things you might think I should have. I didn't hear him fall—or if I did, I just thought it was more of his pacing. I did hear him—well, I thought he was swearing under his breath. It was hard to tell."

"When was this?"

"Just about the time he stopped pacing. You see, Krekor, that was another reason I thought he'd gone. It all fit in. He got tired of waiting for me to come to my senses. He got angry. He swore a little under his breath and then he went."

"You couldn't make out what he said?"

"No, Krekor. It didn't sound like words at all. It sounded more like a moan."

Gregor Demarkian seemed to start, and Hannah looked at him curiously. What an odd thing for him to take so strongly, she thought.

"Is that all you wanted to know?" she asked him. "I'm afraid I can't tell you very much. I was right there and I should know, but I don't."

"One last thing," Gregor told her. "When you came out of the bathroom. What did you do?"

"I opened the door and I looked out. I couldn't see him anywhere. I walked out into the middle of the bedroom and then—"

"Stop. Before you get to 'and then.' Can you remember whether the bedroom door was open or closed?"

"It was closed, Krekor. I looked there first thing when I came out. In case he was just leaving or he was standing on the landing where he could see me."

"I don't suppose you can remember whether you closed the bedroom door when you first came into the bedroom?"

"No, Krekor, I can't remember. I don't think I did."

"Never mind. Go back to the 'and then.' "

Hannah took a deep breath. "Well," she said, "I walked out into the bedroom, and I nearly tripped over him. I remember that. It is all very fuzzy, Krekor, I am sorry, I think I went into some kind of shock. He was lying there on the carpet and there was blood everywhere, just everywhere. And I dropped to my knees and I grabbed—I grabbed that thing—"

"The dagger? Where was it? Was it in the body?"

"It was on the floor in a pool of blood. I could never have taken it out of the body. I grabbed the—the dagger— and then I realized I was cold, so cold, and somewhere in there I started screaming and screaming and in the back of my mind I kept telling myself I had to do something about it. I had to get downstairs and call you or call the police or call an ambulance or something and in the middle of it all I stood up, and she was standing in the doorway to the bedroom with a very odd look on her face."

"By 'her' you mean Candida DeWitt?"

"Yes."

"She was looking at you and she had an odd look on her face?"

"No, Krekor. I don't think she was looking at me."

"She was looking at Paul Hazzard?"

Hannah shook her head. "She was looking over my right shoulder, I think. She was maybe staring into space. I am not doing very well with this, Krekor, but I am doing the best I can."

"You're doing fine," Gregor assured her.

Hannah looked into the bottom of her teacup. "I wish I understood things better . . . . Not just what happened last night, but life. I wish I understood why things are."

"Mmm," Gregor said noncommittally.

Hannah got up and put her own teacup in the sink. Really, it was useless to try to explain things to men.

They never understood anything.

## 2

At the time that Jacqueline Isherwood Hazzard died, Alyssa Hazzard Roderick's only real interest in her will was insofar as it went to prove that Paul didn't have a motive to murder her. That the will was set up in such a way as to pass the bulk of Jacqueline's estate to Paul Hazzard's children when Paul Hazzard died had been explained to her, but Alyssa hadn't seen the point in paying attention to it. After all, Paul was a relatively young man, and a healthy one. He worked out and ate tofu and never touched more than a glass of wine after dinner. Alyssa thought Paul was going to live to be at least a hundred and three. He was going to live much longer than she would, because she was going to be done in by her love of chocolate-chip cookies. Caroline always said Alyssa had an addiction to chocolate-chip cookies. That was the only explanation Caroline could find for why Alyssa would eat them first thing in the morning, sitting up in bed.

It wasn't first thing in the morning and Alyssa wasn't sitting up in bed. It was four o'clock on Saturday afternoon, the day after her father's murder. Alyssa was not sure this was a very good time to do what she wanted to do. Caroline was still sitting downstairs in the living room, working. James was out—but out where? And for how long? Then there was Nicholas to consider. Nicholas was at his club for the afternoon, playing backgammon. How long he stayed depended on whether he won or lost.

Alyssa had no idea why she wanted to hide this little

excursion from her husband, or why she wanted to hide it from anybody else. She just did. She just wanted to go off and get a little piece of private information for herself, on her own, just this once. She'd tell Nicholas all about it later. She really would. She'd tell James and Caroline too, if she had to. Honestly, it wasn't as if she didn't have a right to do what she was going to do. It was just that she wanted to do it on her own and without . . . fuss.

There was a door on the back staircase that led directly from the apartment Alyssa and Nicholas kept on the top floor to the rest of the house. It was never locked. Alyssa never locked it from her side because she didn't see any reason to. Caroline and Paul and James didn't lock it from theirs because they were pretending to be a really close, really involved family unit. At least, that was what Alyssa thought was going on. It was hard to get things straight with people like Caroline and Paul. They talked such fluent recovery that you could never figure out what they were trying to mean, if anything. Alyssa much preferred James. James might pretend to believe in crystals and powders and potions, but he didn't really believe in them, and if you called him on it, he would say so.

Alyssa let herself into the main house and went down the fourth floor corridor to the main stairs. There were several big bedrooms on this floor, but only one of them—Caroline's—was occupied. Alyssa looked in there for a moment, but without much interest. The look of Caroline's bedroom always mirrored the state of her immortal soul. This time it was neat to the point of being antiseptic and as lacking in personality as a room at the Holiday Inn. Obviously, Caroline's soul was being anal this month. Alyssa checked out the necklaces hanging on the jewelry tree—Caroline's inner child had a positive passion for jade—and decided she didn't like any of them. She left the room and went downstairs to the third floor.

The third floor was much more interesting than the fourth floor. Both James and Paul had rooms on it, and there was also a small sitting room James had turned into a kind of museum. This was where he kept the bits and pieces of his trade that had gone out of fashion. This was where he piled up now-useless copper bracelets and discarded pyramids, smooth stones for aid in trance channeling and packets of herbs meant to scent away your psychic pain. Lately, crystals had been finding their way into the collection, first a few, then more and more. Crystals must be about to become passé. What would they be replaced by, Alyssa wondered. Just when you thought the New Age had gotten as silly as it could get—just when you were sure people couldn't get any stupider than they had already been—people like James came up with something new.

Alyssa gave the museum a quick look-over—nothing new there—and then glanced into James's room, just to make sure he wasn't there. Then she went into Paul's room and sat down on the bed. The room was unnaturally clean today. Paul himself had never kept it this neat. Today it had been put back together again by the pair of policemen who had come to take it apart. They had been trained in dustless surfaces and hospital corners.

"Yes?" Caroline's voice suddenly shot up the stairs, sharp and angry. "Yes? Is there somebody up there?"

Alyssa got off the bed and went into the hall. "Caroline? It's just me. I was on my way downstairs to see you."

"You didn't sound as if you were on your way downstairs." Caroline was still on the first floor. Alyssa could tell by the way her voice sounded. It was a relief.

"I stopped in to look at James's museum," Alyssa said. "He seems to be on the verge of giving up crystals."

"You should have called down to me," Caroline told her sharply. "You scared me half to death. I thought you were a thief at least."

Any thief with half a brain in his head would come in on the first floor, in the back, where the kitchen was. That was the easy way.

"I'll be there in a second, Caroline. I just want to use the bathroom."

"I'm going to go back to work," Caroline said. "I hate being interrupted."

If you didn't want to be interrupted, you'd have gone to work in the studio, Alyssa thought. She didn't say it because she didn't want to bring on the lecture on hidden motives and the imperatives of the undiscovered self she was sure it would bring on. Instead, she waited for the sound of Caroline moving away from the stairs. Then she went back into Paul's room. I'd better be fast, she thought now.

She went over to Paul's shoe tree and tilted it sideways. She hadn't told the police about this, and as far as she knew, neither had James or Caroline. Why should they? The three of them had all been through this kind of thing before. The three of them all knew better than to "cooperate" with the police, because cooperation always turned into collaboration and got you in trouble. The three of them hadn't needed to make a pact to say as little as possible. It came to them naturally.

She laid the shoe tree sideways on the floor and pried open the rounded leather bottom of it. She came away with a stack of papers and four heavy gold cuff links. She recognized the cuff links as gifts from Paul's friend, Mrs. Charlow, the silly old cow he had known in Vermont. She put the cuff links aside and went through the papers. There was the deed to this house. There was the number of Paul's Swiss account, with the word "closed" written across it. There was a packet of miscellaneous necessities tied with string: Paul's birth certificate, Paul's baptismal certificate, Paul's old passports. Paul had had a perfectly good safety deposit box in a bank in downtown Philadelphia, but he never seemed to use it. Alyssa couldn't fathom why he kept half the things he kept.

What she was looking for was just under the pile of miscellaneous nonsense. It was in a plain manila envelope folded over twice, but it was clearly marked: JACKIE'S WILL. Alyssa knew it wasn't really Jackie's will. Jackie's will was with Jackie's lawyers. This was just a photocopy. It would do.

She tucked the manila envelope under the waistband of her skirt and pulled her sweater down over it. Then she put the shoe tree back together and stood it up. The bathroom was right across the hall. She went in there and flushed the toilet and ran the water in the sink.

"Caroline?" she called, coming back out into the hall. "I'm on my way."

Caroline didn't answer. Alyssa thought it was a very good sign.

Alyssa thought it was a very good thing that Caroline never paid any attention to anybody but herself.

## *seven*

### *1*

Sonia Veladian was a round-faced, slightly plump, cheerful young woman who looked vaguely familiar, and for a moment or two after Gregor Demarkian opened his apartment door to her he couldn't remember who she was. It was quarter to six in the evening. Before his doorbell rang, he had been sitting at his kitchen table, going over the timetable Mary and Helen had made out for him and worrying over the things Hannah had told him. He had also been eating, but feeling very guilty about it. He had not been eating well. Just an hour before, Donna Moradanyan had emerged from her unprecedented holiday funk to bring him a heart-shaped chocolate layer cake with strawberries in syrup all over the top of it and real whipped cream in the middle. If Bennis had seen it, she would have delivered the lecture to end all lectures on The Virtues of Green Vegetables and The Necessities of Watching What You Ate Once You Got Older. It was Gregor's contention that he did watch what he ate. He watched his bacon and eggs. He watched his pepperoni pizzas and his three-inch-thick prime ribs and his *yaprak sarma*. He was keeping an especially close eye on this cake. It was too bad that that wasn't the sort of thing Bennis wanted him to do.

"I like that police officer they have," Donna Moradanyan told him. "The one who's supposed to be in charge of the case but isn't really, because your friend is."

This took a while to work out. Finally, Gregor said, "Oh. You mean Russell Donahue."

Donna nodded. "He seemed very intelligent. And nice too. Not as if he were the kind of person who would—hound Hannah or anything."

Gregor had wanted to tell her that it was hardly a case of anyone hounding Hannah, but he hadn't had time. Donna had said something about not wanting to leave Tommy alone so long and ran back upstairs. Gregor had retreated to his kitchen and his timetable and a decent knife and fork. He had just written three very important lines at the top of his legal pad, when his doorbell rang.

7:00 to 7:05—SHEILA KASHINIAN HEARS MOAN FROM
SECOND FLOOR
7:48 (or so)—HANNAH KREKORIAN HEARS MOAN FROM
OUTSIDE MASTER BATHROOM DOOR

CONNECT.

There was a connection. He even knew what that connection was. He just had to figure out what to do with it. The doorbell rang and he put down his pen and went into the foyer.

"Hello," the young woman said when Gregor opened up. "I'm Sonia Veladian."

"Sonia Veladian?"

"Father Tibor sent me," Sonia said helpfully. "I'm the one who—ah—went to this workshop that Paul Hazzard's organization ran and Father Tibor said you might want to know—"

"Oh, yes." Gregor backed up quickly to let the young woman inside. "I do want to know. I'm sorry. I just didn't connect for a moment. I thought Father Tibor said you were in Somalia."

"With UNICEF. I was. We were evacuated out about five weeks ago. I've been in Rome."

"And now you're back."

"Visiting my mother," Sonia amplified. She walked into Gregor's living room, dropped down into the club chair, and laughed. "My mother's a mess. She's on husband number five. She's over sixty and she still can't balance her checkbook. If it weren't for my brother and me, she'd probably be on welfare. But she means well."

Gregor didn't go into how many murderers he'd known who insisted that no matter what they did, they always meant well. "Would you like me to get you a cup of coffee?" he offered her. "I only have instant, but in this apartment that's a blessing.'"

"That's okay. I took Father Tibor to lunch. I love to overeat, but this afternoon was too much even for me. Father Tibor said Paul Hazzard was killed here last night."

"That's right."

"I've got to start reading the papers again," Sonia said. "I stopped just after we were evacuated because it was all just too depressing. Well, I suppose I'm not surprised. I remember thinking at the time that he was just the kind of person to get his head bashed in. Father Tibor said Mrs. Krekorian is the prime suspect. That can't be right, can it?"

"I'm afraid it is."

"Well, that's just nonsense," Sonia said crisply. "I've known Mrs. Krekorian all my life. She used to feed my brother and me when Mom would disappear for a couple of days. Her and Mrs. Arkmanian. Does Mrs. Arkmanian still live in the neighborhood?"

"She's got the town house right across the street."

"Dynamite. I suppose you really want to hear about Paul Hazzard. You're investigating the murder. I do see *People* magazine every once in a while."

"I think the less said about *People* magazine the better," Gregor said firmly. "I don't want you to tell me anything that's going to be painful for you to discuss. Not unless you think it has immediate and direct importance in the case under consideration. I don't want you to feel—"

"It's okay," Sonia said. "It really is. I don't mind talking about it at all anymore. Talking about what happened to me, I mean. And you don't even want to know what happened to me. You want to know what I know about Paul Hazzard. Well. Okay. The way it started was, when I was about eleven years old, my mother got this boyfriend, his name was Ern, and Ern had these proclivities. He used to come into my room at night, and do things—if you don't mind, I'm not going to go into specifics here, they don't matter at the moment—and he would tell me that if I told my mother, he would kill us both and I was scared to death and that was how it went on for about six months, when one afternoon my mother came home early because she'd gotten fired from this job she had at a restaurant and there we were. And she blew a fit."

"I can imagine."

"Don't. You have no idea how many mothers in this sort of situation pretend they haven't seen anything. It's like I said. My mother means well. Anyway, there was no end of fuss. Mom threw Ern out, she called the police, she took me to a doctor, there was an investigation. On and on and on. And then it just went away. I just forgot about it. Except that I didn't, of course."

"Of course."

"Mrs. Krekorian and Mrs. Arkmanian were a big help," Sonia said. "And I was good at school and my mother was proud of that, so I worked my butt off and did really well. Then I won a merit scholarship and another scholarship one of the Armenian-American organizations offers and another one, too, for winning second place in a competition this company gave where you had to write an essay on the wonderful things chemistry does for people's lives. And I went to Penn State. And I had a 3.9 grade average right through the first semester of my junior year. And then I fell apart."

"What do you mean, fell apart?"

"Just what I said," Sonia said impassively. "I couldn't sleep. I couldn't eat. I couldn't work. I couldn't think. I failed three courses and pulled Ds in the other two."

"And?"

"And I got lucky. This was, what, at least ten years ago now. It was well before there was all this interest in the sexual abuse of children and adolescents. Nobody knew anything and nobody was doing much of anything except a few people in the self-help field like Paul Hazzard. But my adviser liked me and knew me and he was convinced that I couldn't have had such a terrible semester without something equally terrible happening to me, so he took me out and grilled me until I just started talking about it. And talking about it and talking about it." Sonia laughed. "You'd be amazed what you forget. And the emotions. You know, I honestly thought I didn't feel anything at all about it anymore. And there I was, sitting in this beer bar with peanut shells and sawdust on the floor, getting completely hysterical."

"I hope your adviser kept his head," Gregor said.

"He was cool. He still is. We write. Anyway, at that point we had a problem, because I didn't want to go to individual counseling. The idea of sitting in a little room with just one other person made my skin crawl. Also the campus mental health center at the time was stocked full of Freudians, and you know what that means. You tell them you've been molested as a child, and they tell you it's all in your head."

"So what did you do?"

"Nothing, for a while," Sonia said. "I was a little better just because I'd talked about it and it was out in the open. I was still falling apart, but at least I knew why. Then my adviser came across an article in *The New York Times*—it must have been the Sunday edition, he got the *Times* only on Sunday—about the self-help movement. It had a lot of stuff about Paul Hazzard, and it also had a paragraph about how people like Hazzard were approaching reports of childhood molestation differently from traditional therapists. And it had a phone number."

"So you called," Gregor said.

"I called. There wasn't anything down in State College I could hook up with at the time. Five years later, that town was the state capital of self-help workshops, but not then. There was a group in Philadelphia. I arranged to attend that."

"Father Tibor told me it helped and it didn't."

"It helped in the beginning." Sonia was emphatic. "It helped a lot in the beginning. Look, Mr. Demarkian. People come out of cases like this in all sorts of shape. My own case was relatively easy. The incidents happened, but they weren't of very long duration. Some children suffer through years. My mother was on my side and she took direct and unambiguous action. Some children live through their mothers' deliberate blindness or accusations that the abuse was all their fault or I don't know what else. So you see, all I really needed was a chance to talk about it for a while and work it out of my system and to feel bad and not have to apologize for it. The worst part about being the way I was then is that you want to talk about it and talk about it and talk about it and eventually people just get bored. Even if you don't."

"I can see that," Gregor said. "So what went wrong?"

"It's not so much that anything went wrong, as that nothing really happened. I went to Group every week, and I talked and listened to other people talk, and I began to feel better. I began to feel a lot better. My grades went back to normal. I was sleeping. I had a boyfriend that I'd told all about everything and relations between us were good. And nothing changed."

"In the group, you mean," Gregor said.

"That's right. The thing was, nothing was supposed to change. I hadn't paid much attention to psychological theories when I signed up. I was going crazy. But as I began to get better, I began to notice things. Such as the fact that you weren't supposed to get better. Not really."

"I don't understand."

Sonia made a wry little face. "The theory was, once something like this happened to you, it would be with you the rest of your life. You'd never be free of it. You'd need Group all the time and forever, for as long as you lived. It made me angry. It seemed to me to be saying that the son of a bitch had won. He set out to destroy you and he did destroy you, because you'd never really be you again. You'd always be sick."

"I take it there was more."

"Oh, yeah." Sonia nodded vigorously. "If it had been just that, I would have quit and that would have been the end of it. What kept me in and fighting were the amnesiacs."

"Amnesiacs?"

"Well," Sonia said, "you see, it's like this. Some people who have been sexually exploited as children don't remember that they've been sexually exploited as children. The experience is so horrible, they just repress it."

"I think that's understandable."

"Of course it is," Sonia went on. "The problem is, the

group I was in—all of Paul Hazzard's organization, as far as I could tell—well, they used that fact to their own advantage. I can't put it any other way. Yes, it's true that there are people walking around out there who were abused as children and don't remember it, but the group had a twenty-two-point checklist you were supposed to complete if you thought you had been abused but couldn't remember, and if you came up with yes answers to three or more items on the list, then you were supposed to join a group because you probably had been abused. Let me give you three of the items that were on that list. 'You always think before you speak.' 'You feel a great need to take care of other people and comfort them.' 'You often have trouble getting to sleep.' "

"But—" Gregor said.

"Exactly." Sonia moved to the edge of her seat. "Don't you see? There's nothing in the least pathological about thinking before you speak. Practically every mother on earth feels the need to take care of her children and comfort them. And as for having trouble going to sleep—" Sonia shrugged. "These are disturbed people we're dealing with here. There are a million and one reasons they might have trouble getting to sleep, including drinking too much coffee. You could have all three of those 'symptoms' and not be disturbed in any way at all. But there was more to it than that. There were the other groups."

"That's right," Gregor said. "Paul Hazzard ran a variety. I heard that."

"Shopaholics. Compulsive gamblers. Codependents. Love addicts." Sonia counted off on her fingers. "The groups were held in this big building in downtown Philadelphia, sometimes six or seven different ones on the same night. One night I went around to all the groups and collected their pamphlets. They all had checklists. And guess what?"

"What?"

"The checklists were pretty much identical. Oh, there would be one or two particular items. The compulsive gamblers' list included things like borrowing money to gamble or play the lottery. But mostly the lists were just repetitions. It didn't matter if you were a shopaholic or a love addict or a codependent or a compulsive gambler or a survivor of childhood sexual abuse, the symptoms were all the same. The only thing that determined what kind of sick you ended up calling yourself was what group you wandered into. It was a terrible thing, Mr. Demarkian. These were people in terrible pain. They might not have been sexually abused as children, but they were in terrible pain. In the codependents and the shopaholics, you sometimes just got narcissistic jerks, but with us you got very damaged people. And I didn't see what good it was going to do them to spin them a fantasy about what was supposed to be wrong with them and then keep them locked up in an identity marked 'sick' for the rest of their lives. So I came to a decision."

Gregor Demarkian coughed. "Father Tibor has a great deal of respect for you," he said carefully. "Why does that make me feel that this decision of yours was probably rather . . . extreme?"

Sonia giggled. "I don't know if it was extreme, Mr. Demarkian, but it sure as hell was expensive. This is my senior year in college we're talking about here, remember, and my people don't have any money. Paul Hazzard gave workshops that he ran personally, but they cost over a thousand dollars for a weekend. I didn't have a thousand dollars. So I borrowed it."

"To go to one of these workshops."

"To get myself into a position where I could challenge Paul Hazzard in person," Sonia corrected him. "It took a month and a half to come up with the money, but I did it. It was held in this conference center out on the Main Line. You should have seen this place. It had marble floors in all the bathrooms."

"Did you get to challenge him?"

"Oh, yes," Sonia said. "It was a weekend for survivors of childhood sexual abuse. I came with all the pamphlets and the checklists. As soon as any session I was in was open for audience participation, I started asking questions. I asked a lot of questions. I got a lot of people mad at me. The people who attend these groups don't want to hear that there's anything wrong with them. Not if they've been going for a while. They've got too much of their identities wrapped up in the process."

"Was Paul Hazzard angry with you?"

"Paul Hazzard was thoroughly professional," Sonia told him. "At least, he was in public. Very smooth. Very slick. He had to be. But we weren't always in public."

"Oh?"

Sonia pulled her legs up onto the chair and wrapped her arms around her knees. "The second day, there was a very nasty session right before lunch. I had to interrupt other people to speak, because Paul Hazzard just refused to recognize me. It got very tight there for a while. When it was over, I went to the ladies' room. When I came out of the ladies' room I saw Paul Hazzard standing a little farther down the hall, near a door I thought was probably the men's room. It wasn't. There was another corridor just like the one where the ladies' room was, only on the other side of the building, and the men's room was there. Anyway, Paul Hazzard saw me and motioned me over to him, and I went. I had to have been a good two feet away from him when he reached out and grabbed me."

"*Grabbed* you?"

"By the waist," Sonia said. "He pushed me through the door I'd thought was the men's room. It turned out to be some kind of utility closet. He pulled the door shut behind him and it was absolutely dark in there. And all the time he's got both his hands around my waist and he's shaking me. I was too surprised to scream. Then he slammed me against the wall and grabbed my breasts. Hard and tight. It hurt."

"Good Lord."

"And then he started talking to me," Sonia said, "and it was weird, Mr. Demarkian, because he wasn't angry at me, he wasn't shouting, he wasn't sharp, he was using that same low, lulling voice he always used, the same one he used to talk about giving yourself unconditional love and nurturing your inner child. He was even using the same kinds of words. He was saying I was in denial and that my denial was manifesting itself as a problem with authority and that I was afraid to accept love and understanding. It just went on and on and on like that, and the whole time he was talking he had hold of my breasts and he was not being gentle or seductive or anything else of the kind. He was digging his fingers into me. The pain was incredible. I tried to kick him once or twice, but he was too fast for me. I called him a son of a bitch and he told me that just went to show that he was right. I was exhibiting inappropriate anger. I was still furious with my abuser, but I didn't think it was safe to get angry at Ern so I was getting angry at him instead. At Paul Hazzard. It was insane."

"It sounds worse than insane. How did you get out of there? Did he let you go?"

Sonia shook her head. "I don't know if he ever would have let me go. That's silly, of course. Eventually he would have had to. I guess I mean the situation was beginning to feel eternal, and I was getting more and more scared, and I didn't really know what to do."

"Did you call out?"

"I think I did call out," Sonia said. "I know I must have been shouting, because after it was all over, my throat hurt. I suppose nobody heard me. Maybe everybody was down at lunch."

"Maybe nobody wanted to hear."

"I thought of that too," Sonia said. "Anyway, Paul Hazzard went on and on and on and I kept twisting and turning and trying to wrench myself away from him and all of a sudden it worked. Do you know how that is? His strength must have flagged for just a minute and mine must have had an upsurge and his hold just broke."

"I know how that is."

"Well, I ran for it," Sonia said. "I lurched into the dark in the direction I thought we'd come in, right past Hazzard's body, and I made it. I fell into some debris. Cans of stuff. I couldn't see what they were. I kept stumbling around into things and he kept grabbing me and laughing and I got more and more frantic by the minute, but all of a sudden it was all right. I found the door."

"And you got out."

"You bet," Sonia said. "I went flying out of that closet like Rocket J. Squirrel being launched by Bullwinkle. You've never seen anybody move so fast. I got out into the hall and it was empty. I couldn't see anybody anywhere. I just took off. The corridor was off this big open reception space with couches and plants and things in it. I headed for there."

"Did Hazzard follow you?"

"I don't know, Mr. Demarkian. I didn't look back to check. I just ran."

"And then what did you do?"

"I went back to my room. I packed my things. I called a cab. And I left."

"You didn't report this to anybody? You didn't tell anybody that it had happened?"

"I told my boyfriend when I got back to school," Sonia said, "but if you mean did I report it to the police or something, no. I don't think I would have known whom to report it to."

"You could have charged the man with assault."

"Maybe. But look at it realistically, Mr. Demarkian. Who was I? Just a screwed-up college senior who had been in therapy for nearly a year. Just one more hysterical woman with mental problems. Paul Hazzard was one of the most successful and respected psychologists in the United States. And there had never been a report like that made against him before."

"You could have charged him with assault," Gregor repeated. Then he sighed and shifted on his feet. He had been standing up the whole time Sonia was telling her story. He had been too interested to notice that he was uncomfortable. Now he rocked back and forth and bent his knees. They creaked. "Paul Hazzard," he said, "is rapidly turning into one of those murder victims you feel it's just as well that they're dead. He's headed straight for that category of murder victims that I would just as soon have killed myself. Is that the only time you ever saw him? The first and the last?"

"You bet," Sonia said. "It was the first and I made a point of it being the last. There's all this stuff in the recovery movement about how victims cling to being victims. After you've been victimized, you're supposed to go looking for people to victimize you because that's the kind of relationship you're comfortable with. Well, maybe I never really fit the profile. I not only never saw Paul Hazzard again, I never had anything else to do with his organization. Or with the recovery movement in any form. After that afternoon I never even went back to Group."

Just then Gregor's phone started ringing. He had instruments in the kitchen and the bedroom, and the ringing came to him in stereo.

"Just a minute," he told Sonia. "I'm supposed to be going someplace at six-thirty. That may be the man who's picking me up."

"Take your time," Sonia said.

## 2

Gregor went out into the kitchen and picked up the phone. He looked at the dishes in his sink and the cake on his table and wished he were better at housekeeping. He said hello into the receiver and thought about Sonia Veladian. Gregor didn't know much about psychology in spite of the fact that the department he had founded and headed at the FBI had been called Behavioral Sciences. He hadn't given the department its name. He knew how the minds of serial killers worked. He knew whether the serial killer involved was an out-of-control psychotic or the kind of otherwise sane man whose tastes ran to the violent. He also knew something about the mental life of the people he called acculturated psychopaths—the people who had no more conscience than a Ted Bundy or a Jeffrey Dahmer, but who had sense enough not to actually kill anybody. They just went along, taking what they wanted no matter what effect it had on other people. Maybe that was what the recovery movement meant by "getting your needs met."

On the other end of the line, Russell Donahue's voice sounded strangled. "Mr. Demarkian? Is that you? Can you hear me?"

Gregor came to. "Yes, Russ. Yes. It's me. I'm sorry. My mind was wandering. I take it you're going to be late."

"I'm going to be right on time," Russell Donahue said. "I'm headed your way in a patrol car with all the sirens blasting. We've got an emergency."

"What's an emergency?" Gregor asked.

"Twenty minutes ago Fred Scherrer called the Bryn Mawr police. He reported finding the body of Candida De-Witt, stabbed in the chest and lying dead on the floor of her own living room."

There was a high kitchen stool against the wall next to the telephone. Gregor sat down on it with a thump, stunned.

"Good God," he said. "*Now* what?"

"Now we start all over again from the beginning," Russell Donahue said, "and I get off this goddamned cellular phone and pick you up. See you in a minute or two."

"Right," Gregor said.

He said it to dead air.

*part three*

———

*cloaks
and daggers...*

*o n e*

*1*

People who lived in the Philadelphia metropolitan area tended to think of the city and the Main Line as one place. In spite of the differences in landscape and architecture and social tone, the Main Line *belonged* to Philadelphia, and everyone knew it. Away at boarding school and college, teenagers from Radnor and Wayne said simply that they were "from Philadelphia," and got into the particulars only with people they knew really well. Very social brides announcing their weddings in the *Inquirer* and *The New York Times* said that they were the daughters of "Mr. and Mrs. Whomever of Philadelphia and Palm Beach" in spite of the fact that the houses they had grown up in were nestled into fifteen acres in Paoli. In reality, of course, the towns of the Main Line had very little to do with each other and nothing at all to do with the city of Philadelphia, at least in any official capacity. Radnor had its own police department. Bryn Mawr had its own police department. Philadelphia had its own police department. All the police departments cooperated if they really had to. They preferred not to. There was a streak of competitive jealousy running through their relations as bright and strong as a splash of fresh blood on a white cotton curtain in an English murder mystery.

Candida DeWitt had lived in Bryn Mawr and now she had died there. She had also been one of the chief suspects in a murder case in Philadelphia. She had also been killed in a way that made everyone—even the Bryn Mawr police—certain that she had been murdered by the same person who had murdered Paul Hazzard. Then there was her connection to the death of Jacqueline Isherwood Hazzard. Then there was—

Gregor Demarkian tried to remain calm in the front seat of Russell Donahue's car as it pulled into Candida DeWitt's driveway and coasted down the gravel to the other cars assembled at Candida's front door. It was an unmarked car this time. Russell hadn't thought it was the best idea to come into somebody else's jurisdiction with sirens blasting. Down by the door there were plenty of marked cars with their lights pulsing in the darkening evening. Bryn Mawr had pulled out all the stops.

Russell Donahue slowed to a crawl, looking for a place to park.

"For God's sake. They've got the whole department out here. You'd think somebody had shot the president."

"Fred Scherrer," Gregor suggested.

Russell nodded. "Yeah. Maybe. Scherrer doesn't make me too happy either. Do you mind a bit of a walk? I can't get any closer than this without blocking something."

Gregor didn't mind a bit of a walk. Russell pulled the car to a stop and they got out. This close, Gregor could see that the front door to Candida's house was wide open. Men went in and out of them at irregular intervals, looking grim. A slight man in a trench coat came to stand on the front porch. He looked in their direction, squinted a little, then nodded to himself. Then he began walking toward them.

"Fred Scherrer," Gregor Demarkian said again to Russell Donahue. "You did say Scherrer called the Bryn Mawr police and not us?"

"Yeah. But that doesn't mean anything, Gregor. He might also have called us. I wasn't the person taking the calls."

Fred Scherrer was walking toward them. It was as cold as Gregor could ever remember it being, in Philadelphia or anywhere else. He wished he were in the habit of wearing a hat. He pulled the collar of his coat up behind his ears and wrapped his scarf more tightly around his neck.

Fred Scherrer didn't seem to notice the cold. His trench coat was wide open. His hands were in his pockets, but he took them out often to adjust his coat or stroke his face. He wasn't wearing gloves. Gregor wondered about all the nervous mannerisms. Was Fred Scherrer always like this? How did it affect juries? He was an extremely successful defense attorney. He had to be doing something right.

Fred Scherrer stopped in the middle of the driveway and let Gregor and Russell walk the rest of the way to him.

"Mr. Demarkian?" he said. "I believe we met last night."

"Briefly."

Scherrer turned to Russell Donahue. "I saw you last night too. I'm afraid I don't remember your name."

"Russell Donahue. Detective first grade."

"Good, good. There's a guy in there from Bryn Mawr Homicide who's making no sense at all, but maybe that's normal. Nobody seemed to be making much sense last night either. This is the first time in my life I've ever been this . . . close to it all, if you know what I mean."

"Yes," Russell Donahue said. Gregor said nothing.

"Close to it all in more ways than one," Fred Scherrer said. "Did you know I was staying here for the weekend?"

"Yes," Russell said quickly.

"I've been staying in the guest room," Fred Scherrer said, "but that was mostly a technicality. If—this—hadn't happened, I would probably have changed rooms by the end of the weekend."

"Oh," Russell Donahue said.

"I'm not going on and on about my private life for no reason," Fred Scherrer said. "I want you to know what was going on up front. *They* think I'm hiding something." Fred jerked his head back in the direction of Candida's front door. "*They* think I killed her in a jealous rage and now I'm trying to make it look like she was somebody else's victim. *They* probably think I killed Paul too."

"Did you?" Gregor Demarkian asked.

Fred Scherrer smiled grimly. "If I'd wanted to kill Paul Hazzard, I could have done it four years ago, when I directed his defense after he was charged with his wife's murder. Trust me, that would have been much more effective than stabbing him six times, even if he hadn't gotten the death penalty. It would also have been much safer."

"Something could have happened between that time and this," Gregor Demarkian said.

"It could have, but it didn't. I've barely seen the man in the last four years. Not that you ought to take my word for that."

"I try not to take anybody's word for anything."

"Smart man."

Fred Scherrer turned and looked back at Candida's house. As far as Gregor could tell, the scene hadn't changed at all. The door was still open. Men were still walking in and out. There were still too many lights on everywhere. Fred Scherrer shivered and turned back to them. Gregor thought that he looked feverish, that his eyes were unnaturally bright.

"Come on," the attorney told them. "Let's go up to the house and meet the bozos. Maybe you can do something to get their brains on track."

## 2

The Bryn Mawr police handling the investigation into the death of Candida DeWitt were not, in fact, bozos. One of them, a big man named Roger Stebbins, Gregor knew from previous experience with murder in Bryn Mawr. Stebbins was not as good a police officer as his chief, but he was good, and comparing him to John Henry Newman Jackman might not have been fair. John Henry Newman Jackman, Stebbins's chief, was the single best local Homicide man Gregor had ever met. Roger Stebbins was a man Jackman trusted. That was enough for Gregor any day.

Roger Stebbins was standing just inside the front door, against one wall of the two-story foyer, near a pair of doors that led off into a room on the left. Gregor paused a moment to be impressed with the foyer. The floor was marble. The staircase that led to the second floor balcony was a sweeping curve of polished mahogany and inlaid teak. There was a chandelier hanging from the nearly invisible ceiling by a thick chain, made up of hundreds of tiny prisms that scattered little rainbow arcs of light in every direction. Gregor remembered somebody saying that Candida DeWitt had done very well at her way of life. That seemed to be an understatement.

Roger Stebbins had straightened up a little when he saw Gregor and Russell Donahue come in. Now he crossed the foyer with his hand held out.

"Mr. Demarkian? I don't know if you remember me. I'm Roger Stebbins."

"I do remember you. This is Russell Donahue of the Philadelphia police. Detective first grade."

"Right," Stebbins said. He shook Russell Donahue's hand in a perfunctory way and then shoved his hands into the pockets of his trousers. He looked very worried. "I talked to John Jackman about this," he said. "John sent his regards and said to give you all the help you wanted. I don't exactly know what kind of help I could give. It all seems straightforward enough on the face of it."

"Has the body been removed?" Gregor asked.

Roger Stebbins shook his head. "We left it. John said you might want to see it."

"I do. We do," Gregor said. "Where is it?"

Roger Stebbins looked back over his shoulder at the doors he had been standing next to when Gregor and Russell entered. "It's in there. I've had to post a guard or keep watch myself every minute. That bastard Scherrer is like ooze. He gets into everything."

Fred Scherrer didn't seem to be into anything at the moment. He had disappeared. Gregor started toward the inner doors. Roger Stebbins and Russell Donahue followed.

"This is the living room, more or less," Roger Stebbins said, "except you know what it's like in these great big houses. There are at least three other rooms on this floor that a regular person might call a living room."

Gregor looked inside. The room was an unqualified mess, the way rooms got when they had been worked over by tech men, but the tech men themselves were gone. Aside from a single uniformed patrolman standing next to the body, there was only a white-coated man from the medical examiner's office, waiting. Gregor walked over to the body and looked down at it.

Candida DeWitt had been an attractive woman in an understated way. She was now an attractive corpse, but there was nothing understated about her. Her lipsticked lips looked too bright against the whiteness of her face. Her eyes looked as if she had used kohl on them instead of eyeliner. Her eyes were open. They were very blue.

Gregor got down on his haunches and leaned closer to Candida DeWitt's chest, trying to see what could be seen of the wound.

"Russell," he called. "Come here for a minute."

Russell Donahue came and got down on his haunches too.

"Just one wound," he said. "A smash, bang right in the heart."

"I know," Gregor said. "It looks like the other ones though, doesn't it? The ones last night on Paul Hazzard."

Russell Donahue was doubtful. "We'll have to check with Forensics," he said. "Whatever was used here couldn't possibly have been the same weapon. We have the weapon in the Hazzard murder case."

"Do we? Do you have your lab reports back yet?"

"No," Russell admitted. "But it couldn't have been a coincidence, Mr. Demarkian. The weapon we found being just the right shape to make the wounds and all the rest of it—"

"There's nothing coincidental about it," Gregor said. "The only coincidence in this case happened when Jacqueline Isherwood Hazzard died. Since then, we've been dealing with cold-blooded deliberation."

"You sound like you know what's going on," Russell Donahue said in amazement. "You sound like you know who killed them."

"That's moot." Gregor leaned toward the body again and pointed at the wound. "We're going to need cross-sections, like the ones we're having done on Paul Hazzard and the ones that were done when Jacqueline Isherwood Hazzard died."

"We'll get them."

Gregor pointed to a space just to the right of the puncture. "Pay particular attention to this. Look at that."

"The dress is torn," Russell Donahue said.

"The dress is *slit*," Gregor corrected him. "There were slits like that in Paul Hazzard's shirt last night. Not six of them, of course. It happens only when the force of the blow is particularly strong. It isn't an edge that was deliberately designed to cut."

"What are you talking about?" Russell Donahue demanded. "Mr. Demarkian, if you know who killed these two people, you have to tell me about it. You can't just let whoever did these things wander around loose—"

"I don't know who killed these two people," Gregor said, "at least, not necessarily. What I know is what they were killed with. I held the murder weapon in my hands today. And it didn't even occur to me."

"Wait," Russell said. "What you're implying is that that dagger thing wasn't used to kill Hazzard."

"Of course it wasn't. Why should it be?"

"For one thing, it fits the wound. For another thing, it was lying there next to Hazzard's body."

"It was lying there next to Jacqueline Isherwood Hazzard's body too, but it wasn't the murder weapon."

"When it was lying next to Jacqueline Isherwood Hazzard's body, it didn't have blood on it."

"Have you ever seen the cross-section drawings from the original Hazzard case?"

Russell Donahue shook his head. Gregor stood up and looked around. There was a long, low couch in the middle of the room with a coffee table in front of it, facing the fireplace. There were a pair of delicate-looking end tables with lamps on them. There was a bookcase whose second shelf was a backlit display space holding ornamental china. There was nothing suitable to write on. Candida DeWitt had not been overly fond of furniture.

Gregor searched through the pockets of his coat until he came up with paper and a Bic ball-point pen. His pockets were always full of Bic ball-point pens. The paper was the envelope he had received his last overdue notice from the library in. He walked over to the nearest wall and plastered the envelope against it.

"Take a look at this," he said. "The cross-section of the wound found in Jacqueline Isherwood Hazzard's body looked like this." He drew carefully on one side of the envelope.

"So?" Russell Donahue demanded, studying what Gregor had done.

"Now look at this," Gregor said. "This is approximately what the outline of the dagger looks like."

"Be careful not to get ink on the wall."

Gregor ignored him and drew.

"There," he said when he was finished. "Look at that."

"I am looking at it. They're near enough to identical—"

"No, they're not," Gregor insisted. "Look, that's the mistake everybody has been making, right from the beginning. Everybody's been so impressed with the points of comparison, they've failed to notice the obvious. Which is that these two drawings are nowhere near identical. And neither are the real things on which they're based."

"I don't think you can count the fact that the dagger is longer than the wound is deep," Russell Donahue objected. "Assuming your representation is accurate. I mean, the murderer wouldn't have been able to get the entire dagger into the wound—"

"Of course he wouldn't have. That's not what I mean."

"You mean that little thingy over on the left side."

"Exactly."

"There are a lot of reasons why that might not have shown up in the wound," Russell said. "I'm not pretending to know everything there is to know about forensics—"

"Try using common sense," Gregor told him. "The wound in Jacqueline Isherwood Hazzard's body was deep enough and definite enough so that the medical examiner was able to take a cross-section that looked like this." He pointed to his first drawing. "I've seen the picture. It was unbelievably clear. Do you honestly think, if the wound was that deep and that well defined, that there wouldn't also have been traces of that left side of the handle?"

"Maybe," Russell Donahue said reluctantly. "But Mr. Demarkian—"

"No buts," Gregor told him. "Where's Roger Stebbins?"

"Here," Roger Stebbins said. "I've been right behind you the whole way. I've been listening."

"Good." He turned to Roger. "Have your people searched this room? Have they searched the house?"

"They've done a once-over," Roger said. "They wouldn't do a full shakedown until later in a situation like this. What are you looking for?"

"An envelope addressed to Candida DeWitt. With Hannah Krekorian's return address on it. Probably on the back flap."

"I see what you're getting at," Russell Donahue said. "You want to see the envelope her invitation to Hannah Krekorian's party came in. But would she have kept something like that?"

"I think she would have," Gregor said. "Candida was a very formal woman. Old-fashioned in a lot of ways. She would have expected to write a thank-you note after the party was over."

"After *that* party was over?" Russell Donahue was incredulous.

"Habit is a powerful thing," Gregor told him. "My friend Bennis Hannaford always saves the envelopes, except where she knows the person who invited her very well. Did Candida DeWitt have a maid?"

"She must have had, living in a house like this," Roger Stebbins said, "but maybe it's someone who comes in during the day. There's no one here now except Fred Scherrer. And the body."

"Get me Fred Scherrer," Gregor said. "Maybe he knows."

The two police officers looked at each other in a way Gregor had become used to. They were telegraphing a thought that could be paraphrased: *I don't care what his reputation is, I think he's nuts.* Roger Stebbins left the room anyway, in search of Fred Scherrer. He came back a couple of minutes later with Fred in tow. Fred kept looking sideways at the body and going a little green. Finally, he turned his back to it, squared his shoulders, and folded his arms. Gregor had the distinct feeling that he would refuse to turn around for any reason whatsoever. They could walk around to the back of him and start talking from there. They could sneak up behind him and yell boo. It wouldn't matter.

Gregor couldn't really blame Scherrer for not wanting to stare for minute after minute at the corpse of a woman of whom he had been fond. He sat down on the couch so that Fred didn't have to turn to look at him and said, "Mrs. DeWitt said something at Hannah Krekorian's party last night about consulting you on the subject of libel. Was that true?"

"To an extent," Fred answered. "There had been an . . . incident here. Somebody had gotten into the house and spray-painted some graffiti on the fireplace. Nasty stuff. Threatening death. Candida was in the middle of writing a book about her life. A lot of it was going to have to do with the murder of Jacqueline Isherwood Hazzard. Naturally. She thought—"

"—that one of the Hazzards was trying to warn her off," Gregor finished for him. "This incident wasn't reported?"

"No, it wasn't. I told Candida it should have been. I warned her those people were dangerous. Now one of them's killed her."

"You're sure it was one of the Hazzard children?"

"I find it difficult to think of them as children," Fred Scherrer said, "but yes, I'm sure. From what Candida told me, the house wasn't broken into. She locked up when she left and put the alarm on, and when she got back, the fireplace had been defaced. The doors were locked. There weren't any broken windows. The alarm had been reset. It had to have been someone who knew what they were doing."

"There must have been other people who fit that description besides the Hazzard children," Gregor suggested.

"There must have been plenty," Fred agreed, "but Candida couldn't think of any who might have had a motive. And neither could I."

Motive, Gregor thought. Motive, motive, motive. The classic motives were love, hate, and money—and he would bet on money every time.

"Let's go on to something else," he said. "Did you know that Mrs. DeWitt intended to go to Hannah Krekorian's party last night?"

"Oh, yes. She asked me to go with her."

"And you refused?"

"Point-blank." Fred Scherrer shook his head. "I knew it was going to lead to trouble."

"This kind of trouble?"

Fred blanched. "Of course not. If I'd known that, I would never have let her go. Although I've got to admit, getting Candida to give up doing something she'd decided to do was damn near impossible. I just thought there was going to be a scene, that's all. I didn't want any part of it. That way, if she got sued for harassment or something, I would be in a position to defend her."

"Did Mrs. DeWitt tell you how she came to be invited to this party?"

Fred nodded. "She got an invitation, 'in her mailbox,' as she put it, in the middle of the week. She used the phrase 'in my mailbox' so many times, I finally asked her what she meant by it. She said she didn't think the invitation had actually come in the mail. She said she thought someone had simply put it in her mailbox."

"Did she have reason for that?"

"I don't know. I suppose she must have."

"Did you see the invitation? Or the envelope?"

"I saw the invitation," Fred Scherrer said. Comprehension dawned. "I see. You're right, of course. She would have kept the envelope for the return address. It's probably upstairs in her desk. In her bedroom."

"I'll go check," Roger Stebbins said. He hurried out of the room.

Gregor turned his attention back to Fred Scherrer. "Did Mrs. DeWitt tell you why she was going to the party? Did she give you any indication of what her purpose was?"

"She said she wanted to see what would happen," Fred Scherrer said. "When Jackie—Jacqueline—when Paul's wife died, in the police mess that followed that, Paul tried to throw suspicion on Candida as a way to deflect suspicion from himself. He and Candida had only recently severed a long-term relationship, and it was Paul's idea, not Candida's. I think she's always been very . . . unhappy about all that."

"Did she say anything to you last night, after Paul's murder? Anything about what had happened at Hannah Krekorian's house or who she thought might have killed Hazzard."

Fred Scherrer shook his head. "She said that now that Paul was dead, she knew for sure who had killed Jackie. But it was my impression that she always thought she knew who killed Jackie."

"But this was different?"

"Oh, yes. This was certainty."

"And that's exactly what she said. Now that Paul Hazzard was dead, she knew who killed his wife."

Fred Scherrer closed his eyes, concentrating. "I'll tell you exactly," he said. "We were sitting in a cab, and she'd just explained the whole thing about the invitation to me. Then she said, 'And now that he's dead, of course, it clears everything up. I know just what happened the last time.' I suppose she could have meant how it was done, and not who."

"Especially if she already knew who," Gregor said.

"Especially then," Fred Scherrer agreed.

There was a sound at the door, and they both turned slightly. Fred Scherrer was careful not to turn too much. Gregor watched as Roger Stebbins came blundering through, looking too big and clumsy and out of place among all the delicateness of the room. He was holding a plain white envelope in one hand and grinning.

"Found it," Roger Stebbins said. "There's a little secretary thing in an alcove off the main bedroom. You unlatch the label part and pull it down, and behind that there are a lot of little pigeonholes. It was in one of those."

Gregor put out his hand. "Can I have that?" he asked. "Are you preserving the surface to check for prints?"

Roger Stebbins handed the envelope over. "It's the wrong kind of paper for prints. You think that's going to be of any use to us otherwise?"

"In one way, I think it's going to be a great deal of use," Fred Scherrer said. "Unless Hannah Krekorian is a

lot smarter than she looked last night, I think this takes
care of any suspicion that she sent that invitation to Candida
herself. That was an engraved invitation Candida got,
wasn't it? An engraved blank?"

"Right," Russell Donahue said.

"That's an envelope from Hallmark," Fred Scherrer
said.

"This is an envelope with an uncanceled stamp on it,"
Gregor said. "Mrs. DeWitt was right. It did come in her
mailbox. But not in her mail."

"Wonderful," Russell Donahue said. "Is all this supposed to mean something? What are we supposed to do
now?"

Gregor Demarkian stood up.

"Now," he said, "you're supposed to take me home."

# *t w o*

## 1

Gregor Demarkian sometimes envied the police officers he saw on television, the men and women who leapt out of bed at four in the morning when they fortuitously dreamed a hunch, went chasing all over town waking up suspects to ask just a question or two, and ended up in an eleventh-hour shoot-out with the depraved villain on the roof of an abandoned building. Gregor didn't have much use for shoot-outs or for chasing around town. He liked the Nero Wolfe paradigm, where the Great Detective sat around all day eating shad roe and getting fat and no one dared to lecture him about his cholesterol. What he envied the television police was their ability to forget about time. All the way back to Cavanaugh Street from Candida DeWitt's house, Gregor was acutely conscious of the fact that it was nearly ten o'clock on a Saturday night. It would have been earlier, but Russell Donahue had gotten held up at the last minute by a discussion of protocol with Roger Stebbins. Gregor had opted out of that one. He went to stand in the cold on Candida DeWitt's terrace. The vista was beautiful. After a few minutes, Fred Scherrer joined him. If it hadn't been a useless waste of time when he was eager to get something done, Gregor might have enjoyed himself.

Actually, there was nothing much he could get done.

When Russell Donahue finally pulled onto Cavanaugh Street, Gregor made him stop several blocks from his own apartment. Then he ordered Russell to pull up to the curb and park. Russell complained about the illegality of it all. It was embarrassing when police officers got their cars ticketed or towed away. It wasn't supposed to happen, but it did. Gregor ignored him.

"Do you have a flashlight?" he asked.

Russell Donahue reached into the glove compartment and came up with a flashlight. It was a good big one, the kind that was used in factories and on back lots, heavy and black. Russell handed it over.

"Do you want me to come with you?" he asked.

"Yes."

Gregor stood on the sidewalk in front of Hannah Krekorian's apartment building and looked to the right and to the left. Very few of the buildings on Cavanaugh Street were actually flush up against each other. Most were separated by narrow alleys that led to trash bins and utility sheds. Hannah's building had an alley on each side. Gregor tried to work out which side her bedroom window would look out on, and then realized that the answer was neither. There was actually a view from Hannah's bedroom windows. It wasn't much of a view, but it was a view. That meant those windows had to face the back.

"Come on," Gregor told Russell Donahue, who had climbed out of the car, locked up carefully, and was now standing on the pavement. His ears seemed to be turning blue. "I want to get a look at the fire escape," Gregor explained.

"I got a look at the fire escape last night," Russell protested. He stamped his feet against the cold. "I'm really very thorough, Mr. Demarkian. It's just a fire escape."

"Come on," Gregor said again.

They went down the alley to the left side, which was unfortunately the one that held the garbage for both Hannah's building and the one next door. They emerged into a small courtyard in the back and looked around. There was a scattering of good security lights on the back of Hannah's building and the back of the building with which it shared a garbage station. All the lights still didn't make the courtyard brightly lit. They must have been put in by amateurs. They were aimed incorrectly. Still, Gregor thought, it wasn't a menacing well of blackness back here. It was *possible*.

Gregor shined his light on the fire escapes. There were three of them, one going only so far as one of the second story windows. Gregor thought that one led to Melina Kashinian's bedroom window—although how Howard or anybody else expected an eighty-nine-year-old woman to go crawling down those metal stairs in case of fire was beyond Gregor's comprehension. One of the other fire escapes led almost to the roof level, probably to an attic. Gregor knew that nobody lived that far up. He wondered why Howard had bothered to take the precaution. Howard was not known for spending unnecessary money on anything or anybody but his wife and himself. Maybe he'd intended to put another apartment up there and never got around to it. The last fire escape went to the fourth floor. Gregor walked over to it and shined his flashlight at the bottom step.

"It might as well be a staircase," he said.

Russell Donahue agreed. "These are the best escapes made. They don't fold up. They're wider than the average. They're strong as hell. I'm impressed with the landlord."

"Don't be. He was just making sure he couldn't get sued."

"Whatever the reason, I'd like to have these on my building."

"Let's go around to the other alley and see what it's like."

The other alley was much pleasanter than the one they'd come down. There was no garbage in it at all, just a big metal shed with a padlock on it that probably held paints and ropes and brick cleaner. Gregor walked out to Cavanaugh Street and then back to the courtyard, shining the flashlight up and down, thinking. He finally stopped at the foot of the fire escape that led to Hannah Krekorian's bedroom window and tapped his foot against the flagstones there.

"There would have been a preliminary visit," he said.

"Fine," Russell Donahue said. "A preliminary visit to where? By whom?"

"To here. By the murderer," Gregor said. "There would have had to be a preliminary visit, because this whole operation was very well-planned. Which is a funny thing to say about a murder that in the end depended so much on luck, but there's nothing I can do about that."

"You know," Russell Donahue said, "Cheswicki warned me that you started talking like this after a while. He said I was supposed to keep reminding myself that you're a genius."

"I'm not a genius. And I'm making perfect sense. The murderer had the address of Hannah's apartment, of course, because the murderer had one of those invitations. The problem with that is that everybody on earth seems to have had one of those invitations. Hannah was not being exclusive."

"What about Hannah possibly being the murderer?" Russell asked. "A few hours ago you were recommending that we arrest her immediately. I take it that's off."

Gregor sighed. "I wasn't recommending that you arrest her because I thought she'd killed anybody. I was just hoping to do something to light a fire under this case. This was beginning to shape up into one of those non-events. Murder happens. Everyone freezes solid. No one makes a move. Unless you're dealing with an idiot who scatters clues the way Hansel and Gretel scattered bread crumbs, you never solve a case like that."

"I take it you've changed your mind," Russell Donahue said. "Now you don't want us to arrest her."

"Now I don't think you can," Gregor told him. "We'll have to check, of course, but I'm willing to bet my life that Hannah Krekorian has a rock-solid alibi for the time of Candida DeWitt's murder."

"Why?"

"Because Hannah is being watched over by a bunch of Armenian-American women who worry. If she suddenly dropped out of sight for a few hours, I would have heard about it. Remember. I was sitting in my own living room when you called. I was available."

"Right."

"The murder of Paul Hazzard was definitely planned for last night. The plan was hatched when Paul Hazzard received his invitation to Hannah's party. At that point, the murderer knew something critical. The murderer knew that Paul Hazzard would not only be at Hannah's party, but that he would probably be at Hannah's apartment after the party. I don't mean that he would have slept overnight. I suppose he might have—before all this started, I used to think I knew the women I'd grown up with very well, but I'm giving that up—but the key here is that it wasn't necessary for Paul Hazzard to sleep over for this plan to work. It was only necessary for Paul Hazzard to still be in that apartment when everybody else was gone."

"It won't work," Russell Donahue said. His nose was turning blue. The tip of his nose was turning *bright* blue. "I see where you're going here. First the murderer came out here to check out ways to get into Mrs. Krekorian's apartment, and found the fire escape."

"My guess is that the murderer came out here between five and seven o'clock at night," Gregor told him. "Monday or Tuesday. On weekends we get a lot of tourist traffic out here, but on weekdays the only busy times are between five and seven. People stop at the Ararat and get take-out to eat back home in the suburbs."

"Whatever." Russell Donahue was not interested in this. "The murderer checks out the fire escapes and finds he's got a way in—"

"—or she—"

"Or she. I'm not going to do that over and over again, Mr. Demarkian. It'll make me crazy."

"If you don't, it might prejudice your reasoning."

"Right. The murderer, he or she, works out how to get into the apartment—what about window locks?"

"What about them?" Gregor said. "You can always break a window. Considering what was being set up here, it might even have been an advantage."

"All right. So, on the night of the party, last night, the murderer climbs up the fire escape, meaning to sneak into the apartment, but when he—or she—gets to the landing, there's Paul Hazzard, designated victim, pacing around in the bedroom—"

"No," Gregor said.

"No?"

"That wasn't when the murderer entered the apartment. It couldn't have been. I went all over that with Bob last night. Paul Hazzard would have seen. He would have struggled. He would have cried out. By the time Hannah locked herself in the master bathroom and Paul Hazzard came to pace outside it, the murderer had been in Hannah's apartment for quite some time."

"Really. Since when?"

"Since sometime between seven and seven-oh-five," Gregor said promptly. "That's when, according to Helen Tevorakian and Mary Ohanian, Sheila Kashinian heard a moan."

"Sheila Kashinian," Russell Donahue ruminated. "Is that the one in the earrings and the four-inch heels and the green-and-gold dyed mink coat?"

"That's the one."

"For God's sake, Mr. Demarkian, you can't take that woman's word for anything. She's crazy." Russell Donahue stamped his feet to get feeling back into them.

"She may be crazy," Gregor said, "but she's no liar. Let's go back to my apartment."

"Why?"

"Because I'm cold. And because I want to talk to Bennis Hannaford for a while. Can you get in touch with anybody this late on a Saturday night?"

"Like who?"

"Like your lab and technical people. The ones who are running the tests on the evidence picked up last night."

"I don't know if I can get in touch with the exact people. But Cheswicki put rush orders all over all that stuff last night. There ought to be somebody over there who knows what's going on with our stuff."

"Good. I hate working blind like this. I want some confirmation of what can be confirmed. Like the fact that that idiotic dagger was not the murder weapon."

"Right."

"I've got it almost all worked out," Gregor said. "It's just a question of—well, never mind for the moment. Let's go."

"Right," Russell Donahue said again, bleakly.

Gregor took the alley with the utility shed in it instead of the garbage, and went back out to Cavanaugh Street.

## 2

Bennis Hannaford was on the phone and the front door of her apartment was propped open with *The White Trash Cook Book* when Russell and Gregor came upstairs. They stopped and waved at her and she nodded distractedly.

"I really don't think this is a good idea," she was saying, "I really don't. You have to understand—well, no—well, yes—I've thought of that already, but you can't—oh, for God's sake—no—no—never *mind*—I'll talk to you tomorrow. *Jesus*."

Bennis hung up the phone and walked across the foyer to them. "Sorry," she said. "Is there something the two of you want?"

"This is Russell Donahue," Gregor said.

"We met last night."

Gregor felt awkward. Bennis was not usually this—this stiff? Had he done something wrong?

"Well," he said, "if you wouldn't mind and you don't have anything to do for the moment, I was hoping you'd come upstairs. There was something I wanted to show you. And something I wanted to ask you."

"He's outlining how the murder happened," Russell Donahue said. "It's very interesting. He has me totally confused."

"I heard from Father Tibor," Bennis said. "He said some friend of his was in your apartment when you got a phone call that Candida DeWitt was dead."

"That's true," Gregor said.

There was a clattering from above them and Donna Moradanyan came running down the stairs, her hands full of red crepe paper and silver balloons, her blond hair sticking out in every direction. She saw them and stopped, blushing.

"Hi," she said.

Russell Donahue seemed to stand a little straighter. "Hello," he said. "Where's your little boy?"

"He's sleeping over downstairs at old George Tekemanian's."

"That must be fun for him," Russell Donahue said.

"Yes," Donna Moradanyan said. "Yes, it is."

Bennis ran a hand through her thick black hair. "We're going up to Gregor's apartment, Donna. I'll leave my door open. I talked to Sheila Kashinian. She's got the helium you need for the balloons. When you're ready for it, just call and Howard will bring it over. He stays up until midnight."

"Great," Donna said.

Bennis turned to Gregor. "My brother Christopher wants to talk to you. He knows something about Paul Hazzard. Or he met him once. It's complicated."

"Good," Gregor said. "I'd like to talk to Christopher. Is he around here somewhere?"

"No," Bennis said darkly. "He is definitely not around here somewhere, and quite frankly I couldn't tell you where he was. Nobody ever tells me anything. Are we going upstairs?"

"Yes," Gregor said. "Yes, of course, right away."

"Good."

Bennis wheeled around and started marching up the stairs to the third floor. She reminded Gregor of one of those grim-faced monsters in a Ray Harryhausen movie, a Greek fury processed through Freud.

"Valentine's Day," she said when she was halfway up to the third floor landing. "To hell with it."

Right, Gregor thought.

As soon as he got upstairs, he was going to get back to the murders. They were going to be a lot less complicated than whatever it was Bennis had gotten herself involved with.

## 3

Actually, it turned out to be easy to get back to the murders once Gregor had let them all into his apartment. The change in scenery seemed to cause a change in Bennis. She calmed down dramatically and began bustling around the kitchen. She put the teakettle on. She looked into his refrigerator and made a face. The only time he had what she considered halfway decent food in his place was when Lida or Hannah or one of the other women brought some over—and they seemed to have given that practice up for Lent. If it hadn't been for the Ararat, Gregor would have starved to death this week. Bennis sat down in a kitchen chair and stretched her legs.

"Well," she said. "What is it? Did I accidentally stumble over the murderer in Hannah's living room and not know it?"

"No," Gregor said. "I want you to look at something I've got and tell me what it is."

"Let me make that phone call," Russell Donahue said.

He got up and started to dial from Gregor's kitchen wall phone. Gregor went to the windowsill over his sink and fished around in the little straw basket he kept odds and ends in until he found the single pearl earring he had picked up from the carpet of Hannah Krekorian's guest room the night before. He placed it on the table in front of Bennis.

"What's that?" he asked.

"It's a pearl earring for a pierced ear," Bennis said in mock solemnity. "In fact, it's probably a Tiffany pearl stud."

"Does it belong to Hannah Krekorian?"

"Of course not, Gregor. Hannah's never had her ears pierced."

"Do you know whom it does belong to?"

Bennis shrugged. "Practically everybody I know who has pierced ears has Tiffany pearl studs. They cost about five hundred dollars. They're a really good anniversary gift or birthday gift in the really-special category. Donna has a pair she got from her parents. Lida Arkmanian has a pair her daughter Karen bought her for Christmas a couple of years ago. I have a pair." Bennis pulled her hair away from her face. "I wear them all the time."

"Are any of those people missing an earring?" Gregor asked.

"Donna isn't," Bennis said. "Or, at least, she wasn't this morning. She was wearing hers. I don't know about Lida."

"Was Lida wearing hers at the party last night?"

"No, Gregor. She was wearing her gold shells. Don't you ever notice anything?"

Gregor Demarkian had made a career out of noticing things. These were just not the right kinds of things. Bennis looked curiously at the earring.

"Did you find that in Hannah's apartment last night?" she asked. "Was it at the murder scene?"

"It was in Hannah's guest room. You don't happen to know if Hannah had a guest staying there who might have been wearing earrings like this? Or how often that room is thoroughly cleaned."

"That room is thoroughly cleaned every December first and June first. That's when the cleaning service comes in and does a sweep," Bennis said. "I can't remember Hannah ever having a guest stay over in that guest room except her granddaughters, and they're tiny. They don't wear earrings yet."

Russell Donahue came back from the phone. "I've got somebody checking," he said. "She'll call us back. Have you determined anything important while I was gone?"

"Maybe," Gregor said.

He was still wearing his coat. He was still standing up. He shrugged his coat off and threw it on one of the kitchen counters. Then he searched through his pockets to find the piece of paper he wanted.

"There's never anything around here to write on," he complained. "There's never anything around here to write with."

Bennis got up. The water was boiling. She took coffee

mugs out of Gregor's cabinet and the instant coffee from his pantry shelf and put them on the kitchen table. Then she opened the drawer next to the refrigerator and came up with a pen and a much-used steno pad.

"Here you go," she said, turning back to the refrigerator to get out the cream. The sugar was in a bowl in the middle of the kitchen table. Bennis got some spoons and sat down again. "Are you going to draw a picture? Or are you going to write down the name of the murderer and hide it in the cookie jar, and then when the police finally get around to doing something about the case you'll pull the paper out and show everybody how much faster you were at working it all out?"

"Neither," Gregor said. "I'm going to write down how it happened. Beginning at the beginning. Russell?"

"I'm paying attention."

"Good. Let's go back to what I was talking about before. The first and most important thing was the arrival of that invitation. That invitation provided opportunity. Remember that this is someone who has already killed once—killed Jacqueline Isherwood Hazzard to be exact—and gotten away with it. It would have been a major mistake to murder Paul Hazzard in the same place and in the same way that his wife was murdered. Our murderer does not make major mistakes."

"If that earring belongs to your murderer," Bennis said, "she made at least one major mistake."

"Did she?" Gregor asked. "Even assuming it belongs to the murderer, Bennis, it's only a minor mistake. It wasn't lost at the scene but in another room. It's something that many people have, you said so yourself. It could never be successfully used in evidence."

"It seems to have given you ideas."

"That, yes," Gregor said. He pulled the steno pad close to him and began to write.

1. *P. Hazzard receives invitation*
2. *Murderer checks out Hannah's apartment to see if entry is feasible*
3. *Murderer hand-delivers invitation, repackaged, to C. DeWitt*

Russell Donahue studied the list and frowned. "There's something I don't understand. So what if that invitation was delivered to Candida DeWitt? That couldn't have been enough to ensure that she'd show up."

"There was no need to ensure that she'd show up," Gregor explained patiently. "All along, the murderer intended for there to be two suspects in this case. One, of course, was Hannah Krekorian. The other was Candida DeWitt. I don't even know if Mrs. DeWitt was meant to be a serious suspect. Casting suspicion in this way might have been simply spite. But to cast suspicion, it wasn't necessary that Candida DeWitt actually attend Hannah Krekorian's party. It was only necessary that she could be proved to have known where Hannah lived."

"Oh," Bennis said.

Gregor started writing again.

4. *Murderer arrives at Hannah's apartment and gets in through window, 7:00 to 7:05 last night*
5. *Murderer hides in guest room intending to stay there until party is finished*
6. *C. DeWitt arrives and causes scene*
7. *Hannah goes to master bathroom*
8. *P. Hazzard goes to master bedroom*
9. *Murderer leaves guest room and goes into master bedroom, locking master bedroom door*

Gregor tapped the piece of paper he had pulled out of his trouser pocket, the timetable put together by Mary Ohanian and Helen Tevorakian. "We have to check out the particulars," he said, "but this is how it has to have happened. That's what I mean, Russell, about a carefully planned murder that depended so much on luck. The plan was for a murder later in the evening. The luck was in catching Paul Hazzard the way he was caught. It was a much better setup than the original plan, but it couldn't possibly have been engineered."

"If it happened the way you're saying it did, it must have been someone Hazzard knew very well. It must have been someone he expected to see at that party," Russell said.

"No, it didn't have to be someone he expected to see at the party," Gregor corrected him. "After all, he'd just been ambushed by Candida DeWitt. Another surprise of that kind would probably have seemed relatively minor."

"But it *was* someone he knew well," Bennis insisted.

"Oh, yes."

"As an explanation, this still bothers me a lot," Russell Donahue said. "The times seem all wrong. They're too tight."

"They're much too tight," Gregor agreed. "When I was talking to Helen and Mary this afternoon, one of them said it was impossible. There wasn't enough time in this schedule for someone to have murdered Paul Hazzard. I remember thinking that exposure was inevitable. The odds were enormous that someone would have seen the murderer either going into the bedroom, or killing Paul Hazzard, or going out of the bedroom."

"Is that what you mean by luck too?" Russell Donahue asked. "I don't like it, Mr. Demarkian. It's too many good breaks and too many timetable coincidences."

"Only if the murderer was, in fact, not seen."

"You mean the murderer *was* seen?" Bennis was shocked. "But Gregor—oh, you mean the murderer was seen but the person who saw him, or her, didn't know it was the murderer."

"The person who saw him, or her, was Candida De-Witt," Gregor said, "and she most certainly knew what she was looking at was a murderer, a two-time murderer. That's why she's dead."

"But why wouldn't she have told?" Bennis protested. "She must have been crazy."

"She wasn't crazy," Gregor said. "She was just angry. Very, very, very angry. And she thought she was going to be smart."

The phone rang. Russell Donahue got up from the chair he had dropped into a little while before and went to answer it.

"It's probably for me," he said. "Just a second."

It was for him. Russell picked up the receiver, grunted a few times, and said, "Thank you very much." Then he hung up again.

"Well," he told Gregor and Bennis, "Mr. Demarkian, you were right about one thing. Whatever killed Paul Hazzard, it wasn't that ornamented dagger. They've run it through every test they can think of and it all comes up negative. That dagger had Paul Hazzard's blood on it all right, but it got that blood on it outside Paul Hazzard's body. It was never for a second inside that man's chest."

## *three*

### *1*

On Sunday morning Lida Arkmanian woke up by the alarm clock, got out of bed, went to her bathroom, and took a shower. When she was finished with her shower, she wrapped herself in a terry-cloth bathrobe and went to her closet to pick out a dress for church. She stood in her closet for a good fifteen minutes, trying to decide between the pale blue silk with the princess collar and the jade wool with three-quarter-length sleeves, before she realized what she was doing. It shocked her, more than a little. She hadn't thought about church in a week. She hadn't thought about the *implications* of church in a week. She wasn't really thinking about them now. What she was thinking about was the way the skin on the back of Christopher's neck felt to the tips of her fingers. It was a very odd thing. When she was married—and long before she was married, when she was growing up and first curious about sex and trying so hard not to let anyone know she was curious about sex—the feelings she had always concentrated on were her own, situation passive. The first time a boy had ever kissed her, she had centered herself, feeling what it felt like to have his lips brush against hers, his arm around her back. She had never given a thought to what his lips felt like *to her*— whether they were rough or smooth, whether they tasted of cinnamon or Vaseline. She had cared for nothing but what he had made her feel. That was true, she thought now, of all the years of her marriage. She had paid attention to all the things her husband had made her feel. She had never noticed at all how he had felt to her. It seemed wrong, somehow, backhanded. Were all women like this?

She had the jade wool in one hand. She put it back on the hanger bar and went out into the bedroom again. Christopher was sitting up in bed, waiting for her, expectant. When all this had started, Lida had been sure that it was some kind of joke. Christopher was bored and trying to find something to do he hadn't done before. Christopher had never slept with an old lady and wanted to know what it was like. Over the past twenty-four hours, Lida had changed her mind. She was not a very sophisticated woman, but she had never had any trouble knowing when a man was serious.

Lida belted the bathrobe more tightly around her waist and walked over to the bed. She sat down on the edge of it. When she had thought that Christopher was not serious, he had made her feel young. Now she was far too aware of the slackness of the skin on her face and neck, the fine tracing of lines on the backs of her hands. She did not want to be too aware of getting old. Her cousin Delphinia was too aware. Delphinia spent a lot of time with plastic surgeons.

"Hello," she said to Christopher.

"You had on the alarm clock," Christopher said. "Whatever for? It's Sunday morning."

"On Sunday mornings I go to church."

"Oh." Christopher considered this the way he might have considered a confession of culinary abnormality—"On Sunday mornings I eat fried chicken feet," for instance. Lida thought she ought to be grateful that Christopher knew what a church was. He stretched out a hand and touched her hair and smiled.

"Do you want me to come with you?" he asked.

"Good Lord, no," Lida said. "That's all we'd need."

"Why? You said yourself that everybody on the street knows what's going on anyway, except maybe Gregor Demarkian. What's the matter, if we go to church together, Gregor will suddenly see light dawn?"

"Krekor does not go to church. Or at least he does not go very much. I should go today to be with Hannah, I suppose."

"I think it's a good idea."

"You've never even been interested in religion?" Lida asked him. "You've never for a moment believed in God?"

"I want to know what's really going on here," Christopher said. "Do they disapprove of you, is that it? Do they disapprove of us for doing this?"

"I don't know. It's not what I'm worried about."

"Then what are you worried about? From everything I've seen, Tibor Kasparian is a nice man. He's not going to leap out of the pulpit—"

"—we do not have a pulpit—"

"—and start calling you a scarlet woman. Neither is anybody else. Maybe your friend Hannah will be a little jealous."

"Hannah has other things on her mind."

"And maybe my sister will start fussing—which is par for the course for Bennis, and there isn't a damn thing either one of us can do about it—but I don't think any of these things amounts to a serious drawback to the two of us going to church together. It might even be interesting. I don't usually like churches."

"I thought you didn't."

"I don't like people who try to tell me what I'm supposed to do and what I'm supposed to think and what I'm supposed to feel. I don't like the idea of feeling that I've done something wrong just because I've started to be happy. I don't like the idea of you feeling like that."

"I don't feel like that, Christopher. I don't understand where you get your ideas."

"I watch MTV," Christopher said.

"Well, you should watch Mother Angelica," Lida told him. "I do not think of it as someone trying to tell me what to do. I think of it as a bargain I made. If I am to call myself a Christian in the Armenian Church, then I have obligations."

"One of which is not to sleep with me."

"Sleeping with you does not matter, Christopher.

Sleeping with you for a week when we are not even thinking of getting engaged and not having any intention of
stopping, that matters."

His fingers stroked her cheek. "I'm glad you have no
intention of stopping."

"Christopher, you are impossible."

"I work at it."

"You work at the most astonishing things," Lida said.

She got up off the bed. She felt a little cold and a little
silly, sitting there with nothing but this bathrobe on and a
pair of underpants underneath it. She went to the closet
drawers and got out a bra and a new box of panty hose.

"Christopher," she said, calling through the open closet
door, "do you believe what Bennis said last night? That
Hannah is no longer a suspect?"

"Sure. She got it from Gregor Demarkian."

"It was good of her to call and tell us."

"There was nothing good about it. She was trying to
find out how late we got in."

"I do not think you are always fair to Bennis, Christopher. She is a much nicer woman than you seem to
think."

"She is a much nosier one than you've ever imagined.
What are you doing in there?"

"I'm getting dressed."

Her navy blue linen was hanging to the right of the
jade wool. Lida took that one and put it on. It was one of
the most conservative dresses she owned, man-tailored,
like an elongated shirt. What was she trying to do here?
She went to the built-in drawers again and fumbled through
the top one until she found her silver beads. They were
conservative too.

"I've changed my mind," she said, going to the closet
door as she put on her earrings. "I am going to take you
with me to church."

"Great," Christopher said. "Turn your back. When you
see me naked in daylight, you get embarrassed."

Lida turned her back. She got less and less embarrassed
every time she saw Christopher that way. But there was
no need to tell him that.

"Can I wear jeans and a decent sweater?" he asked her. "That suit Howard Kashinian loaned me fits funny."

"You can wear your jeans," Lida said. "Lots of people do now."

"Great," Christopher said again.

Lida's navy blue shoes were on the second level of the shoe rack. She got them down and put them on.

It was bad enough that she was going to take Christopher to church, she thought. What was worse was that she was feeling irritated with church.

She was also feeling irritated with herself.

All those shoes on shoe racks.

All those dresses on padded hangers.

All those "accessories" in the built-in drawers, color-coordinated or dyed to match.

What had she been doing with her life?

## 2

James Hazzard never woke up to an alarm clock if he could help it. Since he ran his own business and passed himself off as a god to his clients, he could usually help it. Some of his colleagues had expanded their practices by opening quasi-churches of their own. The women started Temples of Diana and the men flirted with satanism. James's position was that it was a mistake to get involved in anything he couldn't carry through with a straight face. That was why he hadn't immersed himself in the recovery movement. He had tried, once, by going to one of his father's seminars—although not one that his father himself was running. Midway through, the participants had been required to write letters to their inner children, and it had just been too much. James had nearly died laughing.

He wished that he could die laughing now, or maybe that he could just die. It was eleven-fifteen on Sunday morning and he was cold. Worse than that, he was with Caroline and Caroline was on one of her patented rampages. He wondered who she had learned her rampages from. Paul had been self-controlled to the point of petrification. Jacqueline had had the emotional life of a sea slug. Maybe their own mother had been histrionic. James couldn't remember their own mother.

"She went searching through his things on purpose," Caroline said. "She was trying to take control of the rest of us. It's a kind of abuse, James."

"Everything is a kind of abuse." This was true. James was sure of it. Having a mother who wanted French toast for breakfast every morning was a kind of abuse.

"You don't take me seriously, James," Caroline said. "That's a kind of abuse too. You refuse to mirror back to me my own reality."

To James Hazzard's mind, his sister Caroline's reality resembled an Escher print. He didn't have time to consider it at the moment, however, because the funeral director was making his way back to them across the enormous reception room. The man was wearing a suitably hangdog expression and holding his hands at his sides the way boys did when they were walking in line at the kind of private school that didn't have a military tradition but wished it did. His name was Arthur Pommerant and James didn't like him much.

"I have very good news," Arthur Pommerant said. "I have discussed the matter with our preparations department, and there will not have to be a closed casket after all."

"Oh," James said.

"Why would we want an open casket?" Caroline demanded. "Why would we want to look at a dead body?"

Arthur Pommerant looked confused. "It's for the wake," he explained. "The deceased is usually on view at the wake. It puts quite a damper on things when the deceased *isn't* on view at the wake."

"I think it's barbaric," Caroline said.

"For God's sake," James told her. "This isn't an arena for getting your needs met. This is something we all have to get through for the sake of the public and the papers and whatever fans Dad had left. Will you just let it go?"

"I see what you're trying to do," Caroline said. "You're

trying to make me look hysterical and unreasonable. Then you can make yourself look like a paragon of objective rationality and get anything you want."

"Oh, for Christ's sake," James exploded.

Arthur Pommerant was looking from one to the other of them. He was not embarrassed. James thought he must have seen family fights a million times before. Maybe everybody squabbled at funerals. Maybe that was one of the ways families got through them.

"Look," he said to Arthur Pommerant, "could you do us a favor? Could you find out whether the suit we had sent over ever arrived."

"I know it arrived," Arthur Pommerant said. "I unwrapped it myself."

"Fine. Wonderful. What about the sheet music?"

"I don't know what you had to have sheet music for," Caroline snapped. "Daddy didn't like music. Daddy was tone deaf."

"The sheet music is in the hands of our organist," Arthur Pommerant said. "We all thought the selections were quite nice. Very nice indeed. A truly spiritual offering."

"What about the menu for the wake?" James was feeling desperate. "You said you'd handle that. I'd like to know what—"

"Oh, it's a little too early for that yet," Arthur Pommerant told him. "We'll have a full workup on the menu by tomorrow. And I want to assure you that we have been quite careful about all the arrangements. There shouldn't be any difficulty at all arising out of the unusual delay we have had here in taking charge of the deceased for burial."

"Oh, my God," Caroline said.

Arthur Pommerant had a look on his face that James would have called beaming, except there was no smile to it. It was as if he had just played a very difficult game and won. For the first time in his life, James was inclined to credit the conspiracy theories his father and his sister had always been so fond of. He was also inclined to tell Arthur Pommerant that he would give the service at the wake himself, and that that service would be a Druid ritual, complete with the blood sacrifice of a bull.

"Well," Arthur Pommerant murmured. "Maybe I

should leave the two of you alone for a moment or two, to talk things over. . . ."

"Yes," James said, relieved. "Maybe you should."

"All you have to do if you need me is to ring," Arthur Pommerant said. "Or you can come along to the back and knock on my office door. Aren't you waiting for someone else?"

"My sister Alyssa," James said.

"She wouldn't come near this place," Caroline pointed out. "She said she would show up only to get us waiting around, fretting about her. It's how she reassures herself that she's still important to the family. It's—"

"I know," James said quickly. "It's a kind of abuse."

Caroline's face got red. "Don't *patronize* me," she said. "I'm a fully adult human being who is perfectly capable of making her own decisions."

"Why don't you just make the decision to *shut up*?"

"I'll be right in back in the office," Arthur Pommerant said. "Really. It's no trouble at all to get in touch with me if you need me. Just ring. Or come on back. I'm always on call."

"Necrophiliac," Caroline said.

Arthur Pommerant disappeared.

The Pommerant Funeral Parlor was on a city street that looked almost residential but was probably mostly deserted. Through the window of the reception room, James could see a hole-in-the-wall deli on the other side of the street with a red heart trimmed in white paper lace in the window. It was the first time it had penetrated to James's consciousness that they were very close to Valentine's Day. Maybe they should bury Paul on Valentine's Day. Maybe that would say something.

James sat down in the nearest chair and looked up at Caroline. "Now," he said, "start from the beginning and get it over with. You're angry at Alyssa. That's fine. Get angry at Alyssa once and for all so you can stop throwing tantrums in public."

"I'm not throwing a tantrum, James. I am expressing my feelings."

"If everyone went around expressing their feelings the way you do, civilization would come to an end."

"She took that copy of Jacqueline's will that Daddy had made. She took it out of Daddy's shoe tree."

"So what? The will is on file down at the lawyers' offices, Caroline. Alyssa could have taken a look at it anytime she wanted to."

"Alyssa didn't go to the lawyers' offices. She went sneaking around in Daddy's room. She went looking in *secret*. She didn't want us to know."

"She was curious on a Saturday night when she didn't have any other way to satisfy her curiosity. The lawyers' offices were closed. She didn't want to face one of your inquisitions."

"I don't hold inquisitions."

"Daddy's will divides his possessions pretty evenly among the three of us, Caroline. Alyssa has just as much right to look through his things as you have."

"She sneaked into his room. She lied to me when I asked her what she was doing."

"Maybe that was the simplest way of telling you to mind your own business."

"She hid the copy of the will under her sweater."

"She probably didn't have any pockets."

"She *lied* to me, James. I'm telling you, she's up to something."

"What could she possibly be up to?"

Caroline walked away and went to look out the window herself. Then she walked away from the window and began to look through her bag. It was her big bag, James suddenly realized, the one she used to carry all that equipment in when she went on trips. She was always complaining about how she hated to lug it around.

Caroline came up with a box of cough drops and dropped one in her mouth.

"Of course, what I really want to do is smoke," she said. "All my addictions are reaching out to me. It's inevitable in times of stress."

James had quit smoking five years earlier. He had never once wanted a cigarette since.

"Why don't you get to the point?" he asked her.

"I am getting to the point," Caroline said irritably.

"Now that Daddy's dead, we three come in for a whole lot of Jacqueline's money, isn't that true?"

"We come into Jacqueline's money, that's true. I don't know how much of it there is."

Caroline dismissed this. "Jacqueline was rich. There's tons and tons of the stuff. I think maybe Alyssa needs it for something."

"Needs it for what? She's married to a very successful attorney."

"Successful attorneys aren't always rich," Caroline said. "Some of them spend too much. Some of them get into trouble."

"Nick Roderick isn't in any trouble. You've got no reason to say he is."

"Maybe it's Alyssa who's in trouble, then. Maybe she wants enough for Nick to retire and go away someplace. Maybe she wants to get away from Philadelphia and everybody who knows."

"Knows what?"

"Knows," Caroline said.

Then she sat down on the couch and faced him, her knees together, her ankles together, a little smile on her face. She was making James feel very queasy. He didn't like her attitude at all.

"I think we ought to look into this," she said, "before one or the other of us winds up dead. We haven't any one of us made a will, you know. If something happened to any of us, our money would go to our next of kin. Wouldn't it?"

"Yes," James said. "It would."

"There, then."

Caroline popped another cough drop in her mouth.

Yes, James thought, Caroline definitely made him queasy, but it wasn't because she'd convinced him that Alyssa was up to something.

It was Caroline he thought was up to something.

## 3

Halfway across town, in the apartment on top of the Hazzard house, Alyssa Hazzard Roderick was putting the final touches on her elaborate Sunday-go-to-the-funeral-home makeup and talking to her husband, Nick. She had a big red heart-shaped box of Russell Stover chocolates at her elbow, open, so that she could pick at it between taking swipes at her lips with her lipstick brush.

". . . so Caroline got all upset," she was saying, "but it didn't really bother me, because that's just like Caroline and I think it was important for me to know. I think it's important for all of us to know. Don't you, Nick?"

"I already knew," Nick said. "You could have asked me."

"You were out. I don't see what all this fuss is about, Nick, really. I just wanted to find out what I wanted to know and not have to explain myself to Caroline. God only knows, nobody in his right mind would want to have to explain anything to Caroline."

"Gotcha," Nick said. "I'm not arguing about that. I'm just saying it would have made more sense to ask me."

"So when you came home, I did ask you. How much did you say it was again?"

"About fifteen million dollars."

"That's a lot of money."

"There's also this house. James isn't going to be a problem about the house, but if we want to stay here, we're probably going to have to buy Caroline out. Will you mind doing that?"

"I don't know that I want to stay here," Alyssa said. "Do you think Caroline will really want to move?"

"Once she has money? Sure. She doesn't like any of the rest of us very much."

"I suppose she doesn't. I suppose I always thought she had money. With that television show of hers and everything."

Nick was doubtful. "It's a local television show, you know. It has had some syndication—"

"—all over the Northeast—"

"—all over the Northeast," Nick agreed cheerfully, "yes, but I don't think it's that big a deal. Not as big a deal as a third of fifteen million dollars. Not as big a deal as Caroline thinks it ought to be."

"Caroline always thinks she's owed. That's what we're going to put on her tombstone. 'I was owed.' I suppose it ought to be 'I was robbed.' More to the point. Do you think I could get away with my sapphire earrings?"

"Not to a funeral home."

"I suppose you're right."

Alyssa put down her lipstick brush—it was a useless exercise anyway; every time she got her lips red she felt the urge for another chocolate cream and every time she ate another chocolate cream her lipstick came off. If she had to choose between lipstick and chocolate, she knew which one she would have to have. She got her jewelry box off the vanity ledge.

"Five million dollars," she said. "Is there going to be a lot of that left after taxes?"

"A few million or so," Nick said.

"And I've got my trust fund too. Not that we'll be as rich as some of those women I do charity work with. Still."

"You'll be completely independent unless you want to get stupid."

"I'm never stupid about money, Nicholas, you know that. Can we go on a vacation when all this is over? You know, after the police business and all that, but before the trial. It'll probably be months before they actually go to trial."

"I think a vacation sounds fine."

"Good. I'm really beginning to feel claustrophobic around here. I—oh, for God's sake."

"What's the matter?"

"Look at this." Alyssa got up and brought her jewelry case across to the chair where Nicholas was sitting, the Sunday paper in his lap. She handed the case over to him and said, "I know it's a mess in there, but just look for yourself. I've lost one of my pearl stud earrings."

## *f o u r*

### *1*

As it turned out, Gregor Demarkian had been able to accomplish one or two things on Sunday. He had talked to Fred Scherrer on the phone. Talking to Fred Scherrer was like talking to any lawyer, only worse. It was impossible to find out anything you really wanted to know in a straightforward way at the same time that it was impossible to avoid revelations you had no interest in exploding under your feet like land mines. Gregor learned all about Fred Scherrer's last two wives, about the arrangements Candida DeWitt had made with the men who kept her, about Fred Scherrer's admiration for Candida as an intelligent businesswoman. He did not learn anything at all about the murder that he did not already know. Fred Scherrer had no alibi because Fred Scherrer was staying at Candida DeWitt's house. At two o'clock on Saturday afternoon Scherrer had decided that he would not be able to live without two dozen Bavarian creme doughnuts from Dunkin' Donuts in the kitchen. He had driven off to the center of Bryn Mawr and with one thing and another—traffic, stopping to buy a disposable razor, deciding to get two dozen jelly doughnuts in addition to the Bavarian cremes—hadn't made it back until four-thirty. Then he had parked Candida's car in Candida's detached garage, walked into Candida's living room, and found the body lying right where he then left it. He was too good and too experienced a lawyer to have touched anything. At least, he was if he wasn't also the murderer. Gregor was aware of that. The problem was that there was nothing in Fred Scherrer's story that could actually eliminate the lawyer as a suspect. Bob Cheswicki and Russell Donahue and his people were working very hard to place Fred Scherrer in all the places he claimed he'd been on Saturday afternoon. In the end, even if they succeeded it would make no difference. Determining the time of death was hardly an exact science. There was nothing to say Fred couldn't have killed Candida before he left the house to buy doughnuts or after he got back.

The other thing of a productive nature Gregor did on Sunday was to talk to Russell Donahue and Bob Cheswicki. They came to Cavanaugh Street carrying computer printouts and cross-section drawings and anything else they had been able to get their hands on that related to the two deaths this weekend but wasn't required to be locked up in an evidence cage or on file with the medical examiner's office. Then the three of them sat down to exactly the kind of busywork that made Gregor's head ache. Check. Double-check. Triple-check. Check again. By the time it was over, Gregor could have reproduced the wound drawings in his sleep. He was glad that Hannah Krekorian was no longer the prime suspect in this case, but if one more person had said The Sentence one more time, Gregor would have gone after the perpetrator with a two-by-four. The Sentence was: "Now that we have a time of death for Candida DeWitt's murder, we know somebody was with Hannah Krekorian for practically every second of the relevant period, so she's out of it." One of the problems with The Sentence was that it was so grammatically and syntactically messy. Gregor kept wanting to edit it.

The last thing Gregor did on Sunday was to watch the transformation of Lida Arkmanian's town house. It was a calculated metamorphosis. Sometime on Saturday evening, the strategy the women of Cavanaugh Street were using to take care of Hannah Krekorian had been judged inadequate and out-of-date. Instead of keeping her safely in Helen Tevorakian's apartment, away from the gossip and the stress, they had decided to "take her out of herself." What they meant was that they wanted to get her thinking about something else. That was going to be very difficult to do. The man had been killed in Hannah's bedroom, after all. Hannah wasn't even going to be allowed back into the room until Monday. Hannah went to church, but it was obvious to everybody that she spent the whole time wondering if people were staring at her. Then there were the newspapers. The newspapers were nuts. Gregor had made a point of not looking at them—he didn't want to see himself described as "the Armenian-American Hercule Poirot" one more time—but he knew what Helen Tevorakian and the others meant. Their problem was what to do with Hannah now that they had decided that something had to be done with her. Their solution was to put her on a ladder against the façade of Lida Arkmanian's town house, three stories up. She was supposed to be hanging red crepe paper.

"You know how depressed Donna has been lately," Helen Tevorakian said when Gregor asked. "Well, now she's feeling better."

"Donna wanted to make Lida's house look like a box of chocolates with lace and a ribbon," Sheila Kashinian said. "It's a very cute idea."

"All we wanted to do was to make sure that Hannah wasn't brooding about it all the time," Maria Varoukian said. "We wanted to take her mind off her troubles."

Privately, Gregor thought there were kinder ways to take Hannah's mind off her troubles than to prop her up three stories over a busy city street in the frigid February cold. He also thought Donna Moradanyan must not simply be feeling better, but getting on to delirious. He wondered why he hadn't noticed it Saturday night. Sometimes he thought he never noticed anything. Still, no matter how crazy the project had been, it had served its purpose in a number of ways. Hannah had been made to feel part of the community again, not singled out by strange things going on in her apartment or under suspicion of murder or anything else. Lida's town house, the front of which Gregor could see from his living room window, looked insanely wonderful, with bright white satin bows on the sash of every window and metallic red-and-white stripes leading from the top of an old and now-unused antenna to the edges of the roof. It didn't remind Gregor of a box of chocolates, or of anything else he had ever encountered in the real world, but it was a nice effect. The women were all proud of themselves too, because Hannah had been so terrified up there on that ladder that she hadn't been able to think about the murders for a minute—or for several hours afterward either.

2

On Monday morning Gregor Demarkian came out of his building to find Donna Moradanyan on a ladder in front of it, tacking a garland of pink chiffon cupids around the edges of the street door. She was being helped by old George Tekemanian, who was sitting on the low side wall of the stoop with a box of spangly things on his lap. Gregor said hello to both of them and they both said hello back, but they weren't really paying attention. Donna was holding a running conversation with herself, not quite under her breath.

"First the netting," Donna was saying, "and then the spring has to go with the red crepe or you'll be able to see it . . ."

Old George Tekemanian looked solemn. "It is a mechanical device," he said. "Every time anyone opens the front door, the box next to Bennis's living room window will open and a cupid will pop out."

Gregor stepped back and looked up. There was no box near Bennis's living room window. Not yet. He told himself he ought to be grateful that the box was not being planned for his living room window. He stepped closer to the building again and turned toward the street. Christopher Hannaford was standing on the sidewalk in front of Lida Arkmanian's town house, looking up at Donna on her ladder. Gregor wondered where Christopher had come from. He wasn't carrying a paper under his arm. He didn't look cold.

Christopher shook his head a little and began to cross the street. Halfway over he called out, "Are you going to breakfast, Gregor? I wanted to talk to you."

"I'm going to breakfast," Gregor said.

"Maybe I will go to breakfast too," old George Tekemanian said, looking hopeful. "I'm cold."

"No," Donna Moradanyan said decisively. "I'll take you over myself when this is done."

Old George Tekemanian sighed.

Christopher had reached them. He had his hands in the pockets of his jeans. His jacket was unzipped. His thick patch of trademark black Hannaford hair puffed and shuddered in the breeze.

"God, it's miserable in Philadelphia in February," Christopher said. "It must have been miserable when I was growing up here, but I don't remember it like that."

"You were too busy being young," old George Tekemanian said.

"We'll see you two later," Gregor told George and Donna. "Good luck with the . . . mechanical device."

Donna paid no attention to him. Gregor started up the street toward the Ararat. His scarf was wrapped tightly around his throat. His coat was long and every available button was buttoned. He was wearing gloves, and his gloved hands were firmly in his pockets. How did Christopher Hannaford stand it, wearing almost nothing really warm at all?

"So," Gregor said. "Bennis was telling me on Saturday that you knew Paul Hazzard, or had met him. That you had something to tell me about him anyway."

"I have something to say," Christopher Hannaford agreed carefully. "I don't know if it will be any use to you at this point. Bennis says you already know what's going on."

"Not exactly," Gregor said. "I know who committed the murder—who committed all three murders, starting with the murder of Jacqueline Isherwood Hazzard. I know what the murders were committed with, and I'm pretty sure that once the police get hold of the weapon, they'll be able to prove it actually was the weapon. I even know why Jacqueline Isherwood Hazzard was killed and why Candida DeWitt had to die. I just don't understand why Paul Hazzard was stabbed six times."

"Is that official, from the police, that he was stabbed six times?"

"Oh, yes. Stabbed six times and stabbed hard. Not so hard that a woman couldn't have done it, but hard."

"I never believed that stuff when I read it in detective stories," Christopher said. "A woman's crime, a man's crime. Even before women's lib I didn't believe it. The women I've known have mostly been capable of anything."

"I know what you mean, but sometimes there are considerations of size involved. If you find a six-foot-ten-inch three-hundred-and-fifty-pound football player lying dead on the floor with his neck broken and the fingerprints of his assailant imprinted in his flesh, those fingerprints might belong to a woman, but she'd be a very large woman."

"I see what you mean. I hope you see what I mean. Do you understand women?"

"No."

"Neither do I. I don't even understand Bennis, and she's my own sister."

"Nobody understands Bennis," Gregor said. "It's not possible."

"Sometimes I think there's just nothing you can do right," Christopher went on. "If you fall in love with a woman because she's beautiful, she's angry at you for that. If you fall in love with her for herself and you don't care what she looks like, she's angry with you for that. If it matters to you how old she is, she's angry with you for that. If it doesn't matter to you how old she is, she's angry with you for that. It's enough to make you want to start drinking in the mornings."

"The Ararat doesn't sell alcohol in the mornings."

"I guess I don't really want any. I think I'm having a bad day."

They were right at the door of the Ararat. Gregor didn't have time to ask him if there was some woman in particular who had caused these ruminations—in Gregor's experience, there always was—or if he was, truly, just having a bad day. Maybe this was the result of a week or so of staying in the same apartment with Bennis. That could do this kind of thing to anybody.

Gregor opened the plate glass door and let Christopher go in ahead of him. Inside, Linda Melajian was in the process of putting out little straw baskets full of heart-shaped candies on all the tables. The baskets had that unmistakable Donna Moradanyan touch. On each and every one of the baskets' handles, a short length of red yarn had been tied into a bow and anchored with a minuscule red-and-white striped arrow.

"Isn't it wonderful that Donna Moradanyan is feeling so much better the last couple of days?" Linda Melajian said.

Gregor took up residence in the window booth. "Wonderful," he repeated.

"I'll go get coffee," Linda Melajian said. "I'll tell my father to get ready for one cholesterol special and one mushroom omelet. Old George isn't still sick, is he?"

"He looked fine to me," Gregor told her. "He's out helping Donna do something to our building."

Linda hurried away, got the coffee, hurried back again. She set them up with a pot and then disappeared on the run one more time, going back to the kitchen.

"So," Gregor said to Christopher. "You and Paul Hazzard. Why do I feel that's an unlikely combination?"

"Because it is." Christopher laughed. "Me and the recovery movement, that's an unlikely combination too. Do you remember when you first met us, when all that happened at our house, when my father died?"

"Oh, yes," Gregor said.

"Well"—Christopher poured coffee—"about that time I was in, I think it was seventy-five thousand dollars' worth of debt in gambling losses. Really crazy gambling losses. Cards. Roulette. Nonsense."

"Illegal gambling?"

"Mostly, yeah. But I didn't do too badly at places like Vegas and Reno when I had the cash. The problem was what I did when I didn't have the cash."

"Meaning run a tab."

"Precisely. I ran a lot of tabs with a lot of people and always the wrong people. More than once, Bennis bailed me out of trouble. The year my father died, I was more than a little overdue. I was getting phone calls threatening me with bodily harm, if you know what I mean."

"Death?"

"No, just maiming." Christopher smiled. "Even at the time I wasn't crazy enough to wait around until somebody was threatening to kill me. Anyway, Bennis bailed me out of that and then she loaned me the money to go to this place in Vermont for three months, where a friend of mine had gone to quit gambling. That wasn't her idea, by the way. It was mine. If you say 'therapy' to Bennis, she spits."

"I know."

"Right. Well. Anyway. I went. And as you can guess, it was a place run by Paul Hazzard's organization. I've been trying to work out the timing. My father died after Jacqueline Isherwood Hazzard did—after by at least a couple of years, I'm sure, which means that I was up in Vermont either while Paul Hazzard was standing trial or after it was over, but not before."

"Okay."

"Okay. Well. I was there for about a month and I was going crazy, only not crazy about gambling. Do you know anything at all about how these therapy programs work?"

"Maybe," Gregor said cautiously. "I've heard a lot of stories since this thing started."

"The stories were probably all true," Christopher told him. "The first day, I was dragged into a room with a psychologist in it and lectured about my 'addictions.' There was no such thing as a simple 'addict.' All addicts had multiple 'addictions.' If I was addicted to gambling, then I had to be addicted to other things as well. The regime at the center was purged of all refined sugar, all alcohol, all tobacco, all drugs, all red meat."

"Red meat?"

"Yeah, well, according to the theory, red meat has a natural tranquilizer in it, an animal protein that acts as a tranquilizer, I don't remember, and a tranquilizer is a drug."

"Oh."

"You're getting that look on your face," Christopher said. "Everybody does when they come in contact with the recovery movement for the first time. You get used to this stuff if you hear it often enough. Anyway, the deal was, we had group therapy at two every afternoon, and what we were supposed to do at Group was testify to the damage our addictions had done to us. To be exact, Mr. Demarkian, we were supposed to tell horror stories. I had some pretty good horror stories about gambling, and I told them, but then they wanted horror stories about my 'other addictions.' Which I didn't think I had. I mean, I smoked marijuana fairly frequently in those days, but I wasn't compulsive about it. It certainly never interfered with my work or my life. The same thing with wine."

"So?"

"So," Christopher said, "they kept pushing me and pushing me. They kept telling me I was lying. They kept telling me I was in denial. I asked them what I was supposed to say if I was telling them the truth—if I wasn't addicted to marijuana or a closet alcoholic or whatever, how did I express that so that they knew I was telling the truth. And the basic answer was that there was no way I could prove I was telling the truth, because there was no way I *could* be telling the truth, because if I wasn't addicted, the question would never have come up. It went beyond guilty until proven innocent. It became guilty with no way to prove yourself innocent. Guilty because you were accused."

"What did you do?"

Christopher shrugged. "I'd signed myself up for three months. Bennis had paid for three months. And I did have a problem with gambling. I decided to give it a shot. One day I staged a big conversion scene in group. After that I just made stuff up."

"Horror stories, you mean?"

"Right. I was good at it too. I was so good at it, I became a kind of institutional wonder story. I got trotted out for all the visiting dignitaries. So, when Paul Hazzard himself showed up in person, I got trotted out then too."

Linda Melajian was back with the food. Gregor accepted his absently and saw that Christopher was paying no attention to his omelet at all. Gregor finished off the coffeepot and handed it back to Linda.

"When you say 'trotted out,' what do you mean?"

"We'd have special therapy sections with the participants picked in advance. Not the usual groups. There were a bunch of us who were considered to be good for the institution's image."

"And there was one of these special therapy sessions when Paul Hazzard visited?"

"Right. The thing is, Hazzard visited for quite a long time, at least a week, maybe longer. He didn't just come in and out for one session. And he didn't come alone. He had one of his daughters with him."

"Which one?"

"Alice?" Christopher asked. "Does that sound right? Thin blond woman who eats a lot."

"Alyssa."

"Is that it? Whatever. She was there, but she wasn't allowed to sit in on our group sessions. So when Hazzard first met Sylvia Charlow, his daughter wasn't there."

"Who was Sylvia Charlow?"

"Woman in our group. Older woman, about sixty-five or so. Fairly well preserved, with all that means. She was in Vermont with one of those codependency things. You know. An addiction to addictions. I've never been entirely sure what they mean by it all."

"Neither have I."

"With Sylvia, her value to the institution was that she talked so well about herself," Christopher said. "She was really eloquent. I kept wondering why she didn't give up therapy and write a woman's novel. She had such a command of prose. When Paul Hazzard met her he was enchanted, and we could all see it. And sure enough, when Group was over he took her aside."

"Aren't there ethical considerations in a case like that?" Gregor asked. "I keep hearing things about Paul Hazzard. They all seem to be—about women."

"I wouldn't be surprised. There are ethical considerations, Gregor, but for God's sake. Nobody pays attention to them. Paul Hazzard sure as hell never did. I saw him later that same evening, after dinner, with Sylvia in tow. They were leaving the main building and going for a walk on the grounds."

"By themselves?"

"Most definitely by themselves. I saw them the next

day too. He had her stuffed into a corner of the main lounge away from everybody else. He was sitting so close to her, his knees were digging into her thighs. She had to sit sideways to accommodate him. And he kept leaning over her. He reminded me of a vulture."

"I think he was one."

"I think he was too," Christopher agreed. "The thing is, this little dance went on for a couple of days, and then suddenly Paul Hazzard's daughter seemed to be aware of it. She was furious. I mean really furious. Every time she saw them together, even if they were just standing side by side in the middle of a crowd of people, she would come over and bust them up. Sylvia wasn't taking this very well. Paul Hazzard was ready to kick somebody. And all that interference wasn't making Alyssa Hazzard any happier. She got madder and madder and madder by the day."

"I think therapy sounds like a wonderful thing," Gregor said blandly. "I thought the point of all this nonsense was to get your life under control. Or at least to get your emotions under control."

"Never mention control to anyone in recovery," Christopher said. "A need for control is a sign of codependency. Maybe they've got a point. Maybe I was watching three completely noncodependent people. They were certainly out of control. I think Sylvia was thrilled with the trouble she was causing. She was that kind of woman. Paul Hazzard was after her anytime his daughter's back was turned. The daughter was getting more and more frenzied. Then, just before lunch one day, Paul Hazzard and Sylvia Charlow disappeared. Poof. One minute they were with us. The next minute they were gone. A minute and a half later, Alyssa showed up to eat. She looked all around the dining room and didn't find either one of them. She looked all around the dining room again. Then she said, 'That goddamned shithead' in a very loud voice and went racing out again. At which point, of course, we all did the inevitable."

"Which was what?"

"Which was follow them, of course. The staff tried to stop us, but there was nothing they could really do about it. We all poured out of the dining room and went racing up the stairs to the second floor. Alyssa Hazzard went straight up to Paul Hazzard's room and started banging on the door. It was locked, of course, but she kept banging. In the end, there was nothing he could do."

"He opened up."

"Of course he did. To give him credit, he wasn't disheveled and neither was Sylvia. There was no reason at all to think they were doing anything more provocative than talking. I don't think Alyssa cared what they were doing. She just started screeching at them."

"Was she screeching anything in particular?"

"Yep. That's why we're having this conversation, isn't it? It was what she said to Sylvia that struck me, a couple of days ago, as having relevance to what's been going on around here. Like I said a little while ago. It's a side issue now."

"What did she say to Sylvia?"

"She said, 'You silly cow. He's after you only for your money.' "

Gregor considered this. It fit, of course, but did it make any difference?

He thought even Hannah now believed that Paul Hazzard had been after only her money. And they all knew Hannah wasn't committing these murders.

"What did Alyssa Hazzard say to her father?"

Christopher Hannaford laughed and poked at his omelet with his fork. "Oh, that was typical. That was right out of a soap opera. 'You old ass,' she told him. 'You know what trouble you got us all into when you tried this the last time. You know what kind of trouble you're going to get us all into again. What the hell do you think you're trying to pull?' It was hysterical, Gregor, it really was. I didn't even blame her. He *was* an old ass."

# *five*

## 1

Fred Scherrer had been dealing with police officers now for better than thirty years, and he couldn't help thinking that he would have made a better one than most of the ones he'd met. He would certainly not be as prone to thinking in tracks. That was why he was so often victorious in his fights against official law enforcement agencies. That was why he was so good at getting acquittals not only for the possibly innocent, but for the flagrantly guilty. Police departments got into ruts and dragged district attorneys down with them. Judges took what was handed to them and never bothered to think a case through. If Fred had been this particular police department dealing with this particular case, he would have gotten out of one particular rut right away. He would have stopped insisting to himself and everybody else that the two murders had to have been committed by the same person. Fred didn't see why that was necessary at all. For the first murder he favored that old woman in whose apartment the murder had been committed. For the second murder he favored himself.

Of course, Fred thought, lying on the made-up bed in the hotel room he had rented at the Sheraton Society Hill, he knew the second murder had not been committed by himself. He'd had a few wild nights in his life, especially in the army, but he would have remembered it if he had stabbed the woman he was interested in to death. That didn't matter. If you thought of the law as a contest—and Fred always had thought of the law as a contest, a gladiators' showdown between the forces of Oppression and the champions of the Individual—all that really mattered was the win and lose. Fred had worked very hard to be the one who always won. That was all that mattered.

It was now eleven o'clock on Monday morning and he was going crazy. *That* was all that mattered. He was staring at the ceiling. He was devising clever prosecution strategies to put his own sweet butt in the electric chair. He was trying to remember if Pennsylvania had an electric chair. He was doing nothing useful at all, and he was about to burst. He still thought it had been the right decision, to stay over for a couple of days now that Candida was dead. This way he didn't look as if he were trying to escape investigation. He wished somebody would come to his door and demand something out of him that he would have to cope with. His room was nice and big and clean and empty. His ceiling was painted in thick cream that looked as if it had been polished. The room service in this hotel was a marvel. He had to *do* something.

"Listen," Sid had said on the phone that morning. "Get out of that room. Go to the library. Let me fax you some work. You know you by now, Fred. If you don't have anything around to occupy your mind, you're going to do something stupid."

"Don't fax me any work," Fred had told him then. "It will only get lost. I've got other things on my mind for the moment."

What he should have had on his mind was Candida on the floor, Candida murdered, Candida the person. What he ought to have been doing was having an orgy of emotion. Fred had never been very good at emotions. They had always seemed to him to be such a waste of time. He preferred to think.

Daggers, he thought now. Walls. Town houses. Jealousy. Money. Everybody thought he needed more money. Billionaires thought they needed more money. There was no end to it.

He sat up on the bed. What hair he had was a mess. He could feel it sticking out of his skull in sharp points. He smoothed it down.

Money, he thought again. Money and the dagger. Those were the keys. It was all so clear to him, sharp as a photograph, except that it wasn't exactly. It was as if he were looking at the picture upside down. Jacqueline lying on the floor of the living room in that town house, lying dead the way he had seen her in the police photographs that had been handed over to him in discovery. Candida DeWitt, talking calmly in the car on Friday night about what she knew and what she didn't know. Candida, lying dead herself on another living room floor. Christ, what was wrong with him? Why couldn't he make it come out straight?

He got off the bed. His coat was lying over the back of the desk chair on the other side of the room. He had left it there when he had gone down to breakfast to let the maid clean up. The maid had picked it up and shaken it out and folded it neatly and left it there herself. Fred shrugged it on and searched around in the pockets to find his gloves. He never actually wore his gloves, but he liked to know he had them with him. He was the same way about the personal confessions of his clients. He liked to know if they were guilty or innocent. He made a point of insisting that they tell him. He was better than a priest at never telling anyone else. It just made him feel better to know.

Fred let himself into the hall, checked the pocket of his pants for his room key, and headed for the elevators. Going down, he went over it all one more time. There were two other people in the elevator car with him. One was a stout little elderly nun in a white habit that reached just to the middle of her knees, and a black veil. She looked mad as hell. The other was a middle-aged woman in a powder-blue suit with a pleading expression on her face. They seemed to be together.

"They make really wonderful chicken salad in the restaurant downstairs," the woman in the pastel suit was saying. "It will be perfect for you. I know how you love your chicken salad."

Fred got out of the elevator as soon as the doors opened on the ground floor. He didn't care if the elderly nun liked chicken salad or not. He passed the reception desk and saw that it had sprouted decorations it hadn't had when he'd checked in on Saturday night. There was a bright crimson cardboard heart trimmed in red paper lace next to each of the check-in stations. The young woman stationed at the cashier's desk was wearing a "Be My Valentine" heart pin on her right shoulder. Fred passed them all and went out onto the street.

Valentine's Day was—when? Friday? Thursday? Decorations were appearing all around him, in the windows of stores, on the doors of restaurants and delis. This was a busy part of the city. Fred walked up to one of the hotel doormen and gave him the address of the Hazzard town house. The doorman was wearing one of those "Be My Valentine" pins on his tunic. It was so cold out here, Fred's face felt stiff enough to crack. The doorman was stamping his feet and whacking his gloved hands together every chance he got.

"I wouldn't bother to pay for a cab to go there," the doorman said. "It's only about ten blocks away. That way." He pointed into the traffic.

"What about the neighborhood?" Fred asked him.

The doorman shrugged. "You shouldn't have too much trouble, even in that coat. But things are the way things are these days. It's a new world."

Actually, Fred thought, it was a very old world. He could have told the doorman things about the crime in ancient Rome that would have curled his hair. He dodged into the traffic and headed out in the direction the doorman had pointed him in. He would have walked a good ways no matter what the doorman had told him. Walking helped him think. Besides, one of the reasons he had picked this hotel was that he'd known it was close to the Hazzard town house.

Daggers. Jacqueline. Living rooms. Stab wounds. Prosecutors. When he'd come to Philadelphia to defend Paul Hazzard against charges of murder, he had thought about the project in purely technical terms. Paul Hazzard was a friend of his. Paul Hazzard was in trouble. Paul Hazzard needed to be gotten out of trouble. Fred had asked Paul the ultimate question—*did you do it?*—and received the ultimate answer—*no I didn't*—and taken enough care to ensure he was being told the truth, but he hadn't gone beyond that. It had been different with Paul, because Paul was somebody he knew. Fred had been reluctant to push the way he might have pushed other people. Fred hadn't even been sure he wanted to know what had really happened there. And now . . .

Daggers. Jacqueline. Living rooms. Stab wounds. Prosecutors. Money. Blood.

It was very cold. Fred Scherrer had been moving quickly. Now he was standing right in front of the Hazzard town house, looking up at its shiny black door. Around him, the city seemed to have deteriorated. One or two of the buildings looked abandoned. There was a vacant lot full of rubbish up the street. Paul had been so proud of this house and his ownership of it. It had been a form of instant background. Fred didn't think Paul had been capable of preventing himself from lying about how he had gotten hold of it. He wondered how much longer Paul would have been able to hold on to it in the middle of all of this. Philadelphia was falling apart. New York was falling apart. It was all going to hell.

Fred went up the stairs to the front door and pressed the bell.

Philadelphia and New York could do what they wanted to do.

He was going to get this straightened out in his head.

## 2

Caroline was in her studio when the doorbell rang, bent over her drafting table under the hot light of a flexible lamp. She should have been at work, but she hadn't been able to face it. First Daddy, then Candida. The local press was having a field day. The national press was probably being just as bad, but Caroline hadn't checked. She hated television. It was a propaganda machine for codependence.

Caroline would have felt annoyed with herself for not going in to work—not guilty; she had purged herself of guilt—except that James hadn't gone in either. She had heard him call Max this morning and cancel all his appointments. Alyssa hadn't left the house either, but there was nothing unusual in that. Alyssa went out only for social reasons anyway. They were all there together and not talking to each other. It was exactly the way it had been after Jacqueline died.

Caroline needed an arch support anchored at the north end of the trellis. She picked up the compass, placed the point of the pencil where it needed to be, placed the swing point where she thought it had to go to give her the sweep she needed, and drew. She got it wrong.

Downstairs, the doorbell rang again. Caroline got up, let herself out of the studio, and went to listen at the stairwell. If nobody else answered the door, she wasn't going to. She didn't want to talk to people today. She was sure somebody would answer though. She knew James and Alyssa far too well.

The doorbell rang for the third time. James came jogging out from the back of the ground floor, from the direction of the basement stairs. He must have been in the kitchen.

"Coming," he shouted as he came.

Caroline leaned far over the railing and saw James stop as he reached the door and go for the eyehole. Then he stepped back and started to open up.

"Fred," he said, "what are you doing here?"

Caroline watched Fred Scherrer come into the foyer. His coat was open and his hands were bare. He looked cold. James closed the door behind him and began walking toward the ground floor living room.

"I'm staying over a couple of days in case they need me for the investigation," Fred was saying. "At least, that was my idea. But they don't seem to need me for the investigation and I was getting a little nuts. I guess I wanted the walk."

"You ought to be glad you didn't come over yesterday,"

James told him. "There were about six reporters stationed out there all afternoon and half the night. I hope they all die of frostbite."

"Who is it?" Alyssa's voice came bouncing out from the same direction James had come in. Caroline thought they must have been back there together. She wondered what they could have been up to.

Alyssa appeared in the foyer.

"Oh, Fred," she said. "It's you. I was wondering why we hadn't heard from you. It seemed only natural that you'd come over."

After that the three of them went off into the living room, and Caroline couldn't see them anymore.

Up on the landing, Caroline stepped back and tried to think. She didn't want to see Fred Scherrer any more than she wanted to see anybody else. She didn't like Fred Scherrer. After Jacqueline had been murdered, Fred Scherrer had been a first-class pain in the ass. Still, he was tricky, there was that. You could never tell what he was up to. It didn't make sense for her to leave him down there with James and Alyssa, where she couldn't hear them.

Caroline went back into the studio and looked around. Her drafting table was a mess. Her black leather tote bag was sitting on the floor next to her drafting table stool, open. Caroline took her equipment off the drafting table and put it in the tote bag. Then she snapped shut the tote bag's magnetic clip and hoisted the bag onto her shoulder. She felt her efforts were halfhearted. She was usually obsessively neat about her studio. Now her drafting table was still a mess and she was going to turn her back on it and walk out.

Obsessiveness is a symptom of codependency. Perfectionism is the essence of codependency. One of these days she really had to get her act together.

Caroline locked the studio door behind her. Then she started down the stairs, listening carefully. This was one of those old houses that was too well built. She couldn't hear anything. She went down a few steps and stood still, waiting. Then she gave up and went down the rest of the way.

At the entryway Caroline could finally hear something. It was Alyssa's voice, high and musical, going on and on about trivialities.

"Nicholas keeps telling me that there's going to be all this money and that the taxes have already been paid on it or the taxes have been figured in, I don't remember which," Alyssa was saying, "and I've been telling Nicholas that after this it's going to be impossible for us to spend any significant time in Philadelphia. I mean it was bad enough after all that mess with Jacqueline, but for this to happen just as all that was beginning to fade from public memory—I just can't stand it."

Caroline walked over to the living room archway and looked through. James stood next to the portable bar, pouring himself a glass of Perrier water. Alyssa sat on the love seat with her legs tucked under her, lotus fashion. Fred stood in the middle of the room, looking up at the weapons on the wall. None of them had noticed her. She walked all the way inside and said, "Hello."

Fred Scherrer turned around. "Hello," he said. "I was wondering where you were. I thought you might have gone in to work."

"I wouldn't have been able to get any work done," Caroline said.

"That's what I told myself." James finished pouring his Perrier and took a sip. "It's just the way I told Max. If I kept my appointments today, everybody I saw would want to know when I was going to channel Paul's spirit so the police could catch his murderer. I couldn't face it."

Fred Scherrer went back to looking at the weapons wall. "I've been thinking about this wall ever since your father died. It's been making me crazy. And now that I'm here, looking at it, it doesn't tell me a thing."

There were all kinds of things on the portable bar besides Perrier water. There was even liquor of half a dozen kinds. It was one of Daddy's hypocrisies. Daddy talked a good game about addictions, but he was the ultimate example of a man in denial. He didn't really believe he could have any addictions himself. Caroline knew she had every addiction on record, in spite of the fact that she'd never actually tried any hard drugs. She knew that if she was ever so much as in the same room with heroin or cocaine, she would fall into a drug-induced swoon and have to be rushed to the hospital. She went through the bottles on the portable bar and rejected each one in turn. The liquor was an obvious no-no. The regular soda had sugar in it and the diet soda had aspartame. The one bottle of "fruit juice" wasn't really fruit juice at all, but a commercial "punch" full of chemicals. Caroline gave up and went to sit down on the long couch that had its back to the street-side window. That way, she stayed well away from Alyssa.

"So," she said. "Exactly what's going on here? Are you holding some kind of investigation?"

"Of course Fred isn't holding some kind of investigation," James said, irritated. "Fred doesn't hold investigations. He defends people after they've been investigated."

"I'm sure Fred holds investigations sometimes," Alyssa said. "He would have to, wouldn't he? Fred has a very interesting theory about all this, Caroline. He thinks the key to it all is Jacqueline. I told him I thought Jacqueline had died so long ago, nobody could possibly know any more about it than they already did."

"That makes sense," James said.

Alyssa waved this away. "Caroline knows what I'm talking about. I wonder what that Demarkian person is doing, that's what I wonder. Fred talked to him yesterday, but other than that, he seems to have disappeared. I think it's creepy."

"I never thought there was any mystery about what happened to Jacqueline," Caroline said. "I thought Daddy killed her."

Fred Scherrer turned around, curious. "Did you? You never had any doubt in your mind?"

"Of course not."

"You don't have any doubt about it now?"

"No, I don't. Why should I?"

"Well," Fred Scherrer said, "there are a couple of problems here. There's the fact that Paul was killed with the same weapon or something very much like the same weapon and in the same way as Jacqueline was. There is that."

"It doesn't mean anything," Caroline insisted. "In the first place, we don't know he was killed with the same weapon, because we don't know what the weapon was that killed Jacqueline. In the second place, it was a famous case, in all the newspapers. It would be easy to copycat that kind of crime."

"Maybe," Fred Scherrer said. He sounded skeptical.

"If I'd thought Daddy had killed Jacqueline, I wouldn't have gone on living in this house," Alyssa said. "Talk about creepy. Did you lock your bedroom door every night before you went to sleep?"

"Of course I didn't," Caroline said. "For God's sake, Alyssa, you're being ridiculous. Daddy wouldn't have any reason to kill me. Or you or James either. We didn't have any money to leave him. And he wasn't screwing somebody he hoped we wouldn't find out about."

"There's another way these two crimes are alike," Fred Scherrer said. "The murder of Jacqueline Hazzard and then the murder of Paul Hazzard. Have you noticed? None of the three of you has an alibi for either one."

Caroline had put her tote bag down right next to her on the floor. Now she reached over and picked it up. She tried to carry cans of plain, unadulterated apple juice around with her at all times. She bought them at an organic deli half a block from the place she worked. The organic deli also carried potato chips that had been broiled instead of fried. They were peculiar.

Caroline found a can of apple juice and took it out. It had an earth-friendly snap top that left no garbage when it was opened. She opened it and put the can down on the arm of the couch. Then she put her tote bag carefully back on the floor.

"Do you know what I think you're doing?" she asked Fred Scherrer. "I think you're trying to work us all up. I think you're trying to say things we're all going to regret."

James laughed. "Hell," he said. "That's what defense attorneys do."

"He's not being a defense attorney in this case," Caroline said. "He's being a suspect, and that's the point. He isn't trying to solve Daddy's murder. He doesn't have to. The police will do that. He isn't trying to solve Jacqueline's murder either. He knows all he has to know about that. He's trying to get out from under what happened to Candida, that's what he's trying to do."

"Caroline, be reasonable," her brother told her. "As hard as it may be to go against your nature, at least try to be reasonable. The same person who killed Dad had to have killed Candida. No matter what did or didn't happen to Jacqueline, even you have to see that."

"No," Caroline said. "I don't have to see it."

"Caroline likes coincidences," Fred Scherrer said, still looking at the wall of weapons. "Big coincidences."

"You're just here to stir us all up," Caroline said placidly. "It's a form of codependency—"

"—oh, for Christ's *sake*," James exploded.

"—but it's a very toxic form of behavior," Caroline went on, ignoring him. "It's really very destructive. It's almost always resorted to out of fear. I wonder what you think this is going to get you."

"I wonder what you think *this* is going to get *you*," Fred Scherrer said, intrigued. "Do you ever actually talk like a human being? Or is your whole head stuffed full of this kind of jargon?"

"Her whole head is stuffed full of cotton wool," James said.

Over on the love seat, Alyssa stirred. Then she stood and walked over to the couch where Caroline was sitting. Caroline moved aside, but Alyssa wasn't coming for her. Alyssa was leaning against the back of the couch and looking out into the street. Caroline turned sideways so that she could see too.

"Quiet, everybody," Alyssa ordered. "We've got company."

"What kind of company?" James asked. "If it's more reporters, I'm going to have them arrested."

"It's Demarkian and those two policemen," Alyssa said. "The ones who were all on the news together Saturday night. They look very grim."

"You're dramatizing yourself," Caroline said. "It's called the soap-opera syndrome. It's a form of addiction."

Alyssa wasn't listening to her. None of them were. None of them ever did. Caroline looked out at Gregor Demarkian and the other two men climbing the steps to the town house's front door. By now, she thought, they all really ought to know better.

## 3

Across town, on Cavanaugh Street, Christopher Hannaford stood in the kitchen of Lida Arkmanian's town house, putting together a salad. He was wearing socks but no shoes, jeans, and a flannel shirt but no belt. His black hair was a mess. Lida was standing on the far side of the kitchen, at the counter next to the stove, putting together the salad dressing. This was at least the fourth time Christopher had made a salad in this room. It had become a routine. It ought to be making him feel wonderful, or at least be making him feel secure. Instead, he felt like cow dung.

"Listen," he said finally. "Why don't you just talk to me? Why don't you just tell me what's wrong?"

"Nothing is wrong, Christopher."

"Of course something is wrong, Lida. For Christ's sake. What do you take me for?"

"Maybe 'wrong' is the wrong word to use."

"Fine. Pick the right word to use."

"You're making too much out of nothing."

He sliced a pile of radish chips the size of Mount McKinley. He opened the drawer in the counter next to the refrigerator and got out a plastic storage bag. He put the radish chips into the plastic storage bag and the plastic storage bag in the refrigerator. Really trivial things were beginning to seem terribly important.

"Lida," he said again.

Lida had the salad dressing finished. She picked up the cruet and walked over to him. She put the cruet down next to the salad bowl and stepped back.

"Nothing is wrong," she said stubbornly. "Believe me. Nothing is wrong."

Christopher Hannaford didn't think he'd ever been handed a bigger crock of shit in his life.

## *six*

### *1*

What Gregor Demarkian liked best about the detective novels Bennis Hannaford sometimes gave him was the part where the detective calls all his suspects into a room and solves the crime in front of an audience. Rex Stout was good for that sort of thing. So were Ellery Queen and Agatha Christie. Gregor much preferred fantasy in his fiction to reality, since the reality was so very seldom really real. Gregor found the fantasy of the gathered suspects enormously funny, and not only because he had never once, in twenty years of federal police work, seen suspects so gathered to receive a solution. Gregor had sympathy for the fictional detectives. He knew why they wanted to bring the dramatis personae into one place. What he couldn't understand were the fictional suspects. Why did they bother to come? Why did they put up with this kind of mock gathering of the clans at all? Gregor had once suggested to a suspect in a kidnapping case that they ought to meet for lunch, informally, to go over the possible consequences of the suspect's descent into perjury. The suspect had told him to go to hell and taken off for a week on the Jersey shore instead.

That the remaining serious suspects in the murder of Paul Hazzard were sitting together in Paul Hazzard's living room when Gregor, Russell Donahue, and Bob Cheswicki drove up was an accident. Gregor knew that. He hadn't called these three people together. He hadn't brought Russell and Bob with him so that they could watch him stage a tour de force and pounce on the killer in an unsuspected leap, eliciting an unguarded confession and bringing the case to a close with a crash. He had come here to get the murder weapon, that was all. And yet . . .

Gregor stood in the foyer of the Hazzards' town house with his coat over his arm and his shoes dripped slush and rock salt into the runner carpet. In front of him, Bob Cheswicki was saying polite things to Alyssa Hazzard Roderick as she took his coat and put it away in the hall closet. Russell Donahue was standing beside him, looking uncomfortable. He hadn't been in plainclothes long enough to be used to houses like this. Over at the archway that led to the living room, Caroline Hazzard, James Hazzard, and Fred Scherrer were waiting. Caroline looked a little defensive. James and Fred just looked bland. Bob and Russell walked away toward the living room and Gregor handed his coat to Alyssa Roderick.

"Don't you people ever call before you show up at the door?" she asked. "We could have been out, you know. I was thinking about being out. The way things have been going, I was seriously thinking of being out to Kathmandu."

She shoved Gregor's coat in the closet and then walked away, passing by the others who were crowding up the entranceway and going straight for the love seat. Gregor watched her sit down and tuck her feet under her. She looked petulant.

"I hope you've come about something important," she continued. "I hope you're close to finding some resolution to this. We're all getting very much on edge."

"Mmmm," Bob Cheswicki said. "Well. Yes."

Russell Donahue put his hands in the pockets of his trousers.

If it went on like this much longer, they would all be frozen into immobility by embarrassment. Gregor looked around the room at the people now arrayed there. Alyssa was still on her love seat. Caroline was still on the long couch and put her feet on the floor, with her knees and ankles together, in the pose Bennis made fun of as "dancing-class rigor mortis." The men were all still standing, however, police and suspects both. It was as if they wanted to be ready for an impending emergency. Gregor considered the situation and made up his mind to it. This wasn't what he had expected, but it was what he'd gotten. He might as well use it.

He walked across the room to a fragile-legged wingback chair and sat down in it. It left his back to the wall of weapons but allowed him to face all the people, which was what was really important. He put his hands on his knees and leaned forward.

"For the moment," he said, "I would like a little information about the financial arrangements in this house. I would like to know about the trust funds Paul Hazzard set up for his children, and about the legacy of Jacqueline Isherwood Hazzard and how it was left. Was there a lot of money in those trust funds?"

James Hazzard folded his arms across his chest. His eyes grew cold. "I don't think we have to tell you that," he said. "I don't think we have to tell you anything without our lawyer present. And even then we don't have to tell you anything at all."

"True," Gregor said. He forbore pointing out that Fred Scherrer was a lawyer, one of the best in the United States, and right on the scene. He didn't know what sort of relationship there was between Scherrer and the Hazzard children. He went on. "Jacqueline Isherwood Hazzard's will is not a secret. It was probated over four years ago. The arrangements made by Paul Hazzard for putting money in trust are somewhat more private, but not by much. This is a murder investigation. It would take only a few phone calls."

"Make a few phone calls, then," James said.

"Oh, whatever for?" Alyssa countered. Her face was pale. "What difference does it make if he knows about our trust funds? They're not that large, Mr. Demarkian. And I'm not sure about the capital. I just know I get about forty thousand dollars a year, and so do the other two."

"That's right," Caroline said.

James shrugged. "What's the old saying? 'Enough to

do anything we want to do but not enough to do nothing at all.' It's too bad Dad wasn't as careful about the money he kept for himself."

"The rumors are true, then, that he was broke?" Gregor asked.

"He wasn't exactly broke," Alyssa answered. "It was more like he just didn't have enough money to go on living the way he had been living. I mean, the upkeep on the house was taken care of—"

"That's in Jacqueline's will," James put in. "She made a trust fund for the house, or something."

"That's right," Alyssa went on. "So we could all live here forever for free and that meant Daddy too, but you know what people are like. He was used to getting his suits custom-made and flashing an American Express platinum card everywhere he went. He didn't want to give that up."

"He *had* to give that up," Caroline said distastefully. "Jacqueline's murder absolutely destroyed him. Nobody wants to go to a therapist who may have murdered his own wife."

"Daddy didn't murder his wife," Alyssa said.

Gregor's chair looked reasonably padded, but it wasn't really comfortable. "Let's go back to Jacqueline Isherwood Hazzard's will," he said. "I take it it wasn't what you all had expected before she died."

"It wasn't what Dad had expected," James Hazzard said uneasily. "You could see that immediately. When he discovered the provisions, he was in shock."

"It had been changed," Fred Scherrer put in. "Just a couple of months before Jacqueline died, she'd moved it all around. We think—although there's no way anybody can be sure about it now—we think it was because she found out about Paul and Candida."

"The original will was much more usual?" Gregor asked.

"The original will gave Paul a life interest in Jacqueline's estate and then divided the estate among Caroline, James, and Alyssa on Paul's death," Fred Scherrer said.

Gregor nodded. "That's not very different from what

the will read in the end, is it, except for the provision for Paul Hazzard himself?"

"It made a big difference to Paul," Fred Scherrer said.

"That's true," Gregor agreed, "but it didn't make any difference to the three people here. Did the three of you know the precise provisions of your stepmother's will?"

"She sat us down and explained the whole thing a few years before she died," James said. He looked suddenly contrite. "We didn't like Jackie much, you know. She wasn't a very pleasant woman. But she'd known us since we were small children, and I suppose she thought of herself as our mother. She was never able to have any children of her own."

"And then Candida DeWitt came along," Gregor said.

"Daddy was like that," Alyssa said. "He was to skirts the way raging bulls are to matadors' capes."

"It wasn't the same with Candida," Caroline said. "It went on forever."

"It was over and done with by the time Jacqueline was killed," Alyssa pointed out. "We think Jackie found out about it and laid it on the line for once. She was such a wimp."

"She was a codependent with severe dependency problems," Caroline said sniffily. "She really needed a group. I don't know why she never went into one. It's not as if she didn't know where to find one."

Alyssa wrapped her arms around her knees and hugged them close to her chest. "Jackie really was a very strange person. She was capable of anything, I think. And she was very upset the few weeks or so before she was murdered. That came out at the trial."

Fred Scherrer nodded. "It did. The prosecution made a big thing of it."

"Yes," Gregor said. "Well, that's only logical." He tapped his hands against his knees, thinking. The rest of them—including Donahue and Cheswicki—looked at him with steady curiosity. That was the worst of playing the Great Detective. People kept expecting you to pull a rabbit out of a hat or do the Irish jig or otherwise behave in a decisive and spectacular manner. They kept waiting for it.

Gregor considered the situation one more time. Sometimes what you intended to do had to be scrapped in favor of what you could do. Especially when what you could do was more. He reached into his pocket and came up with the tiny brown cloth bag Bennis had given him to carry the stray pearl earring in. He got up, walked over to the coffee table, and shook the earring out on its surface. Then he stepped back and looked around.

Russell Donahue and Bob Cheswicki knew what Gregor was doing, and could make a fair guess as to why he was doing it. They didn't move from their places. Fred Scherrer and James Hazzard were interesting. They moved toward the coffee table to get a better look at what was now on it. It was Alyssa Roderick and Caroline Hazzard who were held by what was there. Caroline had gone very stiff and suspicious, as if she suspected a trap. Alyssa looked thoroughly bewildered.

"Is that my earring?" Alyssa asked. "Where did you get it? I went looking for it everywhere yesterday and I just couldn't find it anywhere."

## 2

In some cases, at some times, there is a kind of sea change. The emotional climate shifts. The complexion of the evidence mottles and molts. The angle from which the detective sees the suspects tilts in unforeseen directions. That was what happened in this case now. Gregor had known since Saturday who had committed these murders. He had known how. He had even known why, in a fashion. He knew the sort of explanation of motive that could be given in a court of law. Now he knew something else, something he would never be able to explain to anybody. Now he knew what the murderer felt like.

The little group of people were drawing closer and closer to the coffee table. Alyssa had the earring in her hand

and was turning it this way and that, as if there might be something about it she didn't already know.

"I think it's mine," she said. "They're all so alike, these things. It's maddening. Everybody has them. It certainly looks like mine."

"You are missing one?" Gregor asked gently.

"Yes, I am," Alyssa told him. "I wanted to wear them to the funeral home yesterday, but when I went through my jewelry box I could find only one."

"I don't think you ought to say any more." Fred Scherrer's voice was very quiet. It was also very firm. "I don't think you ought to say another thing until you've got some permanent representation."

"But why not?" Alyssa was bewildered. "Do you mean this was found at the scene of the crime or something?"

Gregor took the earring out of Alyssa Roderick's hand and put it back in its little bag. "It was not found at the scene of the crime," he said. "Not exactly. It was found in the guest room of Hannah Krekorian's apartment, across the hall from the bedroom in which your father died."

"It's not mine, then," Alyssa said. "I've never been in Hannah Krekorian's apartment. And I didn't kill my father."

"No," Gregor agreed, "you didn't kill your father. There was a possibility you had, of course, but the earring takes care of that. What's important here is that you know who killed your father. Just the way you knew who killed your stepmother more than four years ago."

"No," Alyssa said, being very earnest. "I don't know. I really don't, Mr. Demarkian. I have no idea."

"Mr. Donahue," Gregor said, "may I have the briefcase, please?"

Russell Donahue hurried forward with the briefcase, which was nothing more than a couple of thin sheets of leather fastened together, capable of holding half a dozen sheets of thin paper and no more. Gregor took it, laying it down on the coffee table. Then he opened it up and extracted two sheets of tracing paper. Both sheets of tracing paper had the same drawing on them. The drawings looked like this:

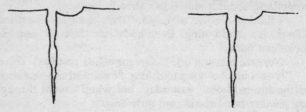

"From the beginning of this case," Gregor said, "from the beginning, that is, the death of Jacqueline Isherwood Hazzard, the unanswered and seemingly unanswerable question has always been: What was the weapon? Eventually this became a question of what was the weapon in all three murders. The dagger was never more than a continual ruse by the murderer. It was a piece of luck, sitting there on the wall like that after Jacqueline was killed. It wasn't planned. It didn't need to be planned. If the dagger hadn't existed, no weapon of any kind would ever have been discovered. Because the weapon wasn't a weapon."

"Wonderful," James Hazzard said. "You talk just like a detective in a book. Do you write fiction for a living?"

"If I did, I would have caught on to this much more quickly," Gregor answered. "You know, sometimes, in a case of murder, you have to know everything, every small and particular detail, before you can arrive at the solution. A friend of mine gives me fiction to read, Mr. Hazzard, in which that is almost always the detective's predicament. Before he can pronounce himself satisfied, before he can emerge triumphantly into the light with the solution in his hand, he must clear up a thousand small details and find the rationale for a hundred thousand random acts—except, of course, that in books nothing is ever truly random. In real life, on the other hand, a great deal is random. Many things happen in a murder case that are in no way connected to the murder at all. And as for the murderer . . ." Gregor shrugged. "It's nice to know all the whys and wherefores, but it isn't always necessary. In real life you sometimes find that all you need is one small piece of definite evidence."

James Hazzard leaned over and stared at the tracing paper. "And this is it?" he asked dubiously.

"These," Gregor said, "are copies of the drawings made by the medical examiner's office of the cross-sections of the wounds caused by the weapon entering the bodies of both Jacqueline Isherwood Hazzard and Paul Hazzard. The one from Jacqueline Isherwood Hazzard's body is on the left. The one from Paul Hazzard's body is on the right. I also have the cross-section taken from the wound in Candida DeWitt's body. I'll get it out for you if you like. There won't be any significant difference."

Alyssa shuddered. "I think we've had enough wounds. Can they really get pictures like this out of flesh? God, that sounds awful."

Gregor moved the tracing paper around. "Cross-sections have become fairly common in stabbing cases over the past few years. They weren't so common when your stepmother died, but the medical examiner at the time was very disturbed by the case. He was disturbed by the wound and by the fact that that dagger was being promoted as the weapon. I don't blame him for being disturbed. He showed more common sense than almost anybody else assigned to the case. Look at that wall up there." Gregor gestured at the weapons wall. "There have to be a hundred weapons up here at least, some of them large, some of them extremely colorful. I've said it before. If you were going to grab a weapon from this wall in the heat of an argument and kill somebody with it, it wouldn't be a small hand weapon on an inconvenient bracket you'd have to reach around to get to. No, there is only one explanation for the recurring presence of that dagger, and that is that it came in handy once—meaning immediately after the death of Jacqueline Isherwood Hazzard—because in a lot of ways it resembled the actual murder weapon."

"The dagger resembled the actual murder weapon," James repeated. He looked dazed. "I'm sorry, Mr. Demarkian, but I've always thought that dagger was a very odd-looking thing. I don't think it looks like anything else at all."

"I know," Gregor said. "I felt the same way after I first saw the drawings in the original case, when I first had

access to the cross-sections taken from Jacqueline Isherwood Hazzard's body. I went on feeling that way even after
I handled the actual murder weapon. I was doing then what
you are doing now. I was trying to think of some weapon
that resembled the dagger."

"But you said there was a weapon that resembled the
dagger," James protested. "You just did."

"No, I didn't." Gregor shook his head. "A murder
weapon is not necessarily a weapon per se. People are killed
with knives and guns and hand grenades, but they are also
killed with bookends and bowling balls and pinking shears.
Some nonweapons are obvious candidates for murder
weapons, like straight-edged razors and fireplace pokers.
Others are not."

"So this is a weapon that's not a weapon." Fred Scherrer
was following the proceedings shrewdly. "Surely the police
know enough to look for something like that. Even assuming it had been cleaned up, whatever it was, why didn't
they find it?"

"They didn't find it because it wasn't there," Gregor
explained. "It was back where it belonged, back where it
always was when its owner didn't have to carry it around.
I don't know if the police ever saw it. If they did, I don't
know how they would have connected it. It would have
been different if they had found it in the house."

"If it wasn't in the house, where was it?" James
sounded exasperated. "And are you honestly telling me
that the murderer kept it? Just washed it off and kept it?
And all these years? Whatever for?"

"The murderer had to keep the weapon," Gregor explained, "because it was not easy to replace, it was needed
for other things, and it would have been missed. Whether
it was kept around for years, I have no idea. Paul Hazzard
and Candida DeWitt may have been killed with a replace-
ment. It doesn't matter. The difficulties, the impossibilities,
of disposing of this weapon do lead me to one conclusion
though. I think Jacqueline Isherwood Hazzard was killed
in cold blood. I also think her murder was planned—but I
don't think it was planned for very long. I think the murderer thought it through for maybe ten or fifteen minutes,
standing in this room."

Alyssa stirred on the love seat. "That can't have been the way Daddy died," she said, "not if you're solving his murder with earrings in people's guest rooms. That could only have been the way Daddy died if that woman did it in a fit of pique then and there."

"If that woman, as you put it, had murdered your father in a fit of pique then and there, that ornamental dagger wouldn't have been at the scene covered in your father's blood."

"What a wonderful way to put it," Alyssa said sourly.

"It had to be accounted for," Gregor told her. "And there was only one way to account for it. It was being used to cover up for the real weapon, to throw suspicion in other directions."

"Why didn't your murderer just use that ornamental dagger on Daddy?" Alyssa demanded. "Wouldn't that have made more sense?"

"Maybe it would have," Gregor said, "but it wouldn't have been so sure. The murderer had no idea if that ornamented dagger could actually kill anybody."

Fred Scherrer snorted. "To hear Paul tell it, that idiotic thing had slaughtered tribesmen without number in its native wherever. He was always very big on how deadly that dagger was."

"What I want to know is where the real weapon actually is," James said. "How do we get to it and what does it look like?"

"Oh, that," Gregor said. "My guess is that the weapon is here."

"Why?" Fred Scherrer asked.

Bob Cheswicki broke in. "Because we already went to where it usually is this morning and it wasn't there."

"Give me a second here."

Gregor leaned forward and got a hand on Caroline Hazzard's tote bag. He had it lifted up off the floor before she had a chance to stop him. He held it close to his chest and looked through it. Then he said, "Here it is" and looked up at the assembled company.

"She needed it for work, you see," he said. "She couldn't just throw it away because it was such an unusually large size; she had to have it made to order. She had to have all her equipment made to order. It was expensive and it was obvious. She couldn't just have it disappear."

He pulled the oversize compass out of the tote bag and dropped the tote bag itself onto the floor. He held the compass up for everybody to see. The big pencil clamped into one point of the V looked dull. The sharp metal tip of the anchor point looked anything but. The metal of the compass had been oiled and shined. It glinted in the light pouring in through the window from the street.

Gregor pulled the V apart as far as it would go and pointed to the sharp-edged flat center arc.

"That's what everybody mistook for the handle of the dagger," Gregor explained. "The fit wasn't exact when matched up against the cross-sections, but cross-sections are often not exact. You see the difference though." He leaned over and tapped the drawings on the coffee table. "The dagger had a curved handle that went to either side of its point. These drawings show something with a flat-edged arc to only one side of the point." He laid the anchor point of the compass on top of the point on the drawing and stood back. They were as exact a match as a cross-section taken from human flesh could ever get.

"Jesus Christ," James Hazzard said.

And then Caroline Hazzard started to laugh.

"It was Daddy's idea, you know, that dagger. He walked in and saw Jacqueline on the floor and he knew exactly what I'd done. He didn't care. We thought a lot alike, Daddy and me. Our relationship was very symbiotic. He didn't start therapy early enough though. He had a tendency to panic."

"Caroline," Fred Scherrer said, "I don't think you ought to go on like this."

"I don't think it makes any difference," Caroline said. "It isn't going to matter much one way or the other. I've been in therapy for years. I'm not going to get convicted of anything. Maybe I'll just say Daddy came into my room and screwed me every chance he got when I was eight. That ought to take care of everything, shouldn't it, Fred? It would even be true on a metaphorical level, and not just when I was eight."

"Caroline, for God's sake," Alyssa said.

"I really think you're all getting far too worked up about all of this," Caroline said. "It's all going to turn out just fine, and you know it. And as far as I'm concerned, Daddy deserved to be dead."

The real question, Gregor thought, was not whether Paul Hazzard deserved to be dead, but whether he deserved to have had Caroline kill him—but that might be a little complicated for this crowd.

Gregor felt better about stepping back and letting Russell Donahue and Bob Cheswicki do what they did best.

*epilogue*

———

*valentine's day
on cavanaugh street
with all
that implies...*

*1*

Tommy Moradanyan went to play group on Thursdays, and because of that Donna Moradanyan had the time between eight-fifteen and eleven-thirty to get things done. This was less expansive than it seemed. What Donna wanted to get done almost always involved climbing ladders and hammering things outside other people's bedroom windows. Looking at the decoration of Cavanaugh Street from a purely aesthetic point of view, it was positively peculiar how so many of the best places to hang red net hearts and pink cupids were directly under the noses of people who liked to sleep late, especially since so few people on Cavanaugh Street did sleep late. Still, it had to be done and it had to be done now. Decorating the street was the only thing keeping Donna Moradanyan sane through Valentine's Day.

"It was absolutely crazy," she'd told Bennis Hannaford the night before. "I'd been going crazy for weeks, so depressed I could hardly even eat, and you know what that means around here, and then the phone rings and I pick it up and there he is. Just like that."

"Did he sound the same?" Bennis asked.

"He always sounds the same. He probably sounded the same when he was five years old. Sometimes I think he is five years old."

"What did he want?"

Donna shrugged. "How am I supposed to know? Even he doesn't know. He wanted to talk. One thing about Peter, Bennis. He surely can talk."

"You could always hang up on him."

"I always want to hang up on him," Donna said. "I always stop myself. He's Tommy's father, after all."

"The contribution of one sperm is a necessary but not sufficient condition for that familial designation."

"You'll have to translate that for me later," Donna told Bennis. "Anyway, the thing is, Tommy's been down for weeks because Peter's not around to pay attention to him. I don't think it's Peter in particular—it can't be; they don't know each other—but Tommy's at the stage when he wants a father around to love him and there isn't one. So I've been thinking maybe I made a mistake, maybe I should have insisted on Peter's marrying me when I had the chance—"

"Raspberries."

"I know, I know. I came to the same conclusion. I mean, there he was on the phone and he's a grown man and he's practically thirty by now and what's he talking about? Baseball cards. He's started collecting baseball cards."

"I think there's money in it."

"Peter being Peter, he'll lose his shirt. Whatever. I just changed my mind, that's all. Tommy and I are better off without him. I'm young. It's not impossible that somewhere along the way I'll find someone Tommy and I wouldn't be better off without. If you know what I mean."

"Sure," Bennis said without hesitation. "Is this someone in particular? Someone you know now?"

"I don't know," Donna answered.

And that was true. She really didn't know. She didn't know much about anything except that if she didn't get this heart up to the roof soon, Valentine's Day was going to be over and she was never going to have the chance. The heart was absolutely wonderful. It was composed of hundreds of small mirrors tinted different shades of red and pink, and whenever the sun shone on it it glittered. Gregor had taken off for the Ararat with Bennis. Old George had promised to pick Tommy up at play group. Donna had nothing on her hands but time.

She tucked the heart and the things she needed to secure it with into a backpack. Then she let herself out on the fourth floor fire escape and started climbing the metal ladder to the roof.

It was a very good thing she had never been afraid of heights.

## 2

Down the street, at the Ararat, Gregor Demarkian and Bennis Hannaford were sprawled across the benches in the window booth, bent over coffee and English muffins while Linda Melajian hurried back and forth from the kitchen, followed by a steady stream of Armenian in a high-pitched voice. The high-pitched voice belonged to Linda Melajian's grandmother, who was spending the day at the restaurant while Linda's father looked around for a new live-in nurse. Linda Melajian's grandmother went through live-in nurses the way a man with diarrhea goes through toilet paper. The word on the street was that she treated those nurses like toilet paper too. She certainly did screech. Gregor wondered why it was no one ever seemed to go about strangling women like this.

Linda had left a pot of coffee on the table. Gregor topped off his cup and sat back.

"In the beginning, I made the same mistake everyone else did," Gregor said. "I kept trying to work out how the murderer—Caroline Hazzard, we know now—how she planned to kill Paul Hazzard in the middle of that party. And it was impossible, of course. She had no way of knowing she would be able to get him alone while that party was in progress. That wasn't what she intended to do at all."

"She intended to kill him later," Bennis said.

"Exactly. She intended to find a handy hiding place and wait until the party was over. Then, with Hannah and Paul in the apartment, she'd have a very dangerous but very useful setup, perfect for her purposes as long as she was careful. She went to a great deal of trouble to make sure there were enough suspects. She stole Paul Hazzard's invitation and slipped it in Candida DeWitt's mailbox. She had no idea that Candida would show up at the party to make a scene, but it didn't matter what Candida did. Caroline was simply trying to establish a certain impression."

"Go back to the beginning," Bennis commanded. "First, Caroline got in through Hannah's bedroom window just around seven o'clock somewhere—"

"Which was the moan Sheila Kashinian heard," Gregor said. "Then she hid in the guest room, dropping one of her sister Alyssa's earrings to throw even more suspicion around. She checked out the neighborhood on Wednesday evening, by the way. Russell Donahue had his people around and they finally came up with something. I knew she had to have been seen."

"She hid in the bedroom," Bennis prompted.

"When Hannah and Paul had their fight, Caroline could see all the running around to the bedroom through the guest room door. She decided to take a chance and it worked. As soon as things quieted down a little, she rushed into the master bedroom and locked the door behind her. Remember, Hannah was still hysterical and Paul Hazzard himself was agitated. Caroline just took advantage of all the confusion to catch him off guard. My guess is that she reached out to hug the man—these people are incredible; they emote constantly—and as soon as she was close enough, she stabbed him with the anchor point of that compass. The six times, I think, were sheer pique. Then she put the compass away—in the inside pocket of this big cape she had, by the way; Russell Donahue found that, too, in her closet with the pocket all crusted bloody—and then she put the dagger down. More diversion. Then she unlocked the door and headed for the window."

"Which is when Candida DeWitt saw her."

"Right. Not all of her, you understand. Just a foot disappearing or the edge of that cape. If it had been anything more than that, anything surer, I think Candida would have told someone. The way things were, she decided to take matters into her own hands."

"Which was stupid."

"Not necessarily stupid." Gregor shook his head. "Remember, Candida had based her life on taking chances. Now she had a book in process that stood to make her a great deal more money than it would otherwise if only she knew the explanation of what had happened to Jacqueline Isherwood Hazzard. And suddenly, she did."

"Did she have to tell Caroline about it?"

"She didn't tell Caroline about it. Caroline simply knew that she'd been seen. She thought she'd been seen but not recognized. She wasn't taking any chances."

"Marvelous person, Caroline Hazzard."

"An incredibly lucky person," Gregor said. "The first time, when she killed her stepmother—because she was afraid of what her stepmother was going to do now that Candida DeWitt was on the scene; Candida was off it by then, but I don't think Caroline knew that—anyway, the first time Caroline just picked up the weapon that was closest to hand and went at it. The fact that there was a weapon on the wall that imitated the one she'd used was a sheer fluke. The fact that her father was the only person in the house who'd been home, and therefore the only one who'd seen, was lucky too. Caroline Hazzard set out to commit very simple crimes that ended up looking complicated because of chance—and because she always knew how to make use of chance."

"And she killed her father because he was seeing Hannah?"

"She killed her father for money. She'd always intended to. Paul Hazzard had no idea what he was protecting in that daughter of his, and neither did Alyssa. Caroline was willing to wait for the money as long as she had her father's exclusive attention. And she did, you know, for almost four years."

"And then Hannah came along?" Bennis was skeptical.

"Hannah is a nice, comfortable middle-aged woman with a good deal of money who would be more than willing to spend it helping someone she loved put his life back together," Gregor said. "Paul Hazzard was used to being a media star. He knew enough about the business he was in to realize he could be one again if he went about it the right way and spent enough in the process. I think he made a very smart move, picking up on Hannah."

"Not for Hannah."

"No," Gregor admitted. "Not for Hannah. What are we going to do about Hannah? Before all this started, it would never have occurred to me that someone like Hannah could be in the market for—uh—for—"

"Sex?"

"I don't think that's the word I'd use, Bennis."

"She's only a year older than you are, Gregor."

"I know. I know. But she seems older than that. They all do. Even Lida."

"Lida's still very pretty."

"Is she? Well, maybe she is. But at least Lida would have sense enough not to get involved with someone like Paul Hazzard."

"That's true," Bennis said. "What about a much younger man?"

"You have a filthy mind," Gregor said. "For God's sake."

Bennis leaned forward across the booth's table and looked out the window at Cavanaugh Street.

"What time is it?" she asked.

Gregor checked his watch. "Quarter to nine."

"They're early."

"What are early?"

"The balloons."

Gregor poured himself more coffee. "Sometimes," he said, "in fact, most of the time, you don't make any sense at all."

## 3

The balloons were indeed early, and there were so many of them, dozens and dozens of them, that Lida Arkmanian didn't know what to say. She was in the kitchen when the doorbell rang, sitting across the breakfast table from Christopher Hannaford. She had sweat on the back of her neck and a pain in her arms that felt like the beginning of tetanus. She had never been so tense in all her life.

The balloons were big silver-and-red hearts. They were filled with helium and each carried little baskets of heart-shaped candy in a heart-shaped straw bag. Lida went into the living room to watch them come in. They came in until they filled the entire room. Lida sat on the edge of her couch and watched them come, carried in in bunches by two men in blue uniform overalls. When it was over one of the two men went up to Christopher and had him sign a sheet of paper on a clipboard. Then the two men left and shut the door behind themselves, and Lida started to cry.

Christopher stopped in the living room door and watched. Lida could feel him watching. She still couldn't make herself stop.

"I don't know why you're crying," he said. "You're the one who's throwing me out. I don't want to go anywhere."

In the old days, women used to carry handkerchiefs in their pockets or their pocketbooks. Why had they ever stopped? There was a box of tissues in one of those fancy-colored cardboard boxes on the fireplace mantel. Lida couldn't think of how it had gotten there. She got up and got a tissue and blew her nose. She always looked so terrible when she cried.

"I know you don't want to go anywhere," she said.

"Can you at least tell me why you want me to go somewhere? You don't seem very happy about the decision."

"I'm not."

"Then what?"

Lida shook her head. "I can't help it. It's all wrong, that's all. It just doesn't fit."

"What doesn't fit?"

"Us."

"Why?"

Lida shook her head again. "Christopher, be reasonable. I'm fifty-eight years old. You're— You're—"

"Less than forty."

"Yes."

"Lida, for God's sake, so what? I don't care. Why do you? We get along together. In bed and out. We more than get along together, for Christ's sake. What difference does it make how old we both are?"

Lida looked away. "I live here, Christopher. I live on Cavanaugh Street. Maybe what we're doing would look unexceptional in San Francisco or New York, but on Cavanaugh Street it will be laughable."

"Everybody knows already. No one is laughing."

"Christopher, why can't you be reasonable? I can't—face people anymore. I can't stand being so conspicuous. And I am being conspicuous, Christopher, we both are. A hundred roses. A hundred balloons at least—"

"A hundred and forty-four. It was easier to order a gross."

"Whatever."

"I'm sorry if they were the wrong thing to do," Christopher said. "I was only trying to make you happy."

"You did make me happy," Lida told him. "You *do*. I wish I could straighten it all out in my own mind. I have liked having you here."

"I've liked being here."

"Sometimes I think I haven't slept in months and months and months," Lida said, "but it hasn't been that long. I'm just so disoriented."

"If you're really going to make me go, I'd better go."

Lida got up and went to look out the big window that fronted Cavanaugh Street. It was warmer today than it had been for a while. Donna Moradanyan was up on her own roof, doing something with what looked like a complicated mirror. Bennis Hannaford was walking back from the Ararat alone, dressed in jeans and turtleneck and sweater and no coat. What was it about the Hannafords that they never could stand to wear coats? Lida thought Gregor must still be at the Ararat with Father Tibor or old George. Lida thought she was lying to herself. It wasn't what people on Cavanaugh Street would think that bothered her. This might look like the old neighborhood, but it really wasn't anymore. The people had changed. The world had changed. The problem was that she hadn't changed, at least not enough.

Years ago, she had been married. Married happily, she had thought. Had she been lying to herself then too? Just three weeks ago she had thought she was happy where she was, as she was. Now she knew that wasn't true. What was happening to her? And why was it happening to her *now*?

"Lida?"

"Christopher," she said. "Listen to me. Are you going to take that new job?"

"The job? Yes, I'm going to take it. I thought we already agreed on that."

"If you take the job, you will have more time off in a week or two, won't you?"

"I'll have a couple of weeks off at the beginning of March. Is this supposed to be going someplace?"

"Yes," Lida said. "I think so. Did you know I have a house in Boca Raton, in Florida?"

"No, I didn't know that."

"Well, I do. I do. I have this house and I go there every year at the beginning of March. Usually I invite someone to go with me, Donna Moradanyan or Hannah or someone. So far this year I have invited no one."

"Are you inviting me?"

Lida turned around to look at him. She loved looking at him. That was the truth. She loved the long lankiness of him, the casual lines, the intelligence in his face. She wrapped her arms around her body and sighed.

"Christopher, it's as if we got into a sports car together a couple of weeks ago and we turned the speed up to two hundred miles an hour and we never stopped. I have to think. I haven't been able to think."

"All right."

"All right."

"I could be there, at my house, by the second of March. If you were there on the third, I could pick you up at the airport. I wouldn't have to invite Donna Moradanyan or Hannah or anyone at all."

"All right."

"I'm making you angry," Lida said. "I knew I was going to make you angry. I don't understand these things, Christopher. I don't know what I'm doing."

"You're doing fine," Christopher said.

Then he walked over to the window where she was standing and put his arms around her. For a moment it made Lida feel as if this whole scene had been a mistake. Christopher would not walk out the front door. The two of them would go straight upstairs again. Everything would be back at the beginning. But instead of kissing her on the lips he kissed the side of her neck and rocked her back and forth a little.

"You can pick me up at the airport," he said, "but I want you to understand one thing right up front."

"What's that?"

"Women are enough to make any sane man nuts."

## 4

A few hours later, when Christopher was back at Bennis's apartment and Gregor Demarkian was doing his best not to read the story about himself in the *Philadelphia Inquirer*, Donna Moradanyan came down from the roof and let herself through the window to the fourth-floor landing. She was just snaking her head into the warm when a tall figure came up the stairs. He looked startled to see her and Donna felt embarrassed to be seen. She pulled herself all the way inside and shut the window behind her.

"Hello," she said. "Excuse me. I was up on the roof."

"Was that safe?" Russell Donahue looked doubtful.

"It's safe enough, I guess," Donna said. "I do it all the time. Do you want to come in for a minute? Were you looking for me?"

"Well," Russell Donahue said. "Yes. I mean, yes. I was looking for you."

"That's nice."

Donna had not bothered to lock her apartment door. She never bothered to lock her door except at night, when she went to sleep, and she did it then because of all the scare stories Gregor Demarkian told about sneak thieves and serial killers. She let Russell in to her foyer and then went around to lead him into the living room. Her kitchen was full of scraps and glue and masking tape and she didn't want him to see the mess in there. Russell walked across the living room and looked out the window. He put his hands behind his back and seemed embarrassed.

"Well," he said. "The thing is, I wanted to ask you something."

"Of course. Do you mean about the case? Is there something about the case that hasn't been cleared up?"

"No, no. The case is finished. That's the point. Now that the case is over, there's no conflict of interest."

"I don't understand."

"There's no conflict of interest if I come and visit you," Russell Donahue said desperately, "and if, you know, if I take you out or something, and of course Tommy too, I didn't mean to leave Tommy out of it, I really like Tommy, and I don't have a whole load of free time what with work and I'm going to law school but—the thing is—I mean— would you mind if I came to visit?"

Donna Moradanyan was finding it very hard to breathe. "No," she said softly. "No, I wouldn't mind."

"You wouldn't? Oh. Good. *Good*. That's wonderful."

"It is?"

"I'm very impressed by you," Russell Donahue said earnestly. He was still looking out onto the street. Donna was looking at her shoes.

"I don't see what there is to be impressed with," she said. "My life always feels to me like complete chaos."

"It's Tommy," Russell Donahue said. "He's a really great kid. And all that drawing you were showing me the other day."

"Oh," Donna Moradanyan said.

"So maybe this coming Wednesday we could take Tommy out to see the machine museum. You know the one I mean? They've got all these machines and buttons the kid can push to make them work and they whir around and make a lot of noise. I thought Tommy would really like that."

"He would," Donna said. "He'd love it."

"Great," Russell Donahue said. Finally, he turned around. "Well, I've got to go into work. I'll see you on Wednesday. Around two o'clock?"

"That's good," Donna said. "Two o'clock."

"Great," Russell Donahue said again. He went back out into the foyer and looked around. He seemed considerably less nervous than he had been when he walked in. Donna didn't know if she was less nervous or not. She opened the door for him. "Well," he said. "I'll see you Wednesday."

"Wednesday," Donna repeated.

"Great," Russell Donahue said for the third time.

He went out the door and onto the landing. The door closed behind him but Donna could hear his feet on the stairs, the clatter of shoes, the sound of a hum. She stepped back and stared at the closed door, and then she did something she hadn't done since she was ten.

She put her hands behind her back.

And crossed her fingers.

*about the author*

JANE HADDAM is the author of ten Gregor Demarkian holiday mysteries. *Not a Creature Was Stirring*, the first in the series, was nominated for both an Anthony and the Mystery Writers of America's Edgar awards. *A Stillness in Bethlehem*, *Precious Blood*, *Act of Darkness*, *Quoth the Raven*, *A Great Day for the Deadly*, *A Feast of Murder*, *Festival of Deaths* and *Dear Old Dead* are her other books. She lives in Litchfield County, Connecticut, with her husband, her son, and her cat, where she is at work on a New Year's Day mystery, *Fountain of Death*.

If you enjoyed *Bleeding Hearts*,
you will want to read all
of the Gregor Demarkian holiday series!

Here is a special advance look
at Jane Haddam's next holiday mystery.
Look for it in your local bookstore.

*Fountain of Death*
*by Jane Haddam*

It was an article of faith with all the people Greta Bellamy knew that spending your nights in bars was supposed to be fun. This was something Greta herself had believed all through high school and the two years she had spent at Southern Connecticut State College. She had at least been able to sit crammed into the corners of hardwood booths for hours without feeling either physically uncomfortable or terminally bored. Now Southern Connecticut State College had changed its name to Southern Connecticut State University, and Greta herself seemed to be going through a sea change. It's because I'm turning thirty, Greta told herself sometimes, although she knew this couldn't be true. Her best friend, Kathy Weddaby, was turning thirty, too, and Kathy was just as happy as she had always been to spend the hours after work investigating the relative merits of Molson golden ale and St. Pauli Girl light.

Tonight, they were all sitting together in a roadhouse called the Avalon—Greta, Kathy, Frank, and Chick. Frank was Kathy's husband. Chick was Greta's boyfriend, and had been, ever since they were all together in the class of '83 at Hamden High. Chick would have been Greta's husband, if she had let him, but every time Greta got started in that direction she pulled back at the last minute. She didn't know what she wanted out of her life, but she did know that it wasn't what Kathy had, or what Chick was able to give her, or what was on offer here at this roadhouse with its third-rate lounge acts bused in from the city and its fat old women in stockings and garters holding up the bar. The booth they were in tonight had a window looking out on the Housatonic River. If Greta craned her neck in just the right way, she could see a row of shuttered little shacks stretching out along the water and then the Stephenson Dam. Greta had a copy of *People* magazine open on the booth table in front of her. She couldn't read the words because of the dimness of the light. She had a bottle of Heineken on the booth table in front of her too, and a glass to pour it in, but she had been ignoring it so long the beer had gone flat. Frank and Chick were smoking Marlboros and blowing the smoke into the circle of light cast by the side light next to the booth. The lounge act consisted of four guys in white dinner jackets and bad skin who had once cut a record for Columbia and appeared on *The Andy Williams Show*. Some of the women at the bar seemed to remember them, and sang along whenever they played. Greta looked down at her magazine and studied the big picture of the heavyset, Middle Eastern–looking man that took up the left-hand page. He reminded her of the men who had belonged to the Shriner's Club with her father, and he wouldn't have interested her at all if it hadn't been for the woman he was with. The woman was small and dark haired and very pretty, but what got to Greta was her attitude. There is a woman who doesn't take shit from anyone, Greta thought. The headline on the right-hand page, in very large type but still unreadable in this dark, said:

**AMERICA'S MOST ECCENTRIC MASTER DETECTIVE**
**PULLS OFF ANOTHER ONE**

Chick was tired of blowing smoke into the light. He turned back to the table, saw Greta's magazine, and snorted.

"Now she's reading in bars," he said. "Jesus Christ."

"It's just *People*," Greta said. "And I'm not reading. It's too dark in here. I'm just looking at pictures."

Kathy turned the magazine around so that it was right side up for her. "It's that murder story again. Don't you think that's morbid?"

"You're the one who bought everything there was to read about Amy Fisher," Greta said.

"She bought everything there was to read about Lorena Bobbitt, too," Frank said. "Christ, I nearly took all the knives in the house and buried them in the backyard."

"I think Lorena Bobbitt was stupid," Kathy said. "Saying her husband raped her and so she cut off his dick. If she wanted to cut off his dick, she should have just cut it off."

"Well, she did," Chick said. "That's the point."

"I liked the Amy Fisher thing much better," Kathy said. "You could understand what was behind that one. Although I don't think I'd do what Joey's wife did. Go back to him like that, I mean. I don't think I'd believe he had nothing to do with it."

"I would," Frank said. "I think that girl was just plain crazy."

Greta took her magazine back from Kathy and turned it around so that she could see it again. The man's name was Gregor Demarkian, but that wasn't important. The woman's name was Bennis Hannaford, and that was. Bennis Hannaford wrote novels about knights and ladies and dragons and magic trolls, and Greta had a copy of one of them—*The Chronicles of Zed and Zedalia*—hidden out of sight right now in her purse.

The lounge act started on a rendition of "Moon River," not a very good one. The piano they were using was flat. Greta took a sip of beer right out of the bottle, made a face at the sour flatness of it, and put the bottle down again. When she looked up, she found Chick staring at her, and blushed.

"I let it go too long." She felt slightly defensive.

Chick flicked his fingers at the beer bottle. "You're letting everything go too long these days. You haven't been paying any attention to business at all for months."

"Oh, she's been paying attention to business," Kathy said sharply. "That's how she got that promotion at work."

"It wasn't a promotion," Greta said quickly. "It was just an upgrade in title. And a little raise."

"Executive assistant." Kathy made a rabbity little face. "Aren't you important."

"I'm being a secretary to Mr. Wilder just the way I've always done," Greta said. "It's just that I did a lot of overtime, and some extra work when we had all that trouble just after Thanksgiving—"

Chick lit another cigarette. He let the match burn down until the flame touched his thumb, but didn't flinch. That was a macho thing all the boys had been into in high school. Chick had never given it up. He dumped the spent match in the ashtray in the center of the table. The ashtray was already overflowing with butts.

"I think that's our point here," he said seriously. "You aren't paying any attention to me. You aren't paying any attention to us."

"It's like you think you're an entirely different person," Kathy said. "It's like you think all of a sudden you've gotten better than us."

"Just because they're giving you a little extra money at work doesn't mean you're better than us," Chick said. "I mean, for Christ's sake, Greta. It's not like they made you president of the company. You're just working for chump change and playing the lottery like everybody else."

"She doesn't play the lottery any more," Kathy said tightly. "She says she's saving her money for something else."

The lounge act had moved past "Moon River" and swung into a tinny version of "My Way." Greta looked at her flat beer and wished she had drunk it. It would really help right now to be a little numb. Chick was right. She hadn't been paying attention to him, to any of them. That was why she hadn't picked up on this hostility before. And yet it must have been there. The raise was new—it wouldn't even kick in until just before Christmas—but the other things, her preoccupation and, yes, that sense of difference, those had been here for months. Now the air was thick with anger turning slowly but inexorably toward hatred, and Greta felt a little sick. The four of them had been together for years now, ever since Greta and Chick had started going out in their high school freshman year. Greta didn't have any other friends, even at work. She didn't have any family left, either. Her parents had died in an accident on the Merritt Parkway more than five years ago. What would happen to her if Kathy and Chick and Frank stopped talking to her, and she was on her own?

She picked up her beer glass and put it down again. "I don't see why I have to buy lottery tickets on a week when I'm feeling short of cash," she said. "There's Christmas coming up."

"I use my Christmas bonus to pay for Christmas," Kathy said.

"She's saving up to pay her way into that health club." Chick smirked. "Five hundred dollars, can you believe that? For this spa. For a week. Fountain of Youth, it's called. Up in New Haven."

"I don't see what's wrong with my wanting to go to some exercise classes for a week," Greta said. "You're the one who's always telling me I'm getting a fat ass."

"I have that week off from work," Chick said. "I wanted us to go to Atlantic City. I even said I'd pay for the whole thing."

"We can go to Atlantic City any week. This was a kind of sale price deal. It's going to happen and then it's going to be gone. I can't afford the prices they usually charge."

"You could have asked me to go with you," Kathy said. "You could at least have thought of the idea. If they charge more than five hundred dollars a week, they must get a lot of rich women going there. I don't think you're going to fit in."

"I don't have to fit in," Greta said wearily. "I just have to do a lot of aerobics and some weight lifting and listen to some lectures on nutrition. I just thought I'd try to improve myself, that's all. I don't understand why it's turned into this big deal."

"I'm going to go up and get another beer," Chick said. "That fat-assed waitress is nowhere."

Fat-assed, Greta realized suddenly, was the way Chick described every woman he was angry with. Even if the woman was as thin as a rail and built like a toothpick, if Chick didn't like her he said she had a big butt. That must mean he doesn't like me any more, Greta thought, but she didn't know what to do with that. He might not like her, but he still wanted her around. He was over at her house every night. He called her at work every lunch hour. He expected her to go out to bars with him as much as he ever had. Greta thought about all those articles in the women's magazines that Kathy bought—*Family Circle*, *Woman's Day*—about men who stalked women who didn't love them any more. That doesn't apply to me, Greta told herself. I still love Chick. I love him more than he loves me. At least I like him.

Without realizing it, Greta had been staring down at her magazine again, at Gregor Demarkian and Bennis Hannaford, at a blurred vision in the background that looked like a very elegant room. Greta hadn't read the article yet, so she didn't know what it was about. Gregor Demarkian sometimes investigated murders that took place in small towns or slums, which were boring. She hoped this murder had taken place among rich people. She put out her hand to touch the cloud of dark hair that floated around Bennis Hannaford's head. Then she took her hand away quickly and closed the magazine.

When Greta looked up again, Frank was gone as well as Chick, and Kathy was leaning far over the booth table, staring at her intently. Why didn't I ever notice how mean her eyes look? Greta wondered. Kathy really did have little piggy eyes in a round and overstuffed face. She had a line of pimples along her jaw and another one at the corner of her mouth. She looked worse than angry. She looked ready to tear somebody apart.

Greta took her magazine off the table and felt around on the booth seat for her pocketbook, so that she could put the magazine away. "I think I'll go to the ladies room," she said vaguely. "I think I need to run a brush through my hair."

"No," Kathy said.

"I think I can go to the bathroom when I want to, Kathy. I think you can't stop me from doing that."

"I got rid of the guys so I could talk to you," Kathy said, "and you know it. I'm not going to let you run away to the ladies room and act like I don't exist."

"I'm not acting like you don't exist. I just want to brush my hair."

Kathy turned sideways and propped her feet up on the bench. "I'm really sick of this. I'm really sick of the way you've been behaving for the past month. We're all sick of it."

"You've all made it clear."

"I wouldn't take anything for granted if I was

you," Kathy said. "Just because Chick has been hanging around you forever doesn't mean he's going to go on hanging around you. You hurt his feelings when you said you wouldn't marry him."

"I wasn't ready to get married."

"Well, maybe Chick is ready to get married. Maybe he's ready to settle down. Maybe if he can't get you to go settle down with him, he'll get somebody else."

"Is this a particular somebody else you're talking about?" Greta asked. "Do you have an applicant for this position?"

"Chick has," Kathy said slowly. "You don't give Chick enough credit. It's not like it was back in high school. Chick has turned out to be a very hunky guy."

"That's nice. Who thinks he's so hunky?"

"Marsha Caventello." Kathy swung around so that she was facing Greta again. She was sitting back farther on the bench, in the shadows, so that Greta couldn't see what was going on in her eyes. "Marsha Caventello has been making up to Chick for the last two weeks. Coming into the plant when she doesn't have to. Dropping her clipboard on his feet and letting him pick it up for her. Telling him how wonderful he is. It's beginning to do the job."

"That's nice," Greta said stiffly.

"Frank told me that Chick told him that if you wouldn't go to Atlantic City, he was going to ask Marsha."

"That's nice," Greta said again.

Kathy leaned into the light. The expression on her face was feral. The smile that was spread across her mouth was as cruel as the smile of an executioner.

"Don't just say 'that's nice,' " she said with satisfaction. "Do something about it. Because if he goes away to Atlantic City with Marsha, Greta, he isn't going to come back to you."

Up at Fountain of Youth, at midnight, Frannie Jay was lying fully clothed on the hard mattress of her double bed, feeling that she really ought to make herself get undressed and take a shower and go to sleep. Tomorrow she had to learn two step dance routines and review the tour literature. She was supposed to be awake enough to participate in a staff meeting at nine o'clock. She had the lights in the bedroom turned off and the curtains on the windows opened. She was telling herself for the fifteenth time that she was only hurting herself by procrastinating like this when she heard the noise outside in the drive.

*Koo roo*, the noise went. *Koo roo clank whoosh*.

Frannie got off her bed and went to the window. The security light on the front of the detached garage cast a wide arc of brightness onto the gravel and the lawn. There was nothing out there that Frannie could see.

*Koo roo*, the noise went again. *Koo roo clank whoosh clank roo*.

Frannie undid the latch on her window and pushed it up. Cold air streamed over her. She leaned out into it and looked across the yard. Empty grass. Empty gravel. A three-car garage with its doors down, closed up tight. Frannie started to back into her room again.

*Koo roo*, the noise started again, but then it stopped, and Frannie stopped too. For just a moment there, she thought she had seen something, close to the house, where there was a small line of evergreen hedges near the back door. She leaned out again, as far as she dared, and squinted into the shadows. Then she backed all the way into the room and went to sit down on the side of the bed.

A foot, Frannie thought, feeling the start of hysterical giggles rising in her throat.

That's what I just saw out there.

A naked human foot.

Attached to a naked human leg.

Sticking out of the evergreen hedges next to the back door.

Frannie Jay put her head between her knees and began to heave.

# BANTAM MYSTERY COLLECTION